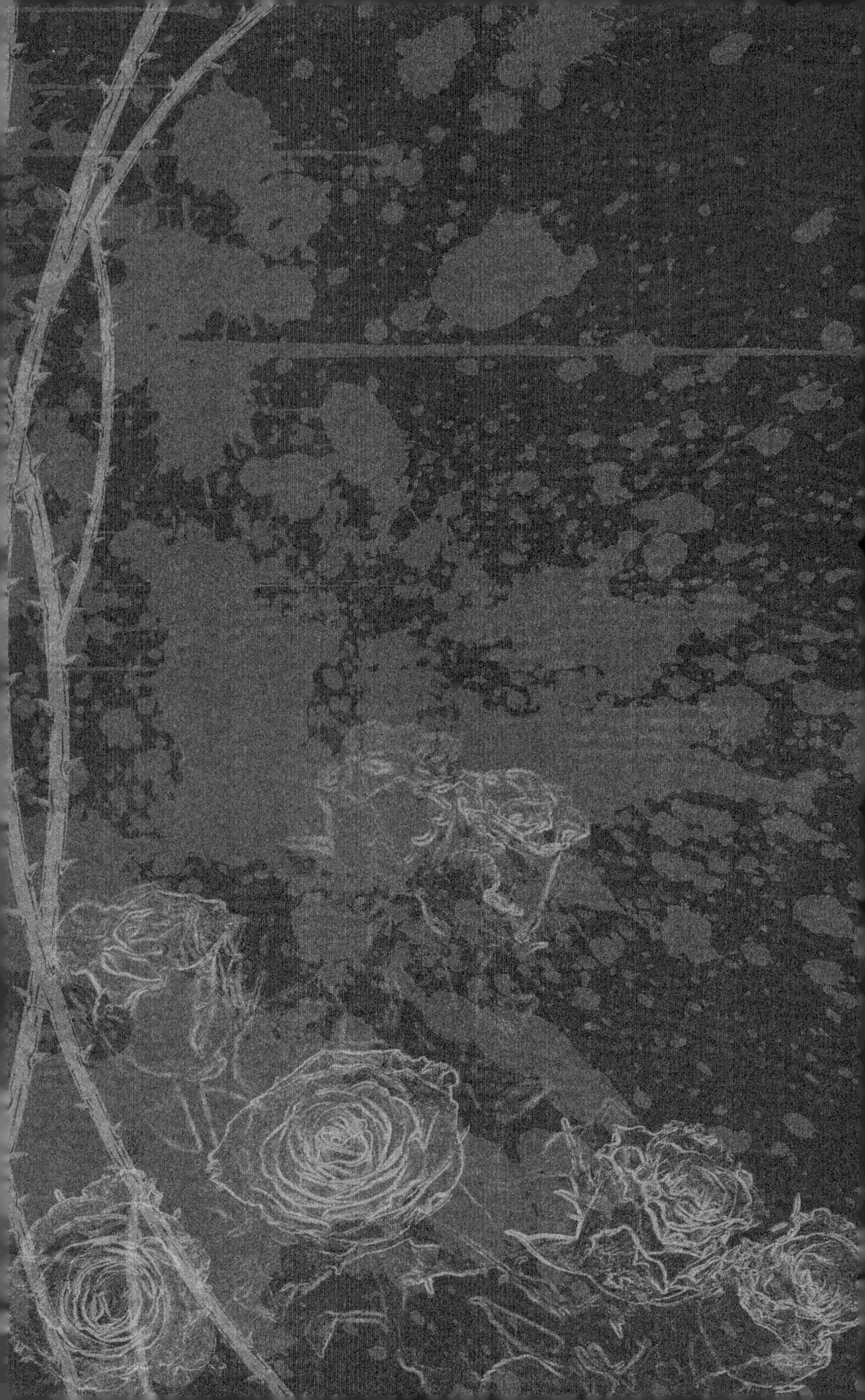

Blood & Steel

Shana J. Caldwell

This book is a work of fiction. Names, characters, businesses, organisations, places, events and incidents either are the product of the author's imagination or are used fictitiously. Any resemblance to actual persons, living or dead, events, or locales is entirely coincidental.

Cover Design: Ever After Cover Design

Formatting: Mallory Kent, The Nutty Formatter

Editor: Tara Routley

ISBN: 978-0-6455788-2-9

To Shalika,
who would have known you'd be into faerie smut?

IMPORTANT AUTHOR NOTE

As this is my very first dark, fantasy romance, I feel the need to warn you that some of the moments in this book are uncomfortable, explicit and confronting. Please take this warning seriously, your mental health matters more than a book.

This book contains very triggering situations such as the mention/hinting of rape. There is also graphic violence, kidnapping, physical abuse, self harm, suicidal thoughts, explicit sexual situations and the death of a baby.

Prologue

Killian Abaddon has walked his life with one hand tightly clasped in death, a steady throb of darkness that constantly poisoned his veins.

A poison he soon learnt to harness and control. No longer was he infected and corrupted, he was whole and wicked and free.

Killian keeps his back straight as he enters the presence of Pantera's ruler. Through gilded golden doors of the throne room, the click of his boots hitting the marble floor echoes. The King of Pantera keeps his golden eyes trained on his second hand, his most trusted Valarki soldier as he approaches.

The Kings long, golden hair reflects silver as it swims around his large olive frame as if it has life of its own. He leans back in his throne made of polished white gleaming bones melded together with gold, his fingers drum restlessly on a human skull as Killian takes slow steps towards him. As if he is the one that rules this place, as if he bares the weight of the crown and its consequences.

"Have I interrupted something?" The King asks, raising a brow. Killian's ice blue eyes holding *nothing* as he looks upon his King. An abyss.

"Of course not, your majesty." Killian's deep voice vibrates over the king's skin as he climbs the dozen stairs of the dais. He moves swiftly, standing off to the right of the king's shoulder. He is nothing more than a shadow, a bringer of death if the king commands.

"Today, we invade." The king mulls over his own words, he twirls a hand in front of him. His olive skin gives way to a glistening gold as he calls his magic forth.

Electricity crackles through the room as a vortex begins to spin in the middle of the great hall, the darkness breaks and zaps away to light that begins to fill the room. The King smiles, resting his chin on a closed fist as his magic opens the All-Seeing Eye.

For centuries the All-Seeing eye has bent to the King's will, finding his next conquest. It's one of his greatest weapons when preparing to send an army.

As darkness clears, the All-Seeing Eye shows the king what he is seeking. Humans move freely through their village, the sun shines brightly and the distant chatter of mortals and animals reach both of their delicate ears. The King delights in their naivety—how he is able to look through the portal like a mirror, its reflection showing the humans so unaware of how they're being preyed upon.

Fifty years the King has been waiting.

Fifty years since he had last given Killian the command to invade the closest villages, taking ten women as slaves to bring back for him and leaving nothing but fire and ash behind. It has been too long since the last conquest, the King's magic has become more demanding; needing to be sated, for the ever growing magic which wove through his bones would turn and begin to feed from his own life source.

Ten women had last graced the King's personal harem ten years ago, women with hatred in their hearts. The King's magic relies on two important practices to be replenished, each female must hold hatred in their hearts for his kind and he must bathe in their blood while drinking their life source. No more, no less, the magic demands ten.

"What has changed?" Killian asks, his voice holding no trace of emotion. Only Killian could ever question the king's motives and not be punished for it. The King rises, his simple white robe flows around him as he stalks down the dais. On cue, three Valarki soldiers walk through the doors with a small pathetic human male grasped between them. Their dark uniforms are in immaculate condition, not one black thread is misplaced.

A grin breaks the King's lips as he clasps his hands before him. The All-Seeing Eye turns and allows the newcomers to peer into its depths. Killian silently approaches and stands beside the King, staring hard at the man who now cowers beneath the brown burlap sack covering his face.

Black tendrils of shadow unfurl and solidify from Killian's hands and spear into the captive, disappearing under his deep tanned skin.

A scream rips from the man's throat as he thrashes against his bindings, the King glances at his general's face. Killian wears a grim smile, his ice blue eyes are dark and leeched of light. Of anything that is good in this world.

The King bristles before squaring his shoulders and straightening his chin.

"You're a twisted bastard." One of the guard murmurs in admiration. The King narrows his eyes at the guard.

Killian slowly takes his eyes from the man, ignoring his screams as Killian's magic inflicts his worst nightmares upon him and feeds on his fear. He smirks.

The King sighs, "Give him here, I'm sending a message."

The guards step away from the human and the black tendrils of smoke emerge from underneath now pale skin, slinking heavily along the ground towards their master. The King prefers to command, needing to reserve his power for when it is vital. Compared to Killian's magic, the Kings is a mere droplet in the vast ocean that is Killian's.

One of the guards tears the bag from the male's head, bloodshot milky eyes stare up at him and he screams pathetically again, the King grabs a fistful of his matted hair and wrenches his head backwards to look down at him, "Do you wish to return home?"

The man nods frantically against his grasp, the stench of piss fills the air. Killian growls his displeasure, standing off to the side.

"Then you're to go with a message."

In a swift movement the King pivots the man towards the All-Seeing Eye, he summons his magic to extend his nails to sharpened claws. He lets the man go, watching as he stumbles towards a false sense of safety. The King grins as he thrusts his clawed hand through the man's back, tearing at internal organs and breaking bones. The force pushes the man through the All-Seeing Eye, the King's arm is through the portal. Screams of terror fill the air as humans scatter, it is music to the Valarkis' ears. The King locates the man's pulsating heart, ripping it from his chest as he withdraws from the portal.

They watch as people scream and run, chaos follows.

A small smile crosses the King's face as he takes a bite of the warm beating appendage in his hand, "Valarki will no longer be weak, forgotten. Pantera will bring ruin to the south of the continent until nothing remains."

"Shall we leave now?" Killian drawls, unbothered. It pleases the King greatly.

"Bring me back fifteen females." The King stalks back towards his throne of bones, slumping down and summoning the All-Seeing Eye to face him once more. No pupil is present, but when the King is alone he can almost feel the prickling sensation of being watched. The scene changes, showing him a lavender field with a slender female laying between the fray. Her auburn hair catches like wild fire in the sun as she sits up, burning amber eyes stare directly through the King, as if she senses not all is right in the world.

His smile grows, fifty years has been far too long. The King has finally risen, and he demands blood.

1. Adalyn

Adalyn

Adalyn Grace is drawn from the depths of her thoughts as a relentless breeze tugs at the strands of the auburn hair that frames her face, demanding consciousness in the present. She blinks back into reality although her thoughts of freedom linger at the edges of her mind like a shadow. Her fingers tighten on the woven basket handle as she looks over her shoulder.

Emilia sits in the middle of a large patch of bright green clovers. A smile tugs at Adalyn's mouth as her younger sister counts them out, looking for one with four leaves that is said to bring the owner luck.

Their father had insisted Adalyn bring her along while she plucked bundles of herbs the family would need for dinner. The herb patch is for the whole village to access and harvest, not only does it grow a large range of herbs but it also has gardens dedicated to flowers and vegetables.

Other villagers work in content silence as they pick their own share of flora, unbothered by the hot sun beating down on them.

"Emilia, we best be off." Adalyn calls, straightening her aching back. She wipes the back of her hand over her forehead, grimacing as beads of sweat dribble down the sides of her cheeks. Emilia's blonde curly hair whips around her face as she looks up at Adalyn, beaming. Her bright green eyes shine deep emerald as the sun basks upon her. She begins to untangle herself from the clover patch, both pockets on the front of her pale blue dress are overflowing.

"When we return tomorrow I'm going to continue my quest to find the four leaf clover," she announces as she reaches Adalyn, holding her chin high. Adalyn scruffs her hair before taking her small hand in her own.

"I'm sure you'll find one eventually." Adalyn squeezes Emilia's hand, looking down at her.

They walk down the small dirt path towards the wooden gate.

Few large trees offer shade to those harvesting, a small reprieve from the sun. Adalyn looks forward to reaching home, being able to strip from the sweat drenched dress that is currently suctioning to her back.

Emilia skips along, swinging her free hand. She has so much energy it's hard for Adalyn to fathom. Although ten years separates the sisters, Emilia has enough energy for the both of them.

"I'll find it. I know I will. Jarhn and Noah aren't going to ruin it for me either, I won't let them touch it at all," she declares. Adalyn grins at the mention of the twins, the youngest boys in their family at only four years.

"Ah yes, those two are little twin tornados of trouble." Adalyn shakes her head and looks forward; they'd reached the end of the path. She lets go of Emilia's hand and unlatches the wooden gate, holding it open for her as she breezes past. Adalyn tethers the rope back onto the post, glancing longingly towards the field of lavender that sits on the other side of the herb patch.

The village is bustling with life at this time of afternoon, Adalyn holds onto Emilia as a draft horse walks past with a carriage. Chickens crow from their crates inside the carriage, the man astride the horse nods once before continuing on his way.

Kids scream as they run past in a game of chase, the grumpy

villagers yell their displeasure while others laugh at the joy. Oakshire has always been a village full of life, from the moment Adalyn had been birthed to twenty one years later. She can't remember a time when the village didn't have the joy and happiness enriched in its very soil.

Although her mother assures her that it wasn't always full of life, that the darkness can always come back and claim this light.

Emilia tugs at Adalyn's hand, pointing towards one of the closest cottage homes as she stops her thoughts from spiralling. Magda, the eldest woman in the village, rocks on her chair in the shade of her porch. Herbs of deep green and violet hang in bunches from the railings while bright pink peonies twist up the side of her home and rest on the shelving of a low window. Adalyn looks both ways before hurrying across the dirt street, Emilia squeals as she bounds up the porch steps and into Magda's open arms. Adalyn's heart fills with light as she follows behind, sighing once she is out of direct sunlight. She leans against the railing, sitting the basket of herbs at her feet.

"What a pleasure it is to see both gorgeous girls!" Magda chirps, patting Emilia's hand with her own wrinkled hand. Emilia grins.

"We've been at the herb patch! Look at all my clovers." Emilia steps back and shows Magda the overflowing greenery that spills from her pockets. Magda laughs, the sound deep and ancient. No one really knows how old she is, just that she has been living in this home from the moment the village was built.

"Oh that's wonderful dearie." Magda pins Adalyn with her light sky blue eyes, her thin white hair is swept up from her face and held with pins. A dark mole sits above her lip, sprouting dark hair. Her simple dark purple dress is stained from a hard morning of work, making healing serums and potions for the village.

"Hello Magda." Adalyn nods, brushing the strands of her own hair back from her face. She silently curses her lousy work of tying the strands back into a bun.

"Adalyn, how was the morning's pick?" she leans back in her rocking chair, resting her hands on her plump stomach. Adalyn reaches into the basket and pulls out a bundle of rosemary, thyme, and parsley.

"I grabbed these for you, mother and father send their thanks for the healing tonic you delivered to us last week for the twins." She walks over and hands Magda the bundle; she takes it with a smile.

"Those two boys know how to find trouble. How are they feeling?"

Adalyn goes back and leans against the railing once more, "Better than ever. It's the last time father lets them play down by the stream."

"Nature is nature, it does not do things with malice; is simply just is." She tucks the bundle into the deep brown leather bag that hangs off the arm of her chair.

"Magda, did you hear about the new family that moved to town?" Emilia asks, clasping her hands in front of her. A few days ago a family moved into the abandoned cottage across the road from their own on the south west border of the large village, Adalyn had only caught a glimpse of the small girl running in their back yard with a small black pup.

"Ah yes, the wife is soon to be due." Magda rises from her chair, knees creaking as she shuffles towards the propped open door that leads deep into her home. "Your herbs will come in handy for the tonic I must make her. Thank you for stopping by girls, tell your parents I appreciate their gift." .

"Come, we best be heading home now." Adalyn grabs the basket and heads down the steps, ignoring the ache in her lower back from bending all day. Emilia is quick to follow behind.

They walk down the less busy roads, heading towards the south end of the village to where their cottage is. Each cottage in the village is made from either clay or wood with a thatched straw roof, every family makes their cottage their own. Adalyn's mother had refurnished a broken wheelbarrow, overflowing with flowers that the villagers may pick freely. She's displayed it under the cottage's front window. It was her mother's idea to not waste the wheelbarrow, father had wanted to chop it up for wood.

Adalyn keeps her eyes on Emilia as she bounds ahead, smelling the flowers from people's gardens before tinkering with woven baskets that are propped against someone's home. She rolls her eyes, unable to stop her sister's curious nature. If there's something Emilia loves to do, it's to be overly curious.

"Do you reckon mother will have lemon water for us once we return?" she asks, skipping up to Adalyn before prancing in circles around her.

"I can only hope, this heat is disastrous." Adalyn wipes the back of her hand across her forehead, blowing out a hot breath. As they reach a curve in the road, they head down the right wider path. The cottages begin to become more spacious, allowing each one a small yard for livestock. Adalyn spots their cottage from where she stands, beyond that is a thick towering pine forest. Oakshire village had been built deep in the forest, circular in shape with the herb patch in the centre as the main source of the villagers' food. The winding roads were created as a defence tactic if the village was to ever befall foul play.

Adalyn scoffs, shaking her head at the stories she'd once believed of darkness and gleaming sharpened teeth and pointed ears. Not once has she ever seen a trace of anything that holds magic or any creature that might. She'd ruled the tales down to just that, tales.

Squealing shatters her thoughts as they arrive home. The twins come barrelling out of the doorway and into Emilia. She tries her best to pry their grabbing hands from her pockets, frowning as they grab a handful of clovers and take off back inside.

"Millie, Addie?" Mother calls, peering out the open window above the wheelbarrow. Wild strands of dark brown hair curl around her heart shaped face, escaping from the messy bun. The large rectangular window currently has two pies sitting on the ledge, steam wafts from their golden crust in the breeze. Mother smiles warmly, her chestnut brown eyes light and full of joy. Nothing makes her happier than a day of baking.

Adalyn ducks in through the propped open door, slipping her boots off and sitting them on the wooden shoe stand under the coats. Wood groans underneath her weight as she moves past the kitchen to the small dining room. Fresh fire wood has been stacked in the mantle beside the clay fireplace, no doubt her father's doing. Emilia escapes down the hall, locking herself in their shared room to count her clovers.

"How was the walk?" Mother asks. Adalyn sits the basket on the wooden dining table, sitting into one of the chairs with a huff. She massages the back of her neck as her mother comes over, sifting through the herbs. Adalyn inhales her herbal scent with the hint of vanilla.

"It was fine, we saw Magda briefly. She sends her appreciation."

Her mother takes the basket from the table and walks back into the kitchen. Adalyn watches as she begins to string the herbs together and hang them from the wall with nails that have been added to the wooden foundation to the left of the kitchen.

"I'm glad she's pleased." Her mother empties the basket, opening the cupboard under the hanging herbs and sits the basket inside. Below the steaming pies from the open window she's begun to prepare dinner. Rosemary has been chopped up with some thyme, a small glass vial is filled with golden oil.

"Where's father?" Adalyn asks, looking over her shoulder to the living room. The twins had escaped to god knows where, the hay stuffed couch is deserted apart from Mitch, the family's grey house cat. He's curled on the top of the chair, tail twitching in sleep around his large body.

"Out the back, one of the lambs broke its leg last night. We're not sure what happened but there's no fixing it." Her mother shakes her head, turning back to the herbs she'd begun to prep, "can you start the fire please? We'll have to put the roast on soon if we want it done by a reasonable hour."

Adalyn rises from the chair and moves from the wooden table, scratching Mitch as she walks past; earning a rumbling purr. She moves in front of the fire and gathers four pieces of wood before crouching down and unlatching the metal cage that covers the open space. She places the pieces in, allowing enough room for her father to place the roast on top.

Adalyn grabs some of hay from the other side of the fire that sit in a metal box, she sits them on the wood before using a small douse of oil and match to start the fire. She latches the gate back in place and gently blows on the orange flame, coaxing the wood to catch fire.

"Does father need help with the lamb?" she asks, wiping her hands on her deep purple dress.

"He might, go see." Mother begins to hum a nursery rhyme as she loses herself in cooking, the one she always sang to Adalyn when she was still a child. Adalyn slips out the front door and walks to the small wooden gate that is beside the cottage. Her father had built the fence around the home himself, using wooden planks and long strands of barbed wire. Brown and black chickens run up to Adalyn as she walks through the gate, chirping as they look at her expectantly.

"I have no food yet, it isn't dinner time." Adalyn walks past them, knowing they'd be right behind her if she looked over her shoulder. Their small farm is large enough to support their family of six. Her mother and father had built a chicken pen when they'd first finished the fence. After that they created a pen for lambs and pigs, although they never usually have more than five livestock at a time.

She spots her father chopping wood in the back right corner of the yard, sweat glistens down his bare tanned back as he swings the axe down. Already a large pile of broken wood has begun to gather around the base stump.

"Of course you'd be out here chopping wood," she calls as she grows closer. He stops and straightens at her voice. His auburn hair glows fire red in the sunlight, his full beard a deep orange. His blue eyes crease in the corners as he grins.

"Ah, my favourite daughter is here to relieve me." His thick accent rumbles through each word. Her father had hailed from Oktavia, a country across the vast ocean when he was only Adalyn's age and had met her mother on the docks. He'd always promised to take her back to his home land one day, where the rolling green hills are endless and the cliffs give way to breath taking views of the ocean. He swings the axe into the base stump before walking towards her. Sweat runs down the deep orange curled hair that covers his chest.

"You need a bath." Adalyn scrunches her nose at him as he loops an arm around her thin shoulders, ruffling the top of her head as he leads them towards the pen for the lamb. She squeals in protest, pushing against his thick body to escape his annoying task. He laughs deeply as he lets her go, walking ahead to enter the lamb pen.

"I need a glass of cold water more than a bath. Have you readied the fire?" he asks, ducking under the wooden shade structure. Two black pigs oink as they sniff through the yellow hay that covers the ground under the shade, Adalyn spots the broken lamb sitting at the edge of the shade. The other four scatter.

"Oh the poor thing." she whispers. Her father gently cradles the lamb in his arms, careful not to cause the creature more harm. It's back right leg is mangled beyond repair, pieces of its flesh hang from the bone while the joint itself gleams in the sun. Adalyn's surprised the skin of its leg it still attached, it turns her stomach as it bleats out weakly before hanging its head over fathers arm.

"I found it early hours tangled in a wild strand of barbed wire, must have been an off cutting that I missed." He shakes his head as he walks past his daughter. She locks the gate behind them as she trails him towards the slaughter block that sits behind the house, dark red stains the earth around the large cinder block.

"You'll have to hold her down for me." Her father places the lamb down, it begins to struggle against him but his large hands are firm and sure. Adalyn steels her stomach as she replaces his hands with her own. She avoids looking at its leg, focusing on its face instead. Her wide eyes are open and scared, she bleats in fear as father walks off to get the axe.

"It's going to be okay girl, you'll feel better soon." Adalyn murmurs, gently stroking the tips of her fingers over the lambs white curls. Her breathing quickens as her father returns, axe gleaming as it catches a ray of sun.

"Must we kill her?" she asks, looking up to him with a heavy heart.

"Have you ever heard of a three legged lamb running around?" Father asks, voice hard but eyes softening. He knows her dislike when it comes to helping him kill the farm animals.

"No." she whispers. She ignores the lurching in her stomach, threatening to make her sick. Her father loops rope from the block around its throat and firmly ties it down; allowing enough room for his axe to make a clean cut.

"Her sacrifice will feed us and keep your brothers and sister happy with a full warm belly. She's in pain Addie, it'd be cruel to leave her like this. Sometimes death is the better option, especially when there is so much suffering." He wipes the wood chips from his axe. Adalyn steadies her breathing, already feeling the gathering tears burning her eyes.

Father readies the axe, saying a swift pray for her soul to pass into Evermore. Adalyn moves her hand from the lambs shoulder, not wanting father to accidently take her hand with him.

"We must all make sacrifices we don't enjoy in this life. Just because I don't want to kill the lamb doesn't mean I will let it suffer and it's a sacrifice that I'm *willing* to make, even though I take no joy from it. It's a part of being human. The only thing that keeps us from the monsters is grieving the choices we make, even if they're necessary. This world can be a very dark place Adalyn, it is best not to forget that."

She looks away as he brings the axe down, as the body underneath her hands thrashes once more before going still for eternity, as the spray of blood catches her flushed cheek, running down into the collar of her dress.

"Go clean up. I'll prepare the lamb."

She doesn't need to be told twice.

2. ADALYN

ADALYN

Adalyn climbs into her small cot, resting against her feather pillow. Her stomach is warm and heavy from the lamb roast they'd had, sprinkled with rosemary and garlic with a drizzle of mint sauce over the tender meat and vegetables. She'd tried not to think about the small roasted body of the lamb, of what she had once been. All thoughts of guilt disappeared once Adalyn had her first mouthful, overcome with hunger and the array of flavour.

Emilia climbs into her cot that presses against the other side of the room, a small dresser sits between the head of their beds. The top holds two glasses of spring water for them throughout the night. She hums happily to herself, tucking her pale nightgown down her side as she lies down. Jarhn and Noah burst into the room, giggling as they come up and climb onto the bed. Adalyn tucks each of them under an arm and kisses the top of their auburn hair.

"Goodnight boys." she coos, squeezing them tightly.

"Night Addie," they say in unison, both giving her a sloppy kiss on each cheek. She smiles as they climb from the bed and jump over to Emilia's. Emilia laughs as the boys tickle her before squeezing her tightly. She whispers her goodnights.

Father ducks into the room, wearing his loose fitting night shirt and pants. "Goodnight girls." He comes over and plants a kiss on Adalyn's forehead.

"Goodnight father, I love you," she says, holding the blankets up to her chin. His eyes glisten.

"I love you too, Addie."

"Daddy can you take the boys now?" Emilia protests. Their father laughs deeply and goes to her bed. He scoops the boys up under each arm before leaning down to kiss her on the forehead. They murmur their goodnights and *I love you* before he turns and heads towards the boys' small room down the hall. The two sisters listen in silence as they beg for a bedtime story, mother hushes them as she goes in with their bottles for the night.

"I want mummy to tell us about the Valarki people again." Emilia whispers, staring intently towards where their parents hushed voices come from. Adalyn turns onto her side and props her head up on her hand, the thin strap of her pale white night-gown falls down her slender shoulder as her auburn hair spills on the pillow. Valarki are the dark fae that are said to roam the forests and rule over half the continent up north, burning villages to the ground and taking women as hostages to bring to their King. Adalyn had never seen or heard of any of their destruction aside from stories, of the group of feral fae that have a taste for human blood.

"You do know they're only stories to tell naughty children?" Emilia sighs and turns those bright eyes towards her sister.

"Stories have to come from some form of truth."

"What are you two bickering about?" Mother's warm voice interrupts Adalyn's reply, that *no*, not all stories stem from truth. Adalyn had told her plenty of tales she'd summoned from the tip of her tongue. Emilia sits up in her bed, the white sheet pools at her waist, "Mum can you tell us the story about the Valarki people again."

Mother frowns, "They're not bed time stories for little girls."

"Please mum!" Emilia begs, wobbling her bottom lip and

widening her eyes. Adalyn shakes her head, unable to supress her smile. No one could ever say no to Emilia when she pulls such a face. Mother relents with a sigh, pulling the stool from the end of Adalyn's bed. She sits between them, resting her hands in her lap.

"Are you listening as well?" She asks Adalyn, eyes shining. She sighs, nodding. She might as well, doubting sleep will claim her anytime soon. Adalyn settles in, keeping her eyes on her mother. She tells a hell of a story. Emilia settles in as well, her eyes bright with glee.

"Once upon a time, in a land far away, a faerie King rose through the ranks of the Valarki. He did not earn his title as King through royal blood, he slaughtered those who dare rose to challenge him. Each kill made him more respected by their people, until there was no one left to claim his title."

"Why would he kill them though?" Emilia interrupts.

"That is their tradition. If you listen without interrupting, you'll learn." Mother glances between both of the girls before continuing.

"The Valarki lived in the sacred mountains near the shore of the ocean, living in the confinements of their stone protection. The king grew restless in the stone walls, learnt to despise the scent of salt and sea in the air he breathed. He gathered his most trusted forces, sending them on a quest. That quest was to conquer the small village that lived at the base of their mountains, a test to see if he was met with resistance.

"They destroyed the village, killing the people and taking women slaves back to their King. He was delighted by this, by the slaves they'd brought him. He was content for mere months, until he grew restless once more and sent out his elite forces again. His force was under the command of his most trusted general, nicknamed the shadow of death. The others in the elite force are weapons and steel, while he is the mind that masters the demise of each village."

Mother pauses, her eyes distant as she recalls the story. A certain terror seizes the depths of her mother's usual warm and inviting eyes, her hands tremble in her lap as she takes a steadying breath. Adalyn can't say it's a memory that her mother is talking about. Refuses to believe it may be.

"Their king was delighted once more but grew bored in short weeks. He formulated another plan, to conquer the entire continent and take the land for himself. His people were more than willing to follow his orders, just as greedy as him. Their forces spread like wildfire, taking down every village they came across. Burning the homes to ashes and taking slaves once again."

"If that's true, why haven't they reached us?" Adalyn asks, unable to bite her tongue.

Mother blinks into reality as she looks at her eldest daughter, "If they ever reach us you best pray they don't take you as a slave. You best pray to any God who will hear you for safety and protection from them."

"Our continent can't be that big," Adalyn grumbles, looking towards the ceiling. Away from the steel in her mother's gaze, from the judgement at her ignorance.

"Our continent is large, in the last fifty years the Valarki King has drawn in his forces. The whispers believe the King has grown content with the land he possess, the riches he now has. His barren lands are far and wide, his people roam freely. The Valarki are monsters, no heart beats in their chest."

"What happens then?" Emilia asks, peering at their mother with new interest. Mother rises from her chair and strokes back Emilia's hair.

"What happens is that we live happy ever after and never have to worry about the Valarki reaching our home. Fifty years has passed and there has been no whisper of them." She leans down and kisses Emilia on the cheek before coming over to Adalyn and doing the same.

"Goodnight girls, I love you both." Their mother turns out their lantern, plunging the room into darkness aside from the moonlight that shines through the window above the bedside table. Adalyn watches as she walks down the hall and goes into her room where father awaits her. The twins snore softly, their soft grunts reaching Adalyn.

"Goodnight Emilia," Adalyn murmurs, rolling onto her side and facing the bare wall.

"Goodnight Addie, can we go back to the patch tomorrow?" Emilia murmurs, voice already heavy with sleep. Adalyn smiles, shutting her own eyes.

"Of course we can. I love you."

"I love you too." Emilia falls into sleep easy, her breathing evens out after a few silent moments.

Adalyn's eyes open on their own accord, her mind and body are wide awake as she continues to stare at the wall. The story their mother had told...the Valarki people aren't real. She simply can't believe it, no one else talks of them or their murderous forces.

She rolls onto her back, staring up at the rays of moonlight.

Mother's been telling the same story from the moment she was born, the conquering King and his evil forces. Human women being taken as slaves for the fae, Adalyn couldn't imagine it. If the King was still alive, why would they settle with no protection against them? Surely they bleed and die like the rest of the humans would.

Adalyn sits up, shaking her head. She is getting nowhere. Most nights the stories don't affect her, she's been hearing them since she was old enough to understand words. But tonight... uneasiness has settled in her bones. She can't decide if it's from the lamb having to die or the unsettled expression her mother wore telling the tale. A late night walk would do best to clear her mind of the horrors that now fill the darkness behind her eyelids. She slides from the bed, stepping lightly into her flats. She glances at Emilia once more; her face is slack with sleep. Peaceful.

She leaves their room, glancing in to see the twins both sprawled on their cots, holding hands between the bars. Mitch meows as Adalyn walks into the dining room from where he sits on the couch, she gives him a soft scratch before creeping towards the front door. The room smells of herbs and spices, of *home.*

She slips through the wooden door, careful to close it softly behind her. Adalyn breathes in the cool air, letting it scorch her lungs as she begins to head into the centre of the village. She wraps her arms around her chest as she walks along, no one in the village stirs. An owl hoots in the distance eerily, sending a chill down her spine.

By this time of night everyone is asleep, dragged into the depths of slumber. Most nights Adalyn grew restless, needing to go for a walk to the herb patch before weariness dawned on her.

There's nothing better than a late night stroll, listening to the nature that comes alive once the sun sets. The moon beams down on her, making her pale freckled skin glow.

The tall towering pine forest that surrounds the village is encased in darkness, the moon light only touching the tips of their deep green leaves that shine black in the night. People barely venture into the forest and definitely never at night time. No one walks further than the large stream that runs down through the trees, no one dares.

Alone with her thoughts, she can admit that just *maybe* there is some truth behind her mother's tale.

Adalyn picks up pace, winding through the empty streets as she heads closer to the herb patch. A shadow flashes to her right, catching her attention. She halts and peers into the darkness of the side street between two small cottages. Her eyes strain, looking for any sign of what it may be.

Adalyn brushes it off, deciding it must have been an owl fluttering past.

She tells herself she's only running for the herb patch to simply make herself tired, not because she's afraid.

She reaches the wooden fence and leaps over it with ease, the moment her feet hit the dirt she continues to run through the dirt path that winds through all the different herbs. The moonlight offers her comfort from the shadows as she reaches the large lavender patch, she halts and rests her hands on her knees. Each breath is full of lavender, calming the racing heart in her chest. Adalyn walks into the middle of the patch and lies down on her back, breaking off a stalk of lavender to hold.

She listens to the chirps of birds, the harmony of crickets. It is peaceful, the purple lavender stalks sway in the cool breeze. It's a pretty contrast against the dark blue sky dotted with millions of white stars, clear of clouds.

Adalyn closes her eyes as she begins to feel that familiar sleepiness settle into her bones, she gently runs her fingers over the lavender stalk that's clutched in one hand. Soon she'd return home, dragging her feet to the warmth of her bed. Emilia will still be asleep once she returns, no one in her family knows she goes for nightly walks to clear her racing mind.

Adalyn's almost drifting to sleep when the breeze changes. Her stomach drops as a sense of *wrongness* overtakes her. She opens her eyes and lay perfectly still, suddenly gripped with terror.

You're being silly, there's nothing out here.

She tries to calm herself, taking deep breaths. The breeze picks up, Adalyn takes a steadying breath as she slowly sits up and peers over the stalks of lavender. She faces towards the way she'd come, towards home. Everything is quiet. Her skin prickles with awareness as she tastes a tendril of smoke in the air. Adalyn looks over her shoulder, towards the other side of the village.

Nothing, she squints—

A orange flame licks at a thatch roof towards the edge of the forest, it's golden light a beacon in the darkness of the night.

Adalyn jumps to her feet and begins to run towards the fence, towards the burning home. Her first thought is to get to the fire, help the people inside. If the people inside can't smell the smoke they won't be able to make it out in time before the roof collapses inwards. She squeezes the lavender strand in her hand as her hair whips at her cheeks and neck. It billows behind her, cascading half way down her back in a river of red. The fence comes into view,

Adalyn pushes herself faster and grabs the railing; vaulting over in one smooth move.

The pounding of her heavy footfalls is all she can hear as she runs through the winding streets towards the burning cottage, there's no animals making any noise, the crickets have even stopped their song. Her stomach twists but she continues to run forward, ignoring how her lungs burn with exhaustion as do her thighs. She can't remember the last time she'd ran this fast.

The crackle and pop of the thatch roof burning fills her ears as the air grows heavy with smoke. Adalyn skids to a stop, eyes widening in terror at what lays before her.

The row of cottages in front of her have caught fire, blazing into the night. She turns her head frantically around, looking for *anyone* who has also noticed.

Her eyes catch on swift movement, now that she's stopped she notices the fast movement that's hidden in the shadows. Movement she noticed earlier and had ignored. A sharp whistle fills the silence before being cut short. Adalyn looks upwards to see a flaming arrow embedding into one of the cottage roofs.

More flaming arrows fly into the night and in the next blink of an eye the fire is spreading rapidly; jumping from roof to roof.

She turns and runs to the closest house that first catches her attention.

"Hey! Wake up! Your house is on fire!" She screams as she pounds on the door, the skin on her hand splinters with each forceful hit. She opens her mouth to scream again when the door flies open. Adalyn falls hard and looks upwards.

A man stands in the door way, mouth gaping like a fish. They both look down to see the tip of a silver blade shining through his chest. Blood spills from his lips as she screams, the sword is pulled out and he's kicked forward. He falls onto her; blood begins to coat the front of her body before she rolls him off. Adalyn wipes the blood from her face and looks to the now open doorway.

A pointed ear male stands before her, grinning with inhuman

glee as he takes a step forward. His tall build is muscled and strong, half concealed in the shadow of the home.

Adalyn's mind empties of all thought, *Valarki.*

A small boy struggles in his grip, the fae has his fingers knotted in the boy's brown hair. He stands tall, looking down at her. His purple eyes glow with joy, his ears point sharply towards the sky.

Adalyn is frozen where she sits.

They are real, they are here and they want *blood*.

In a swift motion the male drags his blade across the small boy's throat. His crying is cut short and replaced by rasping as he falls to the ground and presses his small hands to his throat.

More doors burst open as people run screaming from their homes, more Valarki males emerge from the shadows; all carrying weapons for their demise.

Adalyn rises and begins to sprint down the open street, she needs to get home. She needs to warn her family they're here.

Oh my god they're here.

She pushes herself harder, trying to block out the screams that begin to ring through the air in harmony. She needs to get home, to her *family.* So many cottages have caught fire that she loses count, only knowing that they're a golden blaze in her peripheral vision as she sprints forward.

Adalyn runs past the herb garden, finding Magda on her porch trying to fight against another Valarki. She does not hesitate as she heads for the old woman's burning home, she leaps up the stairs and onto the muscled back of the fae male. Adalyn wraps her arms around his throat and pulls the two of them backwards, he stumbles down the steps and they fall.

Adalyn is crushed under his weight; the breath leaves her as black stars dot her vision. He rolls off her with an animalistic growl, she opens her eyes in time to see him drive his sword through Magda's plump stomach. Magda's scream dies on her lips as she falls to her knees, the light in her blue eyes begins to dim.

Adalyn's heart constricts with pain. She pushes herself to sitting, blinking wildly to clear her mind.

The male towers over her, blood drips from his sword. He smiles ferociously, showing two pointed canines. His orange eyes are as bright as the burning thatch roof behind him. She scrambles backwards, eyes widening.

"What a lovely surprise you are." He prowls towards her, taking his time.

"You—you're a monster!" she shouts. Dirt and blood embeds under her nails. His eyes darken as he swings his sword downwards, she rolls out of the way as the blade just skims her left shoulder. She rolls to standing and begins to run for her home again, the pursuit of his feet from behind is heavy in her ears. A Valarki and human man burst from a home, she crashes into them and sprawls to the ground.

The fae hacks at the man's head, a crazed gleam in his eye as blood coats his hands and dagger, splattering his cheeks.

A hot, blinding pain has Adalyn screaming.

She's pushed forward as a blade slices through the soft skin between her neck and shoulder. It grates against her collar bone as blood spills down the front of her chest. She falls to her hands, struggling to put any pressure on her right arm as she tries to crawl forward. The thin strap of her nightgown falls down her right shoulder.

She can't look at the damage.

A heavy boot comes down on her right calf, has her screaming in pain as she's trapped. Adalyn looks up to see more Valarki pulling people from their homes, children, men and woman are being killed before her. Black smoke coats the air above them as the flames give light to the nightmare before her. A vivid nightmare she cannot escape.

"I might keep you." The male above her says, he kicks her over until she is on her back and staring up at him. His silver blade is pointed at her chest, one movement from him and she'd be skewered.

Adalyn bares her teeth at him, it only delights him more.

"The king is definitely going to like you, I'm sure he won't be bothered if I decide to have my fun with you before we return." He steps back from her, moving as smooth as liquid.

They stare at each other, hunted and hunter. Adalyn becomes fully aware of the blood that coats her, of the blood pulsing from the deep gash of his sword. Of the burning cottages, the screams of the dying people. *Her people.* She manages to sit up on her knees, her hands shake in her lap as her breathing comes in gasps.

God the blood—

3. Adalyn
Adalyn

There's so much blood—

Blood that isn't just her own.

It stains her hands, flecks her face and runs down her bare throat. Soaks into the hem of her torn dress, exposing the deep gash. Her blood drips from his sword and sinks into the earth. It runs down her front, a steady flow that matches the erratic heartbeat in her chest.

Adalyn's knees dig into the soft earth as she stares at the monster before her. A monster she never truly believed was real, only a mere night terror to tell children who had been naughty. His deep brown hair is sleek and long, tied back at the top of his head to expose the shaved sides. His arched ears are adorned with studs. He wears the blood splatter across his angular face like war pain, relishing in it.

How terribly wrong she was.

His unearthly orange eyes gleam with feral delight as his lips pull into a grin, "You're definitely coming back with us."

She can't speak, she can barely *breath*. Surely death will be better than wherever he wishes to take her. He takes a step towards her, his blood splattered boots shine from the cottages that are now blazing, black smoke hangs heavy in the air along with the other tortuous screams that fill the space between them.

"How does that sound? I may keep you as my own personal lamb."

Her bottom lip trembles but she refuses to cower before him, refuses to cry.

Refuses to give him the satisfaction of breaking her.

His eyes darken at the defiance, ready for the challenge she presents him.

Soft foot falls come up behind him, so light she can barely hear them over the ringing in her ears. She can barely focus on anything while her shoulder still ebbs blood, the front right side of her torn dress clings to her now.

Her family—

Hot tears sting her eyes, she doesn't know what's happened to them. If they're alive or—

Smoke parts as the approaching man comes to a stop. He stands tall, his straight raven black hair moves like liquid around his face as he focuses on the fae that stands above her. Two pointed ears peak out from the depths of darkness.

"I believe she's suffered enough." His voice is as cold as death, causing her skin to prickle with unease. The male before her snarls as he slightly turns to look at the newcomer. It allows Adalyn to have full view of the new monster.

"Our purpose is to make them suffer." His hand tightens on the silver sword, knuckles whitening and begging for more bloodshed. Adalyn tears her eyes from the sharp blade and finds herself looking at black leather boots, not one spot of blood stains them.

His dark pants are tight around his muscular legs, carving out the defined lines in his thighs. Her eyes travel further, noting that he's not wearing pants at all. No, he's wearing a battle suit. The tight fitting assortment leaves little to the imagination, defining each curve of his muscle, his broad shoulders and the muscle that coil from his biceps down to his forearm. A lone sword is strapped to his back, still sheathed.

His face—

Gods, his face is carved by the gods themselves.

His ice blue eyes asses Adalyn, cold and calculating. His dark hair reaches the tips of his shoulders, shadows dance across his high cheek bones and hollow out his sharp jaw line. His dark eyebrows raise ever so slightly, the only sign of recognition.

He slides his eyes from her own to the male before him, "Our purpose it to follow our King's orders. We have accomplished that, leave her here to die or bring her with us. I really do not care."

"She'll be coming." The male that had first found Adalyn turns towards her, eyes gleaming in a way that makes her wish for death. "The fun we will have with this one."

The dark-haired male assesses Adalyn once more, dragging his eyes over her ragged form before turning and swiftly stalking off. He disappears into the darkness of the smoke and night. It's as if he hadn't been there at all.

Not all monsters are hideous, some wear faces of the Gods with voices of spun silk.

"Let's go." The male comes forward, so fast she doesn't have time to move as he wraps a large hand around the bicep of her right arm. She cries out as the wound gushes more blood, pulsing with pain and fire. He pulls her up on unsteady feet, dragging her along as he walks down the road.

Adalyn takes the chance to glance frantically around, looking for any sign of her family. She watches in horror as the other fae males break into burning homes, ripping people from their beds and driving their swords into any soft flesh they can find. Bile burns her throat as blood coats the ground, beginning to run in a river down the path they walk.

It's hard to see anything through the smoke that hangs above them, hard to focus over the screams that fill her ears. Adalyn coughs and splutters, smoke and the metallic tang of blood burns her nostrils. She blinks back tears and looks to the baskets that were once propped up against a burning home, now scattered and trampled. She determines they're walking along the path that will take her to her family.

She struggles against her captor's tight grip, tugging relentlessly at his long fingers and clawing at his hand. Nothing she does deters him. Each movement causes the gash in her shoulder to ooze more, leaving her light headed and full of blinding pain.

Her father had once said *we all have choices to make; some of these choices will cause suffering or end it.*

If she wants to survive this- survive them- she has to live. She is nothing without this body, nothing without her life.

She chooses to fight against his hold as the outline of her *burning home* comes into view, throwing the last kernels of her strength into the motion of trying to pry his fingers away. She plants her feet into the dirt as he begins to drag her past her home, the thatch roof burns brightly, the open door is splintered and shattered.

"*Mum! Dad!*" she screams, her eyes skip frantically over the burning structure, looking for any signs of life. Any sign of hope. Her scream causes her captor to pause, looking to what has her frantic. To her shock he releases his hand and crosses his arms over his broad chest and gestures for Adalyn to look.

She doesn't hesitate as she ducks into the burning building. Adalyn chokes on the smoke and falls to her knees, taking shallow breaths as she begins to crawl against the wooden floor boards. The pain in her shoulder is nothing compared to the ache in her heart.

She makes it to the hallway, sweltering heat licks at her back. Sweat runs down her face as she coughs more, holding her right arm against her chest as she tries her best to crawl along.

She crawls into her parents' room, blinking through the tears to see blood – deep red blood bubbles and pops against the heat on the wooden floor boards. The wooden cupboard catches fire, the wood groans against the heat but allows her to see clearer.

Two bodies lay very, very still on the bed.

"*No!*" she screams as her father's pale, blood flecked face stares back at her with lifeless eyes. Her scream is broken and never ending, her entire soul is cleaved in two. She vomits onto the floorboards, knowing her mother lies beside him on the bed. Together in eternal sleep, together on their journey to Evermore.

She scrambles backwards as the bed sheets catch flame, licking at the bodies of her parents. Parents she'll never hug again, never talk to again. She cries as she crawls down the hall, the roof above her groans as the thatch threatens to give out.

She looks into the twins small bed room, her heart bleeds in her chest when her eyes catch both of her little brothers laying in *pieces* on the wooden floor. Small chunks of flesh and limb, unrecognisable apart from the auburn hair that covers their decapitated heads.

She pushes into the room she shares with Emilia, if her body is in here—she will lay right down and die along with them.

Horror turns to a touch of relief when she doesn't see any blood or unmoving bodies in their room, by some miracle she has escaped – or become captive. The thought of her little sister out there in the hands of those monsters has her on her feet, ducking low to avoid the flames that lick towards her. She spots an unmoving grey bundle on the couch; she stops and runs her hands against Mitch's fur. A sob wracks her body at his still form.

A groan and shatter has her pivoting forward, she runs the last steps from the house before stumbling out just as the thatch roof gives in and collapses. Flames burst from the open door and windows. She turns and stumbles backwards.

My family—

My family.

My family are—

A rough hand yanks on her right bicep once more, dragging her forward towards the forest. She fights against his grip, she is so focused on trying to escape his hold that she doesn't register when they escape the heavy smoke, leaving the dying screams behind. It isn't until her foot moves from firm dirt to soft grass that she looks up, only to find the towering forest before her. Adalyn's captor yanks her towards him, causing blinding pain to overtake her vision momentarily.

He snarls in her face, "Continue to fight me all you like. I prefer when they fight, it makes it that more enjoyable."

Her hollow stomach bottoms out at the meaning behind his words, a hint of what is truly in store for her.

"She can't fight you when she's dead." That familiar voice from earlier has her captor flashing his eyes towards him in annoyance. Adalyn takes gulping breaths as she looks towards the forest where the voice came from. He stands at the edge, so still he almost blends in with the very shadows that loom across the expanse of grass from the full moon. Even from the short distance she can see the unearthly glow in his eyes, the stiffness in his shoulders.

"I can still fuck her corpse though." Her captor spits at the ground, continuing to pull her towards the open path in the forest. The edges of her vision begin to haze, her feet take stumbling steps as if she's a newborn learning to walk for the first time.

Adalyn can't find her balance, her mind can't clear.

There's so much pain she can taste it on her tongue, feel it with each breathe in her lungs. Death – a swift death would be more pleasant than this torturous one.

Her sister is out there, the thought of her alive is the only thing allowing Adalyn to cling to this life.

Adalyn may very well be a corpse at this rate. She weakly reaches up and presses her free hand over the gash, feeling the smooth collar bone at the bottom of it. She's too afraid to see the damage he's done.

Foot falls come into step behind them, she feels eyes burning into her back. She doesn't care at this point, he can stare all he likes. Adalyn's eyes threaten to close, they are so heavy and she simply wants to lie down and close them, to give herself over to the heaviness that now bares down over her.

"I've made the orders to return to base camp and leave the village in nothing but ashes. We leave at first light." The voice behind her is clipped, assertive. The male beside her may be holding the sharpened sword, but the one behind them gives the command to wield that sword.

"I believe the King will be interested in the females we return with." The grip on her arm tightens, his voice is filled with pure delight, "I'm hoping he won't pick this one for his harem."

Adalyn swallows against the dryness in her throat, rallying up the embers of fire in her words. She manages to turn and look at him, forcing him to meet her blazing stare.

"Aren't your own females good enough to fuck?" her voice is a weak rasp, but she still manages to spit the words at him. His orange eyes darken, he raises his sword – presumably to drive it through her chest.

A hand wraps firmly around her left bicep, not painful, but enough so that she can't slip from his grip.

"I will take her." His tone holds little room for argument.

"I'll go find another then." The orange eyed brute continues to stare at her, "Speak out of line again and I will cut your mortal tongue out girl."

She presses her lips together as he releases her arm, she almost collapses as blood begins to return to her tingling hand. Her knees buckle as a sense of being slips away. A strong hand holds her upright, allowing her to lean her full weight against his side. He's incredibly warm, it makes Adalyn want to curl into him. His hand moves from her arm, the moment of no contact has her falling to the ground.

She lands hard on her right side, a sob rips from her throat as pain in her shoulder obliterates any fire she had left. It leaves her in shock, the tips of her fingers begin to grow numb; the feeling spreads up her arms.

Warm, strong arms lift her from the ground, holding her under her knees and behind her neck. Her arms hang down while her head rolls to the side. She takes a shallow breath, for a moment the scent of crystal blue waters and black orchid blind her from the pain, replacing the smell of blood and death. She closes her eyes, her heartbeat growing weak in her chest.

"Uht. I don't think so. Open your eyes." That cool tone breaks through the darkness, coaxes her towards the light. Demands she obey. It has her cracking her eyes open to meet his ice blue ones. She sees his face, his expression gives nothing away as he looks forward once more.

"Leave me to die." Her voice is barely a scratched whisper on the wind, his fae hearing picks up the words.

"I'm afraid I can't."

A small smile tugs at the edges of her lips, "I'm afraid you may not have a choice in the matter, monster."

He looks down at her just in time to see her eyes close, his own burning fire simmering. She doesn't open her eyes again, his voice fades until it is barely louder than a murmur.

She collapses into the darkness, letting it carry her away from the fate that awaits her. A fate that is worse than the comfort death can provide.

4. Killian

Killian

The commanding general looks down at the limp woman in his arms, he can scent the stale blood coating her that isn't her own, mixed with the sweet scent of her own fresh blood. Her blood splattered and tear tracked face hangs over his arm, exposing her pale throat and the pulse that barely beats. He looks to the gash on her right shoulder, hissing at the bone and muscle Polarian's sword sliced through. Even now it still leaks blood, draining the life force from her.

He curses under his breath and moves like a wraith through the shadows of the forest around him, each step faster than the last as he heads for the base camp they'd set up only days before. Two healers wait at the camp. After meeting resistance for the first conquest it had seemed wise, especially considering the King desired the human females to be brought to him alive and untouched by the elite force.

Killian glances down to the female's soft featured face, her plump lips are slightly agape and leaching of rose colour with every minute that passes. If he didn't reach the camp soon, he'd be burying her corpse. He doesn't care about the humans— not when the wrath of the King is a reckoning force within itself. Once, he had tried to stop the women being taken as slaves, had tried to stop his comrades from beating and raping them. It hadn't ended well for him. No, it had ended with the King slaughtering his pregnant wife who had been weeks from birthing their child.

From that moment onwards he receded into himself, a shell of the man he once was. He drowned his sorrows with fire whiskey, fucking and death. He knew better to interfere now, had known for centuries. He had worked his way up to being the King's second hand by brute force and cold efficiency, but he had never once called upon the services of the mortal female slaves, had never once taken any human woman –willingly or against their will.

When his wife's life force was sliced from her throat he vowed to never love another female again. For his wife and child he would continue to have his loyalty, the King had been ruthless enough to remind him there are worse things than death in this life. It has been a lesson he has never forgotten.

Ahead fire crackles, the soft murmur of two male voices echo around the currently empty camp. Killian steps from the shadows, casting his eyes over the two fae males that sit by the fire. They stand immediately, bowing their heads slightly.

"She needs healing," he says roughly, crossing the space. Karis, the eldest healer, peers at the female in his arms. His green eyes asses her wound, continuing over her body for any others. His short blonde hair is pushed back by a long hand, he twists his lips in worry.

"That's a mighty wound she has there, even now her pulse barely bothers to beat," he murmurs, gently pressing those slender fingers to her throat. Killian stiffens, looking down at the dying female.

"Is there nothing you can do?" He demands, eyes blazing with hidden power. Karis looks up to him, taking his hand from her throat.

"She will need blood, lots of it. Whoever has done this meant it to be a killing blow."

Killian growls, the sound vibrates against his chest. *Of course* she'd need blood. He pushes all rational thought aside as he takes a seat beside one of the outstretched gurneys for the wounded. He gently places the woman down. She doesn't stir, her chest barely rises with each shallow breath she draws.

"Attach me to her then." Killian begins to roll up the sleeve of his left arm, not thinking too deeply into what he is doing. Why did he feel the need to save this one female? Maybe it was because she'd faced Polarian with her final breath and had spat those words like they held venom that could melt his skin.

"General, I don't believe it is wise," Orios, the second younger healer says hesitantly. Both healers move to her other side, looking at Killian as if he'd gone mad. Killian glares at both of them, a glare that usually sends others fleeing.

"General it is one human female. I'm sure they'll be bringing plenty back. We still have one village to raid before we return, the King will have more than enough for the picking." Karis tries to reason with him, frowning slightly. Of course he's right, Killian knows this, but yet he can't let this female in particular die. He stares down at her face relaxed in unconsciousness, her vibrant auburn hair is a tangle around her head and spills over the sides of the gurney. He picks up the scent of smoke and blood, with a subtle hint of lavender and vanilla.

"We save this one, I will not ask again." Killian rolls his sleeve above his bicep, the vein in the crook of his elbow begins to bulge at the tightness of his sleeve.

Karis sighs, "If you must insist."

The pair of healers work in silent harmony as they summon their magic and open one of their leather medicine bags. Killian props himself on the gurney beside the female, careful not to touch her. He places his arm beside her pale one, Orios crouches down in front of him with the needle ended tube grasped between his teeth.

His white hair curls around his face and arched ears, his pale lemon coloured eyes asses the vein in Killian's arm. He gently stabs the vein, waiting for the blood to begin filling the tube.

"How much will she need?" Killian asks, watching as his dark red blood begins to dribble into the tube. The healers had enchanted it, allowing only one end of blood to flow through. Karis begins to work on the deep gash in her shoulder, covering the torn muscle with a healing balm that will help repair it to full use.

"A lot, she's teetering on the line that crosses to death. Don't be surprised if she doesn't make it." Orios grunts, beginning to thread the sharpened needle through her pale skin. Orios finds the vein in her arm and stabs the other end in, Killian's blood begins to fill the tube and move swiftly into her arm. His own arm tingles around the puncture, sending sharp aches down to his fingers. He hadn't given blood before and could only hope it wouldn't kill her.

"Now we wait," Orios says as he rises, brushing his hands over the loose fitting pants he wears, "would you like something to drink?"

"Water, please." Killian grunts as he watches Karis carefully stitch the gash together, until there are fourteen green lines holding the flesh together. Karis leans backwards, stowing his needle and thread into the leather bag.

"Why this girl?" He asks carefully, not wanting to imply anything. Killian looks over her soft features once more, her small button nose had been shining red along with her cheeks when he'd first seen her kneeling before Polarian; now they're a sickly white colour. A shade from death. When she'd spied him standing there she hadn't cowered like humans usually do, no, she continued to glare right at him with those burning amber eyes.

Orios returns with a jug of water, Killian takes it and nods his thanks before balancing it on his knee. He grabs a rag from beside the fire and dips the end into the water, reaching over he begins to gently drag the wet cloth over her face. Slowly the blood splatter begins to come away.

He'd heard her screams for her parents, seen her rush into the burning building with no trace of hesitation that the flames may claim her life as well. He'd heard her crying for them, finding them slaughtered and still she'd spat words like venom at Polarian. Still she hadn't stopped fighting until she was too weak to do so. Killian continues to wipe her face, only stopping once there's no trace of blood. He dumps the cloth into the jug of water before sitting it under the gurney.

Her screams had sounded very much like his own when he'd been forced to his knees, head held while his wife's throat was slit.

"She has spirit," is all he says, his tone leaves no room for argument or questions. Karis nods once before leaving to speak with Orios, soon the others would return with other females. The carriage that carries the females is in the open under a large pine tree, the light from the fire dances up the thick wooden walls that open to a small barred window. The six females in there make no move to peer through the small hole. They'd travelled with horses and carriages, moving swiftly across the land and covering more distance than on foot. Killian will be happy to return to the castle, bathe in the hot bubbling spring that's hidden under the dungeons of the castle that no one else had managed to find, maybe he'd even indulge in a whiskey or two—

A soft, female groan clears his trailing thoughts. He looks down to the woman on the gurney, her chest rises higher than before, soft curls of air leave her nose from the chill of the night.

She'd lived, even though she may not be happy about it once she's fully aware of what has happened to her. *Who* has saved her.

Killian watches as her dark thick lashes drag upwards, those dull blood shot amber eyes clash with his own. She blinks once more to clear the haze of death, he watches as her reality slams into her. She trembles on the bed, eyes glistening with unshed tears.

I'm afraid you may not have a choice in the matter, monster.

He hadn't forgotten her last words, and from the burning look in her eyes she hadn't either. Killian's so focused on reading the emotions in her eyes that he fails to notice the chunk of wood she's grasped in her other hand that hangs below the gurney.

Fails to notice it until the sharp wood connects with the side of his face, sending him careening towards the fire. The tube is ripped from his arm, the dull sting is nothing compared to the ache that now ebbs in his temple.

Warm liquid runs down his cheek.

He growls as he touches the spot the wood had connected with, his fingers come back with blood. She'd managed to make him bleed. A *human female* has managed to make the shadow of death *bleed*. He looks up from where he still sits on his ass, half furious but slightly impressed.

She sways where she stands, the chunk of wood clasped in her small hands. Her eyes flitter around the camp looking for a route of escape before focusing back on him. Her auburn hair glows red from the light of the fire, casting a red halo around her head.

"Killian—"

"I'm fine." He growls to Karis as he stands, wiping the blood from his fingers on his pants. He would be healed in a matter of moments thanks to his magic. Orios and Karis stay back, silently watching them.

"Let me go," the girls voice rasps. She doesn't cower as she maintains eye contact with Killian, only takes a slight step back when he rises.

"You can thank me for saving your life whenever you're ready," Killian says roughly. His gods damn head aches—

"You lie," she hisses, tightening her hold on the wood. Killian tilts his head and flickers his eyes towards her arm, where the tube now leaks his blood but is still attached to her arm. She looks towards it, finally realising it's there. She swallows hard, her throat bobbing with the motion.

"I'm not going to turn into one of you am I?" She asks, looking back towards him.

He lowers his brows, "No. No one can turn into one of us. It is how we're born."

The thin strap of her nightgown has slipped over her right shoulder, blood leaks from the stitching. He breathes heavily through his nose, of course she isn't going to make it easy. His eyes lower, to where her nightgown is plastered to the swell of her generous breasts; down her slender waist to wide hips—

"Are all Valarki males perverts?" She spits, his eyes flash to her face once more; to find her cheeks a shade darker.

"Only the worst ones," he growls in response, she pales slightly. Her eyes flitter over his shoulder before focusing on him again. She must be remembering that Polarian is the male that first got her into this situation.

"What is this tube?" She keeps one hand wrapped around the wood while the other pulls the long needle out, throwing it to the ground. Karis hisses his disapproval behind them.

"You were dying. I gave you my blood to save you." In the distance Killian hear's the others approaching, picks up the cries of protests from the females they bring with them.

"Why?" She demands, frowning slightly.

"Don't worry. I'm starting to regret it," Killian growls, hands flexing at his sides. He can imagine she'd be in pain, emotionally and physically.

"Let me go," she says again, her body beginning to tremble. She's still missing far too much blood.

"To go back to what? A home burnt to cinders and a dead family?" He questions, knowing he's hit a raw spot. She flinches backwards.

"You're a monster." Her eyes widen as she lowers her arms, chest heaving with the effort to hold onto the wood. Killian prowls around the gurney and closes the distance between them, until he can scent her lavender and vanilla musk. He'd been called much worse. She stares up at him, jaw set in defiance. Up this close he notices the flecks of gold against the amber in her eyes, the scatter of freckles across her nose and cheeks.

"You have two options, you let me escort you to the carriage or you wait for Polarian to return and do so. He'd be more than willing."

Recognition crosses her face, her bottom lip quivers but she manages to whisper, "You."

Killian gently takes the wood from her hand, tossing it behind him on the fire. It crackles and pops as it catches flame.

She wobbles as she walks beside him, his hand anchoring her to the earth at the small of her back. He guides her to the carriage, unlatching the back door. The other females cower towards the back, he lets her go as she gingerly climbs up the two steps and collapses onto the wooden bench closest to the open door and watches him warily. His hand is still warm from her touch. He grasps the two doors, "Next time you draw a weapon on me, I won't be as forgiving."

He closes the door and latches them once more, turning to see the others arrive with another five females. He nods in greeting before prowling towards his private carriage, needing a strong drink.

He may just yet live to regret bringing this woman back to life.

5. Adalyn

Adalyn

Adalyn can only imagine what she is experiencing is shock – pure shock.

The carriage is mainly in darkness, aside from the small barred window above the other bench that sits across from her. Fire light flickers into the carriage, while the cries of the other women reach her ears. She tries to even her breathing as she looks to the other women huddled in the back corner.

She doesn't trust herself to move.

Killian had given her his blood, to supposedly save her life. Why that Valarki bastard had done that, she is unsure. He'd have hidden motives, it might be a calling card for once they return to wherever it is they're taking them.

Adalyn swallows hard, blocking out the images of any of those monsters having their hands on her body. It disgusts her and she'd put up one hell of a fight if any of them even tried to go near her. She may be captured, but there's still hope.

Emilia had escaped, she can only believe her sister got out before they came to their home and took refuge somewhere none of them could find her. Adalyn would come for her, fight until her last breath for her. If it means waiting until she's healed and in full heath, then so be it. She'd endure anything for her, the only member of her kin she now has left.

Oh god, her parents, her brothers—

The carriage doors swing outwards, Adalyn holds a hand up against the light of the fire and slides deeper along the bench; as far as her body will allow her to move. She watches as five females pile into the carriage, smoke clings to them as fiercely as their sobs. The fae male she assumes is Polarian herds them in, a terrifying gleam in his eyes.

Adalyn looks past him, for Killian, only to find no sight of him.

Coward, hiding from what he's doing.

A girl sits to her left while the others take the opposite bench. She moves closer to the carriage door, leaning her head back against the wood. The gash in her shoulder has been stitched, the blood had stopped leaking through once she'd settled. He may have brought her back from the brink of death, but she's going to make him regret *choosing* to save her life. She's going to make all of them regret it.

"Where are we?" A soft female voice whispers from the other end of the carriage.

"Oakshire," one of the girls across from Adalyn sniffles, a voice she vaguely recognises. The women who had climbed in are people of her village, the last survivors of Oakshire. Only taken to be used as cows for slaughter.

"Oh god, we'll be heading to Ravendew before they'll take us back to their lands." The female voice from before whispers, "I'm Allison by the way."

"Synthia."

Adalyn vaguely recalls who Synthia is, she's a few years older than her. Always had been a quite girl growing up. Adalyn closes her eyes, counting breaths. The pain in her shoulder feels like fire and she's still incredibly weak. Each limb feels as if it's a thousand pounds.

Sleep. She needs to somehow sleep.

Images of her slaughtered family flash across the darkness behind her eyelids. The carriage had fallen into the soft silence of sobbing as every female comes to terms with what has happened, with what each of them has lost.

Outside the carriage the hunters celebrate, their cheers overpower the sobs. Their cheerful conversation makes her blood boil, but she's in no position to do anything about it. Not yet. She does the next best thing she can and begins to hum the nursery rhyme her mother had been humming that afternoon.

Her humming breaks in places as tears stream down her cheeks, she forces herself to remember *good and happy* memories of her family, of the life she'd had with them. Of her mother's baking, her father wrapping her in his arms, her brothers bursting with happiness every morning upon seeing her.

Of Emilia sitting in the clover patch, looking for the ghastly four leaf clover.

She wishes she'd found it, maybe then her family could have found some luck.

Adalyn begins to drift into a deep sleep, the darkness so black that no horrible memories dare chase her there. Nothing but the soft comfort of warmth surrounds her as she sinks into it, allowing it to take control of her. In the morning she'd begin to figure out a plan, but until then she'd sleep.

Adalyn awakes to the other girls murmuring. She yawns and straightens, having slumped on the carriage doors overnight. Her neck aches and her shoulder burns but she's alive, learning it's more of a curse than a blessing.

"What's going on?" she mumbles, rubbing the last tendrils of sleep from her eyes. Sunlight streams into the carriage, illuminating the females that had been cowering at the other end of the carriage last night and the few females from her village. Their eyes all shine with fear and that same hollow feeling Adalyn feels in her chest, as if taking each breath is unfair while everyone they loved was slaughtered.

"It's morning...they'll be attaching chain link cuffs to us soon. We'll be led out to relieve ourselves," Allison says, swallowing thickly. Adalyn looks over to her. Her dark brown skin is covered with dried splattered blood and dirt, her white dress is torn mid-thigh exposing a nasty gash. Allison's hands shake in her lap as she looks to Adalyn, her eyes reminding her of caramel mixed with the gold of honey. Dark hair waves around her thin shoulders, reaching her chest before curling at the ends. She's gorgeous.

"Relieve ourselves?" Adalyn echoes, frowning slightly.

She rubs her lips together, "They line us up to piss, watching."

The other few girls who are still trying to face what is happening begin to cry softly into their hands. Adalyn can't blame them but all she feels is her stomach rolling violently. She looks up to the bars, gingerly standing. She wobbles slightly but holds herself up well enough as she takes two steps to reach the window.

She grabs onto the metal bars and looks into the camp.

Acid climbs up her throat.

Valarki males roam around the camp, all dressed in similar outfits. Brown long pants with leather boots laced up to their calves, each carry a weapon of sorts. She can imagine they'd have more hiding between the folds of their shirts and behind the leather breast plate that is laced to their chests. Each male has that *unnaturalness* about them, none of them could be mistaken for anything other than what they are.

Black, raven hair flickers to her right. She pushes her face against the bars but the hair is gone. She scowls.

"Sit back down!" Allison hisses as someone tugs at the ends of her nightgown. Adalyn steps down and turns, the hand lets go of her dress and she sits back on the bench. Allison nods silently towards the door before casting her eyes down. The other women follow lead.

Adalyn can't.

Her dress is stiff on her chest, reeking of blood and smoke. Her skin crawls as she finally notices all the dry blood flaking from her arms and throat, she looks down at her trembling hands to find dark red embedded under her lengthened nails.

She's caught off guard when the carriage doors swing open. Her face jerks upwards, clashing with those ice blue eyes from the night before. Those eyes had been the first thing she'd seen once she'd returned from the darkness of unconsciousness, reminding her of ice and steel. So cold and empty that it had sent a spear of ice through her, freezing her to the bone. Involuntarily her eyes roam from his face, over his broad chest. His black battle suit is spotless, hugging each muscle this man possesses.

"Now who is the pervert?" He *purrs*, those full lips pulling up in a smirk as those eyes glitter with satisfaction.

Adalyn sees red as she flies at him, all common sense empties from her head when her body collides with his own. She hits and claws at whatever part of him she can get her hands onto, they hit the ground hard and he hisses in frustration.

In one movement he twirls them, pinning her underneath him with the hard planes of his body. He breathes heavy, hair hanging around his face. Her hands are pinned above her head, his grip firm on her small wrists. Her chest rises and falls rapidly as the red in her vision clears. Three dark red scratches mar his right cheek, blood leaks from the middle one. She grins violently, half tempted to spit in his face. As if sensing her thoughts his eyes darken.

"You continue to test my patience." His voice is a promise of unpleasant consequences.

Adalyn doesn't say a word, letting the fire in her eyes speak for her. Her awareness prickles as the other males stop to watch the commotion, all eyes are on her.

On *them.*

Her whole body goes rigid against the hard planes of Killian, her soft curves traitorously mould against him. She slows her breathing, keeping her chest from rising high and pressing against his own as it had been minutes ago.

His eyes flicker over her face before looking to the stitching. It stings like hell with her arm held above her head, but she would not give him the satisfaction of knowing he's causing her harm, even if she's going to regret it later when the wound is open and causing her grief.

"General." A male voice echoes in the silence that has fallen over the camp. Adalyn's cheeks heat unwillingly, frustrated with how warm the body pressed against her own is. How the hard planes are sitting pressing against the softest, more intimate parts of her that have never been touched before.

Killian turns his head to the side, looking to where the voice came from. The tips of his hair tickle her nose, she has good reason to grab it between her teeth and yank.

"Get the chains and cuffs. We leave in ten," Killian says gruffly, looking towards her once more. His expression conveys nothing as he hauls the both of them up, lifting her as if she weighs no more than a feather. His large hands still encircle her wrist in front of her, her shoulders sag in relief as a sob is lodged in her throat. Warm blood runs down the front of the ruined night gown, adding fresh stains to the dark brown and red ones.

Polarian comes closer, his orange eyes gleaming like the first rays of sunlight, "You'll be first in line." Rusted metal cuffs dangle from the gleaming metal chain in his hands, it hangs in the dirt and trails behind him. Killian stiffens slightly, jaw ticking as he looks at the chains. Adalyn raises her chin in defiance, not wanting Polarian to see the fear that is quickly rising to the surface, or for Killian to sense it.

"I'll cuff her," Killian says, holding both of her wrists with one large hand. She scowls at him, glad to look away from those burning orange eyes. He takes the cuffs from Polarian and turns to face her, he stares down and narrows his eyes.

"Are you going to make this hard for me?" He asks, arching a dark brow slightly. She pouts her lips, nostrils flaring.

"How's your cheek feel?"

"Examine it since you seem to care so much," he clicks his tongue, angling the scratches towards her. She bites on the inside of her cheek to stop herself from snapping a retort. A click fills the silence between them and she looks down, eyes widening to find two rusted cuffs shackled to her wrists. She can move her hands shoulders width apart, they're heavy and cause her stitches to strain as she holds her hands in front of her.

"Attach the others, make it quick." Killian orders, he glances at her once more before striding away, a scowl on those full lips. She glowers at his muscular back as he stalks off, ignoring Polarian all together. She watches as more Valarki males come closer to the carriage, Polarian strides towards the open doors and jumps in.

The girls scream as they're shoved from the carriage, hitting the earth hard. The Valarki males roughly grab them by whatever piece of soft flesh they can grab and haul them to the cuffs, snapping them around their wrists. It takes all a matter of five seconds before they're all attached to the chain link, with Polarian holding the free end to keep them in line.

"Men, come watch if you please!" Polarian calls, winking towards the closest girl to him who cowers away as tears slide down her red cheeks. Some Valarki men chuckle and hoot as Polarian leads the women to an open expanse in front of the camp, the raging fire from last night is nothing more than a pile of ash and long burnt out embers. He lines them up in front of it, shaking out the chain.

Allison is the first to move, pulling the skirts of her dress up as she squats down. Shame burns her cheeks as she looks at the dirt in front of her face. A moment later the spray reaches Adalyn's ears and then the acidic stench of her piss.

All six women who had been in the carriage before she'd

arrived squat down and piss, all looking away from the Valarki males that now stand in front of their line. Their eyes shine with delight at the humiliation, it makes Adalyn's very soul burn so hot she almost sees stars. One by one the women from her village follow their lead, bowing their heads. Allison finishes first and stands, readjusting her skirts. She looks to Adalyn, eyes flashing with warning.

Adalyn is not pissing in front of them like an animal.

"Squat and piss," Polarian calls, eyes burning into the side of her face. The males turn their eyes towards her, all focusing in. Her cheeks burn as she clenches her hands at her sides. Polarian drops the chain and stalks down the line to where she stands.

"Are you deaf?" He hisses, grabbing her chin with the tips of his fingers. He squeezes her cheeks so hard she tastes blood as the soft flesh grates against her teeth. She refuses to meet his eyes, staring at his snarling lips. She takes a deep breath, he smells of cinnamon and butterscotch. They begin to etch into a smile, "I'll give you one more chance. Get down and piss like the rest of them."

Nothing.

"I was hoping one of you would refuse, I could use some fun this morning. You can't say I didn't warn you."

His hand leaves her cheeks, only to grab the chain between her wrists. He twirls with the grace of a feline as he *throws* her to the ground.

Adalyn lands face first. She coughs out dirt as her hair is wrenched backwards, her shoulder barks in pain as the stitches strain. Spit mixed with dirt dribbles down her chin as a hiss of pain passes her lips, Polarian leers over the top of her with a fistful of auburn intertwined between his fingers.

"I rather like the view of this position, you look utterly delightful on your knees," he smirks, tugging her head back further to prove his point. Her neck strains to the point of hurting, her breathing comes in short rapid bursts.

"You don't want to squat down and piss like the rest of them?

Fine, I'll force you to." Polarian's eyes glow bright as he wields his magic, the air fills with the stench of blackcurrants, each breath she takes causes her stomach to cramp. His magic wraps around her midsection, squeezing her full bladder she had been ignoring from the moment she'd opened my eyes.

His magic is like oil sliding over her skin.

Some of the males standing in front of her whoop with delight, all whistling and pushing into one another as they watch Polarian. He seems to swell from their approval, his ego being patted like a house cat with their shouts.

Adalyn strains against his magic, she clenches her thighs together as that familiar pulsing begins to forcefully happen. Hot tears of *shame* slide down her cheeks as his magic presses down harder, he wrenches her hair upwards and she feels strands rip from her skull.

It's too much—

The sensation is too strong, it's as if someone has taken her full bladder and is repeatedly hammering down on it; waiting for it to burst. It would any moment now and she can do nothing to stop it.

She closes her eyes as wet liquid slides down her clenched thighs, hot and spraying, cuts on her legs sting from the acid. The males laugh and cheer in front of her, her whole body trembles as his magic still continues to press in on her midsection. Crushing —her ribs begin to strain against it.

The liquid stops, the folds of her nightgown are drenched in piss and the acidic smell mixed with old blood has her gagging. Polarian pushes her forward, grinding her face into the dirt.

"Try defying me again and see where it gets you." He growls in her ear, his hand leaves her hair at the same time his magic lets go. She gasps in air and fills her lungs, she pushes herself up as tears drip from her cheeks and hit the dirt.

That god damn *fucking bastard*—

Adalyn's half dragged along as the chain moves, back towards the carriage. She'd be trapped like this, in her own filth until God knows when because she'd refused to give in so easily. She should have listened to the warning Allison had tried sending her. She manages to stumble to her feet, dirt sticks to the folds of the damp nightgown. She's grabbed roughly and hauled into the back of the carriage, she sprawls to the ground and bites her tongue as her shoulder barks in pain.

She looks up to see Polarian grinning ear to ear, nothing sane in his eyes. He slams the door shut and begins barking orders to the other men. She can't distinguish the muffled cries of the women as she manages to sit up, grasping the bench as she drags herself to the carriage door. She pushes herself against it, trying her best to save the girls from the worst of the stench she now emits.

She'd kill that fucking orange eyed bastard.

The carriage jostles as a horse neighs and then they're moving along at a brisk pace. Hunters cry out in joy as the thundering of hooves fill her ears, she looks towards the bars to see the trees all blending. They'd have to be using magic on the horses, on the carriages that had been their camp set up. Somehow they'd been getting through the pine forest with a whole damn entourage, there's no way they'd possibly be able to do that without some form of magic.

Adalyn bites her bottom lip to stop herself from crying. If she gives herself over to the grief that bites at her heels it will consume her completely, she'd have no way of escaping if she became a walking shell. So she harnesses the sadness and sharpens its blade until it's one forged for vengeance and blood.

6. Killian

Killian

Killian rides his black steed at the front of the entourage, the wind tugs wildly at his hair as his magic leaks from him and forces the forest around him to bend to his will. He had not earned being the king's second with parlour tricks and the thirst for blood.

His magic is one of a kind, out of the thousands of faeries born, his magic had been sacred. A magic that not even the king dare questions, but he knows how to keep Killian on a leash that is short enough to enforce rules and commands.

Killian spurs his heels into the stallion's rump, leaning forward as the black magic around him pulses. Trees dissolve rapidly in front of him, leaving only a path of greenery that will soon be destroyed by the hooves of the horses and wheels of the carriages. The path to Ravendew is like a compass in his mind, directing him towards the village as if he is a bee and the village is a blooming flower.

His mind wanders off the longer he stares at the vast nothingness before him, usually he'd enjoy the rides between villages. It allowed him to clear his mind, guard his heart from the horrors he's commanding and to settle into being the *shadow of death*.

He'd received the nickname after his first village coup, leaving everyone slaughtered.

Now, his mind wanders to the female that is held in the slave carriage that rides in the middle of the entourage. After he'd prowled off to ready the horses and make sure the carriages were all attached, he'd sent his magic out to clear the first path of their journey.

He'd observed from a distance what Polarian was doing to the defiant female. He'd humiliated her, forced his magic upon her, reminded her that he is a monster and isn't afraid to act like one.

Killian had seen the atrocities Polarian has committed in the past, the slave women aren't to be touched which are direct orders from the king, but other females in the villages they raid are all fair game. Polarian revelled in the blood shed, revelled in breaking the women before ending their lives.

It disgusted Killian, but he knows better than to interfere. Knows his back can carry no more scars, knows if the whip was brought down upon him again it would be flaying scarred skin upon scarred skin.

Killian wasn't always a monster, but had been broken and melted down into one. When he had nothing to lose, he had everything to gain.

He grinds his teeth together, remembering how the hard planes of his body had moulded to the woman's soft body like two pieces of a puzzle. She was soft underneath him, all curves and her scent was overwhelming, scorching his nostrils and tingling the back of his throat.

It had been the first time he'd *really* paid attention to what she looked like. With the blood gone from her face, she had light brown freckles scattered over her nose and cheeks like stars against the night sky. Her amber eyes are flecked with small splotches of gold.

A curious part of him wants to see if she will break underneath Polarian. He'd witnessed the fire in her eyes, she hated him.

Hated his kind. He couldn't blame her, hatred is a strong fuel for vengeance.

"Commander, we're nearing the borders," Jurian calls, riding up until he is in stride. Killian slows slightly, cutting a glance to his second.

Jurian is a loyal follower, has been from the moment the two had met at the training base. They'd bonded instantly, forming a brother-ship through the hard times. His golden hair flows around his shoulders like water, the sun rays illuminate the cream strands. Most fae males have long hair, it is a tradition broken into all of them from a young age.

Killian had cut his to his shoulders, the only way he could defy his king without dire consequences.

"Twenty yards we set up camp!" Killian calls, his magic catches his words and whispers them into each Valarki male's ear. Jurian looks at Killian, his deep maroon eyes gleaming as he smiles, stretching the scar that runs under his nose and over his full mouth.

"I heard about the resistant female," he says, raising a blonde brow. Killian rolls his eyes and snorts.

"There's nothing to hear. She's a typical slave, like the rest of the females." Killian shifts slightly in his saddle, his only sign of displeasure talking about the female with someone else.

"Ah, but she made you bleed. Twice. She's the first human female in over a hundred years who has drawn your blood." Jurian grins, gleeful at this information.

"Where are you hoping to steer this conversation Jurian?" Killian asks, looking away from his friend. Jurian chuckles, the deep notes roll over Killian's skin.

"I am merely curious. You still bear the cuts on your cheek, why supress your magic from healing them?" he muses.

"It's a reminder." Killian's voice is soft, knowing only Jurian would understand the deeper meaning behind his words.

It's a reminder of the monster that he has become and the

monster he will always be. He'd stopped his magic healing those cuts completely, allowing them to heal naturally.

"Once we return to Pantera, all will be well." Jurian murmurs. The two lapse into comfortable silence, both drawn into the thoughts of returning home. Pantera, the kingdom of the Valarki. Home, a distant place Killian hasn't felt for years.

He pulls his steed, breaking into a slow walk. From here he can hear the villagers enjoying their life, the murmur of life radiates from them in waves.

Their happiness will be ripped from them tonight, and Killian will have no one to blame but himself. He had a full bottle of fire whiskey waiting in his private carriage, he'd be drinking himself into oblivion once this final raid was accomplished.

Behind him the hooves of the horses die out, he looks over his shoulder to find everyone beginning to move and set up camp. The carriages are arranged so they're sitting in a circle, Polarian commands another warrior to begin the fire, throwing out orders to have the camp organised.

Sweat clings to Killian like a second skin, running down his neck and throat. They'd ridden well over half the day. Soon the sun would set, and their real challenge would begin.

Killian throws a kernel of his magic out, projecting a shield to protect and seal them from prying eyes. To someone passing by it would simply look like the forest.

Jurian dismounts, looking up to Killian.

"One more night, brother. One more night."

Killian nods once, holding in his sigh. One more night indeed.

Killian finishes sharpening his blade, strapping the weapon to the leather holster that's on his back. He looks over the empty camp, save for Karis and Orios. They sit across from him on a log, both watching the flames of the fire that separates them. Orange, pink, and purple casts over the sky. Killian looks skyward as the sun melts and gives way to the moon.

It is time.

He'd sent the group ahead to position. In five minutes the archers would be sending their flaming arrows towards the cottages. In ten they'd be invading, slaughtering everyone in their path. Four more females would live tonight, becoming slaves.

Killian stands and heads towards the woods that lead to the village. Unfortunately for him he must walk past the slave carriage. He sees a familiar face peering out of the bars of the carriage door.

For a reason unbeknownst to him, he pauses. She blinks once, as if surprised he'd stopped. His nostrils flare, the stench of acid smothers the usual lavender scent he'd come to identify her with.

"Gone to kill more innocent people?" she hums, wrapping two fragile hands around the metal bars. Her eyes blaze like an inferno. He growls, approaching the doors. She doesn't cower from him, only baring her teeth.

He stops at the doors, pressing his hands heavily on the wood, "You speak of things you do not understand."

"I understand the art of slaughtering the innocent," she hisses, somehow looking down her nose at *him*. It's enough that he barks a laugh, eyes darkening.

"Haven't you seen? I am the master of it."

He spins on his heels and stalks towards the forest, bristling from their encounter. For a slave, she has found every button of his to push. She knows where it will hurt most and strikes with her words. They're the only weapon she has.

His delicate ears pick up the screams before he emerges from the forest. He stays in the shadows on the edge, looking on as the large village burns bright against the dark night. Not even the moon shines tonight, no, tonight's atrocities will be committed in the darkness.

Killian grows cold as he watches his men slaughter the families that spill from their homes, the only comfort these humans have is that they're being sent to the same place as their loved ones. He has no comfort to give them, no mercy. He has a command and he must obey it at all costs.

During the raids Killian is the dictator, the observer. He plans the attacks, the manoeuvres his men will follow. He is the hand and his men are the hammer, destroying everything in their path. A time long ago, Killian had been down there with his men, slaughtering alongside them. Enjoying the bloodshed and the screams of death. He'd earnt his nickname at a great cost, one that had been a steep price to pay.

He spots Jurian storming from a cottage, the roof collapses in on itself a moment later and sends a plume of black smoke into the air. He brings his sword down in a fast and calculated arc, beheading the man that had crawled from the home. His face holds no sign of regret or enjoyment. Jurian simply does what he is ordered.

Killian and Jurian fell from the same tree.

A foreboding sense curls low in Killian's stomach, setting him on edge. He has the sense tonight will not go as planned and it has everything to do with the seething female he'd walked away from.

Polarian emerges from the smoke and flames, dragging a screaming female behind him. She claws at his hands, kicking her feet out.

"Slave?" Killian asks, voice cold and detached from any emotion. Polarian throws the girl at Killian's feet, she moves her blonde hair back from her face and cowers at the sight of him staring down at her. Her blue eyes hold nothing but fear.

"I thought you could use some loosening up." Polarian grins, shaking his shoulders out. Killian looks from the girl, he schools his features to boredom. He'd become a master of it over the centuries, hiding his true heart.

"My loosening up entails a hot clean bath and a goblet of whiskey."

Polarian chuckles, shaking his head, "Alas, I can't let an opportunity go to waste."

Killian's stomach turns leaden as Polarian grabs the female

again, throwing her small body over his shoulders. His magic silences her as he stalks into a dark part of the forest, hidden from others.

Killian can only hope he will make her death quick once he is done with her, once she is broken he will grow bored. Killian looks forward once more, breathing through the tightness in his chest.

One breath in, one breath out.

Jurian stalks up to him, twirling his sword in hand. Fire reflects in his eyes. Blood covers a majority of him, the stench clings to him, over shadowing his usual musk of apple and cinnamon.

"How is it going?" Killian asks gruffly. Jurian steps beside him and turns to the burning village. The screams have begun to die out, casting the forest into an eerie silence.

"Almost finished. Tonight's attack has gone smoothly. No problems. We have four females selected, the men are bringing them up as we speak. I've sent orders to begin burning the remaining buildings down." Jurian looks to Killian, noticing the tightness in his shoulders and clenched jaw.

Killian sighs through his nose, "Out with it."

"You will be free of this one day," Jurian says quietly.

For a moment the crackle and roaring of the fire fills the silence between them. Killian takes a moment to think. He shakes his head stiffly, clasping his hands behind his back.

"I will never be free of this, not as long as the king sees need for me."

Killian would never be free, not when his magic is so rare. Jurian knows this, so together they stand in silence and watch the village burn. The female had been right, they are monsters.

"Go, we won't be far behind now," Jurian says, turning to him. Killian looks at him, knows what relief he is offering him, even if it is only small.

"Thank you," Killian says softly, clasping his brother in arms on the shoulder. They hold eye contact for a moment longer before breaking apart. Polarian emerges from the forest, alone. His orange eyes glow brightly, his release obvious. He roars as he sprints back into the dying bloodshed. Jurian mutely follows after him like a ghost in the night.

Killian turns and walks as fast as he can from the choice he's made, leaving the screaming behind even though he knows their voices will haunt his dreams and ring in his ears for many days to come.

"I want a new dress," a female calls, cutting his unpleasant dark thoughts in half. He stops mid stride and looks to the slave woman, still peering out through those bars.

"Why would I offer you that?" he asks.

"Because I smell disgusting and unless you want to present me to every other Valarki like this then I suggest giving me a clean dress," she states, the darkness hides half of her face. Killian storms over to the carriage, wrenching the doors open. He stands there, chest heaving as he looks up at where she stands. His eyes travel over the deep yellow stain at the front of her nightgown that melts to dark red.

The smell has his stomach curdling.

"What do I get in return for this?" he asks, still holding the doors. Her cheeks burn brightly as she crosses her arms over her chest, chain rattling.

"What could you possibly want?"

He doesn't know.

"A nights rest without you fighting me tooth and nail."

Her eyes flicker to the cuts she'd left on his cheek. She swallows hard, determining if his asking price is worth it. She decides it is, holding her hands out silently. Killian uses his magic to unlock the cuffs, they fall to the carriage floor with a heavy thud.

She massages her red wrists before sitting down and swinging her legs from the carriage. He watches her closely, waiting for the moment she'll try to escape.

The moment doesn't come.

She looks at him, raising a dark eyebrow, *Well?*

He holds out a hand for her, she stares at his offer.

"I'm not holding your hand," she grits, fisting her hands at her side.

"I am in no mood for your antics tonight. Take my hand or stay as you are, I do not care." He growls, offering his hand a moment longer. His magic closes and locks the carriage door behind her.

Her defiance flares at his orders and he knows she hates putting her small hand in his own. Especially when his fingers curl over.

In an instant they stand in the privacy of his modest carriage, he enchants the locks and windows so she can't escape if she tries to run.

She gasps and trembles as he lets go of her hand, a lantern burns brightly on the far right wall. He walks over to the small round wooden table and unclasps his leather holster, hanging his sword on the wall.

"What the hell did you do? Where are we?" she demands from behind him. He sighs as he sits in the single chair, opening the gleaming whiskey bottle. A glass appears in front of him with cubes of ice, his glances over to where she still stands.

Her eyes take in the carriage before her, furs cover the floor in different shades of browns, yellows and white. One lantern burns, casting shadows over the plush red bed that sits in the back of the carriage behind her.

It's bare of anything to indicate it's Killian's, he never leaves anything personal in his carriage when they travel, the others know well enough to never disturb him.

"I used my magic to teleport us into my private carriage," he says simply, pouring a generous amount of amber liquid into his cup. Her eyes watch as his cup almost fills to the brim.

"Where is the dress?" she asks, crossing her arms over her chest. The stiffness of blood cracks and flakes to the fur rugs.

"If you look in the chest beside the bed you'll find some to your...liking." He sips the whiskey, enjoying the burn, "there are no weapons for you to steal in here, so don't bother."

She glowers at him for a moment before turning and walking stiffly towards the deep mahogany chest. She crouches down in front of it and lifts the latch, opening the lid and peering in. She reaches in and pulls out a deep grey fabric.

He's half way through his second drink when she finally stands, the grey dress clutched in her hands. She looks at him expectantly.

"What do you demand of me now?" he growls, fingers tightening on the glass. His anger only seems to ignite hers.

"I want to be *clean*."

He simply watches her, sipping his drink.

"For someone with stupidly long ears you'd think your hearing would be better," she scowls, turning away from him.

"I heard you. I simply chose to ignore you. Try using your manners next time." His head begins to swim, the alcohol pushing away the darkest parts of himself he desperately wishes to escape.

"I will not ask a Valarki *nicely* to be clean." She glares at him, eyes burning with hatred. He grins slowly, showing all of his teeth. He swirls the ice in his glass.

"Then remain dirty. I could send you back to that carriage with less than the flick of my wrist with no clean dress. Fighting me at every command will not work in your favour tonight."

If she was a dragon, she'd be breathing fire through her nostrils. His skin burns under her gaze, he's suddenly all too aware of her.

"Oh your *greatness* may I *please* be clean?" her words are dipped in poison, but she'd said please. Killian looks away from her, pouring a third drink.

"Undress and you'll be clean." He gives her privacy, focusing on the small bubbles that form in his glass.

"You're not touching me," she growls.

"I do not *want* to touch you," he spits, eyes flashing towards her. She flinches back at whatever she sees in his eyes, it takes her a moment more before she turns from him and faces the bed.

He looks away as she drops the clean dress at her feet, gingerly pulling the straps of her nightgown down her slim shoulders. He throws back what little he has left in his drink, catching her bare skin in his peripheral.

He looks at her out of the corner of his eye as the dirty nightgown pools at her feet. Her bare skin seems to glow in the lantern light, free from blemishes and scars. He envies her bare back.

His eyes trace over the generous curve of her hips, the dip in her waist. Her auburn hair is unruly, reaching half way down her back in a knotted mess. A hint of her breasts show as she bends down to pick up the clean dress.

He looks away, jaw set as he waves a hand. His magic washes over her, removing any trace of blood and dirt and piss. The smell disappears with it, leaving the scent of smoked sandalwood and whiskey in the air.

Clothes rustle and settle.

He looks back and surveys her, pushing his sudden arousal down. She pulls her hair back over her shoulders as she turns to him, dirty night gown grasped in her shaking hands. He frowns.

"I...I want to keep it. Could you clean it? Please?" she whispers, the fire in her words kindled to an ember. He senses the utter devastation wafting off her, the despair and heart break.

He blinks and the nightgown is clean. She stares at it, silent tears track her cheeks. She holds it to her chest, avoiding his gaze.

"Why?" he asks, curious despite himself.

"It is the last thing I have to remind me of my family." Her defeat rings in his ears, tightening something in his chest. Another glass appears and he pours her a drink, filling it half way. He extends it to her, she looks up and eyes the drink.

"What is it?" she sniffles, wiping her cheeks.

He shrugs a shoulder, "something to take the edge off."

She hesitates before she drifts closer, her curious nature

besting her. She places the folded nightgown on the table before grasping the drink in both hands, her nose crinkles at the smell.

"It is not pleasant. It's an accustomed taste," he warns, sipping his own. His throat is warm now, his belly a slow burn. Everything is warm. Everything is light.

"To take the edge off..." she whispers, bringing the glass to her lips.

Killian must have lost his damned mind, showing kindness to this female that hates him and sharing a drink with her. He deduces it to being worn down from the day, from the village they'd just destroyed and the lives they'd taken. He hasn't been in Pantera for many moons now.

"What's your name?" he asks, surprising her. She swallows down a small mouthful, cringing slightly.

"It isn't important."

"No, but I wish to refer to you as something other than that insufferable woman." Killian sits back in his chair, stretching his long legs out before him. He itches to change into more comfortable clothing. She watches his every movement, his every breath. No doubt looking for the deception she believes is coming.

Killian is far too tired.

"I will answer your question if you answer mine," she says, lowering the glass. He watches as she moves back and takes a seat on *his* bed, tucking the folds of the simple dress between her thighs.

It's a plain dress, willowy around her curvy figure. It covers her modest chest, with sleeves that reach her elbow.

"A game," he purrs, tilting his head to the side. She flushes, taking another sip. He's beginning to come to the conclusion she hasn't had much interaction with males.

"Where are you taking all of us?" she asks, eyes flashing to his.

"Pantera, land of the Valarki," he says bluntly, jaw twitching. The flush leaves her cheeks, paling her complexion.

"Because we're slaves...to serve who?"

"That's two questions."

She narrows her eyes, “My name is Adalyn Grace.”

Adalyn Grace.

Noble and gracious.

The meaning of her name is a far cry from the female perched on his mattress. He doesn’t voice that, though.

“Killian Abaddon.”

Little war of destruction and ruination.

The meaning isn’t lost on him or the person he’s become.

“My next question, slaves to who?”

He relents. “To the king, if he chooses. We bring him fifteen women to choose from, he chooses ten for his personal harem and the other five are given duties to fulfil around his castle or in the land.”

“I’d rather be a cleaner than a whore,” she spits, seething as she looks down to her drink. Killian’s lips turn up at the corners. Indeed.

“From what I’ve heard he’s a generous lover,” Killian offers, telling the truth. The king is ruthless in many ways, but sex is not one of them. Not that Killian has heard of anyway.

“I’d be generous to cut his extremities from his body if he even tried.” She gulps down the last of her drink, coughing as she brings the glass back down. Her eyes sparkle, a hint of the effects of alcohol overtaking her.

“If you do, send word so I may bear witness.” Killian picks up the return of the soldiers, the four women sob softly as they’re herded into the carriage. Adalyn doesn’t hear them, she just continues to stare at him.

“Why would you want that? He’s *your* beloved king.” She rises from the bed, closing the distance between them. She places the empty glass down, waiting. He pours her another drink.

Yes, he’s lost his damned mind.

“Do you know of the king? What he is like?” Killian asks, genuinely curious. She wanders back to the bed, climbing on and folding her legs underneath her; she cradles the glass in her hands.

“No.” She looks down to the liquid, running a finger around

the rim, "Mother would tell me and my sister bedtime stories about the Valarki invading and taking women as slaves. I never believed her of course, in my twenty one year's I'd never heard a whisper of your kind apart from stories." She swallows a mouthful of her drink. Killian stays silent, knowing the pain she currently feels.

"The night you attacked, my sister had requested the story again and I'd listened. After she'd told the tale I was restless and had left the cottage to empty my thoughts in the herb patch," she confesses, the drink freeing her tongue.

"The stories are all true," he says quietly, studying her.

"I know that now. I didn't before." She blinks through the sadness in her eyes, hiding behind a wall of fire and teeth. This is the woman Killian has come to know.

"There is no happy ending for this story," he whispers.

She studies him, leaving him feeling bare and exposed for the first time in centuries. It unnerves him.

"I know."

7. Adalyn

Adalyn

Adalyn snuggles deeper into the plush mattress, burying her face into the soft silk pillow and pulling the fur rug up over her shoulders. She has never been more comfortable in her life, feeling as if she's floating on a cloud.

She inhales deeply, *crystal blue waters and black orchid.*

Her body sits upright in the bed that isn't her own, her mind tries to catch up as she looks around the carriage she's in. Her heart slams against her rib cage as she looks down to the furs covering her legs, the bed is empty aside from her presence.

Oh god, she'd spent the night in Killian's private carriage.

She looks around as the morning sun rays begin to filter in through the low windows, casting a golden glow against the wooden wall. A soft moan catches her attention, a pained moan.

She silently slides from the bed, her bare feet hit the rugged floor softly. Killian is sprawled on a rolled out blanket, a black fur rug covers his lower half; exposing his toned bare chest that is littered with silver scars against his tanned skin.

She breathes in shallowly, she has the distinct feeling she's witnessing something that is his secret. He moans again, the noise leaving his slightly parted lips. His head twitches, eyebrows furrowing.

She walks a few paces closer, hands twisting together in front of her. He's having a nightmare.

Adalyn looks towards the carriage door – now would be the perfect opportunity to try and escape. She can't hear any other Valarki males rustling about the camp, she'd be free to flee.

She'd have to leave the other females behind. She doesn't know where she'd find the key to the carriage, that is, if it wasn't spelled in magic. She tip toes over to the carriage door, she could go against the odds.

Adalyn ignores the blossoming headache from the drink she'd had last night, after the second cup everything was blurry. She grabs onto the handles of the door, biting her bottom lip as she tries to turn them down to unlock.

They don't budge.

She tries a few more times, whimpering once she comes to the realisation he'd most likely used his magic to keep her from escaping. She glances over her shoulder, eyes catching on her clean dress that's folded on the table.

Killian begins to thrash slightly in his sleep, his moans become more persistent.

She tip toes back over to him, her heart squeezing in her chest. What nightmares plague a monster?

Against her better judgement she finds herself crouching down, she presses her hand against his muscled shoulder and pushes slightly. Warmth seeps into her skin, travelling up her arm. She pushes again, harder.

Nothing.

"Oh come you bloody damned faerie..." she curses under her breath as she presses her hands to his chest and pushes again. Her fingers betray her as they stroke the skin under his collar bone, surprised to find it's soft. Even his silver raised scars are soft.

She shouldn't be ogling at him, she *should* be using this as an opportunity to smother him with his own pillow and solve one of her many problems.

Yet, as she looks upon his sleeping face pulled tight with pain, she can't find it in herself to move. Emilia had nightmares many moons ago, consistently for over a week. Adalyn had comforted her each night, spooning her from behind and whispering pleasantries in her ears until her breathing evened out.

She huffs out a breath and gently begins to push him back and forth.

"Killian? Wake up," she whispers, not wanting to scare him into consciousness.

"This is really annoying you know, having to do this," she tells him, pushing harder. How heavy does this man sleep? She'd never known someone who could sleep so deeply.

She'd need to be a little rough.

She reaches up a hand and taps his cheek, "Come on now."

She leans over him, her upper half covers half his side. Her hair falls around her face and touches his. She slaps his face a little harder, leaving a red hand print behind.

She raises her hand to do it again, wiggling her fingers in preparation. A warm hand closes over her wrist, squeezing to the point of pain.

"You bastard!" she squeals, trying to tug her wrist from his hand. The bones in her wrist grate together and liquid fire begins to seep into her skin from his hand.

She looks to him, panicking to find his eyes wide open and staring up at her, there is no colour to be seen; only that never ending darkness of his dilated pupil.

"Killian, wake up!" she yells, trying to pry his fingers away. She hisses in pain and draws her free hand back, the tips burn a deep blue. Hot tears roll down her cheeks as she sobs, still tugging against his grip. The skin around his hand has begun to turn a deep blue and *god* it burns.

"You asshole, wake up!" she cries, wrenching herself backwards; landing awkwardly on her ass, half pulling him on top of her. His chest presses against her own, as his lower body nestles between her thighs pressing *hard* against her.

He has both of her wrists in his grip now, holding them

against the wooden floor beside her head. Both wrists burn in agony, she can't stop the tears from falling as he continues to watch her with no *soul* in his eyes.

"If you kill me I will come back and haunt your ugly ass," she blubbers, the fires begins to spread to her elbows. The pain is so bright and sharp it has her seeing bright white stars in her vision. Killian growls deeply in his chest, the motion rumbling against her. His lips part slightly as she blinks through tears, warm breath hits her face.

Adalyn needs to break him from this trance before he does kill her, she has no shadow of doubt that's what it will come to if she lets him continue being trapped in this state.

She musters up her courage as she looks at his lips.

She didn't imagine her first kiss would be like this, but she guesses beggars can't be choosers. She values her life more than who she gives her first kiss to.

Adalyn ignores the wrongness of what she's about to do, not letting herself dwell on this choice. She's going against her own hatred for him—going against his wishes of not wanting to touch her.

She leans up and presses her lips to his own, not entirely sure *how* to kiss. He freezes at the contact, his lips soft and slightly moist against her own.

She sighs against his lips as the pain in her wrist halts, leaving behind the feeling of ice in her veins. The cold is a stark contrast against the fire that had been there moments ago.

She's about to pull away when he *kisses* her back.

His lips move against her own, knowing exactly what they're doing as his lips part and his tongue slides into her own mouth. Her tongue dances against his, bumping teeth at the desperation. All common sense goes out the window that this is *wrong wrong wrong* when he grazes his teeth against her bottom lip.

He tastes magical with the hint of whiskey on his tongue.

His hands unpin her wrists as he holds himself above her, mouth still clashing with her own, claiming her.

The fire between them catches and burns, devouring both of them in the growing passion.

Adalyn buries her hands into his hair, running them through the strands that feel like silk sliding through her fingers.

He growls low in his throat, pressing harder against her.

She gasps as he sits backwards, dragging her onto his lap in the process. She keeps her eyes closed, not wanting to *face* what she's doing, but unable to stop herself from the pleasure and desire that is beginning to course violently through her body.

She has never felt so alive.

His large hands run down her back, cupping her arse and grinding her against the hardness of him that strains his night pants. She moans into his mouth and her southern regions turn molten as he continues to grind her against his hard shaft, that tender part of her rubs back and forth against him.

Lava ignites in her veins.

She fists his hair into her hands as she rides herself into him, taking a few moments to get the hang of it. A hand grips her arse tightly while the other slides up her side, cupping her left breast. He gently squeezes, fingers pinching the hard nub softly.

His mouth leaves her own and attacks her neck, sucking at the tender skin on the left side. The stitching on her right shoulder throbs, the slight pain only enhances the pleasure coursing through her.

She's close to exploding.

She groans loudly when his wicked mouth dips down to her breast, sucking at her hard nipple through the thin material. She throws her head back, pressing herself closer to him. She can't get enough of him, she desperately needs more skin on skin contact. He attacks her breast with careful savagery, biting the nub but not inflicting unbearable pain.

His hips buck against her own, her dress has crept up between their feverish kisses. His dampened shaft presses against her drenched underwear, the sensation has her grinding against him harder. He pulls down her sleeve, her left breast falls out and he claims it in his mouth once more.

Her heart is racing in her chest, her body is on fire. She needs *more more more more more.*

His sucks at her nipple, flicking his tongue over the most sensitive part.

She breaks against him.

It's an explosion of fire and light, she cries out as he continues to grind against her; prolonging the high she's riding. He moans against her breast as he finds his own release. His pants grow even wetter, their juices mingling together.

As she finds her *soul* that had left her body, she also finds reality.

It crashes into her hard.

She opens her eyes, gasping. He goes rigid against her, the hardest part of him softening. His mouth lets go of her breast, leaving it tender and peppered with dark marks.

Oh god what have I done?

His breathing is hard and laboured, much like her own. She unwinds her hands from his hair and brings them to her side. She quivers against him, legs shaking and weak.

"I told you I didn't want to touch you," he rasps, still bowing his head near her exposed chest. The tone in his voice has her scurrying off him, she quickly fixes up the front of her dress.

Adalyn is mortified. She stands on shaking legs and takes careful steps backwards. He leans back from where he still sits and looks up at her, the darkness has left his eyes. She makes a strangled sound at the *regret and pain* in his eyes.

"Let me out." Her hands shake at her side, she goes to fold them over her chest. She stops and looks at the dark blue marks that cover both wrists. It looks like an explosion of ink underneath her pale skin, stopping shy of her knuckles and slightly down her wrist.

"What—what did I do?" He frowns as he stands, she looks up at him. She swallows hard, still holding her hands in front of her.

She ignores the wet stain at the front of his light coloured pants, even though her cheeks burn.

"You...you were having a nightmare. I tried to wake you up. You grabbed my wrist and your eyes were open but there was only darkness," she whispers. "You had a hold of both wrists and I felt like I was burning alive. I couldn't get you to snap out of it. So I kissed you."

"You kissed me?" His voice is void of emotion, his eyes go blank as he stares down at her. Her cheeks blossom with heat and leach down her throat, betraying her.

"Yes. I pressed my lips against your own and the pain stopped immediately. *I was pulling away* when you decided to kiss me back." She crosses her arms, anger flares in her chest. She should have let him get savaged by his nightmare. She shouldn't have touched him, kissed him, let his lips roam to her most sensitive parts.

His jaw tightens as he looks away from her, "I am truly sorry. I am not myself when I have nightmares. Usually, it is best to leave me in them."

"How could I have known that? I didn't intend to stay the night. I just wanted to be clean." She snaps at him, she needs to be angry at him. She needs the anger to override the heat that is still swimming in her blood as she continues to look at him. The memory of the desire he'd made her feel aches to be felt again.

Watching his mussed hair, bare muscular chest and bright blue eyes she can't deny the attraction she feels for him, even if it is all physical.

"And did I not give you that without asking for anything in return?" he fires back, looking back to her now. His blue eyes burn with anger, even though his cheeks hold a tinge of pink to them. She's glad she isn't the only one affected by what took place between them.

"*You're the one who gave me 'something to take the edge off.'*"

He snarls as he prowls towards her, she stands her ground

even though she trembles under his gaze. It's terrifying, *he's* terrifying.

"I told you I didn't want to touch you. I don't want to touch you. I am not like them." His eyes darken, holding her in spot. *I am not like them*. That sentence alone has the fire dimming inside of her, the hollowness in his voice.

"You should have sent me back to the other *slaves* then. I'm sorry I was trying to repay the favour for your kindness. I won't in future, I can assure you." She storms past him, her shoulder knocking against his own. "I didn't want to touch you either, but it was that or death."

"Where do you think you're going?"

She doesn't think as she strips down the grey dress she'd dressed herself in last night. She keeps her back towards him as she slides *her* nightgown back on, patting out the creases. Her god damn shoulder is leaking blood again.

"I'm getting the hell out of your stupid carriage!" she charges towards the doors, grabbing the handles and yanking them with fury. They don't budge, she yells out in frustration and kicks at the wood. Her bare foot barks in pain.

"Where are your manners?" His voice is deep, causing heat to ignite in her southern region once again. She glances over her shoulder, narrowing her eyes at him. He stands with his arms crossed over his chest, golden sun rays kiss his skin devilishly. He is achingly beautiful. Standing there with the storm in his eyes she swore he could have been an avenging angel.

"Open the doors." She is breathless.

"You still have *my* mark on your wrists."

Hell, she'd forgot about them.

"Remove them then." She turns facing him, still one hand wrapped around the handle. He smirks, a dimple creasing his cheek as she gets a glimpse of white teeth.

"They'll fade on their own. Think of it as punishment."

Her mind short wires, "Punishment?"

He shrugs, "You need to learn to not disobey me. Three days

they'll brand you, letting everyone out there know," he points towards the doors behind me, "what you gave into."

"That damns you as well. They'll know you obliged." She curses herself for being so blind, so stupid in the moment of pleasure. Killian can shove it up his arse.

"If I willingly obliged in my *right frame of mind*, those marks would be a light blue. No one dares question me or the things I do. I am their commander. You? You are simply a slave."

A slave.

The single word rattles around in her brain. She is simply a fucking slave.

"You are exactly like the rest of the monsters out there," she bites her bottom lip to stop the tears from falling, "I thought for a split second your kindness was real. That *you* might have some compassion underneath that cold exterior." She turns away from him, holding onto the door handles.

"You were wrong." He says simply.

"I will not be mistaken again." She wrenches the doors open, relief fills her as they swing outwards. Sun warms her skin as she climbs from his carriage, not daring to look back to him. Warm magic wraps itself around her and forces her to walk towards the slave carriage, she doesn't bother fighting his magic. It's a warm caress against her body, feeling far more intimate than it should. The doors swing open on their own and her waiting cuffs float in the air.

She deflates as the other females look to her with fear in their eyes. She climbs into the carriage, the cuffs clasp down on her wrists. Killian's magic releases her, leaving her shivering. Adalyn leans against the carriage door, trying to control the sobs that wrack through her body. She wouldn't be mistaken again, because she will never again get that close to him. And the next time she does? She'll be driving a knife through his cold chest.

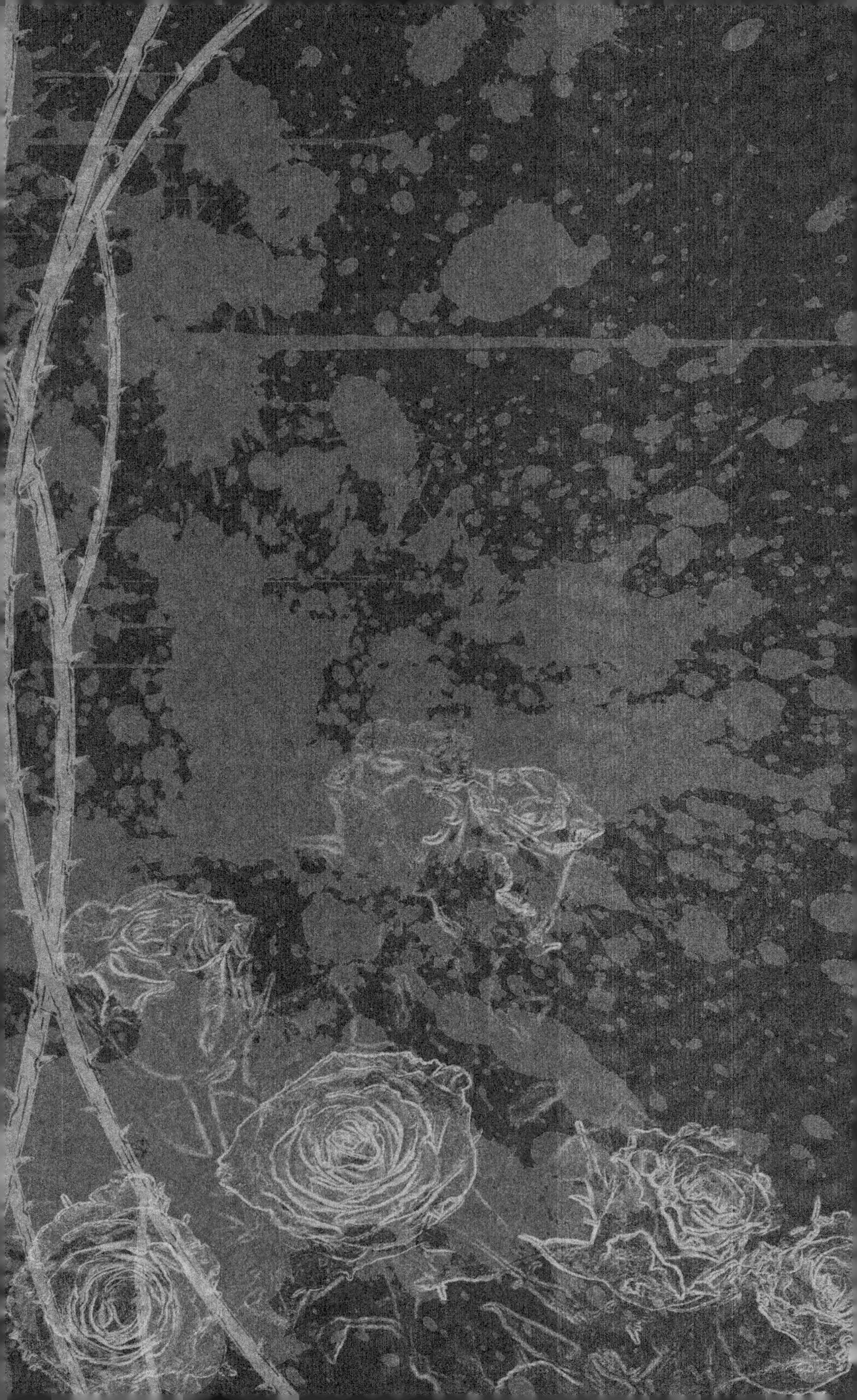

8. Adalyn

Adalyn

Adalyn rubs at her wrist, trying her best to speed up the process of Killian's magic. The deep blue colour has become the bane of her existence. She bites her bottom lip as she rubs harder, knowing if her skin was without the blue it would currently be red raw from her onslaught.

"What happened?" Allison whispers, daring to ask the question she sees in all of the other women's eyes. Adalyn sighs and sits back, dropping her hands to her lap.

"I wanted to be clean and he was nice enough to do that and go a step further in offering me a drink." She looks towards Allison, finding no judgment in her eyes. "I don't remember much, I woke up in his bed and he'd been asleep on the floor. I tried to escape but couldn't. I tried to wake him up to let me out and he grabbed me." Adalyn doesn't know why she's lying about the exact reason she'd woken him up, she rules it down to embarrassment.

"They all have their own magic that can mark us. If it makes you feel any better none of the other Valarki males will harass you until the mark disappears." Allison leans back, keeping her eyes on Adalyn. Understanding dawns on her. Why hadn't Killian told her that?

"How long have you been in this carriage?" Adalyn asks.

Allison half shrugs, looking towards the gash on her leg. The skin around the outside is a deep red while the cut itself is beginning to scab over. It hadn't been stitched or cleaned.

"We come from Arcadia, many weeks away from here. It's along the border to Pantera," she finally says.

How much of a reprieve will they have until they reach Pantera? If Adalyn's to escape and find her sister, she'd need to have all her wits about her. No more distractions and definitely no more going near Killian.

"So we should be leaving today," she murmurs to herself more than to Allison. She looks towards the carriage door. Laughter drifts in through the small window as Valarki males come closer. She shrinks back, not wanting to take the brunt force from whoever is going to open that door.

"Do what they say today," Allison hisses towards her, seconds later the door is wrenched open. Polarian stands there, dressed in nothing more than loose fitting pants. Her eyes betray her as they roam over the contours of his chest, faintly she can see red scratches down the front of him.

Her face drains of colour.

Some of the girls begin to sob again, the noise only makes Polarian grin.

"Come girls, it's time for our final bath," Polarian calls. He grabs the end of the chains, piercing Adalyn with his eyes. He leans in, "Defy me today, and you won't live long enough to see what I do about it."

She nods stiffly, she values her life more than pissing off a murdering monster that has the lead to her chains. She stands and jumps from the carriage. Adalyn holds her head high as Polarian walks across the camp, Valarki males begin to walk beside the line of prisoners. All keep their murmurs from reaching their ears.

Adalyn's back prickles with awareness and then fire. She tenses, her shoulders go taught. A glance over her shoulder has her eyes immediately spotting Killian. He leans against a carriage, arms crossed over his chest. A rather handsome Valarki male stands beside him, his golden hair sits in waves around his chest.

Killian's blue eyes pierce hers and she finds nothing but darkness there. She looks to the other male, finding him smirking towards her. It enhances his handsome features.

She spins forwards, not liking the feeling that's beginning to ignite from seeing Killian. If he's put some sort of enchantment over her or using magic she would kill him.

They walk in silence for a mile before the murmur of a stream reaches her ears. She peers around Polarian's large shoulders to glimpse a river ahead. Her stomach sinks as if a large rock has been placed inside of it.

The river, Polarian being half naked.

He is going to bathe them, himself. While the others watch.

She breathes hard and sharp through her nose, trying to calm the panic that's threatening to drown her. She tries to jiggle her hands out of the cuffs, trying to dislocate her thumb so she can squeeze her wrist through the small cuff. It's useless, *I'm useless.*

Polarian lines them up facing the river, sunlight hits the surface and causes the water to sparkle. He uses his magic to tie the metal chains he'd been carrying to a tree. They have nowhere to escape to, nowhere to hide.

"I think you'll be first, an example for the others," Polarian purrs coming closer to her. She scowls up at him but holds her tongue, she doesn't want him to drown her in front of them all. He looks at her wrists, growling slightly.

"He marked you?" he snarls up at her, as if it's *her* fault she's marked. She quivers under the heaviness in his stare, Allison had been right. No other male can touch her while she's marked.

She gives herself a silent cheer, the only good thing to come out of her night in Killian's carriage.

"Yes. I marked her. You cannot touch her." Killian's voice is deep and rings around the clearing. The other females shrink into themselves as he strides past them, heading straight for Adalyn.

He's wearing nothing more than loose fitting black pants, he'd tied his hair up into a messy bun; the loose strands compliment the angles of his face. Her neck flushes as her eyes roam over his bare chest, knowing exactly how warm he is and how soft he feels.

No distractions Adalyn.

"You gave us orders not to touch the slaves. We're only allowed to touch them after he king has picked out his ten." Polarian argues, flashing his eyes towards her. Behind the anger there is restless desire and possession. If he ever had the chance to get his hands on her, he might be the one that does break her.

"I did. I didn't touch her, she touched me. I marked her for three days as punishment." Killian stops before them, raising a dark brow as he stares at Polarian with cold disinterest. The challenge in his eyes dares Polarian to argue.

"Three days you'll be safe from me," Polarian seethes, dropping her cuffed hands. Her shoulders sag slightly in relief. Three days of temporary safety. She watches as Polarian grabs onto Allison's cuffs. Her mouth falls open as she undresses, standing naked before him. Valarki males come closer, leering at her soft curvy figure.

Polarian smiles wolfishly as he takes both her hands and leads her into the water with him. Allison keeps her head bowed as she's taken into the water.

Adalyn looks to Killian, his jaw tightens as he looks down at her. He gently takes her cuffed hands and unlocks them, still holding onto her wrists. The magic there recognises his touch, warming for him.

"Undress."

He lets go of one of her hands, holding the other firmly. She bites down on her cheek as she gingerly pulls the straps of her nightgown down. Her cheeks and neck burn as she gets out of her nightgown and underwear. Her skin pebbles as a cool breeze caresses the bare skin. She grasps Killian's hand but avoids looking at him. She takes steady steps as he leads her into the water, his large frame blocks Polarian from getting a glimpse at her bare form.

To her surprise he faces her diagonally, her back to the other females and Valarki. He stands behind her, his hands gently holding onto her forearms.

His breath tickles her cheek as he leans his head down, lips grazing the shell of her ear, "I will not humiliate you. Clean yourself."

She sinks down into the water, his hands hover around her but don't touch her again. She's more than aware of his presence at her back as she cups water and brings it to her arm pits. She splashes her face, running a hand through the tangles in her hair.

Killian stays behind her, true to his word.

She ducks her head under the water, wetting her hair. While submerged she drags her fingers through the knots, trying her best to get them out. She breaks the surface and takes a gasping breath, droplets of water run down her face and stick to her lashes as she faces Killian. Her neck burns as her nipples harden involuntarily as water glides down her chest, she can't control the heat that begins to spread through her as she peers up at him.

His blue eyes never leave her face, searching with no emotion. She doesn't know what he's looking for. She crosses her arms over her chest, even though he'd seen one of her breasts. Had become very acquainted with one.

His devil mouth and tongue had been wicked—

She shivers, squeezing her thighs together at the stupid heat that's begun to pool between her legs. Killian's eyes sharpen, his nostrils flare as he goes utterly still.

She looks away from him, digging her nails into her arms to stop her dirty thoughts from progressing. This is not focusing, this is definitely not hating the male before her.

"I'm done," she clears her throat, looking anywhere but at him. This is mortifying. Killian gently tucks her into his right side, shielding her from the other males. One look from him and they don't glance her way again.

"If you think this will change my mind about you, it won't," she says as they reach the bank. Water runs down her naked body and mud sticks to her feet. Killian's magic washes over her like a warm touch, drying her skin.

"I don't want anything I do to change your mind," he says gruffly, angling his body so she can pull her discarded clothes on. She makes quick work of getting dressed, feeling more protected once her nightgown settles around her.

"It won't," she says simply, raising her hands to be cuffed. She meets his blazing blue eyes, unflinching under the conflicting emotions that swirl in their deep watery depths.

"For a human slave, you have a lot of courage with your sharp tongue," Killian says, grabbing onto the metal cuffs and bringing them to her outstretched wrists. His eyes linger at the deep blue that marks her skin.

"You didn't seem to mind it," she snaps back, waiting as he clasps the cuffs together. He grinds his teeth together as he looks at her. She stares at him with the same fire burning in the depths of her eyes.

He tugs her cuffed hands close to him, she stumbles into his chest; her hands pressing to the wet planes of his stomach as he leans down over her and whispers in her ear, "As I can recall you didn't either..." he leans back a fraction.

Adalyn gulps as her heart beats erratically in her chest, dreading his next words.

"You rode me, tasted me as if you couldn't get enough of me. Moaned for me as you found your release using *my body*. Don't act as if what happened between us wasn't without consent...even now I can scent your desire from the words that leave my lips."

Adalyn's blood goes cold, dousing the flame that had grown from how close they both stood and from the words leaving his mouth. She hated the reaction her body had to him.

"Before you panic, no, only I can scent it. Your filthy desires are hidden to everyone else." He leans back, staring down at her; his face void of emotion. For someone who is hot to the touch, he is cold. Adalyn straightens, cursing her hormones silently.

"I'm not going to be your whore, what happened between us

was a mistake. Now if you could kindly *fuck off* and treat me like the rest of the slaves, I'd appreciate it greatly." Adalyn steps away, turning her back to him to watch as the last few girls begin to dress. Her palms sweat as she grasps the folds of her nightgown.

Killian is still behind her, so still she almost believes he's disappeared. Warm lips graze her ear, "Your wish is my command, *Adalyn Grace*."

She shivers as she watches him stride away, unsure if her name on his tongue is a blessing or curse. She hides her gasp at his scar covered back. Not one inch of his back is clean, the silvery scarred skin shines in the sun rays.

It only makes him that more attractive.

She hates herself for thinking that and swiftly turns to face the river, eyes clashing with Polarian's burning ones. She tightens her lips, knowing everyone must have seen their heated little argument.

She could worry about the gossiping later, for now she wanted to rest and rid her mind of anything that involved Killian. Polarian leads the females back to their carriage, forcefully handling each female as he helps them on. He grasps Adalyn's hips and slowly places her into the carriage, dragging her back against his bare chest.

"I may not be able to touch you outright, but Killian has made it clear you're fair game," he whispers in her ear before sending her sprawling onto the wooden floor of the carriage. She scowls as she climbs to her feet, taking a seat. She avoids looking his way as the doors close, locking into place.

Only then does she try to allow herself to relax, as best as she can in this situation, anyway.

9. Killian
Killian

Killian does his best to ignore the inquisitive glances he's continuously getting from Jurian as they ride along in silence. He had successfully avoided his burning questions all morning, even now as the sun begins to sink below the horizon Killian is sure Jurian will hold his tongue.

They'd begun the journey home that morning, five full days of riding are ahead of them although the magic Killian pumps into the horses makes them move swiftly without fault. Each night they rest, sometimes in the remains of villages they'd burned.

Killian watches as the deep blue sky begins to streak with orange, yellow and pink while the sun sinks below for the moon to take over. There's only bare barren land around them, save for the occasional tree. The earth is scorched, only dirt and dead grass cover for miles as far as Killian can see.

They'd done this, destroyed this.

"So...you've been quiet today." Jurian pipes up, glancing to Killian with a smirk. Killian side eyes him, narrowing his eyes. He supresses a groan, he thought he'd escaped questions.

"I'm tired. We have a long journey ahead of us." Both statements are true, but there is also another reason why is he tired.

He'd awoken that morning to his teeth tugging at Adalyn's pale pink hardened nipple, to his hands roaming her soft body and eliciting sounds from her that he doubts have ever left her lips before.

He should have stopped it then, he should have pulled away and rejected her. He isn't sure why he hadn't, but the guilt has been biting at his heels all day. She'd very willingly divulged in what he was offering her, her hatred for him had only fuelled the passion between them.

No matter how hard he tried, he couldn't shake the shame. The guilt. He wasn't like the others, had strived himself to be better than them in the only way he could. Over the centuries he had never seen the interest in bedding a human female, couldn't find the appeal of sleeping with another who doesn't consent. He had never once taken advantage of the human female slaves. Had never laid a hand on any of them, he'd taken out his sexual frustrations with Alissa, a Valarki female who he had known for the last twenty years.

Now a small part of him is intrigued by Adalyn, what her motive was this morning for coming as close to him as she had. For sharing that part of herself with him, for wanting to wake him from his nightmare.

"From what I heard, and every other Valarki male also heard, was that Adalyn was *moaning*—"

"Enough." Killian snaps, lips pulling back in a snarl. He did not want to discuss the fire eyed female with anyone, especially not what had taken place that morning.

"If I didn't know you any better I'd think you quite like this little fire head," Jurian says with a smile in his voice. Killian ignores him, focusing ahead on the path. Soon they'd be setting up camp, the females would need food.

"Well if you're not interested her I'm sure one of my smiles could charm her." Jurian baits him, eagerly watching him with untamed amusement. Killian had always been cold and calculating, far too serious for a majority of his life. From the moment he'd saved Adalyn's life, it's as if a switch has been flicked in him. Igniting the fire of his spirit, it frustrated him to no end.

"I know what you're doing," Killian grits out, "I do not care for the human female. Do whatever you please."

Jurian leans back in his saddle, slowing as Killian gives the silent command to set up camp for the night. "Alright, I'll give the females their portions tonight and have a chat with her."

Killian ignores the souring of his stomach, instead focusing on his magic as he creates a protective shield around their camp. He dismounts swiftly, leaving his horse to roam the enclosed space.

From here Killian spots the slave carriage, three of the males untie the horses that had been pulling it. The girls are going nowhere, so they don't bother with any other form of protection.

"General, would you like the females out?" Polarian asks, coming to walk beside Killian as they move to a large open expanse in the middle of the camp. Killian comes to a stop, surveying the ground.

"Once the camp is set up, have them around the fire for their rations. Jurian will be handing them out."

Polarian nods once, leaving on quiet feet as he continues to throw out orders. Killian rubs his right temple, trying his best to stave off the headache that is coming. He needs a drink—a strong drink at that.

Killian moves through the men and stops in front of the carriage that holds their supplies, he swings the doors open with ease. Dried herbs hang from the ceiling while brown wooden crates are piled on both sides, at the end of the carriage there are stacks of wood. He retrieves ten, using his magic to carry the large logs to the place for the fire.

He works in silence, his thoughts finally turning to a whisper. It helps relieve the tension in his neck and shoulders, he'd need a damn good massage upon return. As the wood catches blue and gold flames, the world is thrown into darkness as the sun disappears.

"I have the rations for the females," Jurian announces, sitting a crate down away from the fire. Most Valarki males lean against their own carriages, talking amongst one another as they share a drink. They won't approach the fire until Killian has turned into his private carriage for the night.

"Get them," Killian commands, rising to his full height and taking a few steps back until he's shrouded in shadows. He crosses his arms over his chest as Jurian approaches the slave carriage, opening the doors with ease.

Killian pointedly ignores what he says, and if the females reply. He knows who stands at the front of their chained line. Jurian reaches in, two small pale hands clasp his shoulder as he helps Adalyn to the ground. She wipes her palms on her nightgown before looking around.

Killian growls low in his throat as her eyes completely skip over him, as if he is a ghost.

One by one Jurian helps the other females down, doing his best to put them at ease. Jurian has a heart of gold and the loyalty of a companion hound. He wouldn't harm these females, it's why Killian likes him as much as he does.

Jurian takes the end of Adalyn's chain and leads the females to the fire. The females cower under Killian's gaze of steel, aside from one.

"Take a seat ladies, I'll pass the rations out." Jurian walks around the fire, eyeing Killian with open curiosity before scooping the crate into his arms. He hands the females their small hessian bags, containing an apple, three strips of beef jerky, a nub of cheese and a chunk of bread.

Jurian comes to stand by Killian, throwing the empty crate into the fire. Killian watches as the gold flames devour the wood —it reminds him of how he'd devoured Adalyn.

"Excuse me," Adalyn pipes up, looking to Jurian. Killian goes completely still, Jurian grins as he rounds the fire to where she sits. He crouches down in front of her, cocking his head to the side. His gold braid spills over his shoulder.

"Yes?" He asks.

"How long does this last us? Should I ration these portions if we're expected to starve before we return?" There's a sharp edge to her words, Jurian takes a moment before he chuckles.

"You'll be fed, from the morning you've had, you need all the food you can get."

Killian expects Adalyn to snarl at him, growl and spit like a feral cat. He looks between them, frowning slightly as she looks at Jurian; her wet lips parted slightly. From here he can see the redness of her cheeks.

"If that's the case, can I have your portion as well?" she raises a brow before taking a bite of the bread. She chews slowly, eyes calculating as she watches Jurian. Jurian takes a seat beside her, stretching his legs out before him.

"Did he really exert you that much?" Jurian asks, smirking at her. His eyes sparkle with amusement and hidden curiosity. Adalyn looks at him with the promise of death shining in her eyes, the other females are smart enough to stay silent and eat their servings.

Killian should turn and leave, he had his own dinner waiting for him in his carriage. Instead he stands there, watching as Jurian talks with Adalyn.

"I've had better..." she trails off, eyes flashing to where Killian stands. The first sign of recognition, he warms slightly, only to be doused in ice water moments later, "and bigger."

Jurian bursts out with rich laughter, clutching his stomach. Killian bristles at her words. She most certainly has *not* had better or bigger. From the innocence and inexperience that wafted off of her, he is certain she is still untouched.

"Oh boy—" Jurian wipes a stray tear, his red eyes glow, "that's the first time I've laughed that hard in a long time. No one else dares make comments about the general like that."

Adalyn shrugs, looking to the portions in her bag, "You can take my freedom but you won't take my tongue."

"You know...we could..." Jurian raises a brow, gauging her

reaction. She narrows her eyes at him, lips thinning. He cracks a smile, holding his hands up, "I would never."

"You're as bad as the big sulking brute across the fire," she grumbles, eyes landing on Killian. Seconds ago she seemed to be warm, full of light. Casting her eyes upon Killian he can only feel the cold of winter and the bite of a blade.

He doesn't like it.

"I like you, Red."

"Red?" she asks, frowning slightly. Jurian reaches out and tugs gently at the end of a red curl that spills over her shoulders. She goes to slap his hand away, but he's fast to remove his hand.

"Your new nickname." He grins lazily, knowing he's getting under her skin. She huffs.

"I should nickname you *annoyance*. I'm trying to eat in peace."

Jurian rises from where he stands, brushing the loose dirt from his pants.

"Okay *Red*, your *annoyance* will be on his way. I take back my portions too, I'm famished after our lovely chat." He winks at her.

Killian watches in hidden amazement as one side of her lips twitch upwards into the form of a smile. As if remembering herself and why she's here, it disappears. She dismisses him, continuing to eat.

Killian stalks away, snarling at any males who even looks to approach him. He's a fool for being annoyed, for feeling anything for Adalyn.

"Killian, wait up!" Jurian calls, jogging to catch up to his friend. Killian continues stalking forwards towards his private carriage. He rips open the doors and climbs inside, he has a good sense to slam the door behind him and lock Jurian out.

"Jesus Christ, Red is right, you are sulking."

Killian plops down into his seat, grabbing his fresh bottle of whiskey and swigging from the bottle, he needs the burn. He needs to focus on anything other than *her*.

"I am not sulking," he finally manages to say, relaxing into the familiar burn of alcohol as he takes another swig of whiskey. Jurian climbs into his carriage, leaning against the far wall as he watches Killian.

"You are." Jurian runs a hand down his golden braid, shaking his head "I only meant it in jest. If I had truly known talking to the woman would get under your skin I wouldn't have."

Killian knows Jurian is speaking truth, but the fact he is annoyed with him for talking to her is another problem in itself. They can't arrive in Pantera fast enough, the sooner he never has to see her again the better.

"That's the problem, I shouldn't give any thought to you talking to her and yet it still soured my mood." Killian frowns down at his bottle. Adalyn hates him, of that much he is certain. He rules down the newly risen emotions to being on the road for so long, for her being the only female to ark back up at him and not cower. The sooner he could bury himself in Alissa and forget about Adalyn the better.

"There's nothing wrong with being fond of a female human," Jurian says slowly, testing the words. This is a topic Killian and Jurian tend to stray away from.

"No, but there is everything wrong with being the one who sent the order to slaughter her family. She hates me, hates *us.* I do not blame her." Killian looks out of his carriage, catching glimpses of the other Valarki males giving the females a hard time. "No woman in their right mind would ever take the monster who destroyed her life to bed. Forgive them for it."

Jurian pushes up from where he stands. Jumping down, he glances to Killian once more, "I don't think that's for you to decide. In another life...maybe things could have been different. We were given this path to walk for a reason." Jurian looks to the fire as males hoot and cheer.

Killian watches as well, growing cold.

Jurian sighs, "For some ungodly reason I believe she was pushed into your life for a reason. It's up to you to figure that reason out. I best go and put the females back in their carriage before the males get too handsy."

"Thank you, Jurian." Killian stands and locks his carriage door as his friend slips away, a saviour to the females even though they may not see it that way. Killian grabs his bottle of whiskey as he rips the shirt from his chest. He collapses onto the bed, bottle to his lips. Tomorrow he would become the cold and calculating shadow of death they all knew him as. Killian has no interest in discovering if Adalyn was sent to him from the gods that have been long forgotten.

If she has, it's a twisted cruel hand of fate.

For she will never – could never – truly be his.

He is a monster and he will do his best to reassure her of that.

10. Adalyn

Adalyn

Adalyn watches in amazement as the deep blue on both of her wrists begins to dissolve, tingling as the prickle of Killian's magic is stripped from her. Taking his mark of protection along with it. Adalyn turns her hands slowly, refusing to blink until her skin has returned to its natural pale colour. She sighs in relief, leaning back into the jostling carriage wall as she lowers her hands into her lap.

After talking briefly with the handsome golden haired *annoyance* two nights ago, she'd found herself in a slightly less murderous mood. He'd been a light against Killian's darkness. She had felt his eyes on her from where he watched in the shadows, knew he could hear her every word.

She had been lying when she'd told the golden hair man she'd had better and bigger, in truth Killian had been her first *everything* when it comes to being intimate.

Her stomach sours at the thought of what could have happened if she'd been too enchanted by him, all it would have taken was a quick slip of clothing and they could have been joined. Adalyn vows to never bed the male, her hatred for him is far too strong for there to be any fondness.

He killed her family. That's all it takes for her to realise how ridiculous she'd been acting around Killian. He's a murderer and his hands are stained with blood, she'll remind him of it every second she gets. It's the least she can do for her family.

She blinks away the tears gathering at the thought of her family, refusing to think of their broken and bloody bodies from the last time she saw them. Instead she focuses on a sweet memory from the last winter they'd shared together.

Her mother had baked an apple pie one afternoon, the house had smelt of apple and cinnamon and it had tainted the air for days after her mother had finished baking. Emilia had been Adalyn's shadow that day, helping her gather herbs and vegetables and bathing with her in the river.

When Adalyn and Emilia had returned home that afternoon the twins had been cuddled up with Mitch on the couch, a wool rug thrown around their small bodies while they both drank goats milk from a cup.

Father had lit the fire, the house was warm and felt of home, a distinct feeling Adalyn had never forgotten. Emilia had plunked down on the couch and snuggled into Noah. Jarhn had reached over and pat her head, his small chubby hand resting in her blonde curls.

Adalyn had walked in to find her mother in her father's strong arms, staring up at him as if he was the man who strung the stars and moon in the sky. She'd always thought her parents had been one soul split in half, destined to find the other in every life. Adalyn vowed that she would not settle for less of a love if it wasn't like her parents. Two halves to a whole. The stars to the moon.

A gentle hand shakes Adalyn out of her memories. She blinks through the wetness in her eyes, reaching up to find her cheeks drenched. A shuddering sob wracks her body and she finds Allison's warm arm coming around her shoulders, pulling Adalyn to her side. She doesn't resist, burying her face into her soft chest and crying.

She can't stop as her heart breaks in her chest, knowing she'll never see her family again. Knowing they're really gone. It's an unbearable pain, it threatens to drag her into its depths and never release her. What is the point of living if her family aren't here to experience life with her? How is she meant to even be *happy* knowing she'll never hear her mother's warm laugh again, see her father's warm smile? She can't even think about the twins who still had their entire life ahead of them.

Emilia though...there is a small spark in the darkness that grows as Adalyn focuses on the thought of her sister. She hadn't seen a body and she refuses to believe the males had gotten to her so she must have escaped. Adalyn can only pray she's far, far away and is safe.

"I know, it will be okay. Cry all you want, I'm here." Allison murmurs into her hair, combing back Adalyn's auburn knots. Adalyn takes a shuddering breath, fisting Allison's dress. She smells of forest berries with a lingering hint of sweetness.

"I'm sorry, I was thinking of my family—of a happy memory. I didn't know I was crying." Adalyn finds the strength to pull back, unclenching her hands. Allison keeps an arm around her shoulders, her own caramel eyes are filled with unshed tears.

"You never, ever apologise for that," Allison assures, squeezing her shoulder gently. She's careful to avoid the still healing cut.

"Thank you." Adalyn blows out a breath, slumping down.

"I see his marks are gone," Allison whispers softly.

"Three days are up, there goes any protection from Polarian and the other mongrels out there."

Allison removes her arm, opting to lean her head on Adalyn's shoulder. She takes Adalyn's hand in both of her own, a comfort in the darkness.

"He's an evil, evil male," Allison whispers, shaking her head.

"He's sick in the head. They all are," Adalyn spits with disgust. She pushes down the tendrils of sadness and instead focuses on that burning red rage. Her revenge is going to be slow and prolonged. She'll make whoever killed her family suffer a fate worse than death.

"From what I've heard the king isn't as vile as these...minions."

"I've heard he's a *generous lover.*" Adalyn says sarcastically, earning a broken chuckle from Allison.

"At least the sex might be good." Allison whispers, "I doubt anything else will be."

"Do you know how long it is until we get to Pantera?" Adalyn asks, eyes skimming over the other women. They all stay silent, defeat wafts off of them like a pungent stench. It curdles Adalyn's stomach, they've all accepted what is to come.

"No idea. A part of me will be glad to be free of this carriage but the other is also fearful of what's going to happen to us. We'll only be switching prisons."

Adalyn sighs, "Hopefully the new prison will have private bathing chambers and a place to relieve ourselves."

Allison falls silent, Adalyn follows her lead. She closes her eyes as the carriage jostles back and forth over the dry ground. Taking deep breaths, she focuses on the noises she can hear. Apart from the pounding of hooves and the distinct creaking of carriage wheels she can just hear birds in the distance, hear the chatter of the jailers that ride beside their carriage.

There's nothing much else to do but rest, so that's what Adalyn does. She closes her eyes, leaning her head atop of Allison's. She conjures another warm memory of her family before she falls into the darkness of sleep.

Adalyn is thrust into consciousness, her body falls from the carriage and onto hard ground shocking her from the last depths of sleep. She blinks rapidly as a hand fists into her hair, dragging her along the ground.

"Let me go!" She screams, clawing at the wrist that has her trapped. She's still disorientated, watching as the other girls fall from the carriage as they're attached to Adalyn's chain. Valarki males hoot and shout as they all watch, their eyes hungry for violence.

She wrangles in the tight grasp, her skull screaming in pain as she catches a glimpse of Polarian hauling her along. He grins down at her with feral, untamed glee.

Her stomach goes leaden as she recognises the gleam of violence in his eyes. Adalyn knows that whatever is coming isn't going to be nice and will most likely leave her in a worse state than she is now.

She keeps a tight grip around his wrist, it lessens the constant burn on her scalp and the urge to cry. She's so sick and tired of being handled as if she is nothing more than a rag doll.

For a split second she wishes she was still marked with Killian's brand.

"Here you go, whore." Polarian spits, his magic slides over her wrists like oil and her chains are broken from the rest. The other girls stumble to a stop, all fearful eyes watch Adalyn as she's dragged further away from them but still in full view.

There's nothing but soft green grass for miles to see, in the distance Adalyn can spot hundreds of sparkling white dots on the horizon. Before she can begin a thought to what they may be, she's forced to her knees. Polarian's magic is vile, roaming over her skin and keeping her grounded. She struggles against the invisible bonds, feeling the vein in her neck strain as his magic forces her head upwards.

He stands before her, his orange eyes glow as he looks down. A gentle breeze stirs his long hair which he'd pulled back into a tight pony-tail. He's armed with weapons, his skin tight clothes leaving little to the imagination.

Adalyn clenches her jaw, refusing to utter a single word.

"It's delightful to see that you have no idea why you're here." Polarian grins, eyes flickering to his right. Adalyn can't turn her head to see who strides this way.

"Killian and Jurian are scouting ahead, clearing a path for the final journey home tomorrow. Do you know what that means little whore?" Polarian crouches down in front of Adalyn, hands hanging between his knees, "It means for the next twenty minutes I can do whatever I wish to you."

Adalyn feels the bile rise in her throat, threatening to choke her.

"Do you know what I wish to do?" he murmurs, leaning in until his warm breath hits her face. She blinks slowly, breathing raggedly through her nose.

He trails a finger down her cheek, grabbing her chin roughly and digging his nails in, "I wish to make you *bleed*."

Polarian releases her, standing once more. He unstraps a dagger from his hip, the silver blade glistens in the dying light. Adalyn's thoughts go blank as she watches the weapon twirl between his fingers.

"The king has given specific commands that none of us may touch the female slaves in a sexual way, but he does condone us breaking you into submission." Polarian looks away from the blade, down to Adalyn's strained form. "I'm going to make you bleed and my magic is going to be the thing that keeps your pathetic heart beating. I won't kill you, I'll make sure of that."

His magic tightens in answer, squeezing Adalyn painfully. She does her best to struggle against its grip but the effort is fruitless. There is no one to save her this time, she can't even save herself. Polarian grins, his only warning as he releases his magic and slams his botted foot into the middle of Adalyn's chest.

She flies backwards into the dirt, wheezing as the breath is stolen from her lungs.

Polarian's large figure looms over her, the other girls begin to cry. "This is the punishment you'll receive if any of you choose to follow the path of this pathetic creature."

Adalyn rolls onto her stomach, clawing at the grass as she tries to drag herself away. The pain in her chest is a deep ache, as if his boot reached her heart and booted it across the open clearing.

A foot comes down over her shoulders, grinding her into the

ground. Her moan of pain is muffled as a hand pushes her face into the grass.

She blinks back tears, she refuses to cry. He can beat her, break her body all he wants, but she will never let him break her mind.

Adalyn stills as she feels the sharp tip of the dagger dig into the soft flesh of her spine. Hissing through her teeth she squeezes her eyes shut, waiting for the next burst of pain.

After several seconds it doesn't come and she opens her eyes, thinking he's stopped.

She is wrong.

He kicks her hard in the side, sending her sprawling onto her back. She tries to curl into her throbbing side but Polarian straddles her, resting the dagger at the base of her throat. Her eyes widen as she feels the skin break, warm blood leaks from the small wound and runs down the side of her throat.

"I'm going to enjoy this." Polarian whispers, digging the blade in deeper.

Adalyn's nostrils flare as she picks up the sharp tang of her blood. It's overwhelming.

Polarian drags the blade from the base of her throat and down her chest, slicing her as he goes. Her breathing comes in sharp gasps as he digs the blade in deeper as it comes to her left breast. She tenses.

Polarian looks down at the blade, taking it from her flesh to stab at the thin material of her nightgown.

"Is this the breast Killian feasted on?" He asks darkly, eyes flickering to Adalyn's. Her entire body goes still, his eyes darken to burnt orange as he stabs the dagger into the top of her left breast.

A guttural scream rips from her throat as blood courses down her front and side. Polarian twists the blade until it scratches bone. Blinding white pain has Adalyn falling into unconsciousness for a split second, only to be pulled back by the pain.

It's worse than any pain she's ever felt. Polarian's magic slides over her skin and she feels it begin to slowly repair the wound. It's enough to make her stomach clench as she tips her head to the side and vomits.

"Let's see how much he wants to touch you now." Polarian growls. He rips the blade out, earning another ear piercing scream. She thrashes against him now, hitting her hands into his solid chest. Her legs kick out while she bucks, trying to dislodge him.

"That'll leave a nice scar," his magic grabs her wrists and holds them to the ground above her head. She watches in disgust as he licks red droplets of blood from his blade. It sends a wave of nausea through her.

She blubbers through her tears, "I'll fucking kill you."

"You won't ever get the chance. I *own* you. Once we return to Pantera you will be mine, the king won't choose you now. You and I have centuries of pain to explore. I will enjoy breaking you, piece by piece." He smiles madly, eyes glowing as he rises from her pinned body.

In a swift movement he sends the dagger flying at her, embedding in her left thigh. She screams again as his magic sinks the blade to bone. Valarki males growl with pleasure, thriving from the scent of blood in the air.

"I'm going to leave you out here as punishment." *Punishment.* Oh how Killian's punishment was a smack on the wrist compared to this. Polarian turns away from Adalyn, leaving her screaming and crying as the blade is still embedded in her thigh. "Put the slaves back in their carriage."

Adalyn manages to stop screaming, her throat raw from the unrelenting pain. Her body isn't her own as she openly cries, the gash in her breast flows with blood while the one on her thigh is a soft bubble around the blade.

She has no real idea why Polarian had done this, a monster doesn't need a reason as to why they do monstrous things. It's what makes them the creatures they are and Polarian is the worst of them, the darkness is like a second skin to him. She can only assume it has something to do with Killian's interest in her.

The sky is thrown into darkness and Adalyn is still held by Polarian's magic to the outskirts of the camp. She groans against the pain, grinding her teeth together. She can't move, can barely think rationally.

She blinks in and out of the darkness beckoning to her, in the darkness there is no pain. There is nothing. She wants to welcome it with wide arms, needing to escape this hell she's currently trapped in.

She doesn't know how much time passes as she lies there, bleeding out while Polarian's magic pumps into her and keeps her alive, keeps the worst of her wounds from killing her.

"Oh my god..." a soft male voice murmurs. Adalyn struggles to open her eyes, her lids far too heavy. Sweat coats her bare skin, the cool night breeze does nothing to help.

A gentle hand touches Adalyn's cheek, stirring her into the present. A broken scream leaves her mouth as the pain in her breast and leg threaten to drown her once more.

"Fuck. Killian, hurry up!" The familiar male voice shouts into the darkness, there's a commotion behind him. Adalyn blinks through the haze to make out the handsome blonde Valarki crouching beside her, his face stricken with worry.

"Hey Red, it's going to be okay. Okay? I just need you to stay with me a little longer." He murmurs, stroking her cheek once more. Adalyn tries her best to remain aware but the darkness is strong and has its claws deep into her. The only thing keeping her in the present is Polarian's magic. Her blood has now created a nice wet carpet around her left side.

Another figure falls to her left side, Adalyn closes her eyes once more. Suddenly Polarian's magic releases her, her arms sag against the ground as the healed wound now reopens and blood begins to gush out once more.

"Fuck!" the blonde Valarki swears, pressing a warm hand against the cut on her breast.

"Karis and Orios are going to be here any second," Killian

says, his voice a calm mask of promised death. "Go grab some clean towels, I'll stay with her."

His friend doesn't hesitate as he jumps up and sprints to his carriage. Killian presses both hands to the wound on Adalyn's breast.

"Adalyn?" He murmurs, leaning over her. His loose hair tickles her nose, distracting her from the immense pain for a moment. She looks up into his blue eyes, they are murderous. His breathing is ragged as he leans over her, his eyes searching her face.

"It's bad...isn't it?" she manages to whisper, her breaths grow shallow.

"You don't strike me as a woman to give up so easily." He whispers, cursing under his breath as blood spills out between his fingers.

"I am tired." Her eyes flutter closed and she embraces the darkness, welcomes it with sick delight as it wraps its warm arms around her frail figure. She nestles deep, inhaling its intoxicating scent.

Adalyn is vaguely aware as her body is picked up from the ground and she's moved—strong arms encase her figure, careful not to jostle her more than necessary. Moments later she's placed on soft bedding, her nightgown is cut down the front and falls away from her still form. More cursing, more rustling.

A warm hand encases her own as she finally slips into unconsciousness, saving her from the world of pain that is about to come.

11. Killian
Killian

Killian grasps Adalyn's limp right hand in his own as he sits close to her right side. His eyes leave her face and look to her exposed chest, to the deep jagged gash that now mars the top of her left breast. Karis swears as he begins to survey the damage.

"It's hit bone, cut tendons and muscle. Any more force and it would have slipped through her ribs and punctured a lung." Karis grasps a silver needle between his thin fingers, threading a deep red string through the pin hole. "I'll need to use my magic to stitch the internal damage before applying a salve."

"Do whatever you can to heal her," Killian says softly, his eyes trail down to the bruise of a large boot that is planted between her breasts, defining the grooves in the imprint. Dark blue and brown blossom on her side from another kick.

Orios works his magic as he retracts the dagger from her thigh, blood bubbles out and spills before he has a chance to press a wad of cloth into the wound.

"To the bone here as well," Orios murmurs, grabbing a needle and thread exactly the same as the one Karis currently uses. The needle works on its own accord as it dives into the wound and begins stitching.

"Who the fuck did this?" Jurian growls from where he stands, watching the display with simmering rage. "We don't touch the female slaves, we keep them safe." Killian feels much the same, if not far, far worse. They'd arrived to the camp later than they'd expected, the males were far too pleased.

Once Killian had picked up the scent of blood, both he and Jurian had made their way to the source; only to find Adalyn sprawled on the ground with blood gushing from two wounds, the cut from her throat down to her breast had crusted over. The other females had refused to speak.

He'd seen red as his mind had emptied of any thoughts.

"I don't know," he grits out, tightening his hold on Adalyn's hand. Her nightgown is ruined, the last shred of her past life is now gone.

Killian isn't sure why that makes him feel uncomfortable, almost bad for her, but it does.

"We need to fucking figure it out," Jurian snaps.

"You think I don't know that?" Killian asks, staring up at him, "I want nothing more than to shed blood after what has been done to her."

Killian's hands shake as her cold hand slowly begins to regenerate with warmth. He sends his magic through their connection to help with the wounds the healers are working on.

"Will anyone out there talk?" Killian asks.

A muscle along Jurian's jaw twitches. "No."

"Then we wait until she is awake to tell us and if she refuses, they all will be punished." Killian lets one hand go and brushes an auburn strand back from her face. His fingers linger, trailing down her cheek.

"They will question your loyalty," Jurian whispers, the disgust evident in his words.

"I am loyal to no one but myself and our king. They are loyal to *me* and if I have to make them bleed to realise their position, I won't hesitate." He'd done much worse when they'd stepped out of line.

"I know...I'm just asking you to see how this looks. The shadow of death who cares for only himself is avenging a slave woman."

"Do you suggest I do nothing?" Killian fires at him, his anger is a live thing that thrums through his veins. Dark magic leaks from him, rumbling the earth beneath them, "Do you suggest I throw her back out to them?"

"Of course I don't!" Jurian barks. "I'm thinking of the bigger picture. You have taken an interest in her and everyone out there fucking knows it. The king will find out and he will use her against you."

"I am aware." Killian sucks at his teeth, drawing in a deep breath. He doesn't stop his magic from taking form and invading all of the Valarki male's minds.

Killians power demands a payment. He sends his magic out to their targets, letting his darkness invade and take control of their minds; feeding from their fear. It keeps his beast sated.

He breaks through their mental barriers and unleashes his nightmares with no mercy.

Screaming starts moments later as the soldiers struggle with an inner battle. No one will win, not until Killian has pulled his claws from their minds.

"You are playing a very dangerous game Killian, a game that could get *her* killed." Jurian looks to her still form, Killian summons a thin black silk blanket. He gently tucks it over her right breast and over her stomach, he covers her mound, his fingers brushing against the soft hair as he tucks the material between her thighs to stop it from slipping away.

"I won't let her die." Killian vows. Jurian snorts.

"Yes, because you're doing a grand job of that so far."

"For the last leg of the journey she will ride with me." Killian slides his eyes back to her face, nothing warm stirs in his chest. No, only ice cold rage.

The Valarki males are wild and untamed, breaking human women is a pleasure they all indulge in. At the village raids Killian gives them leeway, knowing the women will meet their deaths and their suffering will end.

It's sick and fucked up, but he is fucked up far worse than he will ever let on.

The only way he can rebel and not be punished is by protecting the females they take as slaves, they aren't to be touched sexually by the Valarki soldiers. They can be humiliated in other ways, as the king simply wants them untainted. It was his one order, the females aren't to be fucked.

His king doesn't give a shit with what happens in between, but a small part of Killian does.

"Whoever has done this will be punished," Killian says, his voice sounding detached from his body. He closes his eyes as he feels through the dark tendrils of his magic that have created a spider-web underneath their camp, trapping every single soldier.

His blood hums as he feeds off their fear, it's almost an addiction as the sweet rush lulls the blood thirst slightly. He can't be out of his wits once Adalyn awakens, he has to have a somewhat clear mind.

"We've done what we can. I've injected her with pain relief, she should wake in a few moments." Karis' voice breaks Killian from his feeding, he holds out a small vial full of a deep purple liquid. Killian takes it.

"Give this to her once you speak with her, it will put her in a deep sleep and help speed up the healing. There's nothing else to be done."

Karis stands, Orios quickly tucks the blade into his medicine bag as he turns and leaves, not bothering with goodbyes. Killian doesn't care, he slides the material over her exposed breast. It will scar nicely, the skin is stitched in the pattern of a slithering snake.

"Thank you Karis," Killian murmurs, leaning back to look up at him. Karis bows once before leaving his carriage, gently shutting the door behind him. Jurian approaches and crouches down, looking from her pale face to their clasped hands.

"Will you be alright?" He asks.

"I'll be fine. She can't do much in this state." Killian rubs his thumb over the back of her hand, gently beginning to coax her from her mind. He can feel the darkness that covers her, protecting her.

"I doubt that." Jurian huffs, standing, "send word if you need my assistance. If not, I'll speak with you in the morning. I'll keep my ears open for any information I can gather."

"I'll see you in the morning, Jurian." Killian rubs a hand roughly over his face.

"I hope this does not break her," he says softly before slipping from the carriage. He shuts the door firmly and retreats silently. Killian locks the doors and windows with his magic and cloaks an enchantment over the carriage to give them privacy.

He stares down at Adalyn, watching as her chest rises with each breath. Her eyes flutter open, she gasps for breath as her hand tightens on Killian's.

"I'm here," he murmurs, squeezing gently. Her head tilts slightly to the side, her amber eyes are clouded. Killian leans forward, brushing his lips over her forehead as his magic pulses and clears her mind.

She begins to shake, taking shuddering breaths. Tears slip from her eyes as she begins to cry, she trembles from head to toe as Killian moves back.

"*No-no-no-*" her words are raspy and thin, she squeezes her eyes shut as tears continue to slide down the sides of her face in a strong stream.

"I'll get you some water." Killian goes to remove his hand but she holds on tighter, grounding him. He could easily remove her hand, but finds he doesn't want to.

She shakes her head, refusing to open her eyes. He stays by her side, letting her work through her emotions. He can imagine the pain she feels, the horror. He knows all too well that rage will sweep into the room and make home in her bones for blood and vengeance. Whoever has done this to her, will reap the consequences at her hand.

Killian will make sure of it.

They sit like that for several more moments, Adalyn eventually wrangles in her emotions and her breathing evens out. Killian brushes away the last of her tears as she opens her eyes.

Their amber depths burn with the fires of hell.

"I thought I hated you...what I feel for you is nothing compared to this feeling." She whispers, her words barely reach his ears. He smirks, his chest grows cold as he releases his hold on his magic. A heady rush gushes through him as all of the soldier's fear feeds into his soul, strengthening him. It warms him momentarily, an addictive high that he hasn't indulged in for some time.

"This is twice I've saved your life now, Addie," Killian murmurs, running his thumb over the back of her hand. Her breath catches at the nickname, her eyes flicker to their clasped hands.

"You're determined to keep me alive," she murmurs, relaxing slightly as she looks towards the ceiling, "it's annoying."

"Then I shall be annoying for a while yet to come," Killian declares. "May I get you that glass of water now?"

She nods once, letting her hand fall from his own. He stands and moves towards the table that currently harbours his saddle bags. He rummages through and retrieves his skin hide water sack, his steps pause as he looks to where Adalyn lays on the furs that cover the wooden floorboards.

The thin scrap of silk hugs her figure deliciously—Killian begins to grow hard as he recalls how soft she is. He adjusts his front, now is not the appropriate time to be salivating over her.

Gods, I shouldn't be having these thoughts at all. He curses internally. This woman is the devil.

He closes the distance and takes a seat beside her head, he unscrews the cap and holds one hand under the back of her head as he presses the water skin to her lips. She takes a few large mouthfuls before pulling away. Killian lowers her head gently before screwing the cap back on.

"I have a serum that will help you rest if you wish to take it now," he says. Her eyes open as she stares up at him.

"Not just yet...I need to manage my thoughts first."

"Who did this to you?" he asks quietly, staring at her intently. She goes still, refusing to meet his eye. Her hands clench at the thin material as her breathing begins to grow rapid.

"I...I can't say. Not yet," she manages to whisper. "He did this to me because you touched me."

Something breaks in Killian's chest as he stares down at her, for once speechless. She'd been tortured because he'd *touched* her?

"I am sorry this happened to you because of my actions." He whispers, holding truth to his every word. He feels...pained. He feels pained.

The thought throws him off balance.

This is a dangerous game indeed. He doesn't want to *feel anything*.

"I can handle it." She finally looks up to him, "I knew what I was doing when I touched you."

"This is not what happens after a female touches me," Killian growls, "this is the opposite of the things you should feel."

Adalyn gulps, her pale cheeks heating "Trust me, I'm aware."

Killian shakes his head, pinching the bridge of his nose as he lets out a frustrated breath. He'd need some serious massage therapy once they return home and he'd need some creatures to kill.

Lots and lots of creatures.

"Are you going to send me back out there?" she asks, drawing his attention. He shakes his head, keeping his eyes on hers. She relaxes.

"Better the devil you know," she murmurs.

"Come, let's get you into bed." Killian gently wraps an arm under her shoulder. He slides his other arm under her knees as he lifts her to his chest. Her face crunches up in pain, she tries her best to keep her left leg straight as he takes her to bed. Killian silently wills his magic into her, easing her harshest pain. Her face immediately relaxes as a deep sigh leaves her lips.

As he lowers her to the pillows, the silk slip falls from her front and flutters to the floor. Her eyes widen as her hands go to cover her most sensitive parts.

"It's nothing I haven't seen before." He lets her go, looking away as he grabs the soft blanket and pulls it over her slender legs.

She's a dangerous temptation.

"Just what every naked female wants to hear," she says sourly, grabbing the covers from his hands.

"Jealous?" he asks, arching a dark brow as he looks back to her face. Her neck is flushed along with her cheeks as she keeps her heated gaze on his. His blood begins to hum in his veins, liking the way she watches him. As if he's worth something.

"Implying I'm jealous implies I care." She huffs, "which I don't."

Killian can taste the lie as it leaves her mouth, it's sweet with the hint of lavender. He grins as he leans over her, careful not to touch any part of her. His breath fans her face, causing her pupils to dilate.

"You have me thinking otherwise, Adalyn Grace," he murmurs, tilting his head to the side slightly.

"You're mistaken, Killian Abaddon," she says back, slightly breathless. Killian brushes his nose against her own, if either of them moved their lips would connect.

"Mmm I may be...but you can't deny the pull you feel towards me." He doesn't know where these words are coming from, he told himself he would be the monster she thinks he is and yet he's here trying his best to entice a reaction from her.

"The pull I feel is me wanting to stab you." She leans forward, her mouth sliding over his cheek and to his ear, "you may have saved my life twice, but you will live to regret it."

"I will never regret saving you." His eyes flash brightly as his magic dances under his skin, Adalyn leans back into the pillow and wets her bottom lips with her tongue.

"You may not be like the others, but you are still a wolf."

Killian smirks, eyes darkening, "And you are more than a helpless lamb. You are the wolf in sheep skin, waiting for your moment to rip into our throats."

He reaches out and trails a finger down her cheek, under her jaw and down her throat. Her pulse jack hammers wildly against his touch but she doesn't stop him as his fingers tug back the blanket enough that the cut along her chest is visible along with the stitched scar on her breast.

He ignores her hardened nipples, ignores the sweet scent of her growing arousal. If he acknowledges it, there will be no stopping him. He has to have more control over his emotions.

"Do I scare you?" he asks, eyes lingering on the cut.

"No."

He doesn't taste her lie, it makes him smile softly. Of course he doesn't scare the she wolf. He could imagine there are few things that scare her and hell of a lot more things that piss her off.

"You should be scared, Adalyn." He looks back up to her, grasping her chin lightly. Her eyes flicker to his lips as he parts them.

"If you want me to be scared you'll need to try harder." Her silk wrapped words have him hardening, a reoccurring sensation now that they're alone. He growls low in his throat, his chest rumbling.

"Do you...do you think it's ugly?" she whispers, angling her chin down to look at the stitches. The cut. She tugs her bottom lip between her teeth and looks away, "Forget it, I don't care what you think. I shouldn't have asked."

"Your scars will never make you ugly Adalyn, they are a part of your story and the person you will grow to become. Don't shy away from them." Killian traces the jagged cut, the hints of a bruise peak out from under the sheet. "You are still a beautiful temptation."

Her breath catches and her nipples turn to peaks. His hand

trails against the soft skin, the blanket begins to fall away from her perky breasts with each gentle stroke of his fingers.

There's a pregnant tension in the air, a dangerous battle of wills. Will she cave first, or will he? How far will this go before it gets out of hand? It's a dangerous game they play, a game Killian refuses to lose.

"Are you going to stop me, Addie?" His voice is husky, his desire evident in every word. His eyes flash to hers, she grips the bed sheets tightly. Her wet lips are parted, shining in the lantern light. Her eyes...they burn with hatred mixed with undiluted desire.

"There's nothing scarier than losing control..." he murmurs, watching as the blanket falls to her waist. He hungrily eyes each plump breast, wanting nothing more than to explore them with his tongue and teeth.

Adalyn's breathing turns ragged, "It seems you've lost yours."

Killian leans in close to her left breast, groaning as his erection strains against his tight pants. His hot breath hits the tightened peak, causing her skin to pucker with goosebumps.

"No...I'm far from it. But you?" his mouth lowers over her breast, his tongue flicks out and grazes her nipple. She gasps, her thighs tightening under the sheets.

"You have no control left to take." He pauses for one more moment, his eyes darken as he meets hers. The fire and passion... it's a flame that matches his own.

If he does this, willingly, it will only complicate everything that is to come.

She swallows hard, throat bobbing with the movement, "Distract me. Make me forget, even for a moment." she whispers.

A distraction...one Killian can gladly indulge her in. He takes a deep breath, indulging in the scent of her arousal and her musk.

It's addicting, the warmth she stirs inside of him. It's dangerous, the things he's beginning to feel whenever he touches her.

For tonight...he will gladly give them the distraction they both desperately need.

12. Killian

Killian

"I can give you that." He presses a gentle kiss to the side of her nipple, nipping the skin gently as he pulls away to meet her eyes once more, "if you say stop, I will stop. No hesitation."

"Okay." She nods once. Slowly she unclenches her hands from the sheet and brings one to slide through the curtain of his hair, she tugs him towards her gently. He obliges as he lets her guide him, not wanting to startle her.

Her lips hesitantly brush against his own, he doesn't rush her. This is for her...something he has never offered another woman.

"I've never done this before," she admits softly, the fire kindles in her eyes and only leaves desire behind. Killian smiles softly.

"We won't do anything you do not want. I can teach you if you would like." He gently kisses the tip of her nose.

"Okay...okay." She nods to herself, clarity clearing her mind, "I don't know how much longer these pain killers will last, so let's...distract until they wear off."

"Your wish is my command."

"I'll move over so you can lay down."

Killian rises from the bed, Adalyn gingerly shuffles along until there's enough room for him to lay by her side. Once she settles she looks up at him. He slowly removes his shirt, undoing the lace to his pants before sliding them to the floor. His hard erection strains against the material of his undergarments, hiding little.

Adalyn's eyes take in his form hungrily, making his erection throb against the material as she focuses on it, as if her eyes are a gentle caress.

Killian meets her eyes as he climbs into the bed beside her, his own heart beat thrums wildly in his chest as he takes her naked form in hungrily. Finding her how he had tonight had broken his tight restraint of his control.

For tonight they would use each other, but tomorrow they will need boundaries. Not only is he going against his king by having her in his bed like she is, he's going against his own moral code.

But for tonight, with the fire in her eyes, he ignores the rules and loyalties until his head is empty of anything that doesn't involve her.

"Can I touch you?" she whispers, licking her lips. Killian nods once, laying back down as she slowly sits up and gently drapes her top half across his broad chest. Killian shoots his magic through their touching skin and soothes the aches and pains that plague her. The tension between her eyebrows disappears.

"I choose this," she whispers, more to herself than him.

Killian's skin grows hot as her right hand trails along his collar bone, her nails dig in slightly as she makes the way down his defined stomach and reaches the dark hair above the waistband of his pants. "I choose this. I'm so sick of my choices being taken from me."

His right hand clamps down on her round ass, squeezing gently. She takes a shuddering breath as she toys with the hair, her eyes never leaving his.

He leans up and closes the distance between them, sinking his teeth into her plump bottom lip. She moans softly into his mouth as her hand slides underneath the material of his pants. Killian's hips buck as she wraps her small hand around the base of his shaft, her fingers barely touch.

He grasps the small part of control he has, knowing he can't take her how he wants. He can give her pleasure in more ways than fucking her.

"Fuck, your hand is so soft." He growls against her lips as she begins a slow assault of moving her hand up and down, paying close attention to the head. She rubs her hand over his leaking juices and as she grows more confident she picks up more speed.

Adalyn kisses him aggressively, working her hand with the same anticipation. Killian's lips are silk against her own as he gives into her, his tongue slides into her mouth as his hand moves between her thighs.

"It's my turn to please you." He growls, pulling back from her. Her hand continues its tortuous assault as she lies on her back, eyes wide with desire as Killian places himself between her thighs. He makes quick work of removing his underwear.

"I want to please you—" Adalyn protests as Killian gently removes her hand. He kisses her palm.

"You will, after I have my way with you." Killian doesn't hesitate a second longer as he moves back and gently guides her thighs apart, he looks at her glistening folds and groans.

Her hands tangle in his hair as he lowers his mouth to her inner thigh, gently placing kisses along the soft flesh until he reaches the main source of her arousal. It's a sweet musk, begging for him to have a taste.

He blows gently, causing her to buck her hips slightly. One muscled arm wraps under her thigh and presses against her stomach. She will not escape this.

"Killian." She moans his name, tugging at his hair. He chuckles darkly, he gently runs a finger through her slick folds.

"You're so wet for me." His voice is husky with desire, he's drunk off of it. He continues to run his finger through her folds, knowing the pleasure is building.

He brings his mouth down, sucking at the sensitive nub that's hidden. Adalyn's hips thrust into his mouth, her thighs tighten around his head as his tongue begins to explore each delicious part of her.

While he licks and sucks, one finger slowly circles her entrance. She's unbroken and he's vaguely aware he can't break her. The thought has a primal side of him wanting to claim her in every way.

"Killian, please." She begs, trying to thrust into his mouth. He chuckles, sucking at her folds before delving into her with his tongue. He groans, she tastes divine.

"Oh god." Her back arches as she continues to ride his mouth, rubbing her sensitive nub against his devilish working tongue. He bites down and tugs gently, causing a small scream of pleasure to rip from her throat.

"Are you close, darling?" he murmurs, gently easing a finger into her. She relaxes at his touch, welcoming more. He's careful not to break her, he curls his finger upwards to find the most sensitive part that will have her screaming his name.

"So close." She gasps, her thighs shake and tighten as his finger begins to stroke into her. His tongue continues its assault on her nub.

Her moans of pleasure are music to his ears, a high that opium addicts get. This is better than feeding on fear, Adalyn is his new addiction.

A deadly addiction.

His other arm slips from her waist as he grabs his own length, working himself in time to each thrust of Adalyn's hips. Now with free range she grinds her hips relentlessly against his mouth, her moans grow louder and more out of control with each thrust.

"Scream my name," he growls, fingering her faster than before, curling towards her apex. He tugs and sucks at her nub relentlessly, not allowing her to retreat from the high.

He fucks his own hand, he's close. Too close. She needs to find her release first.

"Killian—I'm going to—" her words are cut short as Killian bites on her nub and flicks his tongue back and forth, pulling her to orgasm. Her whole body arches as she tightens around his curled finger. She pulses against him as her juices coat his finger and lips.

"*Killian.*" She half screams, half moans his name as he finds his release at the same time she finds her own. He works her through the orgasm, spilling his seed over the bed sheets.

He licks her clean as she returns to the present, he slowly pulls his finger from her tightness. He wipes his chin with the back of his hand as his eyes find hers.

Fuck. I'm royally fucked, he thinks as her amber eyes burn brightly, enchanting him. Her soft skin is flush with her orgasm, her legs spread and quiver as she relaxes into the bed.

Killian slowly rises, grabbing his shirt as he quickly wipes his seed from the sheets. He refuses to think more into this, for tonight it just is. Tomorrow is for thinking.

Killian slowly wipes Adalyn dry before wiping himself off. He turns from her and pulls his undergarments back on, throwing his shirt to the side he grabs a clean one for her. She still lies there quietly as he passes her his shirt, she takes it sheepishly and holds it to her chest. He chuckles and grabs the water skin, chugging deeply.

Her taste and scent is driving him mad, already he begins to harden again. He splashes water over his hands before passing her the skin. She takes it silently and drinks deeply. Killian crouches down and retrieves the vial for her.

"Now, do you prefer I sleep on the floor?" He asks, running a hand back through his hair. Her eyes narrow as she lets the water skin fall to the ground.

"I don't think that'll be necessary." She struggles to pull the shirt on, so he helps glide it down her arms until it settles over her chest. She lays back and moves over for him.

"Here, drink this." He pops the cork from the small vial and holds it to her lips. She narrows her eyes but drinks the sweet liquid until its empty.

"I still hate you," she whispers, staring at him with unguarded eyes. He tastes the hint of her lie, also mixed with truth. He makes quick work or turning the lantern off, only moon light streams in through the windows.

He climbs into bed beside her, extremely aware of her body beside his own. All he can smell is her. Maybe sleeping beside her will be a bad idea.

He's about to say just that and move to the floor when Adalyn half snuggles into his side. She rests her head against his shoulder, finding his hand with her own.

Killian closes his eyes and focuses on his breathing, Adalyn's breathing evens out and he knows sleep has claimed her. It takes him far longer to fall asleep.

He needs to stop while he's ahead, otherwise these two wolves will tear each other apart and they will have no one to blame but themselves.

13. Adalyn

Adalyn

Adalyn stares at the dress Killian holds, the deep blue material is thin and the trimmings are lined with silver. He holds the two straps up to show case the split that runs down both sides, allowing her to ride a *horse* with *him*.

"I can't wear that." She crosses her arms over her chest, his large shirt pools around her like a dress. She'd awoken to a cold bed, but Killian hadn't been far off.

It took all of her restraint to ignore what took place between them last night, she'd decided Polarian abusing her held ranking over whatever Killian and her had shared. If Polarian even caught hint of what had transpired between them...she may very well not walk away again. She's been near to death both times she's had to encounter his wrath.

Killian narrows his eyes at her, their crystal blue depths blaze with annoyance as his hands clench around the straps, "Yes well you can't wear my shirt and your nightgown is ruined."

"Don't you have anything a bit less revealing?" She asks, slowly rising from the bed. She hisses through her teeth as her left thigh throbs like a heartbeat, whatever she'd taken last night had pulled her into the best sleep she'd ever had. It doesn't stop the pain today though, she holds her left arm across her stomach; lessening the movement of the skin near the cut on her breast.

"I'm all out," Killian grinds out.

"I'll find my own outfit then." She ignores the fire in his eyes as she turns from him and limps towards the large chest. She silently curses him with each slow movement, the pain only works to irritate her even more and shorten her patience.

Adalyn pops open the lid, leaning against the edge as she looks down. She blinks once, twice, before snapping her head towards Killian with a snarl. "Where are the clothes?"

There are only empty bottles of whiskey residing in the chest. Her hand curls around the neck of one.

"You will wear this dress. It doesn't restrict your movements and it covers what you need it to. Have you ever ridden a horse before?" He demands, throwing the dress onto the bed before turning around. Adalyn watches in silence as his hand flexes around the neck of his current full whiskey bottle. His fingers tremble around the glass.

He doesn't deserve to be internally tortured, no, that's Adalyn's role. She throws the empty bottle towards the wall of the carriage, it shatters on impact and has Killian forgetting about the whiskey.

"Are you out of our god damn mind?" he barks as he stalks towards her, his long legs eating the distance between. She rises to her full height the best she can, refusing to cower before him.

"I will wear your *stupid* dress. Turn around." Adalyn moves past him, her heart skipping stupidly as her shoulder brushes his own. She steels herself against her chaotic heart, knowing she'd need to get herself together. He'd informed her that morning she'll be riding with him for the rest of the journey, meaning she'd be plastered to his chest for relentless hours.

That may have been completely fine if he hadn't *distracted* her the night before, tasting her and exploring her in ways she didn't even know were possible.

Her cheeks burn at the memory of her pale legs spread and his head buried between her thighs, more than happy to stay there.

"I can scent your thoughts from here," Killian grumbles, wooden boards creak as he makes his way to the other end of the carriage.

Adalyn snaps, "You weren't involved in any of them."

Although he holds his tongue, Adalyn can feel his resentment to her words, the way the temperature drops with his foul mood. She grabs the dress, running her hand down the silk material. After struggling slightly with Killian's shirt, she manages to get it off, finding herself completely naked.

"I don't have underwear," she grumbles, slipping the dress over her head the best she can. Once it's settled against her curves she can silently appreciate the dress is a good choice, it covers the cut on her breast and the bruises. She hadn't ridden before, but she'd have to ride with both legs over the same side. It won't be possible for her to ride normally.

"I don't keep a clean pair of women's underwear for the rare occasion I might need them," Killian drawls. Adalyn turns towards him, pulling her hair back to braid down her left side. He leans against the carriage wall, his tight black battle suit is as dark as his hair. The hilt of his many knives gleam in the morning sun.

"This ride is going to kill me." Or she might kill him, or pull them both from the horse. She doesn't care too much at this point, but now that she's recovered her energy, that festering hatred in her soul has grown.

Polarian *will* pay and she is going to make him suffer every second knowing a human female will be his end.

"That makes two of us. Come, the rest are ready." Killian turns from her and opens the carriage doors, jumping to the hard ground with the stealth of a mountain cat. Adalyn refuses to look at him as she lowers herself to the floor boards, sliding her legs down and gingerly reaching for the ground.

Killian remains silent, watching her with that steady gaze. She can't determine what he's thinking so she doesn't bother, brushing away the thoughts of the man in front of her, she looks around. Horses covered in black shimmering armour march around the camp, terrifying Valarki males are atop them armed to the teeth.

Adalyn keeps her head high as she follows after Killian, doing her best to keep the limp from her steps. It's easier said than done, she falls behind quickly as he strides for the front of the triage.

"Bastard," she growls under her breath, grabbing the dress in her hands as she picks her way barefoot along the hard ground. She does her best to avoid the prickles and sharp rocks, Valarki males watch her with the intensity of lions. She has no room to escape, not that she could if she wanted to try.

"Of course he'd come to your rescue." Polarian's voice cuts through her thoughts like a blade through skin, the deep tone of his voice douses her like a bucket of ice water as she comes to a halt. She glances over her shoulder, tipping her head back to find him on a gorgeous chestnut mare.

"He might have, but *no one* will come to yours." Adalyn feels her top lip begin to pull back in a snarl. She feels Polarian's rage wafting off of him, threatening to suffocate her. It spikes a small kernel of fear in her that she does well to hide.

"You'd be best to watch your back once we arrive at the castle," Polarian says softly, leading his horse right past her, "I'm not the only male who wants a piece of you."

She watches, mouth dry, as he canters towards the front of the group. Killian exchanges words with him, looking behind his shoulder and scowling when he finds Adalyn nowhere in sight. She's half tempted to hide, just to push whatever buttons she can.

It's her only way of grasping any form of control, because the more time she spends with Killian the more she's beginning to lose it. She'd meant what she said last night, only needing him for a distraction. In the darkness of his carriage and the comfort of his bed it'd been far too easy to slip into denial, that they're just two lovers tangled in the sheets.

That he didn't murder her family.

That she isn't out for blood.

Once they arrive at the castle, Adalyn will force herself to forget about Killian and the distraction. She refuses to think any deeper into it, knowing her emotions will rise from the cold slumber she'd sent them into. All she needs to feel is burning anger and hatred, a rage so strong sometimes she has to blink through the darkness of it to clear her vision.

Before, she never would have been described as a violent girl.

Now? Violence is all she craves.

"I haven't run away." Adalyn calls, finally parting through riders to find Killian talking with the handsome annoyance in hushed tones.

"Red, it's good to see you on your feet." He steps forward, offering her a wicked smile as his maroon eyes brighten, "Let me introduce myself, I'm Jurian. Killian's second in command."

"I care why?" Adalyn asks, raising a single brow. Jurian barks out a laugh, unaffected by her sour mood. His golden hair spills down his front, a section is braided with a green vine.

"I just simply wanted to tell you my name, I'm sure you'll offer yours soon enough," he chirps.

Adalyn limps forward, heading to the horse Killian has in his grasp. His eyes track each step she takes, her every intake of breath. "Doubtful."

"If you ever want to switch riding partners, I'm more than happy to tag team," he calls, grinning before walking to a palomino mare and leaping onto her saddled back with ease. Killian says nothing, waiting as Adalyn reaches up the black stallion's side.

Killian's large hands enclose around her waist as he pushes her up into the saddle. Adalyn bites her cheek as her wounds cry out in pain, grabbing the horn with both hands to steady herself. Her left leg leans against the front of the saddle as she sits on her side.

In one swift movement Killian mounts behind her, both of his large legs encase her as he brings his arms around her midsection. He picks up the black reins in his tanned hands and clicks his tongue.

"Do you have any pain killers?" She asks, the jolting of the horse walking has tears stinging her eyes as sharp pain spears through her.

"No."

"Oh, so we're back to that now," she grumbles, sitting taller so her back doesn't press completely against his hard and warm chest. It's far too tempting to lean back and nestle into him.

"We never left," he whispers into her ear.

Adalyn is about to give him a taste of his own medicine when she feels the warmth of his magic seep from him, it swims over her skin in loving recognition before hitting the ground and bursting forward.

In an explosion of darkness the barren land rumbles, greenery bursts through the darkened cracks in the earth. Killian's magic goes far and wide, covering the area beneath them. Their stallion grows impatient from the energy now coursing through his veins, with the click of Killian's tongue the stallion bursts into a gallop. The others follow behind, the thundering of hooves and jolting of carriages can hardly be heard over the sound of wind howling in Adalyn's ears.

Adalyn watches in stunned awe as the barren field begins to spurt with life, for miles green grass begins to grow as well as yellow wildflowers. Adalyn leans slightly over the saddle and finds that the hooves cut a clear path between the flora. She furrows her brow in confusion, isn't Killian the shadow of death? How can he be growing life?

"I'm going to portal us to our border," Killian calls to Jurian, who rides right beside them in stride. Jurians eyes light up with excitement and he grins. Adalyn can't hide her curiosity as Jurian looks to her. "It's safe Red, it'll land us right on the borders of our lands and yours."

"How far into Pantera do we need to travel until we reach the castle?" She asks.

"To the mountains on the northern border, it'll probably take the entire day of riding to get there. Are you excited?" Jurian is eager to return home, it sends a pang of sadness through her.

She doesn't have a home anymore and doubts she ever will again.

"Why would I be excited by switching jailers?" She asks softly, looking away from him quickly. "A cage is still a cage, regardless of how pretty it is. I'm nothing more than a bird to you all." *But you won't break my wings,* she thinks to herself. Her nails dig into the horn of the saddle, leaving indents behind. Killian leans into her until her entire back is flush against his chest, his hot breath fans the side of her throat and sends a thrill through her.

"What a sweet song you sing," he murmurs softly. Adalyn tries her best to not let him get under her skin although the huskiness of his voice has her clenching her thighs tighter.

"You won't be a distraction to me ever again Killian, you aren't going to be my jailer anymore," she whispers back. The magic around them builds rapidly until ahead Adalyn begins to see a black vortex splitting open in the middle of the now flourishing land.

"You're right," he brushes his lips against her ear, "I'll be something far worse."

He straightens, although her back is still plastered to his chest. In their murmured conversation he'd slipped an arm around her waist, casually holding onto her hip.

He raises the arm that has hold of the reins, Jurian whoops in delight as the vortex splits open with the thunderous crack of boulders colliding. The earth trembles beneath them as the vortex grows and begins to illuminate multiple houses with Valarki moving about. Heads turn to the noise and they all scramble backwards.

Adalyn shrinks into herself as she feels the deep magic pulsing through Killian's raised hand. She'd known he was powerful, but this? He could level this earth with a mere thought and doom them all. This power is dangerous and it makes Adalyn wonder what his king has over him to keep him on this leash.

The thought of Killian being leashed to the king makes her skin crawl, she pushes the feelings of sympathy away. He doesn't deserve sympathy from her. Although he has saved her life twice now.

Twice too many, she thinks as they head straight through the rippling vortex. Her skin explodes with heat and just before it becomes unbearable, they appear on the other side. Adalyn gasps, looking at the multiple crowded buildings before her. Valarki cheer and roar as the rest of the entourage file through the vortex. The tang of blackcurrant is heavy in the air, indicating how much magic swirls before her.

Buildings of stone walls and metal roofs go on as far as Adalyn can see, the midday sun bears down on the red earth relentlessly. Sweltering heat bites at her heels, causing her brow to break out with beads of sweat. The Valarki here range from cream skin to skin as dark as night and all their glowing eyes are directed at Killian, the shadow of death.

At Adalyn, a soul he's claimed.

Some parents hold their children on their shoulders, allowing them a glimpse of the large group. Adalyn can visibly see their magic hanging in the air around them, still too young to wield it. The sight of happy families has her heart breaking again, tears gather in her eyes.

These Valarki will never know the loss Adalyn has faced, they will never have to live looking over their shoulder in fear. They will never know what it is like for their homes to be swarmed and watch as the people they love and have grown up with are slaughtered before their eyes.

Adalyn trembles as her sadness mixes with sharp anger. Their happy cheers only work to darken her mood until she feels it like a living being residing in her chest. She wishes for nothing more than to scream at them, to silence their happiness.

She will never be happy again and she can only blame the man that she rides with.

Adalyn glances to Jurian, finding him beaming with pride as they continue to canter through the wide street and head deeper into Pantera. He smiles at the other Valarki, waving and blowing kisses.

Despite herself she looks up and over her shoulder to Killian, he sits rigid behind her with his dark eyes focused ahead, a muscle feathers in his jaw as he glances down his nose at her.

"You aren't happy," she murmurs, a statement more than a question. Killian studies her for a moment before tearing his eyes away, his hand tightens on her hip as she sucks in a breath and waits for his answer.

"I haven't been happy for a long time, Adalyn." His voice is lost to the wind but Adalyn catches the few words. They're enough to have her facing forward in the seat once more, far too many eyes fall to her as they pass the folk.

Something in her chest tightens, if she were to escape, she has no doubt in her mind the Valarki surrounding them wouldn't hesitate to eat her alive. Silence falls over them as they continue to ride down the stretch of the wide sandy dirt road. The deeper they head into the heart of Pantera, the tighter Adalyn's chest feels.

Her hand falls to where Killian's rests on her hip, she slides her fingers between his and leans into him. He shudders against her but relaxes a moment later. She feels Jurian staring at their clasped hands but he's wise to keep his comments to himself. She may be changing jailers, but for some insufferable reason she wishes Killian could remain hers. There would be no better revenge than a blade served with justice sliding into his unexpecting cold, beating heart.

14. Killian

Killian

Killian is far too aware of the small, warm hand that is intertwined with his own. Of the warmth that seeps into his chest, the soft body that now leans against him. He's also aware of the looks Jurian is not so subtly giving him. He grits his teeth against snapping at his closest friend.

Last night had been too close for Killian and Adalyn. He'd woken this morning with her small body flush against his own, she'd nestled into his side as they'd slept and made herself at home.

He'd silently crept from bed, not wanting to disturb her or give her a chance to read the emotions he couldn't control. Killian had known then that whatever was happening between them had to stop, if the king was to get word of his *fondness* of Adalyn, it would put an even bigger target on her back.

He could have eased Adalyn's pain with the flick of his wrist, using his magic to soothe her. After waking with her in his arms, he came to the decision to put this to an end. No more distractions for either of them. If the king is to choose Adalyn as one of his ten women, Killian will have to see her almost every day. If he began to feel any form of warmth towards her, it would be his down fall.

A downfall the king would make him pay handsomely for.

"Are you excited for the feast?" Jurian asks as the cheering crowd fades behind them. As they head deeper into Pantera, the crowds thin. Killian is aware of the human slaves that the Valarki keep, he spots a few peering out of the buildings they're no doubt bound to.

He's glad Adalyn hasn't seen them, and if she has, he's glad she hasn't said a word about them.

"The feast is the last thing I'm excited for." Killian sighs, the beginning of a headache blossoms at the base of his neck. With any luck it'll leave him too unwell to attend the feast that will be held in their honour tonight.

"Free wine, food and women." Jurian looks to Adalyn, "even the slaves are welcome to join in the celebration of our return. You get limited freedom for the night."

"Do you really believe I want to *celebrate* the murder of my family? Of other innocent humans?" she spits, her voice full of disgust. "You're more deranged then I first thought."

She pulls her hand away from Killian's and sits straighter in the saddle. Killian glares down at her, knowing she's no doubt reliving the moment she'd run into her burning cottage. Had seen what remained.

"A simple no would have sufficed," Jurian grunts, narrowing his eyes at her. Killian knows he means well, even though he gets under her skin.

"Do I look like a simple 'no' woman?" Adalyn asks, glaring right back at him. She'd be the only female willing to bite back at either of them. Jurian gives her a crooked smile, flashing his white teeth.

"No, but I'm sure after a wine or two you'd be more than willing."

"You're a pervert," she hisses, turning abruptly to face forwards once more. She trembles in the saddle and Killian can't decide if it's from anger or fear. Jurian howls with laughter causing Killian to grin. Killian ignores their bickering as he faces ahead once more, large black mountains dot the horizon and cast a shadow over the valley in front of them.

They'd reach the castle just before nightfall if they kept at this relentless pace. It only worked to spur Killian to go faster, the sooner he was home the sooner he could forget about the disaster of a trip this has been.

"Just come to the dance, have one drink with me and then I'll escort you to your chambers," Jurian whines.

"You're pretty but you're not that pretty," Adalyn snaps back. Jurian gapes at her, floundering like a fish. Killian snickers at his expression, it takes a certain type of wit to outsmart Jurian. Jurian points an accusing finger at Killian.

"So you'll let him do god knows what to you, but you won't have a simple, innocent drink with me?"

That wipes the snicker off Killian's face. He growls.

Adalyn merely shrugs, "Any distraction is a good distraction. It could have easily been you."

Killian fights the urge to throw her from the horse.

Jurian sucks in his cheeks and faces forward, avoiding looking to Killian. He steadies his breathing, blinking through the growing darkness inside of him. He had been a distraction for her, that's exactly what she asked for so why does hearing her say it make him want to commit murder and break bones?

"If I knew insulting Killian would get you to shut up, I would have done it a lot sooner," she remarks, sneaking a glance towards Jurian.

"There's a difference between insulting me and disrespecting me," Killian grumbles, his chest hits her back with each word.

"You've done nothing to earn my respect and you sure as hell have done everything to earn my insults." He can practically hear the scowl in her words.

"If I recall, I've saved your life twice," Killian snaps back.

"Did I fucking asked to be saved?" She looks over her shoulder and up at him, her eyes swirl with one emotion after the other;

anger, sadness, despair and back to anger. It makes the amber depths burn brightly.

"You didn't need to." He bares his teeth at her, digging his hand into her hip knowing it'll leave marks behind on her pale skin. He doesn't care at this point. She's done nothing but be ungrateful, she doesn't realise what he's put on the line saving her those two times.

"You killed my entire family," her bottom lip trembles, "by saving me twice you have taken me from returning to *them.* What is so good about my life that I must live it? So I can be some brute faerie's slave?"

"Do you think you are the only one to know suffering?" Killian's voice is deathly low, touching on a past he wishes to never revisit, especially not with her. Not in the light or the open; his demons come to him at night time. He doesn't wish for them to rob him of his days as well.

"I know I'm not and now that I do suffer, I would never wish it upon another. You can all rot in hell for all I care, once you wipe your hands of me it'll be a fucking blessing to not look at you again." She turns forward in her seat, leaning even further away from him. Killian says nothing, breathing fire through his nose. The truth of her words are enough to have him falling into that memory of his wife kneeling on the marble tiles, of her throat being slit and her crimson blood spilling down her front.

She was simply a punishment for Killian. She'd been softly spoken, beautiful and caring. Had never once hurt a fly and that is the end she was met with, all for loving him.

She thinks she knows everything, that she is the only one to know loss.

Jurian doesn't say a word, his lips twist as he looks to Killian; understanding flashes in his eyes and he nods once. Killian can't ride with her anymore, not when his darkness is so close to the surface and she's there.

He never claimed to be a good person with morals. Oh no, that hasn't been Killian in a very long time.

Killian leans back and wraps Adalyn in the invisible hands of his magic, she yelps in surprise until she's dumped in front of Jurian to ride with him for the rest of the journey. Killian clenches his jaw as he gallops ahead, feeling her burning stare on his back as he leaves her behind.

Killian slows his horse to a walk as he reaches the end of the now black dirt path, broken skeletal trees claw towards the greying sky. There are no plants or life here, only black crows that litter the sky, flying above and around the multiple peaks of the stone castle. The sun begins to set, casting skeletal shadows across the ground. His stallion walks forward, bowing its head twice as they approach the large stone wall that encases the castle.

Six guards stand in the two guard posts that rise beside the wood and steel gate, they bow in unison as they see who stands before them.

Two flames flicker beside the arched gate, large enough for carriages to pass through. The stone around the arch is decorated with the carvings of war, above the arch and staring at all who enters is the skeletal head of a dragon, slain a millennia ago. Above the gate, perched on the stone ledge are two grey gargoyles facing each other.

His sensitive ears pick up Adalyn's gasp behind him, Jurian murmurs something that has her going quiet once more. The only noise to be heard around them is the hooves of the horses hitting the dead earth and the creak of carriage wheels.

The castle goes on for miles before them, protected by that high stone wall that's encased in the king's magic. High peaks of each building rise into the sky, crows circle each peak/ From where Killian is, he can spot each guard that patrols along the stone walls or the stone bridges that connect the high rise buildings. In each window golden light burns, the only sign of real life inside.

It's a cobblestone fortress and an impossible labyrinth for

those who wish to escape. If they don't get caught by the guards first, usually the hounds pick them off.

Killian urges his steed forward, grim faced as the gate begins to creak open, exposing the jostling courtiers racing back and forth as they prepare for the celebration.

Killian focuses forward, not sparing any of them a second glance. He reins in his magic, drawing it back to the depths of his soul. Around the first courtyard there are carriages propped against stone walls, guards patrolling and barking at the few human slaves. Courtiers dressed in finery move in a flurry, going from one stone entrance to another.

Killian's headache blooms even more as he steers his stallion down a wide path to his right, leading to the large stables that reside at the back of the castle. It's also where they store all their carriages after a conquest. A stone archway perches across the stone wall and the building to their left, carvings flare golden as they walk through. No one lingers on this path, no one dares.

"This place is terrifying." Adalyn whispers behind him.

"You get used to it," Jurian murmurs back, riding directly behind Killian. He stays silent, not caring if they talk at this point.

She isn't his problem now.

"How could you? This place is so...dreary. It's all grey. The only sign of colour was on the Valarki back there."

Jurian chuckles, "The courtiers, they dress like that regularly."

"So what...happens to me now?" Adalyn asks, a slight tremor in her voice. Killian grinds his teeth together, urging his stallion to walk faster.

"You'll be taken to a shared room with the other women where you'll be bathed and dressed and then you'll have to attend the celebration. Tomorrow you'll meet the king." Jurian keeps his voice low, "You best keep that sass back behind these stone walls, the king isn't one to put up with that."

"He can't be that scary," Adalyn grumbles.

"He's worse than us," Jurian whispers, not wanting to risk the others behind them hearing.

They finish the lengthy walk and emerge before the large wooden stables. Three large pits of fire burn before them, Valarki soldiers throw wood and body parts into the orange depths.

Killian dismounts as a stable boy emerges before him, the small faerie isn't a dark Valarki, but a distant relative. He's half the size of Killian, his pointed ears reach to the back of his head while thin white brows frame his overly large eyes; bottomless depths of milky white. His skin is the colour of teal, his white hair moves like liquid around his narrow face, as if it has a mind of its own.

When the king couldn't find human slaves for the stables, he enslaved the weakest of their kind.

"Horses are to be brushed, fed and watered. Carriages are to be cleaned. The king will be checking tomorrow morning to make sure they meet his standards." Killian crosses his arms over his chest as the stable boy takes the stallion's reins and leads him towards the large stone stable before them. The scent of hay and horse is mixed with smoke and death.

"Just stay close for now," Jurian says. Killian turns to find him helping Adalyn dismount the horse. Once her feet touch the ground she hisses, nails digging into Jurian's arm.

The scent of blood hits him a moment later.

Killian looks down to her thigh, to the split in her dress. Blood runs down her leg, old and new.

"Why didn't you say anything?" Killian demands, walking over to them. Adalyn lets go of Jurian and throws her shoulders back, careful to not put pressure on her left leg.

"I did. You chose to ignore it, so I did as well."

Killian's mood darkens, Jurian looks between the two of them and huffs. The other soldiers begin to dismount and head towards the stone archway that leads them back into the heart of the castle.

Killian and Adalyn stare at each other, a silent challenge.

Killian growls, opening his mouth to reply "You—"

A small screech has Adalyn turning away from him, most of the soldiers have departed, save for Polarian and the small group he hangs around with.

One of the stableboys cowers before him, curling in on himself. From here Killian can see his two paper thin wings, both bent at the wrong angles.

Adalyn pales and dashes towards them, Jurian curses as Killian storms after her. Polarian grins, raising his hand towards the faerie.

Adalyn jumps in front of him, the slap echoes in the open expanse. Her head snaps sideways, she stumbles backwards into the stableboy.

The faerie looks horrified, grabbing her arms to keep her upright. She spits blood, blinking through a haze before facing Polarian once more.

"Now isn't that a nice surprise." Polarian grins, stepping forward. She braces her feet apart, protecting the faerie behind her. It has Killian's cold heart wrenching in his chest.

"Leave him alone," Adalyn says with bite in her words. Polarian towers over her, a viper ready to strike.

"He wasn't here in time and I had to wait. This is his punishment."

Killian prowls closer, causing Polarian to stiffen. Adalyn looks over her shoulder and scowls, she reaches behind her and pushes the small faerie back, away from the both of them. Killian doesn't need to look over his shoulder to know the other stable faeries can see what she's doing.

"Enough." Killian barks, his temper snapping, "I've had enough of your attitude *slave* and you," he whirls towards Polarian, letting the damper on his power lessen, knowing darkness churns in the depths of his blue eyes. "You have been nothing but fucking trouble this entire journey. I won't hesitate to strip you of this right, remember your ranking and fuck off."

Polarian deflates, his skin paling. He nods once, staring daggers at Adalyn before stalking off. His small followers hurry after him, only once they disappear through the stone arch does Killian rein in that small kernel of power.

"Leave the stable boy." Killian growls, turning away and

stalking towards the stone arch way. Two male guards dressed in gold armour emerge, they are the ones who escort the females to their shared room for the night.

Jurian falls into step beside Killian, they walk in silence as they head into the castle.

Killian needs a god damn drink.

15. Adalyn

Adalyn

Adalyn ignores the throb in her thigh, in her breast. In her very soul. She sags once Killian and Jurian disappear, turning to the faerie that is behind her. He stares up at her beneath his white silken hair, his large milky eyes shine with tears.

"Are you okay?" she asks, looking over his pale blue skin and dirty brown rags. He smells of horse and leather, with a subtle hint of salt water.

"My...my wings." His voice is high, each white tooth ends in a sharp point. Adalyn hides her grimace.

"Let me take a look." She says softly, gesturing for him to turn, he's so much smaller than her. Anger chokes her, of course Polarian would hurt someone who couldn't fight back.

She hisses as she sees the translucent wings bent at the wrong angles, sagging against his bony back. White membranes pulse along the arches of his wings.

"I think they might be broken," she murmurs, not daring to touch them in case she causes more damage. The faerie turns towards her once more, clasping his overly long fingers together.

Two other stable boys run towards them, assessing Adalyn warily before standing beside their friend.

"Thank you," the one on the left rasps, their pale green skin is covered with flecks of mud and dried blood. Adalyn manages a soft smile.

"There is nothing to thank me for. Polarian is a bastard."

"We cannot speak ill of the warriors," the same faerie whispers, the one on the right keeps an eye on the other Valarki that walk around them.

"Well I can." A guard in gold armour approaches Adalyn, their eyes a blank expanse as he stops before her. The three lesser faeries scuttle off, towards a shack that's hidden in the shadows beside the stable.

"I suppose you're here to take me to my room," Adalyn says, turning to find another guard in gold holding the chain that has the other fourteen females. The guard says nothing, grabbing her bicep and forcing her towards the line.

Adalyn bites her tongue to stop her cry of pain, ignoring the trickle of fresh blood that runs down her leg.

Allison smiles weakly as she turns to Adalyn, relief washes through her to find the others still in one piece. The guard re-shackles Adalyn to the chain of cuffs and begins to lead them towards the large stone arch.

"I'm glad you're okay." Allison whispers, reaching out and brushing her hand against Adalyn's shoulder. A touch of comfort.

"I'm glad you are too." Adalyn whispers back, earning a sharp glare from the guard in front of her. She shuts her mouth and decides to focus on their surroundings.

The dirt beneath their feet turns to hard stone, Valarki dressed in finery sneer down at the females. Adalyn ignores each sneer, ignores each nasty comment that is meant to bring her down.

She mentally maps out the castle as best as she can, so far they've only been walking straight. Multiple paths lead off the one they walk, Adalyn looks down each one to find more stone paths and walls.

Ahead, the golden guard leads them through a black wooden

door as the alley comes to an end. It swings open on its own as the passage torches find flame.

The difference has Adalyn looking at the hall they walk down with awe, a red carpet runs underneath their feet while portraits of Valarki in crowns and riches are hanging on the walls with golden flames between them. Adalyn stumbles over her own feet as she finds herself staring up at Killian's painted face.

His blue eyes are piercing, his black suit immaculate as his hair hangs down around his waist. This must have been painted long ago. Even in portrait form her heart kicks into gear.

She wishes she could pull the flame from the wall and light it on fire.

The guard hauls her forward, forcing her to look away from the painting.

They reach another curve and turn left, the hallway opens up and human servants now walk these halls. Some carry food while others push carts full of bed linen.

Not one glances towards the girls. Not one of them seems to be aware they're even there.

Adalyn's stomach churns with fear at the vacant look in their eyes. Is that what's in store for her? Is she going to be a husk of a person, doing someone's bidding and not even know?

"These are your chambers for the night. Bath and dress, we'll return in thirty minutes to retrieve you all. There are clothes in the drawers." The guard stops them before a double wooden door, they swing inwards just as the cuffs on the female's wrists are unlocked and blinking out of existence before Adalyn's very eyes.

"Leave the room at your own risk. There are guards and ghost hounds waiting around every corner. They will return you by any means necessary." The guard narrows his eyes at Adalyn, she scowls but limps past him. Seven single beds run down the left side of the large room while eight run down the opposite side. At the back of the room is a stone arch way, revealing a large marble bath. Adalyn limps towards the bathing room, needing to relieve herself desperately.

The other girls file in behind her, taking a moment to settle in the room. Adalyn relieves herself with a sigh in the privacy of the bathroom. It'd been far too long.

Allison walks in, eyes going straight to the large tub full of steaming herb scented water. It would easily fit six of the girls at once.

"I'm going to bathe," Adalyn announces. She strips herself from the dress Killian had given her until the cool air nips at her bare skin. She gingerly hops into the water, biting her lip as the cut on her left thigh throbs. Allison follows suit, lowering herself into the water on the opposite side of the tub.

Her caramel eyes survey Adalyn, flicking down to the twisted stitching on the top of her breast.

"What happened after they found you?" she whispers.

Adalyn lowers herself into the water until it touches her chin, the water is warm and helps relieve the tension in her muscles. Her auburn hair fans out around her, she gingerly wipes the blood off from the cut on her leg.

"Once you were all taken back to the carriage I was...stuck there. Killian and Jurian arrived, they found me immediately. They took me back to his private carriage and stitched me up." Adalyn shakes the memory from her head, ignores the darkness that threatens to swallow her at the memory. She can't give herself over to it, not yet.

"I am so sorry. We couldn't do anything," Allison sniffles, wiping a few stray tears away, "as much as I don't like the Valarki I'm thankful the general saved you."

"He's still one of them, regardless if he saved me or not," Adalyn murmurs. Allison's eyes shine with sympathy.

"I know and I know it doesn't change anything but...I think if it was any other female he wouldn't have done the same."

Adalyn snorts, "He only did it for himself."

"How are you feeling?" Allison asks softly.

Adalyn swallows around the tightness in her throat, "I'm feeling a lot of things. This is all a lot to take in. Jurian said we meet the king tomorrow and that he'll decide our fate, pick ten of us."

"We'll be okay, as long as we have each other. I know at this celebration I plan on eating as much as I can."

Adalyn chuckles softly. "Trust me, that's my plan too and maybe getting my hand on a glass of wine. We get limited freedom so I'm going to make the most of it."

They fall into comfortable silence as some of the other girls join them in the bath, a few still have that far away vacancy in their eyes. Adalyn climbs from the bath and finds folded white towels under a marble sink, she wraps herself in the soft wool before walking back into the bed chambers. At the large wardrobe she pulls the doors open, dresses of various colours assault her eyes.

She grabs one of deep red. Golden lace encases the bottom of the dress's skirts and rises as if it's fire.

Adalyn shakes her head as she limps to the closest bed, throws the dress down and dries herself quickly. She pulls the dress on, ignoring the fact that she still has no underwear.

Smoothing the clinched bodice of the dress down, she lets her wet hair hang down her exposed back where the dress dips. It's far too nice and easily the most expensive thing Adalyn has ever worn.

Adalyn gently sits down on the bed, fighting against the exhaustion that threatens to consume her and drag her into its dark depths.

She is so tired.

The noise of the others girls getting dressed is white noise in Adalyn's ears. She keeps her eyes on the closed dark wooden doors and waits.

The doors suddenly swing inwards, announcing the arrival of the two golden guards. Adalyn rises, the silk slippers she'd found keep her steps light as she limps towards them, once they arrive to the celebration she'd need to walk without the limp.

The other Valarki don't need to know she's weak.

The guard on her left snarls at her, causing her to snarl right back.

"Act like a dog and I'll act like one back," she snaps, glaring up at him. The other just huffs, gesturing for the gathered females to follow him. They walk deeper into the castle, passing other guards, slaves and courtiers.

They leave a hallway and emerge in a large towering chamber, the archway doors have been propped open. Soft music spills out of the room with the chatter of conversation, the large expanse before Adalyn is crowded with Valarki who are all dressed in finery, females turn their sharp eyes to the humans.

Adalyn keeps her chin raised as she walks into the room, ignoring the beating of her wild heart, ignoring the sweat gathering in her palms at their attention.

She can feel their hate from here.

The guards disappear among the crowd to leave the human females to their own devices. Adalyn turns, wanting to find Allison and get to the edges where conflict is less likely.

She finds the other girls gone and is greeted by sneering Valarki.

She takes a deep breath, it'd just be her then. She gathers the skirts of her dress and walks towards the closest large white pillar, draped with red silk ribbons. She reaches the stone without any causality and leans against it, taking the pressure off her injured leg. Thankfully the thick straps of her dress cover the scar on her left breast.

"Well, I never thought I'd see you here." Jurian's warm voice startles Adalyn, she turns to see the crowd parting for him. Her eyes rake over him, his golden hair flows in waves around his chest while the deep green tunic he wears display every inch of muscle he has. The gold trimmings are a nice touch, complimenting his ruby eyes.

"You can compliment me whenever." He grins, spinning slowly for her to see his entire outfit. One hand clasps a half empty champagne glass. Once he's finished his twirl, he tucks his free hand into his pocket.

"You look..." she hums, tapping a finger against her lips, "like an annoyance."

"Oh please, you were sulking by yourself here. I was being a good friend and giving you company." He laughs, taking a sip of his champagne. Adalyn rolls her eyes and crosses her arms back over her chest, looking out over the crowd.

"How did you settle in?"

"Fine," she says, distantly aware he now stands beside her and is looking out over the crowd as well. The music is soft and lovely, a mixture of piano and violin and other instruments she can't place. When was the last time she had heard such nice music? Had she ever heard music this lovely before?

"Killian is here somewhere," Jurian says casually.

"Why do you think I care?" Adalyn looks up at him, raising a brow. Jurian grins, his face is rather handsome if Adalyn's being honest.

"You get under his skin, it's entertaining for me."

Adalyn huffs, still staring up at him. She finds herself appreciating his narrow nose and soft rose coloured lips that are set in a smile, his cheeks are sharp and hollow out his jaw.

"Are you...admiring me, Red?" Jurian grins, eyes flashing. Adalyn scowls and snaps from her trance, slapping his arm as she turns away from him.

"You're mistaken. Take your stupid faerie eyes somewhere else," she snaps, refusing to look at him. He laughs loudly, causing the closest Valarki to scowl at her.

"What's so funny?" Killian's deep rumbling voice comes from behind them, Jurian turns and holds in his laughter, nodding his head in acknowledgment.

"Just something Red said." Jurian turns back to the crowd as Killian steps up beside him. Adalyn can just see the outline of his black suit, a hand is wrapped around a champagne glass.

She knows if she looks at him she might not be able to look away.

Killian steps in front of the two of them, encasing them in a circle as if they're old time friends, sending a clear message that no other is welcome to join their circle. Adalyn stares at his polished black gleaming boots.

"Have you had something to eat?" Killian asks. She feels the intensity of his eyes roving over her dress that is rather generous to her figure.

She finds her traitorous eyes travelling up his tight formal pants, trailing over the black jacket that hangs open to reveal yet another black button up shirt. She finally reaches his face and loses the breath in her lungs.

He'd washed his hair, it hangs around his face and grazes his shoulders, curling slightly as it dries. His blue eyes are kind but guarded as they meet hers, his lips tighten slightly.

He is the most attractive man she's ever seen.

And she *hates* him all the more for it.

"No, I haven't," Jurian announces, breaking the stare they'd been holding. They both look towards him, his cheeks are slightly stained pink.

"I haven't either," Adalyn admits, knowing the growling of her stomach will be heard by their sensitive ears if she doesn't eat soon.

"Let's go and get food then." Killian gestures towards the wall closest to them, Jurian doesn't need to be told twice and he's already heading in that direction. Adalyn walks in step beside Killian, both of them keep their eyes on Jurian.

"What is this place?" Adalyn asks.

"The royal ball room," Killian says, sipping from his glass, "it's where the king hosts ridiculous parties and has most of his meetings."

The crowd moves for the three of them as they reach a long length of table covered in white silk cloths, foods of all kinds litter the surface. Adalyn audibly gasps at the array of sweets that are presented before her. Jurian stops a step from the table, looking back to where Adalyn and Killian stand side by side.

Jurian smirks, eyeing Adalyn as if she's as tempting as the multiple sweet desserts splayed out on the table behind them in the grand ball room. Killian scowls at her side, her shoulder brushes his own as she takes a step towards Jurian, she feels the warmth of Killian's magic reach for her.

"You look utterly ravishing." His words send a sharp thrill through her, she meets his bright ruby eyes and sees the hidden challenge.

"Shall I go splay myself upon the table alongside the other desserts to be feasted upon?" She arches a brow, feeling the heat from Killian intensify at her back. Broody, over possessive faerie asshole. Jurian chuckles, flicking his eyes over her shoulder to the large towering presence that has stepped closer to her.

"Red, the look on Killian's face right now says that you're one word away from getting your wish."

Adalyn steps back into the warmth of Killian, hiding her surprise when one of his large hands automatically settles on the curve of her right hip and grips her firmly. She ignores the heat flooding between her thighs, hoping neither of them can scent the sudden arousal. She allows herself a small, secretive smile, "Annoyance, you know there's nothing I love more than a challenge."

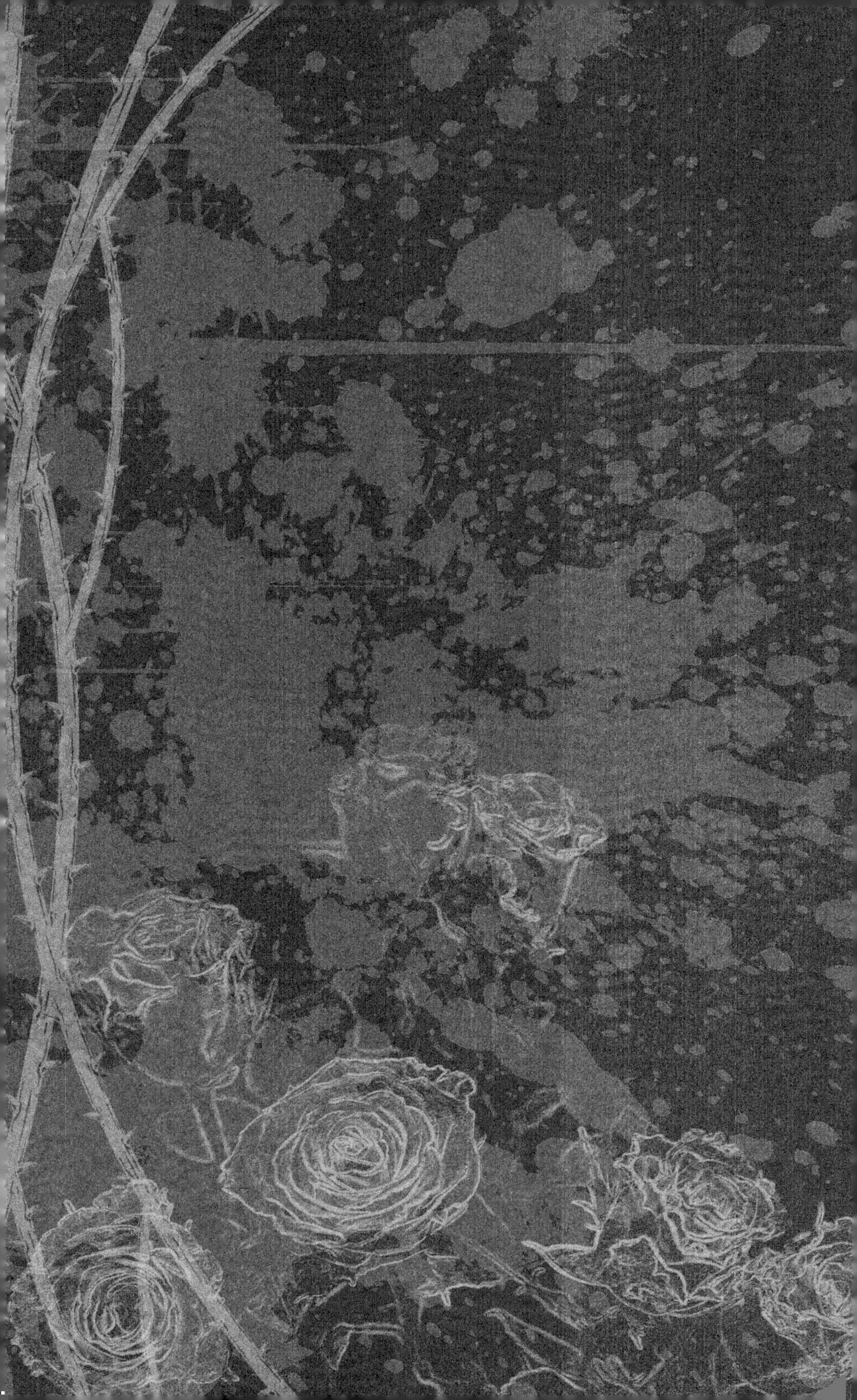

16. Killian

Killian

She'd be the death of him.

Jurian laughs before turning back to the table of desserts. Killian looks down to find Adalyn peering up at him. Her eyes flash before she steps from his embrace, stalking towards where Jurian now piles a silver plate with desserts. Killian notices the subtle limp and ignores it.

He doesn't move from his spot as Jurian recommends sweets for Adalyn to try and helps pile her plate. She leans over the table, reaching for a red cupcake on one of the golden stands.

Killian rakes his eyes over her small waist and bare back, the skin smooth. His eyes reach the curve of her ass and he forces himself to look away. He'd picked up the scent of her arousal when his hand had touched her, had to think of horrible things to stop his own.

Jurian and Adalyn turn back towards him, both carrying ridiculously large plates. Jurian grins as they walk back towards Killian, he leads them towards a vacant table towards the back of the ball room. Valarki males bow their head as he passes while the females undress him with their eyes. He keeps his expression neutral, shoulders back and spine stiff.

He hates this part, he hates the celebrations and court finery.

He slides into a seat and rests an elbow on the table, staring unseeing out into the crowd.

Adalyn and Jurian sit beside him, Adalyn in the middle of them. She begins to pick at the food, sniffing each portion with caution before taking a bite.

Soon Killian could retreat to his chambers and rest.

"So this is it?" Adalyn mumbles around a mouthful of caramel tart, "you eat, drink and dance for the rest of the night?"

"Pretty well. The king is here somewhere, no doubt at the front of the room sitting on his throne," Jurian says back. Adalyn contemplates that in silence.

"What happens to the ten of us he chooses?" She asks carefully.

"Ah...Killian, do you want to answer that?"

Killian blinks once and sighs through his nose, turning to look down at Adalyn. She has a few crumbs lining her lips as she stares up at him, silently chewing.

"You'll join his personal harem. Do what he asks, cater to his needs. For the five women not chosen they'll be branded as slaves and sent to whichever district needs them, unless he chooses to keep them in the castle."

"Will the harem be under the influence of magic like the other human slaves?" she asks, her skin pales. Killian is slightly impressed, of course she'd pick up on that small detail, not many other humans did.

"No, they're under their own free will."

"So what happened to the last lot of his harem?" she asks, twisting her mouth.

Killian goes still, Jurian doing the same.

"I'm not sure," Killian says stiffly, looking back towards the dancing crowd. He needed another drink, badly. He gestures for one of the human servants, the small female carries a silver tray full of sparkling wine. Killian grabs six, passing one to Jurian and Adalyn before sitting the four in front of him. The servant wanders off, unseeing.

"Oh...okay then." Adalyn mumbles, taking a generous sip of the wine.

Killian settles into his chair, he can't find his focus. He can't concentrate. Too much has happened in the last few months, the last thing he needs is to be here in a room with Adalyn, the lead cause of his broodiness.

He could find Alissa, she'd be prowling the crowd somewhere trying to hunt down a man for the night. Jurian and Adalyn fall into safe areas of small talk. Killian finishes off his four glasses in quick succession before standing, tucking both hands into his pockets. He needs a distraction.

He looks down to find Adalyn staring up at him, her amber eyes shine in the lights of the ballroom. She looks lovely, not that he would ever admit it to her. It's too intimate of a compliment.

"I'm going to retire to my chambers for the night. Have a good evening." He nods once to Jurian before striding into the crowd, keeping an eye out for night sky hair.

He's almost to the propped open doors by the time Alissa appears. She squeals when she sees him, closing the distance with her long cream legs before she throw her arms around his neck.

"I've missed you," she purrs, squeezing him to her. He chuckles, gripping the dip of her hips. The blue sequinned dress hugs her curvy figure, splitting at the thigh on either side to expose her long lean legs. She steps back, her black hair had been curled and pinned back from her soft face.

Her lilac eyes are lined with dark kohl, sweeping away from her eyes. She grins, her red plump limps brighten her features. She's stunning for a Valarki female, more so than the other women that fill the ball room and she knows it as well.

She steps back, brushing a hand down his chest. Her large breasts threaten to spill from the tight confines of the low dipping dress. Silver chains drape from her throat and cascade between her breasts before clinching at her waist.

"You look beautiful," Killian says.

"I know, sometimes I really outdo myself." She sighs, "are you leaving?"

"I was looking for you actually." His words are strained. Understanding flashes in the depth of her eyes, her smile softens. She'd been his best friend for ten years now, she knew what he needed in this moment.

"Come on then, I've been waiting months for your return." She slides her arm into his as they leave the ball room, the music and chatter die away the further they head into the castle. Killian's room is on a level above them in a private hall, they reach the steps and nod to the passing guards.

"How was the journey?" Alissa asks, idly stroking his arm.

"A disaster." Killian growls, "I made a mistake."

Alissa laughs, the sound is almost enchanting, "The big bad shadow of death made a mistake? I don't believe it."

"I did, with a human woman," he murmurs, blocking out the memories of his face buried between Adalyn's soft thighs. How he's never tasted anything sweeter in his life.

"Killian...I thought you'd never touch one of them?" She whispers, peering up at him, "you didn't fuck her did you?"

"Goodness no, but I did save her life twice." He winces.

"Why? You've never bothered before."

Her guess was as good as his, he didn't know why he saved her life either. Maybe it was his guilty conscience finally catching up to him after the many years of unjust and relentless slaughter.

"She's...different to the others. She doesn't fear me." It's the best, weak excuse he can come up with in the moment. Alissa considers his words, humming to herself as they walk down his private hall.

"If that's the case, the king will most likely pick her as one of his ten," she relents, looking up at him as they reach his chambers. He opens the door and slides out from her embrace.

He undoes the top buttons as he stalks towards his large black silk bed, the dark wooden four poster frame reaches the roof. A fire to his right is the only light in the room, he reaches the bed and turns. He sits down, discarding his jacket on the ground.

Alissa closes the door behind her as she enters, slipping from her heels as she peels the straps of her dress down. Her large breasts peak with need as she struts towards him.

Killian forgets every thought of Adalyn, forgets every touch and conversation they've shared. Alissa stops before him, helping with the last of his buttons before discarding his shirt on the ground.

"How do you want this?" she whispers, running her hands down his toned chest. Killian grasps her wrists gently, looking up at her.

"Hard."

He pulls down the rest of her dress until she stands bare before him, already the sweet tang of her arousal fills the air around him.

He leans forward and grasps one of her pink nipples in his mouth and bites down, earning a hiss from her. She buries her hands into his hair and leans back, allowing him more access.

It's only a matter of moments before they're a flurry of teeth and needy hands, he flips her onto the bed before ridding himself of his shoes and trousers. She pants as she stares up at him, spread and slick for him. Killian growls.

"Turn, I want you on your hands and knees."

Alissa happily obeys, raising her ass for him as she lowers her breasts to the bed. Killian climbs behind her, grabbing her generous hips in his hands before thrusting hard.

Alissa moans as he fills her to the hilt, her need for him runs down her legs as he begins to pull out to the tip before thrusting back into her. He reaches down and wraps her silken hair in his fist, yanking her up as he slams back into her.

He doesn't go slow or soft. He doesn't take his time with her, he takes what he needs and she gives it right back. She's trapped in his embrace as he impales her with so much force the bed frame groans. She cries out as his other hand lowers between her legs, circling that bundle of nerves.

He drives into her harder as she tightens around him, reaching her climax. Killian closes his eyes as he leans his forehead on her shoulder.

Behind his eyes the body before him transforms into someone smaller, softer. Instead of black hair clasped in his hand, it's auburn strands.

Killian groans as release comes upon him quickly, far quicker than it had before with Alissa. As she clamps down around him and cries out, Killian spills his own seed into her. They stay joined, panting. Once Killian stops throbbing he releases her hair, pulling himself from her before climbing from the bed. Alissa sprawls out, breathless.

Killian stalks into his private bathing chambers, a hot bath awaits him with a tray of scented soaps. He doesn't bother inviting Alissa as he lowers himself into the water and grabs a soft wash cloth.

She leans against the archway, naked with both of their release sliding between her thighs. Her cheeks are flushed red as she smiles down at him.

"It was good to see you missed me as well," she says.

"You're my best friend, of course I did," Killian says, looking to the tray of soaps. He chooses one and lathers himself. Scrubbing every inch he can get his hands on.

Alissa stalks forward and takes the cloth from him, cleaning herself before dumping it back into the water. She strides from the bathing room, reappearing moments later, dressed once more.

"I'm going back to the celebration, are you going to be okay on your own?" she asks, adjusting her hair.

"Yes, I will be. Thank you. I'll find you tomorrow at some point and discuss more of the journey."

"There's no rush, take your time." She blows him a kiss before leaving him, he waits until his door closes until he leans back in the marble tub and closes his eyes, resting his arms on either side.

He shouldn't have been thinking of Adalyn while buried in Alissa, it was wrong. He huffs as he sinks lower into the water, closing his eyes and welcoming the darkness. If this is what he needed to do to get Adalyn out of his system, he'd do it.

He could only hope she'd be out soon, there's only so much drinking and fucking he could do.

17. Adalyn
Adalyn

Rough hands drag Adalyn from her bed, she opens her mouth to scream but a gloved hand clamps down and cuts the noise off. She blinks the last tendrils of sleep away, head pounding, as she surveys the room. Valarki soldiers have a hold of the other females, the two golden guards stand in front of their open bedroom door.

Adalyn finds her feet, cheeks burning as she is forced in front of the soldier that has a hold of her. All of the females are dressed in their night dresses, the material so thin Adalyn feels as if she's wearing nothing.

Dread coils in her stomach like a serpent. Her heart thunders as she tries to think of where the guards might be taking them. Is this Polarian's doing? Is he waiting for them in some darkened room?

"Don't fight me, slave." Her guard hisses low in her ear, hand tightening painfully on her bicep and around her mouth. She breathes heavily through her nose, the cut on her thigh and breast are throbbing and she feels the blood running down her leg. He'd been too rough when he'd grabbed her from her bed, she's thankful the fatal cut on her right shoulder has mostly healed.

Still disorientated, Adalyn shields her eyes as they walk into a large throne room. The lanterns burn brighter than ever, while the full moon shines down through the glass ceiling.

Atop a dais sits a throne of white bones, melded together with gold.

On that throne is the king of Pantera.

His golden and silver streaked hair catches in the moonlight as he leans forward, his golden eyes miss nothing as the guards line all fifteen girls up before him. Adalyn can't take her eyes from him, noting the defined muscled chest that is on display along with the many scars marring his caramel skin.

Adalyn is forced to her knees, the jolt brings tears to her eyes. Her guard steps away, as do the others until the girls kneel before the king. He hums to himself, sweeping over them all. Adalyn swallows the dryness in her throat, a flicker of movement catches her eye to left of the throne.

Killian's blue eyes blaze in the moonlight as he stares down at her, half hidden in the swarming shadows that seem to swallow the back of the throne room.

"Good evening ladies. I'm sorry to have pulled you away from slumber so suddenly, but I find myself impatient to wait until tomorrow morning to meet you all." The kings deep voice is as sensual as a lover, a gentle caress that has her skin pebbling.

"Out of the fifteen here, I will be choosing ten to serve in my personal harem. The other five will be given other duties to attend, whether that be in the castle or in the many districts of Pantera. One by one you will rise, tell me your name and something you enjoy." He points towards the opposite end of Adalyn, "You will go first."

The girl at the end of the line rises on shaking legs, covering her chest with her arms as she looks up to the king, "I-I'm Clare, I enjoy gardening." Her dirty blonde hair plasters to her throat and the sides of her narrow face. She kneels once more, bowing her head.

"I'm Allison, I enjoy music." Allison rises on steadier feet, raising her chin as she meets the king's eyes. He smiles slowly, causing even Adalyn's cheeks to heat. Allison kneels.

"I'm Sam, I like books." Sam rises, all bones and sharp angles. Her voice is as sharp as a blade, even though her chocolate eyes show her soft nature.

Adalyn looks back to Killian, still finding his eyes on her. Her heart begins to pick up pace as she allows herself the chance to look over him, his hair is tangled and his clothes hang from him, his open shirt reveals his chiselled chest, as if he too was pulled from bed for this.

He offers her a small, secretive smile.

It makes her toes curl.

The girl beside Adalyn nudges her with her foot. Adalyn looks away from Killian, cheeks burning as she looks to the king. He stares down at her, having risen from his throne.

"Are you deaf?" he questions, taking a step down the dais.

"No." Adalyn rises, hissing through her teeth as she presses her hand against the trail of blood. It's left a small mark on the white marble floor. The king is in front of her in an instant, gently taking her hand away from her leg.

He frowns as he leans down, gently touching the skin around her cut. Up close his scent consumes her, smoked sandalwood.

"I didn't mean to bleed on your floor," Adalyn murmurs, all too aware of the soft sweep of his fingers. He looks up at her between the gaps of his long silk hair, his golden eyes glow slightly. He smiles, the corners of his eyes creasing.

"Nonsense, there's been plenty of blood spilt on these floors before."

Adalyn pales, his statement does nothing to make her feel better.

He rises to his full height, towering over Adalyn. He takes both of her hands in his large ones, rubbing his thumbs over the top of her hands, "What is your name?"

"Adalyn." She whispers, tipping her head back to meet his eyes. He assesses her as if he is a warrior and she is the enemy. She doesn't cower or retreat under his gaze, only meets his unflinching stare with her own; letting a small kernel of that hatred show.

He grins like a feline, letting her hands go before turning and walking back to his throne. He sits down, looking back over them all once more. Adalyn goes to kneel, looking down to find her thigh is...healed. The stitches are gone, all that remains is a small golden scar.

She frowns as she kneels, avoiding her small puddle of blood.

"I have chosen my ten," He declares, "Clare, Allison, Sam, Elain, Danah, Maddison, Brittany, Ariel, Imogen and..."

Killian goes rigid.

"Adalyn."

She snaps her head up, mouth half open in protest. The king simply raises a sharp brow with a slit in the end, she closes her mouth and bites back her retort.

Five guards come forward and grab onto the other five females that weren't chosen, they're lead away. Adalyn looks over her shoulder and watches them go, stomach churning. Is she any better off?

"From this evening onwards you will have your own private chamber in my hall. You will wear the dresses supplied in the wardrobes. You are free to roam this castle but you are not entitled to leave. You will answer when called or face the consequences." He leans back in his throne, waving a hand. Adalyn's left wrist burns with ice cold fire, reminding her of the brand Killian had placed on her. She looks down to the inside of her wrist to find a golden dagger piercing a lilac rose branded on her skin.

"That is my brand. You are my property from this moment forward. The guards will take you to your new rooms, tomorrow I'll meet with you all personally and get to know you better. Guards, escort them out."

Adalyn looks up to find Killian staring at the king, a burning hatred lives in his eyes. It's much the same as the one Adalyn has.

Her guard drags her up and pushes her back, she stumbles

before finding her feet. They leave through grand oak doors and head to the left, after twenty steps the hallway opens to a large spiralling stair case carved with gold. Adalyn has all of a second to admire the detailed design of flowers and vines before she's forced up the stairs. She walks as fast as she can, still reeling with everything that's happened in the last thirty minutes.

She'd been chosen by the king, healed by the king.

She conquers the stairs to find herself in a large hall, the ceiling towers high above them. Intricate details of vines have been moulded into the white wooden pillars that tower on each side of the hall. At the end, two large golden doors are sealed shut.

Adalyn doesn't need to be told that's where the king resides, and the ten rooms spilt between the two sides of the hall...she can only guess what he might need when calling on one of them.

Her guard takes her to the first room on her left, she hides her relief with a scowl as he forces her into the room. She crosses her arms over her chest once he lets go and waits until he leaves before she turns.

Her breath is taken from her all over again.

A large queen sized bed sits to her right, the white comforter is half consumed by gold and white pillows that are propped in a tower like manner. Adalyn walks over to the bed, running her hand along the soft material as she takes in the rest of the room.

Her room is large, ridiculously so. A red fur mat covers a large majority of her white marble floor, beside the bed in the corner is a small red brick fireplace. A single black love chaise sits in front of the darkened fire, a thin blanket draped over one arm.

Adalyn moves over to the towering wardrobe that's plastered against the wall to her left, she pulls open the two wooden doors to find it overflowing with dresses of all colours and materials.

She runs a hand over each one, tears run down her cheeks at the finery of them. She doesn't deserve this. She stumbles from the open cupboard, choking for breath as more tears continue to stream down her cheeks.

She doesn't deserve this. She lived while her parents died.

They suffered and she's here, playing dress up for the person responsible for her family's murder.

She runs to the closed wooden door that's near the fire, bursting into her private bathing chambers and slams the door behind her. In the darkness she stumbles towards the large empty marble bathtub and lowers herself in.

She curls in on herself, crying and muffling her screams with her hands as her body convulses.

She doesn't deserve to live, to admire the castle she now is forced to live in. Would her parent's ghosts hate her for finding that she hasn't thought about them since she arrived? That she's been so busy trying to ignore the warmth she feels for Killian that she's forgotten about them in the process?

Adalyn's thoughts spiral into darkness, until she's questioning whether she should just finish the job Polarian had started.

She doesn't belong in this world. She hasn't belonged from the moment her mother and father ceased breathing, when her brothers were dismembered.

Emilia...Emilia is still out there, somewhere. She has to be. I have to have hope.

It's the first time she's dared allow herself to think of her sister, the last family member she has. Emilia may very well be alive and well, waiting for Adalyn to come and find her.

Adalyn tries to grasp the hope that is her sister in the darkness, but the hurt she feels has other ideas. Thoughts of self-inflicted pain swarm her mind, a small release to focus on anything that isn't the overwhelming sadness. A release.

Adalyn scrambles from the tub, half manic and hysterical as she throws open draws and looks under the basin for something sharp that may bring her temporary silence.

She needs silence.

Adalyn looks into the mirror that's hanging on the wall, she opens the bathroom door and grabs onto the fire poker that's propped against the fireplace. She braces her arms as she swings and breaks the glass. A large spider web crack swallows half the side of the mirror, Adalyn drops the poker and pries one of the lengthy shards from the mirror.

She climbs back into the empty bathtub, lying on her back as she hiccups through her tears.

Do it, no one will notice. No one will care. Why would they? You are nothing now, you are a slave.

Adalyn closes her eyes as she lowers the sharp end of the glass toward her thigh, pressing the point into her soft skin. One slice and she would stop. Just one to end the screaming in her mind. She's never intentionally harmed herself before, so although she isn't sure the pain of splitting her skin open will help dull the pain in her heart, she takes the risk.

Maybe it won't take away the pain she's feeling, but maybe she can bleed some of it out.

Make it bearable.

You have no one. You are nothing more than a whore for the king's taking, you don't deserve to end your pain. You deserve to suffer it.

Adalyn goes numb as she drags the glass atop her thigh. Her skin splits and blood bubbles down and soaks her underwear. Her hands shake as she takes gasping breaths. The bloody glass clatters into the tub beside her as she trembles.

The screaming in her mind has stopped.

There is only silence.

Adalyn's tears continue to spill down her cheeks, the stinging in her thigh takes all concentration she has left. She lays in the tub, head throbbing as she holds onto the silence. Blood spills down into the tub, she tilts her face down and watches as the red liquid flows from her.

It's...calming. Releasing, liberating.

It's the one thing she can control in her life, even if it's hurting her.

In a daze, she runs a finger through the slow stream and holds it up to her face, feeling comfort as she takes in the dark red contrast against her pale finger. The metallic stench burns her nostrils, but it's a small price to pay. She's content that she took the risk, taking the pain and making it her own.

Adalyn is utterly numb, and if this darkness is always going to be this welcoming...she isn't sure if she'll ever be able to drag herself out of it.

18. Adalyn

Adalyn

Adalyn emerges from her private room, dressed in a pale pink gown and slippers. She lets her brushed hair spill down her shoulders as she looks down the hall, all of the other doors are shut, including the king's chambers. She heaves a sigh of relief as she turns and takes the steps slowly, wincing at the slight pain that shoots up her right thigh with each lengthened step.

She'd woken a few hours earlier, puffy faced with dry blood cracking on her thigh. She'd lit the fire and burnt her undergarments and had hidden the sharpened glass in a crack inside the chimney.

She'd cleaned herself up once she'd hidden the evidence, relieved to find the cut on her thigh hadn't needed anything more than a firm bandage.

Today she'd explore the castle, mapping out every exit route she can find. Her stomach grumbles, calling for her to find the kitchen first. Adalyn finishes her first set of stairs to find another private hall that she hadn't seen last night, too distracted to take notice.

Killian emerges from one of the rooms, straightening a black lapel jacket as he begins to stride towards the stairs. He runs a hand through his straight, shoulder length hair before looking up. His blue eyes crash into hers immediately.

She straightens her shoulders, burying her clenched hands into the skirts of her dress as he slowly strides towards her. She's far too aware of his lingering gaze, devouring her from head to toe.

"What are you doing here?" she asks once he's standing in front of her. He narrows his eyes slightly, all warmth dissolving.

"I live here if you can't recall." He drawls, tucking his hands into his pockets. He has the air of bored confidence about him.

"Where can I find the kitchen?" She asks, "I'm hungry and I don't really wish to see the king until he...calls for me." She grimaces at her words and looks away, down the last spiral set of stairs.

"I'll walk you to the kitchen, the king's called for my presence but I'll make the time for you." Killian walks past her and begins a swift decent down the steps. Adalyn hastily follows, grasping the banister as she takes two steps at a time.

Curse him and his long legs.

Killian takes a sharp left, leading her away from the hall she'd been in last night. She keeps in stride with him, ignores the stinging in her thigh and plasters on a scowl.

"How did you like your room?" Killian asks.

Adalyn glances up at him, "It's ridiculous and unnecessary. We're his slaves, why aren't we in shackles and out in the stables?"

"I told you he's a generous lover, I wasn't lying. From now until the moment he deems any of you unfit for him, you'll live like royalty," Killian murmurs, glaring at a few golden guards that stand post. They lower their heads, avoiding his gaze.

"And what happens when does?" Adalyn demands, grabbing his arm to pull him to a stop. Killian looks to her clasped hand and up to her face. She releases him and takes a healthy step away.

"I don't know. I don't dabble with his affairs. I am his second in command and a war general. The last thing I have time for is a lover's quarrel," Killian growls, eyes flashing. Adalyn feels her top lip rise above her teeth, her own anger ignites under her skin.

"The last thing I have time for, is to be standing here begging for information," she hisses.

"Don't beg then Addie darling, it doesn't suit your hateful demeanour at all." He turns swiftly and continues walking, not caring if she follows or stays rooted to the spot.

"Damn you, damn you, damn you," she mutters under her breath with each step she takes as she follows after him. Hunger urges her onwards, even though she wants to revolt and go anywhere but where he's leading her.

His arrogance can be felt from where Adalyn trails behind him, along with that delicious scent of his that has her hating him even though her blood warms and thickens.

Has her thinking of how his wicked tongue had made her feel all sorts of pleasure, had quieted the screaming of her mind.

The way his tongue had moved as he'd inserted a finger inside of her—

"Where are your thoughts?" Killian calls over his shoulder, daring a glance towards her.

"Where do you think they are?" she shoots back, blushing furiously.

Killian chuckles darkly, "In the gutter. From the sweet scent—"

Adalyn rushes forward and barrels into him, slapping a small hand over his mouth. He stumbles forward but supports her weight as she practically climbs onto his back, wrapping her other arm down to keep a hold of his chest.

"Don't you *dare* finish that sentence Killian Abaddon or you will not see the light of day." She hisses into his pointed ear, her breath stirs the hair that frames his face. She squeals as he licks her palm, but she keeps it clasped over his mouth.

"Killian don't play dirty—" She shrills as he nips at her palm, sending tingles through her arm. She loses her grip on his mouth but manages to keep a firm hold of his shoulder. He reaches around and grabs onto her thighs, stopping her from slipping.

"Are you done?" he asks, tipping his back to look at her. Her breath mingles with his own as she stares down at him, all too aware of her body pressing against his own. He seems to realise it as well as he goes rigid against her, although he doesn't take his eyes from her.

"Yes," she gulps, looking away from him. Too close, she'd gotten too close. She curses herself internally, *what happened to hating him and wanting to drive a blade through his cold heart?*

She looks back to him, tugging her bottom lip between her teeth. His pupils dilate as he watches her every movement. They stand in the middle of a hall, completely transfixed by one another.

Ah, that's right. I forget how devastatingly handsome he is and my resolve crumbles into nothing when I'm around him. Especially when he looks as me how he is now.

Their noses touch and Adalyn's heart threatens to explode. Is he going to kiss her? Does she want to kiss him? Will she be hurt if he *doesn't* kiss her?

Someone ahead clears their throat, it's enough to break Adalyn from whatever trance Killian held over her. She scrambles off of him, her neck and cheeks burn like a wild fire as she looks to see Jurian standing in the arch doorway. He cradles a hot cup of coffee between his hands, steam wafts from the dark blue mug.

"Oh do continue, it was just getting good," he remarks, grinning as he looks from Killian to Adalyn. She storms up to him, slapping his arm as she passes him.

"Shut your stupid fat mouth Jurian," she barks as she slips past him into the large kitchen.

She stops, her blood going cold as she looks at each human slave. Their glassed over eyes are enough to have her appetite dissolving. They work in silence, as if someone holds strings to their movements as they prepare grand meals and slave away over sinks and flaming stoves. They're barely more than bags of bones wearing costumes.

"Fuck, I shouldn't have brought you here," Killian growls from behind her, his voice sounding far away. Adalyn grabs onto one of the human females walking past her, she simply shrugs from Adalyn's grip and continues walking towards the back of the steaming kitchen and disappears into a large pantry.

"Come on Red, I'll take you to the gardens." Jurian stands in front of Adalyn, gently he wraps an arm over her shoulder and steers her from the kitchen. Adalyn trembles as she keeps her eyes glued to the skirts of her dress. Killian doesn't say a word as Jurian leads her past him, heading down yet another hall.

She'd been distracted and half joyful once again. If the slaves weren't a slap in the face to her small reprieve, the utter agony in her chest would be.

"Would you like to talk about it?" Jurian asks softly, gently rubbing his fingers over her shoulder. She shakes her head, lost for words. He nods in understanding and sips his coffee, continuing to guide them down a steep decent of stairs.

"I think you'll appreciate the gardens." Jurian chatters away, "they're stunning in the warmer months. The flowers here are interlaced with magic so it's even more special once they bloom."

"I...I like gardens," Adalyn mutters, dragging herself from the hollowness in her chest. She looks up to find Jurian's golden hair pulled back from his face, tossed in a messy bun that has strands flying around his face.

"I do as well, my mother loves gardening," he admits, smiling softly.

"Does she live in the castle?" Adalyn asks, needing any sort of distraction to pull her from the guilt. She'd been too close to Killian once again, and she knows deep down that it must come to an end eventually.

"No she lives in the south west coast of Pantera, it's safer for her to be among the other water folk. They're the nicer Valarki, if there's such a thing." Jurian releases his grasp on her to open a small wooden door, he props a skull shaped rock against the open door as Adalyn trails him out. Warm sun greets her as she takes a breath of fresh air.

"Behold," Jurian spreads an arm wide, Adalyn steps from behind him to find the most extravagant garden she's ever laid her eyes upon. Tall deep green hedges line the outer walls of the garden from prying eyes, it's a small courtyard with a stone fountain, bubbling water in the middle. Adalyn walks through the rows of midnight black roses as she makes her way towards the fountain, admiring the rearing horse as water spills from its mouth.

Jurian trails behind her, gently touching a few flowers as he walks.

"Who...who takes care of this?" she asks, looking over the wine stained orchids that line the first part of the garden bed. Behind them yellow and white chrysanthemum bloom, their petals curling and uncurling as they drink in the rays of sunlight.

"The king himself. Despite being utterly wicked, he has a soft spot for flowers." Jurian walks over to a patch of auburn lilies, the same colour as Adalyn's hair, "He likes pretty, soft, breakable objects."

Jurian plucks a lily, standing to look at Adalyn, "You may be soft and pretty but you are far from breakable. Don't believe otherwise."

"Why are you being so nice to me, Jurian?" Adalyn whispers, watching as he closes the distance between them. He smiles as he slides the flower behind her ear, making sure it's secure in her hair. His hand lingers on her cheek, the tips of his fingers are warm.

His red eyes are prettier than the flowers that surround them, warmer than the sun that beats down on them, "Because I am tired of being something I am not. Aren't you?"

Adalyn clasps his hand that lingers on her cheek, "We may be from different worlds...but I think we might be the same. You and I."

"You're trapped in this world, as much as you detest it. Just because you are human does not mean you are not worthy, I know there will be certain Valarki who will try to tell you otherwise."

Adalyn lowers his hand, letting him go as she grimaces, "Yes. I have one face that comes to mind."

Jurian falls into silence, his eyes churn with emotion and thoughts as he watches her. She looks away and clears her throat, not wanting him to stare long enough to see through her cracks.

"You think I'm pretty?" She asks, steering the subject away from any serious topic. Jurian chuckles, the sound has her looking back to where he stands in front of her.

"Oh Red, I've been trying to woo you from the moment I met you at the camp fire. Of course you're pretty."

Adalyn rolls her eyes, snatching his half empty mug from him. He whines in protest but doesn't stop her as she takes a sip. The bitter taste of coffee is a strong remedy to her churning feelings. She shoves them down, building that iron wall around herself once more.

"Well, you're pretty too," she murmurs, glancing up at him. He laughs, snatching the mug from her once more. He leads her over to a stone bench that rests under the shade of a towering building to their left. She sits beside him, feeling at ease as she leans back and lengthens her legs before her.

"Careful now, I might think you're the one doing the wooing." Jurian winks, resting one arm over the back of the chair. Adalyn snorts, crossing her arms over her chest.

She may never admit it...but Jurian had temporarily saved her from that darkness that plagued her the night before. Without knowingly doing it, he offered her comfort in the only way he knew how.

"Do you agree with the king's idea of keeping human slaves?" Adalyn asks, finding the courage to talk to him about her thoughts. She doubts she'd get a straight answer from Killian.

"I...have to be careful of what I say. There's eyes and ears everywhere in this damned placed." Jurian mumbles, his eyes flicker over the garden before them as if he can see the invisible eyes and ears he speaks of.

"Well I don't have to be. I don't understand why the king needs to continue his plague down the continent. Why does he need more land? He has more than enough." She looks to Jurian, "Is something coming? Is there a reason why he needs land and slaves?"

"You're smart Red, too smart for your own good. I don't know much, Killian is the one who has all the information. I'm simply his second hand once we're sent out on a conquest."

"Right and I can barely squeeze conversation out of him as it is."

Jurian chuckles, "he's a hard man to talk to. It's like talking to a rabid wolf sometimes, trying to prod at him until he snaps back. He has his reasons."

"You have that right." Adalyn sighs and looks back out to the garden, breathing in the floral scent, "I feel so useless, I have no purpose but to be the kings lap dog. I hate it."

"Whatever you're planning in that pretty head of yours, I suggest against it," Jurian warns, tapping her knee with his foot.

"I'm not planning anything," *Lie.* "I just wish I had another task to occupy my time."

"Explore the castle and see what the grounds have to offer. It's large enough that it'd take you some weeks until you've journeyed into each room." Jurian suggests, "there's a library hidden in the catacombs but it's guarded by hounds so I advise against going that far."

"What are these hounds anyway? The golden guard mentioned them to me before." Adalyn drums her fingers restlessly on the stone arm, eyebrows furrowing. A library could hold some answers she's desperately seeking, it would give her the upper hand if she ever managed to escape the kings claws.

"They're a creature the king created from his own magic. As large as a horse and as terrifying as a skinned wolf. Even the Valarki are unsettled by them."

"How do you kill them?"

"How you would kill anything, a sharp blade to a soft vital spot." Jurian rises from the chair, stretching his arms over his head. The hem of his shirt drifts up, exposing toned tanned muscles.

"Are you leaving?"

"Yeah I should probably go and dress and see what the king wanted with Killian. Enjoy the sun, you're safe in this garden. No...enemy of yours would dare find you here." Jurian smiles once before spinning on heel and striding to the small propped open door. He turns at the last moment, grabbing a puch from his pocket, "here, it's some cheese and crackers. You should eat something."

She reaches out and grabs the pouch he throws, her heart warms slightly at the gesture. She rests the pouch in her lap before she turns from his retreating figure and gathers her legs onto the stone seat beneath her. She rests her chin on her knees and drinks in the only colour this ghastly place has.

It isn't until the sun gives way to the moon does Adalyn drag herself from the stone chair, stretching her stiffened legs as she journies back into the castle.

Each step in the stone wall feels like a chain tightening on her throat, and there isn't a damned thing she can do about it.

19. Killian

Killian

Killian watches as Adalyn leaves with Jurian, the warmth he'd felt in her moments ago when they'd shared each breath had been leeched the moment she stepped foot in the kitchen. He'd been too focused on wanting to see what the king wanted from him to really pay attention to how it might affect her, seeing human slaves under the king's magic.

He shakes the darkening thoughts from his mind as he makes his way to the throne room, Jurian would look after her. May even pull a rare smile from her, if he used his charm and wit.

Ahead two golden guards stand post, clasping their golden swords in each hand as they stand on either side of the propped open throne room doors.

Killian wears his cold mask with ease, it's almost become a second skin to him, acting as though he is heartless and feels nothing. Having any sort of enjoyment in this cut throat castle is an easy way to be punished. His back is evidence of that.

Killian meets the blazing golden eyes of his king, ignoring the power that leaks towards him as a display of ownership. He lounges in his throne made of human bones, each human he'd killed himself. He'd created this throne with his bare hands, evidence enough of how ruthless he can be.

Loose white pants cover his lower half, his broad caramel muscular chest reveals golden swirls of ink that cover each pec and spread to his biceps. An ancient Valarki dialect each king receives once they take the throne. Killian bows once he reaches the base of the dais, falling to one knee. He'd only ever bow for his king.

"Rise."

Killian does, keeping his spine straight and face indifferent. Polarian and his small group of followers stand against the far wall to Killian's right, a line of six golden guards stand on either side of Killian.

"How may I be of service your majesty?" Killian asks. The king stays silent, surveying Killian from head to toe. Killian had long ago mastered his display of emotion, or lack thereof. Even though it feels as if the king strips his skin from bone, Killian simply stands there.

"I've been informed you've taken a liking to one of my females," he finally states, arching a golden brow.

Killian's sudden blink is the only sign of surprise he shows. He should have known the king would find out eventually, it isn't as if he'd been careful about it. Especially not moments ago when he'd almost kissed Adalyn in the hall for anyone to see.

"There was one female I saved twice, yes. I wouldn't say I've taking a liking to her," Killian says coolly, shrugging one shoulder as he tucks his hands into the pockets of his pants. He's the image of boredom.

"Yes so I've heard, Adalyn is her name." The king taps a bare foot, each thud expels restless power.

"That is correct."

The king smiles, exposing two sharpened canines, "I'm giving you a small side task. For punishment of becoming fond of this female, you will have four weeks to bleed her. If she is still un-bled at the end of the four weeks, Polarian may have her for twelve hours to do whatever he wishes and then she is to be returned to me."

Killian's mind goes utterly quiet.

The king grins, one of satisfaction. He knows how much Killian hates the human females he takes, had seen the distaste in his eyes over the many years when any have offered themselves to him.

"I've been thinking about this since last night when I finally met who this Adalyn woman is. She's a sight for sore eyes. If I'm being honest Killian, I would take her for myself, but I find this far more enticing." He leans back in his throne, muscles rippling as he rests an elbow on the thigh bone of the chair's arm. He twirls silk gold and silver strands of hair through his fingers, the ends spill over the seat.

"How will you know if she's bled?" Killian asks, reining in his anger.

"She will be spread before me and probed how the others are." He turns his golden eyes towards Polarian, "thank you for volunteering this information. If Killian fails I know you will not."

"I will not fail," Killian says softly, he unleashes a small hold on his power, a silent reminder that he has not forgotten what his last punishment was for going against the king.

That even now he will do his bidding without hesitation, even if the thought destroys what's left of his broken cold heart.

"Good, she'll be with you for the next four weeks starting in seven days. For the next week I will get to know her. Enjoy it."

"Is there another reason for you calling me here?" Killian raises a dark brow, narrowing his eyes. Darkness churns in the golden depths that stare back at him.

"Yes. There's...a sickness plaguing the north east coast of Pantera. We're getting reports of hundreds of Valarki turning up dead. I want you to travel there and find any information you can, who or what may be behind it. Why they're dying." The king drifts in his thoughts, eyes glazing over momentarily.

This is the first Killian is hearing of this, "What sort of sickness do you think it is?"

"I'm unsure. The deaths are unusual from what I've gathered

in the many reports. It's best if you saw the bodies yourself, use that dastardly power of yours to detect anything."

"And I'm supposed to take Adalyn with me?" Killian questions.

"Yes. I will tweak the brand on her wrist. She may leave this castle with you and must always be in a fifty foot radius once you step outside these walls. If she thinks of running, the agony will be enough to have her crawling back to you."

"I see." Killian breathes heavily through his nose, he needs a strong drink. After this conversation he'd love nothing more than to lose himself in a bottle of the finest whiskey he can find.

"Don't fail me, shadow of death. These are our people dying out there."

"I know. I will comb through the library beneath and find whatever information that may help me."

"Go, I grow bored of looking at your blank face." The king waves his hand, dismissing Killian.

Killian bows his head once more before turning on his heel and striding from the throne room. He doesn't dare glance towards Polarian, knowing the male would be gleeful. His blood threatens to turn to lead in his veins as he prowls down the empty halls, aiming for the stairwell that will lead him to the catacombs.

Adalyn hates him and he knows a small part of her wants nothing to do with him. He vaguely feels the same way. Not once had he touched a human woman before her, had never felt the desire or need too.

The king believes he will fail at this, wanting to hold the vow he gave to his now deceased wife all those years ago. All he has left is his word to her, to their unborn child.

What the king doesn't realise is that somewhere in Killian's cold chest, a small warmth has stirred. A warmth Adalyn herself has caused, as if she's the kindle and he's the flame. He'd been too close to claiming her lips this morning, had almost given into his desire when he'd scented the sweet tang of her arousal in the air.

She tasted like sweet honeydew, feasting on her was as addictive as looking down the bottle of one of his most prized whiskeys. He isn't sure if he'd ever get his fill of her, if he'd ever itch that scratch he can't shake off.

Not even Alissa had managed that, how he assumed she would.

If anything, it had left him with guilt and now this task... there's no way he'd be able to even look twice at Alissa if he did manage to take Adalyn to bed.

He runs a hand through his hair, snagging on small knots. If he was her first, she'd never forgive him for it. Would look at him with even more hatred in her eyes. He wouldn't blame her, it'd be a welcome embrace.

It'd be what he deserved.

And now with Valarki dying without cause, it's one cluster fuck after the other. He wanted to return and have at least a week of reprieve and relaxation before being given his next task.

Killian reaches the iron clad door, two torches flicker on either side of the haunting structure. He pushes the door inwards and begins the sharp descent down the crumbling stone stairs. The air is stagnant, each step stirs dust and disturbs the critters of darkness. At the base of the stairs more torches flicker, hanging from the skull wall.

He wipes down the front of his black lapel jacket and faces the catacombs. Thankfully the library is down this same hall, not somewhere beneath the castle in one of the many mazes of catacombs.

Two hounds sit before the library door, they're as large as a horse with the shape of a wolf. No fur covers their bodies, only thick leathery black skin. Their skeletal figures stir, swivelling their wolven heads towards him.

Black smoke streams from their nostrils, their red eyes glow faintly as they rise on their haunches.

"King's orders," he grunts, waving his hand in the air. They growl but allow him safe passage, not even they dare get on his bad side. Killian pushes through the two wooden arched doors, immediately candles light as the doors shut behind him.

Starting on his left and working their way in a circle towards the ceiling, the candles create a spiralling ring of fire that illuminates the many rows of forgotten leather-bound books. A grand fireplace to his right lights, wood cracks and pops as the fire feeds and warms the room. This library is enchanted to become welcoming once there's a presence in the room, Killian had heard many years ago that it has a personality of its own, but he's yet to witness it.

He walks over to the large rectangular oak table, running a finger along its length as he walks past and down the first row of books. His eyes skim the titles, some in the ancient Valarki dialect. He grabs three black leather-bound titles from a high shelf down and carries them towards the table, each volume focuses on unnatural causes of death.

He's a chapter in, discussing what death is, when the library doors open. He looks up, mildly irritated as he sees Alissa and Jurian walk in. Alissa looks at the library in awe while Jurian grumbles and walks to Killian, leaving her to gawk.

"Sorry I couldn't find you earlier. I ran into a smug Polarian and he said I'd find you here sulking." Jurian collapses into a seat beside Killian, looking to the books spread before him.

"I'm not sulking." Killian leans back, "How is she?"

"Better. It took some coaxing, but I showed her the king's garden, told her she looked pretty and plucked a lily for her." Jurian shrugs, "I think she's lonely."

"As long as she was more..." Killian trails off, loss for words.

"Alive? Once she snatched the coffee from my hand, I knew she was safe to be alone." Jurian grins, winking towards Killian, "what was that display I saw before rudely interrupting?"

"What display?" Alissa asks, perching herself on the arm of Killian's chair. Her subtle rose scent has him nudging her into her own chair.

"Oh, it was with Red and Killian here." Jurian juts his thumb towards Killian. Alissa arches a brow, looking to Killian slightly confused.

"Who's Red?"

"The slave girl we saved," Jurian confirms. Alissa leans back in her seat, fiddling with the hem of her pale blue silk crop top.

"Ah, the one that's been giving you trouble," she purrs.

"The king has given me an impossible task." Killian growls, massaging his temples as he leans on the desk. He closes his eyes, "he wants me to bleed her in four weeks, while I also take her with me to the north east border to fulfil duties."

"What!" Jurian blanches. Alissa throws her head back and laughs.

"Oh my, this will be the first task you've failed him." she says, amused.

"What—what happens if you don't?" Jurian's tone demands Killian's attention, he opens one eye and looks to his friend.

"Polarian has his way with her for twelve hours."

Jurian pales.

"So? She's just another slave," Alissa says, tapping her lengthened sea blue nails on the table. Killian bites his tongue, not wanting to argue with her.

"You know what Polarian is like. She'd hardly be a person once he's done with her, if she survives it."

"Again...I'm having trouble figuring out why we care so much about a slave. Killian you detest the humans, have vowed to never take one to bed, let alone *bleed* one." Alissa places a hand on Killian's arm.

"It's not that simple." He grits his teeth together, leaning out of her touch while he pinches the bridge of his nose. No, it has never been easy for him from the moment he took his first breath.

"It is. Take her along with you, let some other desolate Valarki male have his way with her while you're on your travels. Saves you and her from Polarian's grasp."

"If you met her you'd understand why that is definitely not an option," Jurian murmurs, flickering concerned eyes towards Killian.

"I don't like the humans, they're nothing more than vermin. You've both always know this," Alissa chirps, rising from her chair to wander over to the fire.

"The last thing we want is for her to find this out." Killian mumbles, more so for Jurian to only hear, "If she does, she'll definitely be handed to Polarian."

"You're the lesser of evils," Jurian says sympathetically.

"I'm still the villain in her story." Killian stares down at the open book, unseeing.

"We're all the villains in someone's story, we can't all be heroes." Jurian rises from his chair, clasping Killian on the shoulder. "Be safe brother, I've got personal affairs to attend but call me if you need."

"Thank you, brother." Killian watches as Jurian strides towards the doors, grimacing as they open on their own accord. He never did like the hounds.

Alissa lingers.

"What is it?" Killian sighs, not having the energy or patience to withstand any more conversations. Alissa walks over to him, wrapping her arms around his neck while she nestles into his cheek.

"We'll still have our fun before you leave, right? I missed you." She murmurs, her breath hot in his ear.

"Maybe. I have a lot I need to think about." Killian gestures towards the door, "you'd best leave now."

"Don't push me away, Killian." She presses a wet kiss to his cheek before flittering from the room, racing to catch up with Jurian. The doors close with a content sigh, clicking into place.

Killian pushes all thoughts of Adalyn and Alissa from his mind until there is nothing but the books in front of him and the dying Valarki on his mind. Not even his demons torment him here.

20. Adalyn

Adalyn

The next morning Adalyn finds herself back in the king's private gardens, a hot cup of black tea in her hand as she aimlessly walks through the many rows of flowers. She'd placed the auburn lily on her bed side table, smiling stupidly at the small gift Jurian had offered her. A gift of peace in the circumstance they'd found themselves in.

Her appetite hadn't returned, but she'd been craving the warmth of something. Tea had been the best she'd come up with, relieved to find no slaves had been haunting the kitchens when she'd snuck in to make herself a cup.

It'd taken her longer to find the gardens than she'd like to admit and knew it would take her double that length of time returning to her room. She hadn't seen any of the other women since they'd been escorted to their rooms, Adalyn makes a mental note to check on Allison once she returns.

Light footsteps draw her attention from the fountain, towards the propped open door. The king himself stands in a ray of sunlight, his caramel skin glows as his hair is set aflame.

Those golden eyes swirl with mild surprise and amusement as he takes in Adalyn. She'd dressed in a simple, teal dress that clinches at her waist and cascades into many light skirts around her legs.

"I-I'm sorry, I can leave if you wish," she stutters, beginning to stride for the open door.

"Stay, I insist." The king steps into her path, she draws up short and hides her trembling hands by clasping her hot cup of tea between them. The corners of his mouth lift, his golden eyes are nothing but warm as they assess her.

"Okay..." she nods and turns to the side, controlling her breathing as she looks at the roses.

"How are you liking the castle?" he asks, standing beside her. She stiffens slightly, a small tremor of fear shoots through her...he owns her. The brand on her wrist is answer enough. She's one of his consorts, for him to do whatever he wishes to her.

"It's...nice. This garden is my favourite part," she admits, running her finger around the rim of her mug. The steady movement has her nerves calming and hiding the hatred.

"Yes, the garden is my favourite part as well. It's a shame there isn't more out there."

He sounds...sad.

"A shame indeed." Adalyn takes a small sip of her tea, savouring its warmth, "what brings you out here?"

"I come here to think when I find it too crowded in my mind, the fresh air and floral scents help that cause." He chuckles deeply, the noise a pleasant sound. Adalyn finds herself tilting her head back to look up at him, wanting to see the smile that may accompany that laugh.

Snap out of your lust filled mind.

"Yes...it does help." She scolds herself as he meets her eyes, as he trails a light touch down her arm before striding a few stops forward to admire the roses.

She's puzzled by him.

He's this blood thirsty killer that wants to conquer the continent and yet he's out here...in his personal garden admiring the roses.

Adalyn knows better than to believe he might be speaking truth. Knows better to not let her eyes deceive her, with his smooth words and handsome face it wouldn't be a surprise if some of the other women have already taken a tumble in the sheets with him.

"There's going be to a small gathering tonight in the ball room, I extend the invitation to you as I have with the other women. Wear something nice." He looks over his shoulder at her, "I expect to see you there."

The brand on the inside of her wrist burns slightly.

"Of course...your majesty," she addresses him, uncertain if he has a preferred name. He smiles and turns away from her, content with the title she'd given him.

Arrogant ass.

"I'll see you tonight Adalyn."

The dismissal is obvious. It makes Adalyn pissy as she leaves the gardens, clenching her mug in her hands. She'd escaped here, wanting to quite her mind. Why did he have to come along and kick her out?

She wanders through the castle, peering into empty bedrooms and finding only cobwebs and dust. Nothing interesting catches her eyes, nothing that might allow her to snoop.

As she walks along unhurried, she thinks over what the king had said to her. She must attend a small gathering and must wear something nice. Two things she detests, the only good thing that may come from it is seeing all the other women the king had taken into his harem.

She ignores the oily feeling that scuttles across her skin at the thought, she hadn't even had one man and the thought of sharing one makes her stomach revolt. Are the other girls okay with this outcome? Can they sit and be the pretty lap dogs the king wishes them to be? Adalyn isn't sure, but she knows she won't sit and heel.

After more hours of aimless wandering, taking mental notes of each hallway and window and exit, Adalyn emerges at the stairs that will take her to her room. She forces her tired legs to take each step, as soon as she returns to her room, she'd be running a hot soapy bath.

Killian leaves his chambers, locking the door behind him with his magic as he goes. His sharp blue eyes find her and they *burn*.

"Have you finished eye fucking me yet?" he growls, prowling towards her. Adalyn backs into the railing until it's digging into her lower spine. Killian stands before her, towering over her with nothing but darkness and the promise of blistering cold. His eyes still burn, and Adalyn finds herself enticed by the flame.

"I would never do such a thing with the likes of *you,*" she snaps back, gripping the railing on either side to support her. She hadn't been eye fucking him, but now memories of him shirtless and hard before her plague her mind. Killian encases her on the stairwell, pressing the hard planes of his body against her own. She tilts her head back, licking her lips as he watches her.

"You think very, very dirty thoughts about me, darling," he snarls, the railing groans under his grip. Adalyn pushes her chest against his own, her nipples peeking through the thin material.

Distraction. Killian can be a distraction from the darkness that's waiting to pounce once you return to your room.

"Those thoughts of me impaling you with a sword are filthy indeed." She's breathless, her quick wit is quickly turning to dark desire for him, a forbidden desire she craves.

"So you've never thought of impaling yourself on my hard cock?" he murmurs against her throat. Adalyn isn't sure when he'd moved; too lost in her own thoughts of desire. His words are filthy and have her toes curling in her slippers, unable to help the wave of need that goes through and has her pulsing for him.

Distraction.

"I hate you," she whispers, letting her hands fall to his chest. She feels the staccato beating of his heart under her right palm, erratic as her own.

"And I hate you. Hatred mixed with pleasure is the best kind."

Killian nips at her ear lobe, earning a soft mewl from her. He licks the column of her throat, knowing exactly what he's doing to her.

More. More. More.

"Prove it to me." Adalyn pushes him back gently, enough to look into his eyes, "take me to my room and prove it."

"I'm not going to fuck you Adalyn..." her face falls, "yet. When I do, I'm going to take all day pleasuring you in ways you've never considered. There will be no interruptions."

"Less talking, more proving." Adalyn wraps her arms around his neck as he hoists her into the air. His large hands grasp her ass firmly as she wraps her legs around his waist, her thigh stings with the movement.

"First door on the left," Adalyn murmurs against his neck, breathing his scent in greedily. She allows herself this small pleasure. Jurian may be able to distract her from her pain momentarily...but Killian can offer her an escape. He consumes all logical thoughts and feelings, she burns when he touches her.

She needs to escape, even if it does involve his body.

Killian doesn't hesitate as he opens her door, locking it behind them before he strides over to her bed and throws her down. She bounces once on the mattress before he has a hold of her legs, her chest heaves as she slowly removes her slippers.

The fire in the room stutters to life, crackling and popping. Adalyn supresses the memories that threaten to consume her at the noise. Killian climbs over the bed and perches himself on top of her, his need for her hard and restrained in his pants.

"Is this what you want Adalyn?" he murmurs against the skin over her right breast, she squirms underneath him as she clenches the bed sheets. He chuckles darkly, spreading her thighs with his own.

"You want me so desperately and you hate me for it." His breath is hot as he sucks at the soft skin over her breast through the dress. Adalyn moans, arching into his touch.

"Tell me it's true. That you want me and hate me," Killian

demands gruffly, trailing a scorching trail down her side as his hand grips her hip.

"I want you—" Adalyn moans sharply as his hand lingers between her legs, "I hate you."

Killian growls as he sits up, Adalyn follows the movement. He gently unzips the back of her dress, letting it pool around her waist. She hastily pulls the material off until she's bare before him.

She hadn't worn underwear this morning, unable to find a clean pair with her rush to escape her room. Killian chokes, looking at the soft hair that curls between her thighs, at the evident slickness waiting for him. Adalyn throws the dress to the floor and begins to unbutton his own shirt, her fingers tremble with each button.

Killian helps her remove his shirt until he's breathing heavy, his toned stomach tense. Adalyn runs her hands down the planes, marvelling at the softness of him.

She needs more. If she didn't have more she might just combust.

Killian unlaces his pants, rising from the bed to pull them off. His undershorts go with the material, he fists his hard length with a softness she hasn't seen from him before. Her cheeks heat, she'd never been able to fully admire his naked form before....but it has her mouth watering as she greedily drinks in all of him.

"Touch yourself over me." He pants, bracing one hand against the frame of the bed. Adalyn leans back into the pillows, spreading her legs wide as her hand dips between them.

He watches each swirl of her finger, each gentle caress as she finds a familiar pattern that brings her pleasure. Killian is breathing like a rabid wolf, barely any of the blue in his eyes is visible as his eyes are glued to her wet heat.

It's enough to have Adalyn biting her bottom lip, moving her fingers faster and faster.

"Would you like to try something new?" Killian manages to ask, tearing his eyes from her fingers to her face.

"Yes."

Killian takes her hand as she reluctantly stops pleasuring herself, throbbing and aching with the need for release. He helps her stand before he lays himself down on the bed, he reaches for her.

A lifeline.

Adalyn sits her small hand in his own as he guides her back onto the bed, "I want to taste you." Adalyn's core clenches in response.

"Show me how," she breathes out, letting him guide her until she's on all fours with his hot breath between her thighs. She leans on her left arm, taking the large hard length of him with her right hand. He jerks into her hand, earning a hidden smile.

"You don't have to," he rasps, his hands spread her cheeks and he curses. "You have no idea how much I fucking crave your taste."

"I want to," Adalyn replies before licking away the small bead of his own need. As she begins to work her hand up and down she uses her tongue and lips to focus on his head, unsure if she'll be able to get much of him in her mouth.

As her lips wrap around the tips and moves lower, he feasts upon her. Adalyn pushes against his face, eyes rolling back in her head as pleasure instantly burns low in her stomach. He sucks at the bundle of nerves before licking her clean down the centre, tugging at her lips before diving his tongue into her heat.

Adalyn sucks him faster, pumping her hand in movement with her bobbing head. She returns the favour, twirling her tongue around his shaft while softly grazing her teeth.

He thrusts into her mouth and she gives him control, using her other hand to gentle stroke at his tightening balls.

"Addie if you keep that up, I'm going to come before you," he says into her heat. Adalyn lowers her mouth even more, feeling him hit the back of her throat with each thrust. She wants to please him as much as he's pleasing her. She *needs* to feel his release, finds herself wanting to swallow down whatever he has to offer her.

One finger circles the tightness of her ass while he gently slides another into her tight heat, careful not to make her bleed. He curls that finger upwards, hitting that ridged spot that has her crying out as she rides his face while he uses his tongue to focus on that bundle of nerves.

He presses his thumb against her ass, light explodes behind her eyes as she orgasms, screaming out around his cock. He thrusts even faster into her mouth, throbbing as his quick release approaches. Killian removes his finger and rapidly circles that bundle of nerves, driving Adalyn into her second orgasm.

Her hand tightens on his balls as he groans his release, spurting into her deeply. She swallows each mouthful down, the tang of him is slightly salty on her tongue but not unpleasant.

He softens in her mouth, her thighs shake as she rises on all fours and collapses onto her back. They lay there, unmoving as they both pant.

Adalyn shuts her eyes, the quiet in her mind is bliss. Utter bliss.

Killian sits up, running a hand through his hair. Adalyn opens her eyes to find him staring at her, he offers her a rare smile. His eyes trail lower, the intensity of his gaze has her nipples hardening again.

Gods, she just had him and she's ready again?

His eyes move lower.

He goes utterly still, unbreathing. Adalyn freezes, horror overcomes her as she realises what he's looking at. She scrambles from the bed, half falling to the floor as she grabs at her dress and covers her chest and thigh. It's one thing for him to see the wounds others had given to her, it's another for him to see the wound she's given herself.

"Adalyn..." Killian looks to her, a wild desperation in his eyes she had never seen before. Panic claws at her throat, she needs him to leave.

"Get out." Her voice is soft. He frowns, climbs from the bed and strides towards her. Adalyn backs up until she bumps into the chaise, the warmth of the fire at her back has nothing on the fire in front of her.

"When," he demands, eyes darkening. Adalyn feels her anger rise once more. She harnesses the anger like a shield, protecting herself from him.

"The first night I came to this god forsaken room," she spits, clenching the dress tighter. She needs him to stop looking at her like *that*.

She refuses to acknowledge the emotions in his eyes. She needs him to leave and will use any means necessary.

"Why didn't you come and talk to me?" he asks, standing deathly still and stark naked before her. It makes her heart throb painfully at the words that are about to leave her mouth.

"Why the fuck would I get you for? You murdered my family and kidnapped me. You don't care for me so don't act like you do. Get the fuck out of my room, you've served your purpose." She leans back into the chair, eyes burning with tears. "All you're good for is a distraction. I hate you with every single part of me and it's not because I want you. It's because I hate myself just as much. Why else would I let you take me to bed? Have your way with me?"

Killian takes a step back, eyes hardening. She barrels on, already knowing her next words will hurt him. She'd seen the vulnerability in him when they'd shared a few moments alone.

"You're no better than the rest of the Valarki males outside of this room, taking advantage of a female human. Get out! You're not wanted here. Go warm someone else's bed." Adalyn turns from him as the first few tears fall, she stares into the fire and hopes he can't scent the saltiness of her tears. Footsteps retreat and clothes rustle. She hears her door crack open.

"And you're no better than the mindless slaves here," he spits, disgust obvious in his tone, "no wonder why you got fucking caught. Stop being a coward Adalyn, you act as though you're already the king's whore."

The slam of the door echoes around the quiet room.

Adalyn breaks.

21. Adalyn

Adalyn

It takes her longer than she admits to piece herself back together, to gather the sharp broken pieces of her soul and to try and make them fit inside of her. She splashes water over her face, scrubbing her burning eyes. She leans on the white basin and stares into her reflection, shadows hang under her bloodshot amber eyes.

There's nothing she can do to hide it. It'll be obvious to anyone who looks at her close enough.

The king expects her to attend this dinner, he didn't say she had to stay long or socialise with him. She throws her shoulders back.

You can do this. You didn't come this far to break now.

Adalyn takes deep breaths as she leaves her room, counting silently in her mind to lessen the churning dark thoughts. After that first night she'd truly broken, it's hard for her to keep them at bay.

Sometimes, she finds herself seeking out their vice.

Allison emerges from her room, she startles as she looks up to see Adalyn. Adalyn squeals and rushes towards her, the skirts of her maroon dress fly out behind her as she wraps her arms around Allison's slender shoulder.

"I thought I'd never see you again," Adalyn murmurs, pulling back to look over Allison. She smiles, finding that it reaches her eyes. She wears a simple white dress, the sleeves are lace and clinch at her wrist while the rest of her dress hugs her figure.

"I've been trying to find you but you're never in your room." Allison admits, squeezing Adalyn's shoulders. Her caramel eyes are filled with warmth upon seeing her friend. Adalyn finds herself blurting out what had happened with Killian, what they'd shared together and what she'd said to him afterwards.

She keeps the incident with the glass shard and her thigh to herself, Allison has enough to worry about.

"Oh...Addie," Allison gasps, wide eyed.

Adalyn runs a hand through her hair, "I know. I was a bastard to say those things but I just...I'm so angry."

"I'm angry too but I'm trying to make the best out of this situation." Allison links a dark arm through Adalyn's and steers them towards the stairs. "A few of the other girls are having a hard time but most of us have just...accepted it. There's nothing we can do and the brand on our arm is our life now. I hate being here as much as you do, but what do I have left to run back to?"

"Freedom," Adalyn whispers, clasping a pale hand through Allison's, "we have our freedom."

"What is freedom worth if only to be hunted like game? Is it worth your life?"

"I'm not sure. I..." she almost admits she believes her sister is still alive, out there and waiting for Adalyn to come home to her. She hasn't let herself consider that Emilia may not be alive, and that she has nothing left beyond these stone walls.

"Be careful where you voice these thoughts. I've spent time with the king and he doesn't seem horrible, but I doubt he'd react fondly to hearing one of his women speaking of rebellion."

"Have you...shared his sheets?" Adalyn murmurs, glancing to Allison. They'd finished walking the stairs and now stride down the hall that takes them to the ball room. Adalyn's stomach flutters with stone butterflies, Killian is going to be at this dinner.

"Well..." she trails off, her dark cheeks staining deep red. Adalyn gasps, her eyebrows raising to her hair line. Allison breaks into a laugh and slaps her arm. "Yes, I've shared his sheets. It's pleasurable, although I sort of want in on the action between you and Killian."

It's Adalyn's turn to laugh, it breaks from her chest like a wild animal. The sound is foreign to her ears, when was the last time she truly laughed?

"What? He's really sexy." Allison pouts, tugging her towards the open marble doors. The two golden guards ignore them, deeming them no threat. Adalyn finds herself smiling, leaning into Allison.

"He is very sexy indeed and he is definitely not lacking in the areas that matter most." She whispers to her friend, a light shines in Allisons eyes as she chuckles. It warms Adalyn's heart.

"I think you need to speak with him, if only to clear the air. If what you're doing with him isn't what you want, then don't. Call it off and mean it. But if you do want to keep doing whatever it is, tell him. He seems like the most reasonable Valarki male here." Allison pulls her to a stop, stepping close as the other fine Valarki dining sneer towards them.

"There's nothing wrong with what you're doing. No one defines your choices but you, no one gets to judge how you put your broken pieces back together. If you want to ride Killian into the sunrise then go ahead, if only it brings you a moment of peace." Allison squeezes her hands, tearing her eyes from Adalyn to look at the crowd. Adalyn looks around as well, surprised to find the crowd as large as the one from their first night.

Two large wooden tables have been decorated with various foods and wines, displayed against the opposing back wall of each other. Adalyn catches a human servant leaving through a small side door, hidden behind a large marble pillar.

Her heart beat picks up, could she slip away unnoticed and try and speak with one of the humans?

"He's here," Allison mutters, drawing Adalyn's attention

away from the hidden door. Adalyn follows Allison's gaze towards the throne where the king lounges, two of the other girls perch on his lap and sip from their own wine glasses. The other six stand in a line to his right, faces void of emotion.

To the king's left, stands Killian.

His stare cuts through Adalyn before he looks away, focusing on the crowd once more. A muscle in his jaw feathers. Her chest caves, she'd never get the chance to talk to him in front of everyone.

"Come on, let us go talk to the king," Allison suggests, linking their hands together and begins to slip them through the crowd. Allison holds her head high, not bothering a second glance at the scowling Valarki.

Adalyn scoffs under her breath, it's as if they think they want to be here.

"Your majesty," Allison says, bowing at her waist. Adalyn looks up to the king, finding his golden eyes already roving over her. The two girls slide from his lap, joining the line of the others. The king leans forward, two pieces of braided hair swing in front of his face.

He's still shirtless.

"Do you not own shirts?" Adalyn blurts, unable to help herself. She sucks in her cheeks the moment the words leave her mouth, he goes still.

"I didn't—what I mean is—"

He bellows out a laugh, startling half the crowd behind her. Adalyn twists her hands in front of her, waiting for some sort of reprimand for speaking out of line. His smile is hypnotising, out of the corner of her eyes she sees Allison blush furiously.

"I'm glad you took me up on my invitation," he finally says, controlling himself even though that devastating smile stays in place.

"Of course your majesty," she says softly.

"Do you like music?" he asks suddenly, rising from his throne of bones. Adalyn hides her grimace as one of the skulls begins to wobble loose.

"Ah yes. I didn't hear many sorts in my village though," she says wearily, taking a small step back. She doesn't dare look to Killian as the king walks down the few steps and stops in front of her.

"We shall share a dance then, you've humbled me." He reaches for her hand, his hands are smooth as she slides her own in his palm. He looks to Allison, his smile softening, "Hello, little bird."

"Hello." She bows before scurrying up the few stairs to stand in line with the other girls, leaving Adalyn alone with the king.

It shouldn't scare Adalyn as much as it does.

"I hope you're a good lead because I don't know how to dance," she admits, letting the warmth of his palm help to ease her nerves. He leads her towards the dance floor, soft notes from the piano and violin reach her ears. The crowd gives them wide berth, Adalyn's neck grows hot from their attention.

"I've been dancing for many years, I'd like to say I'm quite grand at the art." He pulls her close, laying a palm against her lower back while his other hand takes her free one.

"What do I do with this arm?" she asks, shaking her right shoulder. He grins.

"Slide it around my waist. Also step onto my feet, I'll carry you through each step." She does as he says, marvelling at the ripple of muscles in his back. He's warm and soft, she toys with the strands of golden hair that brush over her hand.

"You aren't wearing shoes."

"Magic, sweet one," he murmurs, leaning close enough to share breath with her. Her heart kicks into gear as she looks into his eyes.

A bitter taste is left in her mouth as the king's magic washes over her, her feet float over his on their own accord. He holds her firmly to him, her soft body curving against the hard planes of his.

One step, two step, three step, spin.

Adalyn holds her breath as he continues the pattern, gliding them around the room with ease. Not once does he take his eyes from her, as if she's the most enchanting thing he's ever seen.

"Relax," he whispers.

So she does, leaning into his hold as they make their way around the room once more. The others around them are a blur in her peripheral vision, the sad notes of violin and piano pull at every broken piece of her. If the king wasn't holding her up, she'd be little more than a puddle on the floor.

"Is this enjoyable for you?"

Adalyn blinks once, realising he's talking to her, "Yes, I enjoy this."

He licks his lips, "We shall dance more often then."

They fall into an easy silence, Adalyn eventually rests her head against his bare chest and listens to the steady beat of his heart.

Could an evil king harbour a heart of gold? Is it possible? It's almost too easy for Adalyn to imagine herself accepting the life that's been offered to her, letting go of her hatred and simply existing in this grand castle with one of the most gorgeous Valarki males she'd ever laid eyes on.

In his arms nothing else seems to matter that much, Adalyn isn't sure if it's his magic working its way through her or her own thoughts.

"Stop using your magic on me," she mumbles into his chest, the skirts of her dress swirl between her legs with each step as she lets her eyes close.

He chuckles, the sound vibrates into her, "My apologies."

The warmth lingers but the oppressing thoughts dissolve, leaving her fully aware and sober that she is in fact dancing with the king of Pantera.

The king finally spins her to a stop, the bitter taste leaves her mouth as he retracts his magic. She steps quickly off his feet, clearing her throat as she lets her arms fall to her side. The king smiles down at her, amused.

"And to answer your question," he leans down, his breath

tickles her ear as his lips run against her cheek. She can't convince her limbs to move, "yes, I do own shirts. But why would I wear one when I can see your reaction?"

"You must be mistaken," she says breathlessly, bitting her bottom lip. He chuckles darkly and rises to his full height, towering over her.

"Run along sweet one, we'll have time together soon." He leaves a soft kiss on her cheek before turning and walking to his throne. He gestures for the other women, Allison is one of the lucky few who have the opportunity to perch in his lap. Adalyn wipes the wetness of his kiss from her cheek and looks to where Killian had been standing. She curses, how long had she been dancing for? Had he left?

Allison meets her eyes, Adalyn gestures towards the table on her right. Adalyn slips through the crowd as Allison murmurs something to the king before sliding from his lap.

Moments later Allison emerges, "What is it?"

Adalyn gulps down the three large mouthfuls of foul tasting wine, sitting the empty glass aside, "I'm going to go and speak with Killian. Could you come to my room once you've finished here?"

"Of course. Good luck." Allison kisses her cheek before melting back into the crowd. Adalyn grabs another glass and finishes its contents in record timing before walking along the back wall towards the open towering doors.

She isn't sure what she's going to say once she sees him, if she'll apologise or swear at him some more. But talking with him will help the stupid heavy weight she feels in her chest.

Adalyn leaves the hall unnoticed and rushes towards the stairs, the guards pay her no mind as she runs down the large open hall before skidding to a stop in front of the grand stair case.

She climbs the stairs swiftly, each breath burns her throat and scorches her lungs. Once on the level for his room she walks down the hall with light steps, her stomach revolts. She's going to be sick if she can't speak with him soon.

Adalyn gathers the skirts of her light gown, hesitating infront of Killian's large wooden door. Her stomach violently twists at the memory of the fight they'd had only hours ago, her words were blades and Killian had been on the butchering block. She raises a hand to knock, cursing herself to find it tremble.

She shouldn't be here. She shouldn't care if her words hurt him. Everything is hurting her, why should she give anyone anything less? She straightens her shoulders and knocks lightly once, the door opens silently with magic that isn't Killian's. She'd know his magic in death.

Adalyn's arm falls to her side as she takes a deep breath, forcing her eyes from the deep red fur rug to the large oak bed.

She freezes.

A strangled choke leaves the confines of her throat at the scene before her, she can't tear her eyes away, not as tears run down her cheeks with a mind of their own.

A gorgeous female Valarki rides Killian, her large creamy breasts bounce with each of her movements. His hands are all over her, seeming as if he can't get enough. He hasn't noticed the open door, or Adalyn standing there with silent tears streaming down her face as her heart breaks even more. The women's lilac eyes snap to Adalyn and darken to midnight black. Her black curled hair cascades in waves down her back as she offers a small possessive smile.

As If she'd won something Adalyn hadn't known they're competing for.

Heart pounding, blood rushing and stomach churns, Adalyn manages to take a step back. She can't move through her emotions fast enough, can't un-hear Killian's breathless moans of pleasure as he pounds into her. Seeing this woman with Killian...has Adalyn wanting to be sick in the worst way. Had what they shared meant nothing to him?

It crushes her and she knows then that she's fucked up by letting him get as close as he has. She should have known who he was, what he is.

Deep down she did know, she just chose to ignore it.

For once she just wanted to be *wanted* by someone.

The reality has her reeling, leaving only that sharp ache of loneliness in its wake. A sob breaks from her lips, she needs to leave. She's going to break and –

Killian's head snaps sideways, towards the small noise she'd made. That foreign magic has disappeared, as if it had been allowing Adalyn to watch without Killian noticing. He stops mid thrust, eyes widening.

"I'm—" Adalyn can't finish her sentence before she's spinning and running down the hall, towards the staircase that will be her salvation. She presses a hand to her mouth as she feels the bile rise in her throat, she's going to be sick.

She careens up the stairs and rushes into her room, she barely makes it to her bathing room before she's hurling into the sink. She'd managed to close the door behind her, by some short miracle.

Tears stream down her face, but she refuses to think of them. She wipes the back of her mouth with her hand and trembles. How could he have been with her, shared what they did and then go and bury himself in someone else?

Did she really mean that little to him?

More hot tears burst from her eyes, as her sobbing echoes around the bathroom. All she knew recently is how to break. She stumbles into her room, the fire burns down to low embers as she tears the dress from her body.

She climbs on numb legs into bed, sliding under the heavy covers. She huddles around a pillow, staring into the last remnants of flame. Allison would be there soon, her lifeline.

She'd been a fool for thinking of Killian as anything other than the bloody thirsty murderer he is. For the first time in her life she'd decided to find the small amount of light in something that is wholly made of darkness.

It had been her own mistake, turning out her own lights to join him in the dark.

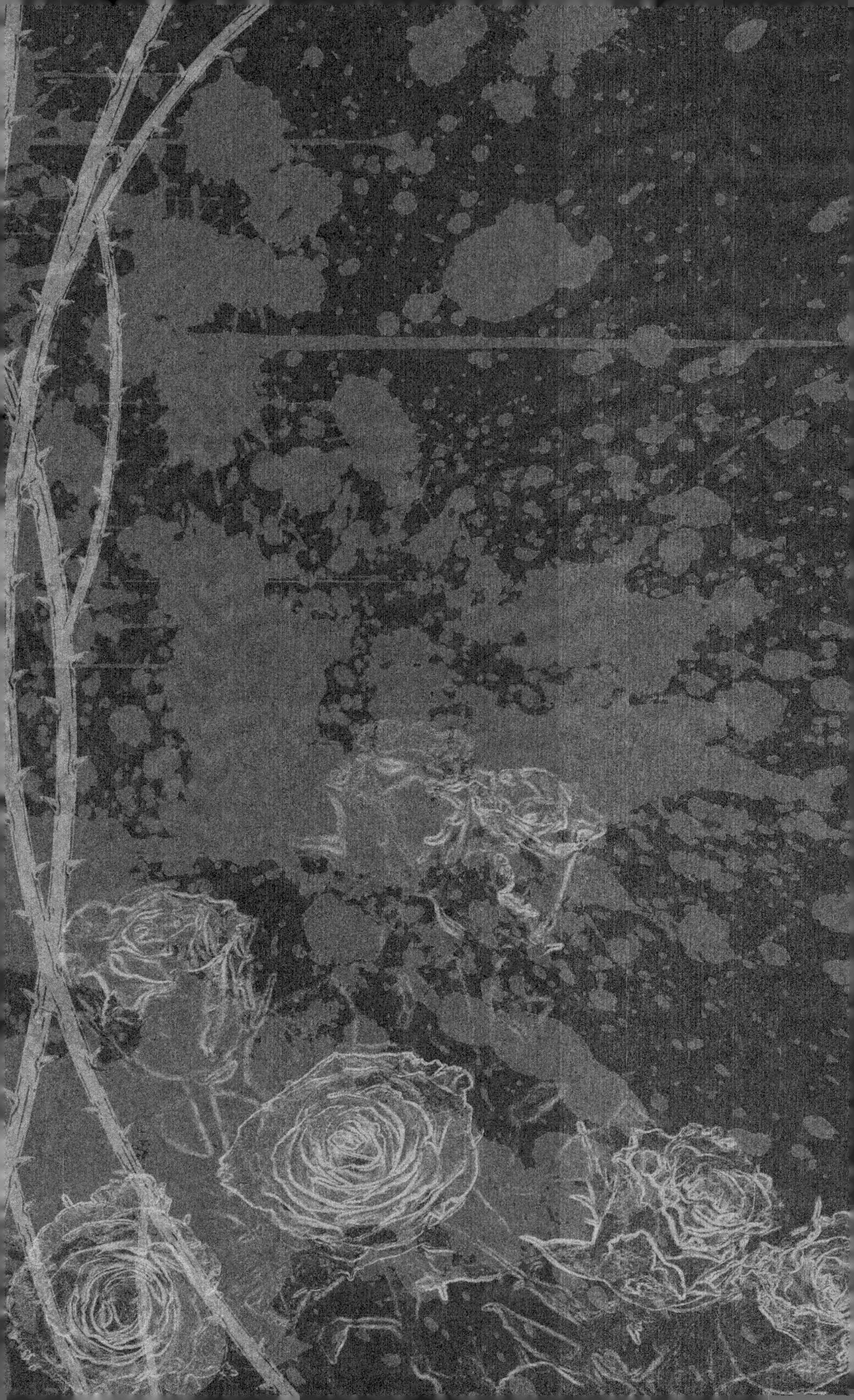

22. Adalyn

Adalyn

Adalyn isn't surprised when Jurian finds her hiding in the king's gardens once more, resting on the stone bench with a warm cup of coffee between her hands. She looks up to find him striding towards her, he smiles slowly. Kindly.

"I thought I'd find you here." Jurian chirps, coming to a stop in front of her. She drags her eyes over him, he'd dressed as if he's going riding, the long brown pants compliment his height while the thin material of his white shirt hides little muscle.

"What could you possibly want?" she asks, arching a brow. Her fingers strain on the mug, her heart a heavy weight in her chest. It'd been the first time she'd managed to drag herself from under her sheets, needing the sun on her face and the fresh air.

No one had bothered her, not that she cared.

"Care to accompany me to the stables?" Jurian holds his open hand out for her, gold rings glint in the midday sun rays. Adalyn slouches back in the stone chair, staring at him. He sighs, leaving his hand outstretched towards her.

"I heard about what happened." He finally relents, sitting beside her. Adalyn ignores him, choosing to stare down at the dark coffee as it swirls around softly.

"Talk to me, Red," he says softly.

Adalyn shrugs slightly. "There's not much to talk about. You obviously know some things have happened between Killian and I. I just..." she trails off.

He waits patiently, his company gives her the courage.

"I just thought that maybe he was good. That underneath the cold exterior he was warm and could have been someone I could eventually forgive with how I arrived here, even call a friend." She mutters, her eyes burn with unshed tears, she's so sick of crying. "He's just like every other Valarki male. It's my fault for assuming he could be better than what he is."

"Red...Killian is a complicated man. He's always been that way, when his wife was still alive he actually vouched for the humans. He would help slaves escape whenever given the chance, would always go against the ruling and try his hardest." Jurian's voice is pained, as if the memories he's recalling hurt.

"He was married?" Adalyn asks, finally turning to look at him. Jurian leans his elbows on his knees, resting his chin in his palms as his fingers tap his cheeks.

"Yes, he was. But you heard nothing from me." Bright ruby eyes dart towards her, "I won't tell you her downfall but that day changed Killian. He was no better than a ghost, he hasn't been for the last ten years. When we destroyed your village and took you, it was the first time I'd seen him unhinged in ten years."

Adalyn trembles, recalling the horrid night that haunts her nightmares. The charred bodies—the thick smoke.

"I'll always be honest with you Adalyn. I know what my people are. I know we have practices that need to be outdated. I was given an order and I followed it, it was my life or other's and I will choose myself each time." He finally looks to her, eyes swimming with emotion. Golden strands of his hair catch in the sun, floating on a phantom breeze.

"What would happen if you said no?" Adalyn asks.

"We'd be executed or the people we care for would be. As

horrible as it sounds, I would rather keep my life, I know the methods the king can use against traitors." His face pales slightly.

"Do you know which Valarki killed my family?" Adalyn whispers, ignoring the strands of her own hair that float in the breeze in front of her face. Jurian goes as still as stone, mouth slightly agape. She reaches out, placing her hand on his shoulder, "please Jurian, I need to know."

"You can't kill them and it wouldn't be from a lack of trying," Jurian says gently, placing a hand over her own. "I would have to talk to the soldiers that went on the conquest and see if a similar scent to your own lingers on them. Would knowing help you heal?"

Adalyn doesn't tell him this is a gaping wound that will never heal, no matter how many minutes or hours or days pass, that black depthless pit will always be sensitive to touch.

"I think so." She draws her hand back, letting it fall to her lap. Jurian combs a hand through his hair, blowing out a heavy breath.

"I'll do my best then, but only if you agree to come for a walk to the stables with me."

"This isn't time to bargain—" Adalyn begins to protest.

Jurian rises, holding a hand out to her, "I don't want to hear you complain. Come on, I don't like seeing you sad."

Sad.

Adalyn sits her cup down on his vacant seat and takes his hand, letting Jurian pull her up. To her annoyance he slips her arm into his own, clasping his free hand over hers. She glares up at him, earning a devilish grin.

"I'm not some show mare to prance around," she grumbles, only half meaning the malice behind her words. Jurian chuckles, leading her through the winding hallways of the castle. Adalyn looks at each human slave, knowing they'll never see her.

"You're my *friend* and I want others to know it," he says simply, as if it is that easy to be friends with the enemy. Adalyn rolls her eyes, gripping him tighter. They reach a small door, walking out to find themselves in the courtyard. Valarki sneer at her, careful to avoid Jurian's gaze.

"You know they all hate me, right?" she whispers, flinching away from a large soldier that snarls as he walks past them. Jurian pulls her in closer.

"I don't care what they think, Red."

It soothes something broken in her chest.

The scent of horse and leather rides the breeze as they step out of a stone arch way. In the daylight Adalyn can finally see how large the stables really are. Almost towering half the size of the castle wall, the stable runs back for miles. Stable boys flitter back and forth, some leading horses and others simply working.

Three large fire pits are lit in between Adalyn and the stables, soldiers stand in front of the fires and throw questionable items into the blazing flames. She's thankful she can't scent the burning flesh on the breeze.

"It's magic," Jurian says, staring with indifference at the fires.

"What're they for?" she asks, happy to stay where they're standing.

"To burn the bodies of our enemies, traitors or just dead things." Jurian grimaces, "sorry, I forget you're human."

Adalyn weakly waves her free hand. "No hard feelings."

Jurian guides her between two large fires, the heat has sweat beads running down the sides of her face and throat until they break the confines and reach the stables. The cool wind a sweet relief, a stable boy stops and peers up at her.

Something about him seems familiar, though she can't place it.

"You saved me," he chirps.

Her knees threaten to give out on her as she remembers. She lets Jurian go and wraps her arms around the small faerie creature, joyed to find his wings are in working order once more. He squeals, uncertain of what she's doing.

"I'm sorry—it's just good to see you alive and well," she says weakly, letting him go to step back. Jurian watches them with curious eyes. The stable boy twiddles his long fingers together, his milky eyes churn as he looks to the brand on her wrist.

"You and I are one and the same," he whispers, sadness etching into every feature. It crushes Adalyn, making it hard for her to draw her next breath.

Humans aren't the only race being wronged by the Valarki.

"Yes, we are. Us little people have to look out for one another." She looks over her shoulder, "this is Jurian."

"I know who he is." The stable boy steps back, his wings flitter nervously, "I'm sorry for what's to come."

He turns and flees back into the castle, no doubt running from the feral look on Jurian's face. Adalyn frowns, crossing her arms over her chest as she faces Jurian. He looks away from her.

"What really happened with the last ten females of the king's consort?" She demands.

"If you want to know so bad you can find out for yourself. I can't tell you." He looks to her, "it won't change anything."

"It may not but...what hope do I have of escaping?" She asks, clenching her fists, "am I really to be trapped here as the king's whore until I die?"

He flinches, as if she'd hit him.

"What you choose to do is in your hands. Your life is a series of choices you make, if you choose to...find some way out of the brand, then I wish you well."

"Is there a way I can get this brand off?" she asks, taking a hopeful step forward. Jurian shakes his head, unable to look at her. It deflates her.

But...she can find out what happened to the last women and have an idea of what's in store for her. If the king has his harem now, he may not make a move to conquer more human villages so soon.

"Where would I find the catacombs?" She steps closer, lowering her voice so no eavesdroppers can hear their conversation. It has her leaning into his chest, resting her hands on the hard planes.

His hands wrap around her small wrists, "That would be suicide."

"I don't have a life worth living regardless. I need to do something Jurian, I can't sit around and do nothing." *I can't be useless, accepting of this fate that I despise.*

"It's under the castle, through an iron door. Hounds guard the doors, you'd need to either disable them or kill them to get into the library." He looks down at her, eyes hardening, "I shouldn't have told you about it."

"Well you have and my choices are my own. Shall I steal your sword as well?" she tilts her head to the side, letting her loose waves fall over her shoulder and down the front of her dress.

"How about we make a deal?" He smiles slowly, smugly. Adalyn flattens her eyebrows, pressing her lips into a thin line.

"What?"

"If you give me a kiss, I will give you my best blade."

She scoffs, waiting for him to laugh.

He doesn't, only grins down at her as if he knows she will say no. That she'd rather be burning in hell than to kiss another Valarki male.

Her heart-beat stutters in her chest as she digs her nails into his chest, the material of his shirt is smooth beneath her fingers. Before he can react or stop her, she launches herself at him; rising on her toes as she slides her arms around his neck.

Her lips press to his, he stumbles back at the sudden assault. His warm hands burn into her sides as he slowly kisses her back. He tastes of warmth and light, his tongue dances with her own as he holds her close to him.

With her lips and tongue joined with Jurian, she thinks of how easy it would be to love him. Even easier to be his friend, someone she could rely on.

Heat sparks in her veins as he tugs gently at her bottom lip, before claiming her lips once more. His kiss is intoxicating and she finds herself leaning into him, digging her nails into his chest.

A large, warm hand rests against the back of her head,

allowing Jurian better access to her mouth. The heat sizzles in her veins, aiming between her thighs. Killian makes her feel as if her very soul is on fire, while Jurian makes her feel as if she's standing too close to a fire.

Killian.

She finally pulls back, drawing in a large breath. He stares down at her as if he's never truly seen her before. A soft pink tinge covers his cheeks, his lips glisten. She blushes furiously, running her tongue along her bottom lip before gathering her thoughts.

"Sword, please." She steps out of his arms, holding out a hand. Her heart beats wildly in her chest.

"You devilish woman," Jurian laughs deeply, the sound makes her heart flutter. His laughter tapers off as he uses his magic, summoning a sword as long as her arm. The silver blade is covered in intricate blue writing, while the leather handle is well worn down.

"It's yours for the day, it will return to me tomorrow morning." Jurian uses his magic as the blade floats towards her, she grabs the handle with both hands. The light weight makes it easy for her to wield, arcing it through the air to find some familiarity.

She's never used a sword before, it'll be her uprising or downfall. She hasn't decided yet.

Her skin prickles uncomfortably, she glances to her right. Her eyes snag on a large male leaning against one of the towering maple trees that sits away from the fires. His blue eyes are vibrant, even in the distance. Darkness and fury radiate from his utterly still form.

Killian.

Jurian follows her line of sight, cursing under his breath, "I don't suppose he showed up after you ravished my lips."

Adalyn scowls, "I was simply upholding the end of my bargain, it is not my fault you find me so kissable."

"If you ever decide to switch teams, I'll gladly have you." He winks, blowing her a kiss.

Adalyn *smiles.*

A light enters Jurian's eyes, a softness.

"Adalyn," her name is barely more than a whisper, "my name is Adalyn."

"Adalyn." He sounds it out slowly, tasting the syllables. He smiles, shoving his hands into his pockets. "If you survive the hounds I'd love to hear how, Adalyn."

"Okay *Jurian*, I'm sure you'll be the first person I'll track down to throttle," she replies sweetly, bobbing her shoulders. "Is he still staring?" she asks lightly.

"Like a hawk." Jurian looks over her shoulder, wincing. She throws her shoulders back, holding the sword awkwardly. It's time for her to get some answers and an iron door somewhere on the lower levels will be her salvation. She walks past Jurian, reaching up on the tips of her toes to press a kiss to his smooth cheek.

"You're going to get me killed Red," he groans, glancing down at her. She shrugs and walks away, careful to hold the sword as though she does know what she's doing with it. Jurian might be even more of a fool than she first thought if he'd given her his blade and hints.

Is he sending her to her death, or does he simply believe she's too cowardly to track down the library? She'd prove him wrong.

"Hopefully I'll see you again, if not, thanks for the last kiss," she calls over her shoulder, sauntering under the arch and through the castle grounds as if she owns the place.

She ignores the snarls and sneers, her mind solely focused on the task before her; even though the ghost of Jurian's lips haunt her.

For a moment she lets herself wonder, wonder what it might be like if Jurian is the one she chose.

23. Killian

Killian

He hadn't been able to move when he'd seen Adalyn and Jurian walk into the stable area, he'd leant against the large tree and simply observed. He hadn't seen her since she'd opened his door, finding him impaling Alissa.

After she'd run he'd barked for Alissa to leave, needing time to sort through his fucked up thoughts. He'd been furious after their fight and seeing her in the king's arms had made him feel things he hadn't in ten years. Killian had needed an escape, a release, and Alissa had been there to offer it.

Restless thoughts had kept him from sleep, why had she been there? What could she have possibly wanted to say? Two days had passed and the king was still yet to announce their little adventure together for four weeks.

He may as well hand Adalyn over to Polarian now, there's no way she'd want to touch him after what she'd stumbled across. Alissa had been furious when he'd kicked her out, snarling that it hadn't been her place to keep his senses trapped in a bubble.

He hadn't seen her for the past two days either, not that he minded much.

Killian observes Adalyn wrap her arms around the stableboy, they speak briefly before he scurries into the safety of the stables.

From the look on Adalyn's face and her posture, Killian's positive he hadn't left her with warm words.

Adalyn suddenly launches herself at Jurian, wrapping her arms around his neck and sealing her lips to his. Jurian had been surprised, but had succumbed. Their kiss turns passionate, consuming.

Killian contains his anger, his very bones scream from the strain it takes him not to walk over there and rip them apart. He deserved this, gods he's this upset over a kiss, how much had Adalyn felt?

She pulls back, waiting for something.

Dread dampens his anger when Jurian's finest sword floats to her waiting hand. She shares a few words, growing still before looking over her shoulder and meeting Killians burning eyes.

She doesn't so much as blink before turning back to Jurian, Jurian has the good sense to look worried at what he sees on Killian's face.

Killian focuses back on Adalyn, studying the side of her face, the flush in her cheek and the soft curve of her throat. He'd only been buried between her thighs two nights ago, tasting like his ruin.

He braces himself against the tree as her soft, plump lips turn into a smile. She'd never given him a genuine before.

It is heartbreakingly beautiful.

Jurian says few words, Adalyn walks past and presses a kiss to his cheek before sauntering away, swinging her hips as she disappears through the stone arch into the castle. Killian prowls forward, keenly aware of the darkness that covers his broad shoulders and caresses his throat and jaw.

"Before you kill me and stake my head to the castle gate, I didn't think she'd actually kiss me," Jurian bursts out, raising both hands as Killian comes to a grinding halt in front of him. Soldiers send questioning glances their way, never staring for too long.

"She wanted my sword and I gave her a fool's bargain for it, a kiss. I never believed she'd kiss me," His cheeks heat, causing Killian's jealously to stir even more. What are Jurian's feelings regarding Adalyn?

"She's the king's property, it doesn't look good on her or the king if she's out here shoving her tongue down your throat," Killian snaps, his hands shake at his sides.

"Clearly Alissa's pussy isn't that good anymore if you're angry at me over a little kiss." Jurian snaps, eyes hardening. "You don't get to be angry or jealous after what she walked in on. You don't have the fucking right to lecture me when I know you were in her room two days ago, enjoying everything she offered you."

"Shut your mouth." Killian stalks forward, aching to throw his fist into Jurian's smug face. It wouldn't have been the first time they'd beaten each other to a pulp before finding familiar ground.

One of the many perks of being brothers, they aren't afraid to knock each other down a peg.

"Or what? What is so special about Adalyn that has you acting like an asshole? You detested the human females before you met her, so what's changed Killian?" he demands, crossing his arms over his chest.

Killian can't voice that he has changed, that saving her life that first night has damned him to the depths of hell because somehow he can't get enough, doesn't think he could ever *have* enough of her to be satisfied.

"She told you her name?" he asks instead.

"Yes, she did. I earnt the fucking right to know it. I'm her friend Killian, she needs one desperately right now." Jurian shoulders past Killian, "get your shit together man, you have a task in front of you to accomplish. Either you have her or Polarian does and I know who I would rather she give herself to."

"She will never touch me again." Killian half turns towards his retreating figure. Jurian pauses, sighs and looks back to Killian.

"As much as she won't admit it, she would. She sees right through you, or thought she had until she saw you with Liss." Jurian shakes his head.

"She won't forgive me if she ever finds out my task." Killian voices one of the fears that have been chasing him from the moment the king informed him of what he must do. They all expect him to fail but the only person he is going to fail is Adalyn and damn himself in doing it.

"She may not, but I'd rather her angry and alive over dead." Jurian turns away from him, shoulders tense, "I don't care if you sleep with her Killian. Just because we declare something it doesn't mean we have to uphold that vow forever. People change, *you* change and there is nothing wrong with that."

"I'm sorry—for acting how I did." Killian looks away, over the dreary castle wall to the gathering dark grey clouds on the horizon.

"She's gone to the library if you want to play hero, that's why she wanted my sword. I refused to tell her what happens to the king's consorts, so she's gone hunting for the information on her own."

Killian splutters, balking as he snaps his head to Jurian.

"How does she know about the library?" Killian almost yells. Jurian grimaces, smiling painfully as he turns to face him.

He has the good sense to retreat slowly.

"I may have accidently told her when I found her in the gardens."

"The hounds are going to devour her." Killian feels himself tremble.

"You better hurry along then." Jurian turns and flees into the safety of the stables. Killian turns and runs into the castle, snarling and shoving people aside through the courtyard until he reaches a small hidden door that works as a short cut through the castle.

He could find his way through this castle blind, having lived here for centuries. The library is in the catacombs, the iron door sits at the back of the castle in a lower, forgotten level that no Valarki inhabit.

Killian sends a pray to the forgotten gods, asking them to keep her alive until he can arrive.

He leaps over the railing and sails to the floor, landing with a thud. Dust explodes around him in a wave as he rises.

The iron door hangs open, the golden lights flicker.

Two growls not of this world reach his ears just as a delicate scream is ripped from a feminine throat.

He launches towards the door, rallying his magic, *Adalyn.*

Please don't let me be too late.

Killian leaps down the spiral stairs, cloaking himself in utter darkness until he is nothing more than a shadow to Adalyn. He's half afraid she'd let the hounds have her if he came to her rescue.

She stands, hands shaking violently as droplets of blood drip from her hands to the ground before her. The two hounds snarl and snap as they tower over her, he isn't sure where the blood comes from but he's relived to see her alive.

He'd kill Jurian himself for sending her down here.

"Get back!" She shouts, swinging the sword wildly.

Killian sends a rolling wave of his darkness out, the hounds stiffen and shrink. Whining as Killian's magic wraps around their minds and shows them their nightmares. Adalyn heaves in each breath, the scent of her tears fill Killian's senses as she lowers her sword.

Killian stays silent and still, feeding on the fear that funnels through the connection to the hounds. It'd been too long since he'd allowed himself the release, the fear of other magical creatures always kept him sated for longer.

Killian went by many names.

A general.

The king's second hand.

The shadow of death.

But no one ever whispers about the notorious trait that everyone should truly fear from him. Once, in the ancient dialects his magic had been recorded.

A dark Valarki, a rare mutated kind that gave the new born powers that no creature should have ever possessed. Killian is death and darkness himself, every few weeks he must feed from fear he inflicts on others.

Soul eater.

Dream destroyer.

It's the one thing he hopes Adalyn never has to discover about him, that he truly is as twisted as the other Valarki, if not more. He is darkness while she is light.

She doesn't cower from the two hounds, now pressing themselves into the ground and clawing at their faces. They know better than to get on Killian's bad side and hurting Adalyn had earnt them a one way ticket to torture.

A groan echoes along the skull walls, Killian watches as the library doors open inwards. Soft golden light illuminates the room as a fire crackles.

Adalyn keeps the sword clenched tightly in a knuckle white grip as she runs through the two hounds, barrelling into the safety of the library.

Killian slowly walks over, watching as she stands before the large columns of old books. Her gasp of awe slightly relaxes him. She drops the sword on the table, half in a daze as she walks to the closest row of books. A pale hand runs along the spines as she walks deeper into the library, slowly reading each title.

He could happily stand here all day, watching her human emotions control her so thoroughly and visibly. She pulls a thin book from a row up high and walks back to the table, she pauses and looks to the fire.

He bites his bottom lip to stop a chuckle giving him away, she grabs the back of one chair and drags it towards the fireplace. Once she's happy with it she collapses into the seat, cracking open the pages. The library seems to sigh with relief, more than happy to keep her safe and enjoy her company. The doors close, locking Kilian out.

He lets the darkness fall from him, he grabs the snouts of each hound and forces their ruby eyes to focus on him as he releases his hold on their mind.

"You touch her again and you *die.* Is that clear?" He snarls. The hounds whine, hiding their bony tail between their legs. He releases their jaws, stepping back. He brushes his hands down his suit and straightens. She'd be safe once she left, whenever that might be.

Killian reluctantly leaves the catacombs, shutting the door behind him. It's best no other Valarki suspects she's down there.

As he reaches the first civil floor a human servant approaches him, her brown hair is dull while her cheeks are hollow. The emptiness in her eyes is much, much worse.

"The king requires your presence," she rasps. Once the message leaves her lips she turns and stumbles away, her rail thin body barely keeping her standing.

Killian shoves down his disgust and hatred for what his kind do to the humans.

Once he'd been a dreamer.

Killian slowly makes his way to the throne room, mentally preparing himself for whatever the king is going to tell him. Knowing Killian's luck, it isn't going to be anything good.

He'd endure it, had endured it for so long already.

Knowing Adalyn's safe is enough for him to fall into the easy mask of being an unfeeling monster, the role he plays far too well.

Maybe it isn't so much of a mask anymore.

Killian strolls into the throne room, sliding his hands into his pocket as he looks up to see the king leaning back in his throne.

The king gives him a poisonous smile. "We have a traitor in our midst."

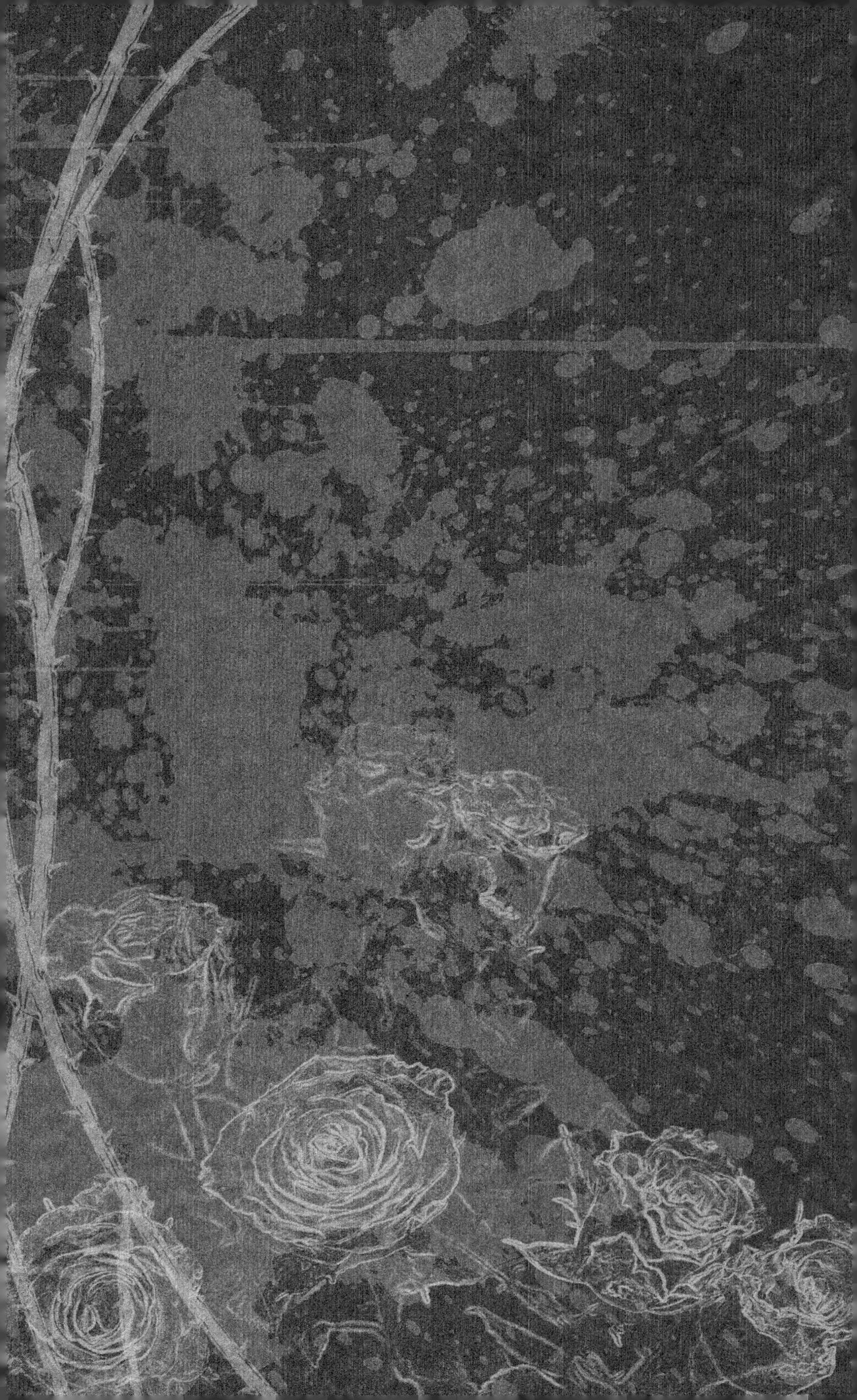

24. Adalyn

Adalyn

Adalyn occupies the small catacomb library into the late hours of the night, a large pile of books written in Valarki text are piled in front of her, towering high above her small form that sits right in front of the round table. She leans back, arching her back in a satisfied stretch; trying to work out the persistent ache that had begun bugging her after the first five minutes of hunching over the first book.

Dust had covered the higher books that Adalyn couldn't reach, only the tips of her fingers had rubbed against the base of their thick spines in writing and runes she couldn't understand. Adalyn had barely been able to read the human language in the books she had managed to find. The library had been created in the catacombs before the castle had towered above it, a small nook crafted from raw magic.

The library looks after itself, as if it has its own heart and soul. Adalyn had been more than perplexed when a warm meal had suddenly appeared on the open book she'd been trying to decipher, her stomach had growled in appreciation. After eating the contents of the hearty soup Adalyn had wandered between the towering aisles once more, plucking each book from its perch and looking for any sign it may tie to the king and his personal affairs. So far she'd found nothing.

Adalyn grumbles as she slouches in the chair, drumming her fingers on the arm rest. Dry blood coats her right hand, dark red flakes coat the table and floor. She'd suffered a small cut when she encountered the hounds made from nightmares. She glances towards the closed library doors, as if she could see through them to the guards that menacingly wait for her.

Adalyn couldn't say what had stopped their attack but she hadn't thought twice before dashing into the safe confines of the books, more than content to spend as many hours as she could in here. Would they attack her once she left?

Voices rumble through the closed doors, startling Adalyn. She leaps from the table and runs to the last row of books that lean dangerously close to the stone wall. Skidding to a stop she plasters herself against the shelves, willing her breathing to slow. She peers through the small opening in the books and looks to the table, relieved to find the books gone and setting undisturbed.

Thank you, she mouths to the library, gently brushing a hand down one of the books.

She swears the air around her warms.

"How long do you reckon it will last?" Jurian asks, strolling into the open library doors. Killian trails after him, running a hand through ragged knotted hair. His shoulders sag slightly, the only sign of exhaustion he shows.

"I don't know. How does he expect me to do all of these missions at the same time?" Killian demands, slumping into the seat Adalyn had been seated at only moments ago. Jurian perches on the table beside him, his golden hair is swept up from his face. He grins lazily, splaying his hands in front of him.

"Because you are Killian Abaddon, bringer of death and guider of destruction. If anyone can accomplish what he's tasked, it's you." Jurian leans back on muscular arms, staring over Killian's head and into the crackling fire.

"He has to know there are many would-be traitors in his mist.

The king does not rule fairly or kindly, our kind still suffer under his hand as well as the other races. Does he want me to kill them all?" Killian idly wonders.

"You're starting to sound like the Killian from before." Jurian murmurs softly, "like the Killian who fought for the injustice of others."

Killian laughs without humour, the sound ringing in the too quiet space.

"Yes and look where wanting to be the hero has gotten me," Killian rests his chin on his palm, staring at the wall in front of him. "My wife and unborn child were murdered, I was tortured for ten years with Alissa being my only momentary escape. The king has held my leash from the first moment I voiced my displeasure for his slaves."

"You are not the villain, Killian." Jurian looks to him, eyes shadowed.

"You are in the wrong tale then, my friend. No matter, I suit being the villain best. It is easier for others to hate me than understand me."

"That's because you don't let anyone close enough to understand you." Jurian retorts.

Adalyn doesn't dare breathe. She should not be here for this conversation.

"It would only be one more thing for the king to hang over me. I don't want anyone else tortured and killed because of my actions or choices." Killian leans back in his chair, combing a hand through his hair once more. "Once I return from this task I will need to leave, if only for a week to clear my head."

"It's going to hurt her," Jurian barely whispers.

"I know." Killian rises from the chair, its wooden legs scrape noisily against the cobblestone floor. He stalks towards the fire that sits directly in front of Adalyn. Her eyes widen as she continues to lean against the book case, unable to take her eyes from him.

He shoves his hands into the pockets of his pants, the orange flames reflect shadows across the hard angles of his face.

Haunted.

Adalyn's mind goes silent as she takes him in, he looks haunted— no— he *is* haunted. Running from the ghosts of his past that won't stop knocking on his back door. Who is he going to hurt? Is it the mysterious woman Adalyn had seen him with?

What could he possibly do that would hurt her? They both looked more than pleased with each other when Adalyn had stumbled across them, coming to apologise like the soft hearted fool she once was. The woman that she had been before her parents had been slaughtered.

The library darkens with Adalyn's mood, though she doesn't notice the drop in temperature or the shadows beginning to gather on the high ceiling. Torches flicker as a breeze stirs through the library, a warning. Jurian peers around, eyebrows raised.

"What's the go with the library?" He scoffs, "has it taken a liking to Adalyn's human ways?"

"I could still kill you for that," Killian growls as he cuts Jurian a stare. Jurian still sported aching ribs and a bruised ego from the beating Killian had given him.

Jurian scowls, remembering how he'd gotten his ass handed to him. "She's stronger than she looks."

"No, she isn't. She may be as quick as a viper with her words and wit but she is human—" Killian's face strains, as if it pains him to say these thoughts out loud, "she is *human* Jurian. Painfully so. We both have the habit of forgetting that crucial detail."

"She lived, didn't she?" Jurian sulks, crossing his arms over his chest. He winces with the movement.

"You are a pain in my ass." Killian turns back to fire, falling into silence as he gives himself over to his no doubt troubled thoughts. Adalyn breathes softly through her nose, exhaustion wars with her good sense to stay alert. How long had she been down here for? She desperately wanted to curl into bed, forgetting all of the bad things that seem to seek her out.

"Someone in this ghastly place has to keep you alert. Are you going to stay here and brood or are you ready to return to your rooms?" Jurian asks, rising from the table. He strides for the closed doors, dressed in loose fitted pyjama pants and shirt. He arches a brow pointedly, "You have a long week of preparing ahead of you, come. You can dwell on the darkness later."

"There is only ever darkness," Killian whispers, clenching his jaw. He turns from the fire and strides to Jurian, swiftly walking to his side. Together they leave through the open doors and Adalyn glimpses the two sleeping hounds.

Once the library doors close the room brightens once more, warming. Adalyn slumps down against the shelf, extending her legs out before her. Walking up the multiple stairs was going to be her greatest challenge. She had failed her task, finding nothing down here.

A pillow and folded quilt blanket appear at her side, hitting the floor with a soft thud.

"Thank you, library." She picks up the pillow and quilt, manages to drag herself to the small area in front of the crackling fire. She sets herself up, lying on her side and snuggling into the soft quilt. The torches blow out and the fire stops crackling, even though its flames continue to burn and comfort Adalyn.

Sorrow gnaws at her bones as she lets herself fall into her memories of her family, of her past and moments that had once brought her tremendous amounts of joy. Silent tears stream down her cheeks, soaking the pillow. She doesn't care, can't seem to find the energy to wipe them away.

She is falling into herself, finding nothing to tether her to what has become her present.

What shall keep her present, when there is nothing but despair waiting for her?

. . .

Adalyn emerges from her room, her bones stiff and aching from sleeping on the library floor. She'd awoken, feeling slightly lighter than she had in days, if not weeks. It's as if the library had taken her pain away and given her warmth and comfort in return.

She mulls over the conversation Killian and Jurian had, unable to piece anything together. She feels utterly stupid, she was never meant for a life of sneaking around and spying. Adalyn had planned for a simple life and this had not been what she's bargained for.

A slim figure bumps into Adalyn, jolting her backwards.

"I'm sorry—" the human slave splutters, turning fearful eyes towards Adalyn. She cowers before her, hiding her scrawny brown hands in the skirts of her apron. Adalyn stands there, mouth slightly ajar.

"You—you can talk?" Adalyn asked in a hushed tone, leaning forward. Fear ignites in the women's dull green eyes, which once would have been a stunning shade of jade and emerald.

"Please, please do not tell his majesty," she begs, almost falling to her knees.

"Of course I won't, why would you think that?" Adalyn gasps, quickly checking both ways down the narrow hall. They're alone, for now.

"The other women in the king's harem—his last lot—they had not cared for the other humans here." She keeps her voice light, eyes straining at the corners. Few scars mar her cheeks and throat, obvious signs of past torture. It curdles Adalyn's stomach, knowing she's felt similar pain.

The cuts on her body hadn't given her any trouble once arriving, the king had healed the one on her thigh while the one on her breast and shoulder had healed unnaturally fast. Adalyn had ruled it down to the type of poultice they'd slathered in before stitching the gashes closed.

She still hadn't exacted her revenge on Polarian for what he'd done to her.

Soon, she promises herself, *soon I will make him suffer.*

"How are you present? All of the other slaves are empty shells walking around, none even acknowledge my presence." Adalyn buries her hands in the fine silk skirts of her dress, feeling guilty that she is being treated so much better than the women in front of her.

"I don't know. I'm assuming the magic they spell over us has worn off over the years. I can't recall much, but recently the veil has been lifted and the fog has cleared." Her gaunt figure shudders violently, "If we are caught talking I will be taken away."

"Can we go somewhere else?" Adalyn pleads, the women looks at her and furrows her brows, "I need answers I can't find elsewhere. The Valarki refuse to give me answers, the library held no hope. I have nothing. What happened to the other women in the kings harem?"

The women pales, her brown skin blanching.

"Is it that bad?" Adalyn fears it might just be, maybe knowing what is to come is far better than not knowing. After all, she is magically bound to the king. He could use his magic and force her hand in whatever he chooses or does with the women once he grows bored.

"It is. I don't know what happens, but once they entered his throne room they never left. Whatever he does with them, it isn't natural." She brushes deep brown strands from her face, her hair is patchy in places on her skull.

"He kills them?" Adalyn feels her hands begin to shake as she struggles to wrap her mind around it. It explains far too much.

Her fate was doomed from the start, from the moment she stepped foot in this castle she was destined to be slaughtered.

"I think so, I wish I had more answers for you. I must be going, I have duties to attend." The women steps to retreat, her dark blue dress is dull and hangs around her bony frame.

"My room is the first on the left in his private hall, if you ever need help or *anything* please go there and hide. I don't care, the door is always unlocked. I hope we can speak again soon." Adalyn swallows her growing fear, knowing any second they could be caught.

"Thank you." The women smiles sadly, "it was nice to meet you. Someone who isn't fry brained."

Adalyn forces herself to smile, if only to ease her company, "As it was you. I'm Adalyn by the way."

"I'm Tabitha. Be safe, Adalyn." Tabitha turns and walks from the hall, slumping her shoulders and dragging her feet. Adalyn is almost certain their conversation had been her imagination with how *unalive* Tabitha currently looks as she walks along.

That is until she flashes Adalyn one last small smile before retreating around the corner.

Adalyn turns and continues through the castle. She mulls over the new information. Should she tell the other women that the king is eventually going to kill them all? What if he doesn't and word reaches him that she's been saying he will? There are far too many things that could go wrong if she isn't careful with how she treads.

For now, she decides to keep the information tucked away, saving it for a rainy day.

Adalyn reaches the castle grounds with ease, dragging herself from her thoughts. Valarki dressed in finery walk to and fro, some sneer while most opt to ignore her. She is more than happy to ignore them right back. Valarki soldiers stalk the high walls, long bows strapped across their backs with their sling full of metal arrows.

From where Adalyn stands she can take in more details of the castle she hadn't had the chance to notice when she'd first arrived. A network of thin cobblestone bridges connect each tower, appearing like a maze. Each bridge has soldiers strolling back and forth, small dots to Adalyn's squinted eyes.

As she silently admires the intricate detail on the stone gargoyles that are perched throughout the castle towers with no order, shouts pull her away. She looks around, slightly bewildered.

Shouts turn to screams, Adalyn's feet take off running before her mind can comprehend who is screaming and why. Heart thumping wildly in her chest as pressure claws up her throat, Adalyn careens through the large arch way and appears before the three large fires.

Deep churning orange eyes meet hers, halting her next step.

A scream rips from Adalyn's throat as Polarian throws the stable boy Adalyn had helped into the closest fire.

No.

No.

No.

NO—

Almost immediately his wings evaporate, his skin melting from bone. His screams pierce Adalyn's ears, leaving a trail of blood leaking from both. She stumbles forward, hand outstretched hopelessly as she watches the small boy die.

Polarian cackles as he grabs another stable boy, the small faerie screams and claws at his muscular arm violently.

Adalyn moves faster than she ever has before, heading straight for Polarian.

Too focused on the stable boy clutched in his hand, he doesn't realise he's left his entire front open for an attack.

Adalyn collides into his chest with the force of four thundering horses, Polarian shouts in rage as his hand lets go of the stable boy.

Adalyn has one last breath of life before the force of colliding with Polarian sends both of them into the raging fire, it opens its flames hungrily.

Furious orange eyes meet her own before she feels the heat encase them.

She truly screams.

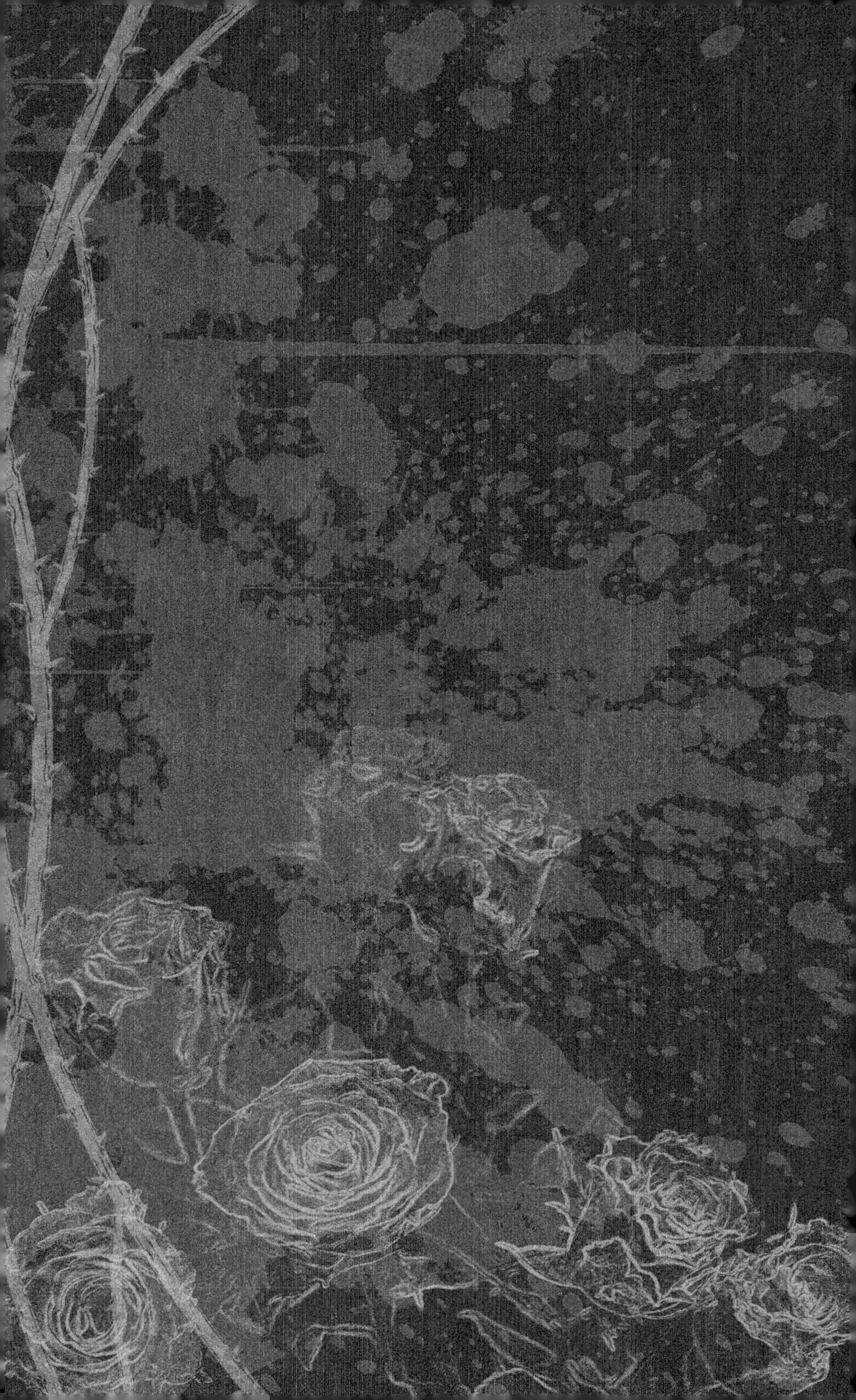

25. Adalyn

Adalyn

Blistering flames threaten to devour Adalyn, hovering a hair's breadth away from her skin. Sweat runs down her face, throat and back in rivets. Adalyn squeezes her eyes shut, waiting for the flames to devour her as they had the stable boy.

She takes a deep breath, and then another.

Large hands dig into her waist painfully, enough to leave bruises. Adalyn forces her eyes open, they water against the heat. Polarian snarls up at her, the rage in his orange eyes matches the flames that dance around them.

"You are only protected because the king has ordered it, otherwise I would not hesitate to hold you while you burn." He digs his nails into her skin for good measure, Adalyn feels her fury rise and that familiar spark of *anger* return with a vengeance.

"You are a coward and you deserve to rot in the depths of hell," she seethes, "I would happily take my own life if it meant taking yours as well. You are nothing more than a self-righteous, arrogant murderer who thinks he's so important. You're not and you will have your day. All the horrible, detestable things you have done are going to come back and haul you away."

Polarian glares at her, saving his words. The roar of the flames is the only sound to be heard around them, the protection Polarian has over them the only thing to keep the flames from consuming them. Adalyn's fierce eyes stray from his face, looking around the bottom depths of the fire they now currently reside in.

Black bones gleam and coax the fire, most shattered and nothing more than a kindling. Adalyn's feels her small breakfast begin to rise.

"I'm getting out." Adalyn begins to struggle for breath, pushing shaky arms against Polarian's chest. He'd landed on his back in the large pit, Adalyn wished he'd impaled himself on one of the gleaming bones poking through the ashes. She'd landed on top of him, her body flush against his.

"You can't get out without me." Polarian wraps his arms around her, "do not think for one second I want to be touching you."

Adalyn holds back a vicious retort, he might still leave her behind for the flames. He rises, his arms wrapped around her small form keep her plastered to his broad chest. He climbs from the fiery pit with ease, throwing Adalyn to the ground once they emerge.

There's a flurry of commotion all around them.

Warm hands find Adalyn, fluttering over her as though she's an injured bird. She lays on her back, gulping in fresh air. Already the burn in her lungs begins to lessen, the bile leaves her throat and settles once more in her stomach. She cracks open her eyes to find Jurian crouching above her, he shudders with relief.

"I thought—I thought you'd died," he barks, his relief morphing to anger, "what the fuck were you thinking?"

Adalyn struggles to rise on her elbows, annoyed that he's shaking her shoulders like a child. "He was throwing the stable boys into the fires." She snaps, "the one...the one I protected when we first arrived went into the flames. He did it to spite me Jurian, I couldn't stand by and do nothing."

A soft, small part of Adalyn curls in on itself. Polarian, a man in her frequent nightmares. Still neither of the Valarki she'd grown to tolerate knew what he'd done to her, knew that he was the one that had skewered her and left her to die.

Jurian grinds his teeth together, his eyes flash a deep shade of red. That is the only warning Adalyn has until Jurian is slamming his fist into the side of Polarian's face, wiping the smug grin off completely.

Adalyn lurches to her feet, blood rushing to her head as Jurian begins to beat into Polarian. They fall to the ground in a flurry of blurred fists and wild spurts of magic. Soldiers bark orders and some scurry off, no one dares interrupt two of the most dangerous Valarki here.

No one except Adalyn.

She spins and runs to the stables, the stable boys scatter like flies as she bursts through the open doors and grabs a rake. She sprints back towards the fight. Jurian is underneath Polarian, his nose is bloody and his bottom lip is split.

Adalyn uses her speed as she spears forward with the rake, a cry breaking from her throat as the four metal prongs groan in resistance before piercing Polarian's back. He roars in pain, looking over his shoulder.

If looks could kill, Adalyn stumbles back; falling over her feet as fear overtakes her.

The three second distraction is what Jurian needed, he gains control of the situation and uses the rake protruding from Polarians back as leverage.

"*STOP!*"

The fires flutter into bare embers at the king's command. All commotion stops. No one dares breath, or move. Jurian drops his raised bloody fists, looking up to see the king furiously striding through the arch entryway. Adalyn drops her head in relief, if the king is here that means the fighting has come to an end.

"What is the meaning of this?" he demands, barely restraining the rage against the situation before him. Adalyn can feel the pulse of his magic as it lashes out at the space around him.

"Polarian was throwing the stable boys into the fire. Adalyn stopped him." Jurian answers, meeting the kings blazing golden stare. His hair floats unnaturally around his tense figure, the late afternoon sun catches on every gold, silver and cream strand.

"Adalyn stopped him?" The king looks towards where she's sprawled ungracefully in the dirt. She props herself up onto her elbows, blinking through the sting in her eyes. He looks ethereal, like an avenging god risen from the flames.

"Yes," she croaks, forcing herself to sit up. She rubs at her throat before continuing, well aware of the many eyes trained on her. "The stable boys have done nothing wrong. I will not stand around and watch innocents be slaughtered."

The king's face darkens, the only indication she's angered him further.

"You are my slave, Adalyn. You will not fend for those who are weaker, you will not interfere with official soldier's duties and you will not defy me." His statement burns into her, she cries out in pain as her brand sends fire up her arm. "You are leaving with Killian for four weeks. You have no say, I order you. If I hear of ill behaviour or another stunt like this, they will be your last four weeks breathing."

Adalyn trembles, four weeks with Killian.

It's almost worse than burning in the eternal flames with Polarian.

"Clean yourself up. You will be collected tonight and escorted to my throne room, I will inform you of your duties. You have disgraced me. I have half the mind to hand you over to Polarian for the night." A growl breaks from Jurian's throat, the king glares at him, "Both of you are suspended of your duties for the rest of the week. You are soldiers, not *children*."

Spinning on his heel, he stalks back into the castle. Once he's gone from view the very earth underneath them seems to relax. Jurian shoves Polarian from him and rushes to Adalyn, ignoring the blood gushing from his nose and other multiple cuts and bruises that litter his handsome face.

"Jurian, your face!" Adalyn breaks into a fit of coughs, Jurian pats her back as she leans on her knees.

"You forget I'm a soldier Red, I've had far worse than what you see."

Adalyn looks at him over her shoulder. "Are you okay?"

Worry creases the lines of his forehead. "I'm worried for you," he whispers.

"Don't be. Lady luck is on my side," she replies bitterly, chasing away the scratch in the back of her throat. "I need water and to bathe. Will you see a healer?"

"I'm heading there after I walk you to your room. I don't trust Polarian." Jurian gently takes her hand in his own and leads them towards the archway. Guards stare mutely at them while the other soldiers snicker. Adalyn can't find it in her to bite back at them, so she ignores their comments and laughs. Adalyn ignores Polarian, who still kneels on the ground. One of his followers attempts to pull the rake from his back. Adalyn grimaces, if only she'd aimed for his throat.

"Smart thinking by the way," Jurian comments, guiding them into the castle. Out of view of prying eyes and listening ears, Adalyn sags, feeling her feet begin to drag. Flashes of the small stable boy going into the fire reply, his screams ring in her ears as she is forced to relive the horrible moment he was burnt alive.

They begin to make the journey to her room, a path she's becoming familiar with. Idly she says, "What was?" She peers up at his battered face. He'd gotten hurt because of her, it seemed to be a pattern she couldn't outrun.

"Using that rake against Polarian, hopefully the bastard feels it tomorrow." He simply grunts, his tongue flicks out and dampens the spilt in his lip. They fall into silence as they finish the walk to her room. She lets her hand slip from his and opens her door, lingering at the threshold.

Adalyn meets his piercing gaze. "Thank you Jurian, for having my back with Polarian. No one has ever gone out of their way for me like that before, not to that extent anyway."

"I hope, regardless of the circumstances, that we may become friends one day Adalyn."

Adalyn has clarity for a rare moment.

A friend.

She finds herself smiling softly, despite the horror that has been the last hour, "I think I may like that a lot. Now go and get cleaned up, the ladies won't love the bloody and battered look."

Jurian laughs, the sound warms Adalyn. If he can laugh through a time like this, then surely she can be strong enough as well.

"Addie, the ladies love this look. I'm tough and badass and notoriously handsome."

Adalyn chuckles, "not this one."

"Killian would kill me if I ever tried."

Adalyn ignores his comment, slamming the door on his stupid grinning face. Once his footsteps retreat she leans against the sturdy frame of the door, the shock finally wears off as she comes to the realisation of what had just transpired.

Screaming rings in her ears, chasing her into the confines of her bathroom.

Adalyn releases a small noise of frustration as she tries to knot the thick swad of silk material around her body, after hurling her guts up she'd entered her room to find a dress folded neatly on the bed, the reek of magic had lingered. No doubt the king's doing. After spending the few hours she could spare hiding under her sheets she'd finally managed to pull herself up and out of her stupor, but now she is beginning to regret it.

Adalyn covers both breasts and winds the material around her waist and ties it off to her left hip, exposing a dangerous amount of her leg. Her back is on display for everyone to see, her cascading hair the only protection she has from roving eyes.

She closes her eyes and takes a deep breath.

She'd made progress today, even though the morning took a

disastrous turn of events. Once her presence wasn't needed she'd be slipping away to pay her respects to the stable boy that was lost today. She would allow herself to mourn before dealing with the other problems at hand.

The king might have killed his last consorts—but why?

Adalyn begins to pace, unable to connect any dots. None of it makes sense to her, did they grow too old? Lose the desire he had first found in them?

A knock startles Adalyn, she turns in time to see Killian opening her door. She sucks in a sharp breath as his eyes meet hers, their blue depths churning. Straight raven hair frames his angled face, only working to accentuate the dark uniform he wears.

He looks regal, ready for war.

Her throat dries. She hadn't spoken or seen him over the last few days, she'd done everything to avoid him at all costs. The last time she'd seen him he'd been buried deep inside—

"Why do you look like you're wanting to spill blood?" Killian asks, raising a dark brow. Adalyn scowls, clenching her hands at her side.

"Because I've had the misfortune of looking at you. Why are you here? I'm capable of walking myself to the throne room," she snaps before stalking over to him. She breezes past him, making a conscious effort not to touch him or inhale his scent.

It takes more willpower then she'll ever admit out loud.

"King's orders," he says smoothly, seemingly not phased by her mood. He walks beside her with ease, eyebrows drawn as his eyes flicker over their surroundings.

The soft echo of their feet hitting the floor fill the silence between them, Adalyn does her best to ignore Killian. She bites down on her cheek, casting her mind to why she must hate him. She forces herself to seem interested in the minimal decoration as they head towards the throne room. There's a certain warmth that lingers in the air, it makes her feel at home.

She frowns, *I bet that's magic. I bet they use that tactic to keep us locked in here.*

"How much did you see?" Killian asks roughly, as if the words pain him to voice. Adalyn allows herself a humourless laugh, after all that has happened today, dealing with this is the last thing she wants to do.

"I saw enough. I don't need your pity. I knew better than to think..." she shakes her head, ignoring the pain in her chest. That's another problem she refuses to think about, can't allow herself to consider. "Never mind. I don't care. You can do whatever and *whoever* you so choose."

"She came to see me and I was angry after our argument."

"I don't care. I don't want to know because if you tell me details I might just stab you." Adalyn huffs, glancing at him out of the corner of her eye. He looks good enough to eat and she hates him for it.

"Are you jealous, Addie?" Killian steps in front of her, the hall around them is deserted and allows them a moment of privacy. Adalyn stops short, glaring up at him with as much disgust as she can muster. She doesn't think it would ever be enough.

"Being jealous would imply I actually care about you. Which I don't," she says evenly, refusing to look away. Killian raises his hand, she doesn't think she breathes as he caresses her cheek with the fondness of a lover; running his calloused palm down her throat to cup the back of her neck.

Killian closes the distance, pulling her to him as his other arm wraps firmly around her waist. She moulds against him perfectly, as if they were built for this. Built for each other. Her hands fly up between them and rest on his chest, nails dig into his shirt but neither know if it's to push him away or bring him closer.

"Your lies taste as sweet as you do." He murmurs, leaning down until his nose grazes hers. All thoughts quiet at his touch, the warmth that now seeps into her. She searches his eyes, looking for any reason to push him away. Looking for a reason to hold him closer.

Adalyn can admit she's all over the place, that nothing in her life right now is stable. That she is broken and may be beyond fixing.

"You need to let me go," she whispers, throat bobbing. Killian chuckles, the broken notes sound sad to her ears.

"Trust me, I would have if I could by now."

"What does that mean?" she demands, frowning up at him. He shakes his head.

"It means I want to kiss you Adalyn and I don't want you to stop me."

The world stops spinning as she's cemented in this moment. Adalyn's silent as she tries to comprehend what he's just said.

"Why would I want to kiss you after I saw you buried in that gorgeous woman, hours after you'd had me?" The feeling of warmth dissolves and turns to hurt and anger. She pushes from Killian, putting space between them. "I don't want whatever this is you're trying to do. I sure as hell won't be your pathetic rebound. You may not respect me more than that, but I do."

Adalyn storms past him, raw and angry. The nerve he has to approach her and demand a kiss. She scoffs as she strides down the hall, she'd rather plaster her lips to Jurian's again than his. Adalyn rounds the corner and walks through the gilded golden doors, Valarki crowd the entire space while human servants cater to their needs.

Moments later Adalyn feels Killian's warm presence at her back. Her body stiffens, getting ready to turn around and give him another outburst of her real thoughts.

"Adalyn—" Killians whisper is lost on Adalyn as the gorgeous woman he'd shared himself with strides towards them with confidence of a hundred women. Her luscious red lips curl seductively as she stares at Killian, her scraps of cloth are barely a dress that cover her generous breasts and wide hips.

Adalyn feels her heart bleeding in her chest, she feels pathetic standing here in something similar, knowing she must look disgusting compared to this woman.

She can’t catch a break.

The woman stops before them, finally acknowledging Adalyn. Her gaze is as sharp as a blade, “ah, so you’re the king's new whore.”

Her words cut with precision, flaying Adalyn from the inside.

26. Killian

Killian

Killian watches Adalyn with anticipation, wondering and waiting with what she might snap back to Alissa. He can't take his eyes from her face as he waits for her anger to rise, for the tell-tale sign of her lips dropping at the corners and her eyebrows drawing down slightly. Adalyn blinks slowly, looking Alissa from head to toe. Killian watches as the fire gutters out from her eyes, leaving dull amber depths behind.

He expects violent words and the threat of death, what he doesn't expect is for Adalyn to bow her head. Her very soul seems to recede into the shell of her body as her shoulders curve inwards. She doesn't utter a word, simply moves around Alissa and heads for the king's gleaming white and gold bone throne. Alissa grins, watching her small figure part the crowd. Other Valarki stare down their noses at Adalyn and utter sharp words of hate that ring in Killian's ears.

It makes her seem smaller. Frail. *Broken.*

"Was that necessary?" He asks, glaring as Alissa finally turns to face him. She shrugs, sipping from her glass of wine.

"I was simply stating the facts, it's not my fault she's upset over it." She scrunches her nose up. Killian tries to rein in the roaring in his mind. He looks past Alissa to see Adalyn bowing before the king, the empty look in her eyes has him moving through the crowd.

He'd heard what she'd done to Polarian today, how she threw both of them into the fire. Was she willing to forfeit her life? Had she known the flames wouldn't harm the either of them? It had left Killian furious, but it had given the king the opening he needed to bring down his task for Killian.

Alissa shadows Killian, eager to see.

"Adalyn, you've met Killian before," the king rumbles, peering down at her. She rises from her bow, gazing up at him. Killian stops at the edge of the crowd, Alissa lingers slightly too close for comfort to his left.

"I have." Her words ring hollow, empty.

How could she let Alissa get under her skin so easily? Does she not realise she's much more than that?

"For the next four weeks you will be accompanying him on a mission I've ordered. Your required skill set is needed, if you try to run and escape there will be consequences. Killian will temporarily own you for this time, whatever he says you do, you do not argue or fight against him. If you have concerns you go to him." The king leans back in his throne, pinning her to the spot, "he is your master and you his slave."

Adalyn winces, looking down to her branded wrist. The golden brand alters with the king's magic, droplets of golden blood appear around the daggers sharpened tip. It'd be beautiful if no one knew the meaning behind the brand.

"Tomorrow morning you will be in his care. Do not displease me."

Adalyn nods once, breathing deeply. She doesn't protest, simply bows. It unnerves Killian, seeing her so vacant and submissive. He combs over their recent argument, trying to piece together why she's suddenly taken a back seat in her mind.

You're nothing but the king's whore after all.

Killian's stomach lurches as guilt weighs down on him.

He'd called her that out of anger, wanting to hurt her how she'd hurt him. Only to have Alissa do the exact same.

"Of course, your majesty." She rises from her bow and waits for dismissal. The king smiles down at her, pleased with her subdued reaction. He waves a hand and the festivities begin once more. Adalyn melts back into the crowd, as if she hadn't occupied the space moments ago.

Killian takes a step towards her retreating figure when Alissa wraps a hand around his arm, pulling him up short. He glares at her.

"You are not running after a *human slave* in front of the most important people of this court," she hisses into his ear, earning a scowl.

"She's upset."

"Who cares? She's a slave Killian, the sooner you realise that the better. You know she has mere months before the king performs the ritual. Don't let yourself get caught up in the rush."

Killian goes utterly still, recalling the ritual. The brutality of it all.

Alissa smiles with fake sympathy, patting his cheek. "Come now, let's have a wine or two and feast on the cheese and assortment of crackers. I've been waiting all day for this."

Jurian finds them moments later, a glass of ale in one hand and a bread stick in the other. They both lead Killian towards one of the empty tables at the back of the room, piling a plate of different nibbles in front of him and a glass of whiskey over ice.

Killian gulps the amber liquid down, closing his eyes to memorise the burn.

Tomorrow would be the first step towards utter hell.

Killian stumbles down the hall, the world around him teters sideways, or maybe that's him. He isn't sure. After Alissa and Jurian had dragged him to one of the feast tables he'd gobbled down glass after glass of whiskey. He hadn't seen Adalyn since she'd stood before the king and gods be damned he wanted to see her. They're to be in each other's presence for the next four weeks, he didn't like the thought of her not talking to him.

He didn't like that he thought that, either.

Killian continues to walk up the spiralling stair case, past his private chambers, past the king's private hallway. Killian goes up another three levels, finally finding the short hall that will lead him out to a small balcony, to give him some fresh air and peace. He uses the stone wall as a guide as he walks down the hall, frowning to find the wooden door ajar.

With a gentle push the door swings open, silver moonlight spills over the balcony. Killian can't see anyone until he takes a step out.

Adalyn leans against the stone ledge furthest to the right, she faces the moon with her eyes closed. Killian goes still, raking his eyes over her. She'd donned a large white knitted jumper, it swallows her small frame and gathers at her wrists.

She hasn't heard him.

He walks to the ledge, bracing himself against the cool stone. He doesn't make his steps silent, wanting her to know he's there. He looks over the balcony, watching as guards patrol the stone bridges that breach between each tower. Most towers have a small balcony for reprieve as well, if the hustle and bustle of the castle becomes too much.

Killian hides out on the balconies or below in the hidden hot pool that's in the catacombs. He'd been meaning to go there since he'd returned, and with tonight being his last night he's in no state to be submerged in water, lest he drowns.

For a moment they're both silent.

Adalyn sighs, "What do you want?"

"I came for fresh air."

"And you just happened to come to the same balcony that I occupy?" she snaps, there's a hint of exhaustion in her voice. Killian grinds his teeth.

"What would you like me to say? No matter what comes out

of my mouth it makes you recoil." He glares at her, meeting her amber eyes. A line forms between her brows as she watches him, huddled in the warmth of her jumper.

"You're right." She looks away from him, deciding to stare out over the castle wall and to the squabble of buildings that surround it. Once it hadn't been such a sore sight, when the population wasn't so overcrowded. The homes were kept in nice shape, there was room to breathe. Now there's a layer of grime in the air as the Valarki and human slaves live atop one another.

"Is it possible to form a truce between us?" Killian asks, "if only for the four weeks. Once we return you can carry on hating me."

"I don't hate you Killian." Adalyn makes a frustrated noise, "not totally, anyway."

"Is it because of Alissa?" He asks, daring to approach the reason as to *why* she's suddenly repulsed by him.

Adalyn tenses, a muscle in her jaw clenches and for a moment Killian braces himself for her wrath and fire, but it never comes. Adalyn deflates.

"So that's her name."

"Yes. I've known her for millennia but we've only been friends for the last ten years." Killian pushes away the memory of his family's murder, tonight is not the night to expose his secrets. Not to a woman that currently hates him. Adalyn scoffs, causing Killian to look at her once more.

"Right, just a friend."

Killian feels his cheeks heat, he scrubs a hand down his face, "It is just how Alissa is. I am not the only male she beds."

"I don't want to hear it Killian." Adalyn steps away from the balcony and stares directly at him. "I don't want your excuses or explanations. I just want to forget."

"If you'd let me explain—" he takes a steady step towards her.

"You don't get to explain and I don't want to hear it." Adalyn squeezes her hands into fists, the white jumper falls down her right shoulder, exposing the thin strap of her night gown and the sliver of a scar from when Polarian had used his sword against her.

That moment feels so long ago.

"Adalyn—" Killian reaches towards her. She shakes her head as she walks past him, careful to keep out of his grasp.

"You're drunk Killian, go and drink some water and go to bed. This is pathetic, even for you." She slips back into the hall and disappears from sight. Killian listens to her soft foot falls until he can no longer hear them. He slumps against the railing and looks towards the swollen moon.

"You took a wife and unborn child from me, and now you've given me...a beautiful human who hates me. Why?" He asks, knowing he won't get an answer.

Maybe, he thinks, *maybe this is my punishment. Maybe I deserve to suffer.*

27. Adalyn

Adalyn

Adalyn finishes braiding her thick auburn hair, using a piece of white ribbon Allison had gifted her to keep it from unravelling. She lets it hang over her left shoulder, it just reaches the waistband of her brown riding pants. She'd truthfully never ridden a horse on her own before, but she refuses to ride with Killian again. Adalyn runs a hand down the front of her white shirt, tucking it in at the hem. After donning a simple black cloak and clasping it at the base of her throat she grabs her saddle bag, full of clean clothes and hidden fruit, dried meat and a full water skin. Not having to wear a dress has liberated her, especially the fur lined boots she now wore. Allison had agreed to help her pack the night before, after she'd gone looking for a place to clear her mind and had found the balcony.

A drunk Killian had found her not long after.

She pushes all thoughts of him from her mind as she begins to count each breath, journeying through the castle to the stables. Her heart constricts for the stable boy who had been thrown into the fire and had turned into smoke and bone.

She hadn't found the courage to visit the others, afraid her presence might also make them a target for Polarian's sick and twisted ways.

Adalyn emerges into the stable yard, the three fires roar today as soldiers continues to throw pieces of meat and other questionable items into their hungry depths. They all ignore her as she stands off to the side, patiently waiting for Killian. It's still early morning, the warmth and golden rays of the sun are only just beginning to kiss the land.

Tapping a foot to expel her nerves, Adalyn mulls over why the king had punished her with this. What need would Killian have with her for the next four weeks? What assets could she possibly possess for Killian to utilise? She doesn't even know what his mission is or where they're going.

For all she knows, he could have been asked to take her deep into the mountains and feed her to the other monstrous creatures that lay in wait. No one would know, or care.

That's not true, Allison and Tabitha would care.

Adalyn rubs her eyes, *you may hate Killian now for what he's done, but you know he wouldn't kill you.*

She hated that the small voice in her mind was right.

"Don't look so stricken, it's only a horse." Killian's deep, warm voice jolts her from her thoughts. She releases her bottom lip from her teeth and finds him towering before her with a black stallion at his side. The horse is dressed in black scale like armour that covers his throat and front legs, as well as his hide and back legs.

It's the stallion Killian had been riding when they'd returned from their conquest.

The horse snorts his impatience, stamping a heavy black hoof into the dirt. His dark eyes are so brown they're flecked with black.

Adalyn finds her voice, tearing her eyes from the horse to glare at Killian, "I know what a horse is." She refuses to meet his eyes and instead finds herself staring at his pointed ears. He's wearing his hair half up and half down, exposing his Valarki heritage.

He sighs, running a hand down the horse's black face.

"This is going to be a long four weeks."

She ignores his comment, “where’s my horse?”

He raises a dark brow, gesturing to his stallion at his side, “we’re doubling.”

“Like hell we are.” She snaps her gaze to his, curling her hands into fists. Maybe she could flee to the king, beg him to punish her in some other way and not send her on this outrageous task. Killian’s eyes darken, his face as hard as stone.

“Just get on the damn horse, Adalyn.”

“No.” She crosses her arms over her chest, praying he can’t hear the uneven beating of her heart. She tears her eyes from his, looking towards the slave Valarki that tend to other horses. They peer towards her with wide milky eyes, curious and careful.

“I’m not having his argument with you here in front of everyone to witness. Get on the damned horse and once we’re out of the castle gates you can unleash,” he growls.

Her heart thunders.

Her fear is mingled with the slightest hint of arousal at the demand in his voice, at the depth of it. His words had skittered over her skin, warm and demanding. She pushes all thoughts of desire from her mind, focusing on the hurt.

He doesn’t understand that the thought of being so close to him makes her sick, will make her want to peel her skin from her bones and flee. He doesn’t realise how much what they’d shared had meant to *her.* She was still coming to terms with how much she cares for him, to share her body with him. She wrangles that thought in, not wanting him to read her emotions that would be written on her face as plain as day.

He simply stares at her, waiting.

She waits as well, she could do this all day.

“Do you even know how to ride a horse?” He relents.

“Yes.” *No*, but she isn’t going to tell him that.

He turns, striding towards the stables as his black stallion follows beside him. He pauses in front of one of the stable boys, gesturing into the stables and nods once. The boy scurries off, Killian turns and gestures for Adalyn to approach. She adjusts her saddle bag at her side with shaky hands and slowly walks towards him, thankful his back is turned so he can't see the tremor that courses through her.

Can't see her admiring the view from behind, how his pants sculpt the muscles in his backside.

Damn you! She curses silently, *why do you get to look good enough to eat?*

The stable boy returns, leading a saddled white mare behind him, her long mane is braided with red roses while her large blue eyes look around.

"Here you are, general," the stable boy squeaks, his wings fluttering nervously behind him. After he passes the black leather reins into Killian's open hand he scurries off, hiding in the stables. Adalyn scowls, annoyed that Killian hadn't even thanked him.

"Here's your horse," Killian says between gritted teeth, holding the reins out for her to take. She gingerly plucks the leather straps from his open palm, her fingers skim the warmth of his skin. The mare simply looks at her with ocean eyes, white tail swishing.

Adalyn watches silently as Killian throws his reins over the stallion's thick neck, grabs onto the saddle and mounts in one smooth move. He stares down at her, blue eyes narrowing. Adalyn clasps her saddle bag to the leather saddle before copying his movements, finding it far harder to climb into the seat.

Once she's righted and her boots are in the stirrups she straightens, clasping the reins and the saddle horn with both hands for dear life.

"I asked for a placid mare. She will follow, all you have to do is hold on," Killian says, clicking his tongue. His stallion begins to walk forward, heading for the path that runs along the castle wall. Her mare follows, Adalyn tightens her thighs as she gets a feel for the odd jostled movement.

"I know you can't ride." Killian says, his words floating over his shoulder. Adalyn bares her teeth at his broad back where two long swords are sheathed, of course he's armed. She hadn't even thought to grab a weapon.

"I don't know what you're talking about."

"I can taste your lies, Adalyn," he replies coolly, his form now tense. Adalyn blushes as she recalls how sweet he mentioned her lies are. Almost as sweet as her.

"I wouldn't have to lie all the time if you didn't speak such rubbish," she grumbles back, huffing as she runs her eyes up the large cobblestone wall that surrounds the castle. Her heart picks up in anticipation, she may still be a slave but she'd be out of this damned castle and have some free rein to relax.

Killian barks orders ahead of them as they reach the large arched stone gates. Adalyn peers up, finding the two stone gargoyles facing each other; their stone expression frozen in snarls of rage. She wonders...are they living things beneath the stone? Have they been spelled to be frozen as decorations for an eternity? It's definitely something the king would do.

A cold wind ruffles Adalyn's hair and cloak as the large gates are opened, exposing the grey barren land that surrounds the castle. Adalyn keeps her head high, refusing to acknowledge her fear. Killian leads his steed through the arches, wisps of darkness fall from him and curl into the ground before disappearing. Adalyn urges her mare forward, avoiding the stares of the guards that are now focused on her.

With a subtle click the doors are closed and locked behind them. Adalyn doesn't bother glancing back, she looks around and takes a deep breath. Flexible freedom.

Adalyn stays silent as they walk through skeletal trees, the thudding of hooves is all that can be heard for miles. They reach a cross road, a wooden rickety sign has been nailed into one of the larger dead trees. Adalyn squints, trying to decipher the language that's been burnt into the moulding wood.

"It's Valarki. You won't be able to read it," Killian says, studying the wooden sign. Adalyn pulls her mare to a stop beside him, a spark of satisfaction zings through her when her mare listens without complaint.

"Where are we going?" she asks, sneaking a glance his way.

"Towards the mountains that surround the castle and then through the forest." He gives her the bare minimum amount of information. She presses her lips into a thin line, not wanting to pry. Prying would only spark an argument between them.

Killian clicks his tongue, turning his horse towards the left. Adalyn follows, falling back behind him. For miles all she can see are the grey skeletal trees, it unsettles her immensely. There's something wrong about ground they walk upon, the air that hangs heavily around them.

"What's wrong with this forest?" She asks, knowing he's the only one who can give her answers. He'd been somewhat honest with her before the Alissa situation, so she can only hope he'd give her the truth.

"It's cursed."

"Why?"

"Because it is," he huffs, tensing in his saddle.

"Oh my god, do I have to pry the answer out of your stupid mouth?" she snaps, her frustration getting the best of her, "What happened to the truce you wanted?"

"You've made it clear you don't want anything from me, so why should I bother? You'll get sick of hearing yourself talk and shut up eventually," he snaps back, his words so deep they blend with a throaty growl. From where she sits she can see him clench his fists. She's struck a nerve.

"So you just expect me to sit in silence for the next four weeks?" She digs her heels into her mare, urging her forward. She walks beside Killian now, glaring at him. His eyes slide towards her before focusing ahead once more.

"Yes."

She feels her hackles rise.

"You know before we arrived here, I thought you had a good bone *somewhere* in your body. After we messed around and then

I caught you with Alissa hours later, I realised the only good bone in your body is the one in your pants. Even then, it's tainted." She funnels her hurt into anger, wanting to hurt him how he'd hurt her. "Now you're just being an ass to me for the sake of it."

"Do you expect me to grovel at your feet for forgiveness?" He demands, finally turning to face her. His eyes blaze with anger, their blue depths glow eerily. Adalyn would admire the contrast of his eyes against the grey background if they weren't in an argument.

"I—"

He cuts her off, "You said moments ago what *we* were doing was just messing around. Nothing serious. So why should I have known sleeping with Alissa would have upset you? From the start you have shown me nothing but disdain unless it's my finger curled inside of you."

Adalyn feels her cheeks heat with anger and embarrassment, "Yes and what a mistake that has turned out to be!"

He laughs dryly, "So now it's a mistake?"

"You know what? Yes, those times I shared with you were a mistake. I should have saved myself for someone who actually gives a shit about me. It's clear I've been nothing but a distraction for you from your own horrible life." She bares her teeth at him, "News flash, Killian, everyone has a shit life. You're not the only one who suffers and is plagued by demons."

"So I make one wrong decision and now everything we shared is a mistake? You're accusing me of using you and I have never once used you." His voice echoes between the trees, "I could say the exact same back. You used me to get away from the horrors of what happened to your family, of the current situation you're in right now. Don't you *dare* sit there and accuse me of things that are false."

"Yes!" Adalyn throws her hands into the air, startling her mare. Her eyes burn, but she carries on. "I have never been with anyone before you. Everything I *gave* you and *shared* with you were firsts for me. Being that intimate with someone actually means something to me."

Killian's eyes darken.

"After having you so intimately and then to find..." her voice breaks, she forces herself to look away from him, "and then to find you buried inside of her. It was a slap in the face. It hurts. I know I am nothing special, I know I am human and I can never be as stunning as the Valarki females are. I thought what we were doing meant something to you as well."

"It did."

"Don't lie to me now Killian." Adalyn brushes away the few tears that have fallen, "if what we shared meant anything to you, the thought of being that close with another female wouldn't have even been a thought crossing your mind. When I look at you now, I am reminded of that moment I opened your door. I can't just see you anymore, I now see you buried in her."

Killian falls into silence. It's deafening.

They continue walking in silence, Adalyn sniffles. Her heart is aching, which only makes her eyes water more. She'd been foolish to tell him the truth, to put her heart on the line and tell him exactly why what he did had hurt her.

Naïve. She'd been naïve, thinking she could mean anything to him.

Adalyn gets lost in her thoughts, avoiding looking in his direction. She'd made an even bigger mess of things, splurging her pain to him. As if he could fix it. He is the reason it all broke in the first place.

"May I explain?" Killian asks softly. His voice startles Adalyn, they'd been walking in silence for that long she'd almost been able to forget he was walking beside her. She tangles her fingers in her mare's mane, nodding once. She may not believe a word he says, but he'd feel like he accomplished something.

"I have never once been with a human before. The thought had never crossed my mind. After seeing how the other Valarkis treat your kind I made it my personal mission to never get entangled with one. I actively showed my distaste for them," he begins.

"If you're going to sit there and tell me how being a human is my downfall, save your words," Adalyn mumbles.

"Can you simply listen and not interrupt me?" he asks. Her silence is answer enough for him. "Before I led the conquest I was sleeping with Alissa, yes, but it was a release. I care for her because she's one of my best friend's but when we slept together it wasn't anything more than chasing a temporary release. Alissa sleeps with any male or female who shows her attention, it's who she's always been. I can guarantee after you saw us together, she would have found another to bed that night.

"I lead the conquest, intent on returning home with the women the king wanted and then making myself scarce. I never planned to save you. I never schemed ahead of time. I never seduced you or used my charms to get you in my bed." Killian takes a steadying breath, "You are not what I expected. You surprise me at every single turn, you have a fire inside of you that refuses to go out. For the hundreds of years I've been alive, no other human woman has ever caught my attention the way you have."

Adalyn bites her bottom lip.

"What we shared does mean something to me. It has from the moment you woke me from a nightmare with your lips against mine. You know exactly how dangerous I am, how dark it is inside of me and you still tried to help me after everything I'd done."

Killian pulls his horse to a stop, her mare stops in time with his own. His warm fingers gently grasp her chin and turn her face towards him. Her leg presses against his own as she finds herself leaning into his touch, staring up into his eyes. He searches her face, brushing his thumb against her cheek.

"If I had known we were both on even ground with how we felt, Alissa wouldn't have been a thought. It is hard for me to show any emotion, especially in that castle. You are enslaved to my king and it enrages me. I can't actively do anything about it, his magic is chaotic." He leans his forehead against Adalyn's. "I care for you Adalyn, deeply. As much as we go for each other's throats, I have come to find comfort in your touch."

"Killian..." Adalyn trails off, her heart unsure of what she should do. She's still hurting and his betrayal still feels fresh, but she can't deny that she does care for him. She wouldn't be so upset over what he did if she didn't care.

"I don't expect anything from you Addie, I needed you to hear my side and try to understand why I did what I did. It was foolish and I let my emotions rule over me. I never intended to hurt you and I truly am sorry, but there is only so many times I can say sorry."

Adalyn swallows the tightness in her throat, "I...I just need time."

"I know sweetheart, and I will give you as much as you need. If you decide that I'm no longer a person of interest, I can respect that decision and keep it civil. We're together for four weeks and I was hoping we could find common ground for the duration." He brushes away a stray tear, offering her a soft, sad smile.

"I'll try not to go for the throat next time," Adalyn mumbles, her cheeks heating slightly.

"I would appreciate that," he chuckles, "although seeing you fired up does wonders for my *one good bone*."

Adalyn slaps his shoulder, barking out a broken laugh, "you are insufferable."

He grins, a hint of light sparking in the blue depths, "I know."

"Truce then?" Adalyn asks, tilting her head to the side gently. Her nose brushes his own, the simple movement has her tensing in her seat as arousal sparks deep in her belly. He still grips her face, his touch a gentle caress. His nostrils flare slightly, making her cheeks burn.

"I can live with that. Shall we continue?" His voice is a deep rumble in his chest, anticipation claws up Adalyn's throat. She fights with the side of her that begs for his touch, begs for his attention. She's still upset with him and if she gives in now, he might use her weakness against her. He towers above her, she'd rested her hands against his thigh at some stage. She digs her nails into the thick material.

"Yes, we...probably should." She says breathlessly, losing herself in his warm touch and deep words. *Think with your brain, not your lady bits.* She repeats the chant in her mind, feeling his hot breath hit her mouth.

"We'll set up camp tonight once we reach the forest." Killian rumbles, brushing his nose against her cheek. She locks up in her seat, her entire body keenly aware of his simple touch. She can't form words, too focused on just how close his mouth is.

"If you keep looking at me like that Adalyn, I may just kiss you." He swallows hard, chest heaving. She's glad to know she isn't the only one affected so deeply when they're this close. She takes her bottom lip between her teeth, sucking before letting it fall from her mouth.

"Then do it." She closes the small distance, brushing her lips against his own. They're soft and damp, as if he'd been waiting for her to make the decision. Giving her the power to decide how far this may go. Adalyn reaches up and intertwines her hands into his loose hair, opening her mouth and tangling their tongues together. Killian's large hands travel down her side, in one swift movement she's plucked from her saddle and straddling his lap. Her mare doesn't move, unphased.

He kisses her back with the desperation she feels. As if she could never get enough. She plasters her chest against his own, rubbing her breasts into the material. Killian runs his large hands over her thighs, reaching around to grasp her ass tightly. He grinds her against his very obvious arousal. Adalyn moans, Kilian captures the sound with his mouth.

They're a tangle of teeth and tongue, kissing the other as if it's more important than the air they breathe. Adalyn thinks it may be, nothing has ever made her feel as good Killian has. Not even close.

He grabs her bottom lip between his teeth, sucking and biting gently. Adalyn gasps at the sudden sharp pain, the tang of blood fills her mouth. Killian breaks the kiss, breathing heavily. Adalyn stares at him, wide eyed. His wild eyes rein in the desire and heat. He rests his forehead against hers, wrapping his arms tightly around her waist. She presses her hands onto his chest, feeling the rapid pulse of his heart.

"We can never just have a simple kiss can we?" Adalyn says, still wrapping her head around how she'd gotten onto his saddle. He chuckles, shaking his head gently.

"No, I don't think it will ever be that simple when it comes to us." He leans back, brushing auburn strands back behind her ear. He gently places a kiss on her nose before grasping her chin in his hand and lowering his mouth to her own.

His mouth is gentle, tender. The kiss is slow and soft, making Adalyn's heart spasm in her chest. She moves her lips softly against his own, melting into his embrace. This kiss is more intimate, more personal. Killian breaks away first, kissing her forehead.

"I'm placing you back on your mare now otherwise we'll both get carried away," he declares, settling his hands on her hips. Adalyn nods, trying to convince herself that riding her own horse is definitely a safer option.

"Time Addie, time," he murmurs into her ear as he gently helps her back into her own saddle. Adalyn settles into her saddle, looking up to find Killian adjusting his pants. His cheeks are flushed, his hair tangled from where she'd bury her fingers into the silk strands.

"Let's go then," Adalyn sighs, tapping her horse into a walk, "otherwise time will be the least of my worries."

Killian's deep chuckle chases after her, warming her from her toes to the tips of her ears. Adalyn hides a smile. He's right, they do need time. If only so Adalyn can forgive him for past mistakes and find her trust in him once more.

If he continues to kiss her like that, she'll dive head first into all that he is. If she doesn't work through her feelings for him before then, their relationship would be tainted from the start. Killian trots past her, winking as he goes. He urges his stallion into a smooth canter, Adalyn's mare is quick to follow his lead.

A weight lifts from Adalyn's chest as she follows after him. Maybe the gods are on her side for once.

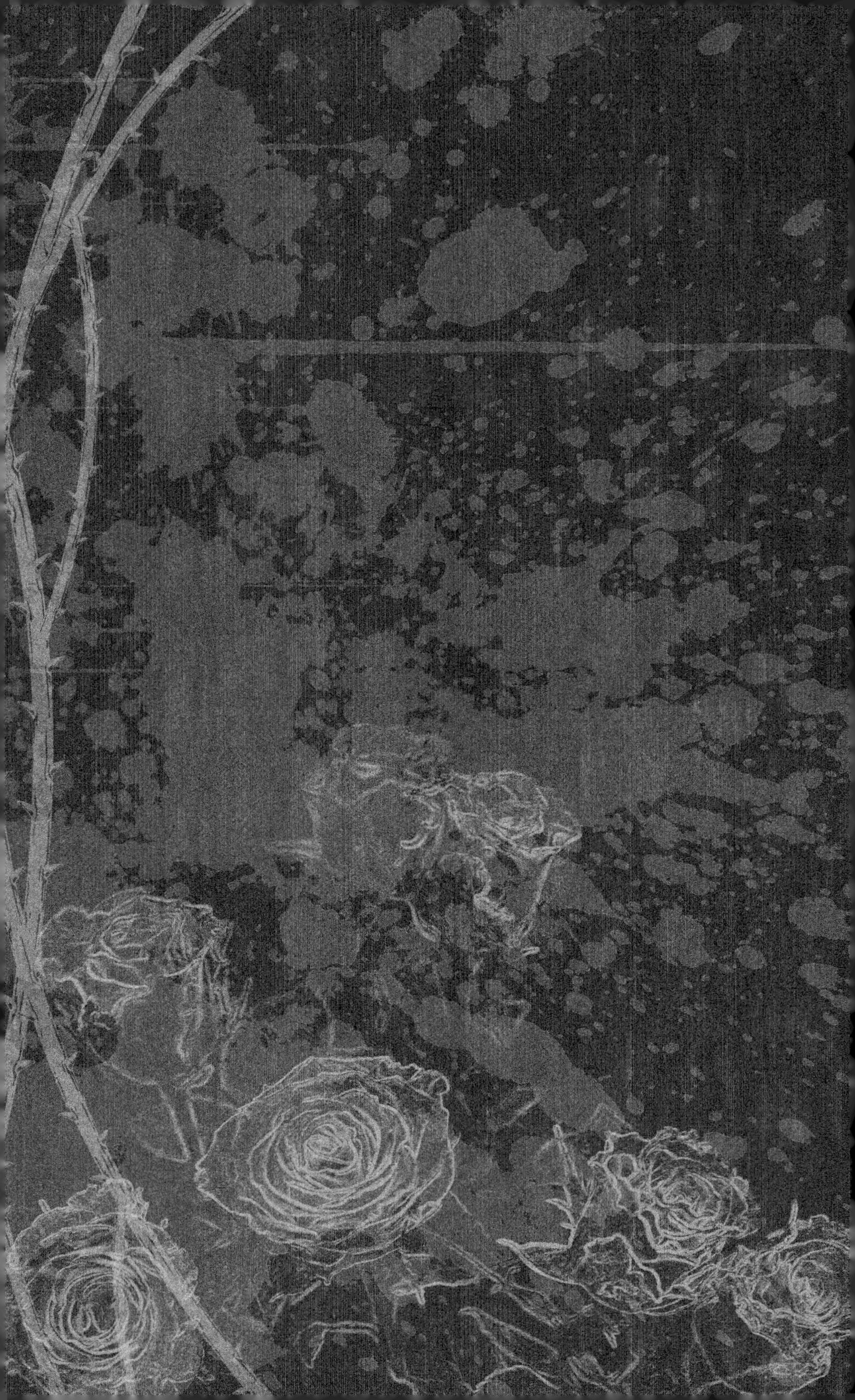

28. Killian

Killian

Killian steers his stallion down the narrow path, urging him forward slowly to avoid any trips that may be fatal. After breaching the skeletal forest that surrounds the castle they'd emerged on the top of a large cliff, below, a lush forest stretches on for miles; breaking in random sections to the small Valarki villages that border the cliff. Killian's magic had been tied to following the traitor from the moment the king had bestowed this mission upon him, he refuses to think about the other request that the king demanded of him. He only wants to focus on the sickness and the traitor.

"Holly gods," Adalyn gasps, her mare begins the descent down the cliff face; happy to follow Killian and his stallion. Killian doesn't dare look over his shoulder, knowing even the slightest loss of concentration could be the difference between life or death.

"Stay calm and don't panic. I've made this descent hundreds if not thousands of times. It'll be another half hour or so before we reach the bottom." Killian grimaces as loose rocks tumble down the cliff side from his stallion's heavy hooves. He doesn't tell Adalyn that most of the times when he'd taken this path with others, more than one in his group had slipped and never lived to tell the tale.

"I'm...I'm afraid of heights. What if my horse falls?" Adalyn's voice borders on panic. Killian goes against all instincts and turns in his saddle, trusting his stallion to be surefooted. He sends a wave of magic into his stallion and Adalyn's mare, lending them the strength and courage to keep all of them alive on this descent.

"She won't fall, she's made this descent as well," he assures, anxiously looking over Adalyn. Her hands are white where she grips the horn of the saddle, all the colour has drained from her face; brightening the constellation of freckles over her cheeks and nose.

She doesn't take her eyes from him, trying her best to control the short rapid breaths that become smaller with each inhale. Killian feels himself begin to really worry. It's one thing for a Valarki to travel down the path of the fallen, it's another for a human. He forgets Adalyn isn't like him, doesn't know this land or have the experience when travelling it.

"You need to calm down Addie," Killian's sleek raven hair ruffles in a sharp cold breeze. Adalyn trembles in her saddle, fear grasping her in its deadly hands. The last thing he needs is for her to panic, panic on a cliff side is a one-way ticket to death. He'd seen it happen far too many times.

"I—I" her wide eyes look away from him, and down to where the forest is a green expanse to their right. She begins to teeter sideways, losing her grip of reality as fear digs its sharp talons in.

"Adalyn!" Killian snaps, desperate to get her attention. She snaps her eyes to him, terror shining in their amber depths. Auburn strands whip around her face as another relentless breeze tries to tug her away from the safety of her horse.

She trembles violently, managing to right herself in the saddle. She squeezes her eyes shut and begins to count, each number a wheeze.

"I'll tell you about the time my mother took me to the ocean for the first time," Killian says, still twisted in his saddle and wanting to distract her. She pops one eye open, meeting his. He watches as her throat bobs before he continues.

"I was only a little boy and I'd never been before but I'd been nagging at her for weeks to take me. She finally relented on a day she didn't work, it was only an hour ride away and we'd doubled on the old mare we'd kept. She'd been in the family long before I was born." Killian chuckles at the memory, shaking his head slightly. "We hit Oris, a small village that's only a short walk from the ocean. The people there are lovely, we stopped and got fish on a stick."

Adalyn has both eyes open now, her focus entirely on Killian. He relaxes slightly, sending another wave of his magic out to calm the horses. He doesn't dare take his attention from Adalyn, afraid if he looks away she'd slip from her saddle.

"What's...a fish on a stick?" She manages to ask, licking her lips a few times. Killian watches the small movement, knowing her fear has dried her mouth out.

"Literally that. A whole fish speared and cooked over a fire, it's already scaled so it's only white flesh meat and the head and tail. You'd enjoy it."

"What else did you do?" She takes a deep breath, trying her best to relax.

"We walked on foot to the beach, it's a black sand beach but it's truly incredible. The ocean is the brightest and deepest blue at once, the colours bleeding together. Imagine salt in the air every time you took a breath."

"Black sand?" Adalyn asks, a light entering her eyes, "my father always talked about the ocean when I'd help him chop wood and ask a million questions about the world. He'd only ever been to the golden sand beaches."

"I've only ever been to the black sand beach, but I don't doubt it. This world is far larger than we think. My mother was an avid water lover." Killian smiles gently, fondly remembering his loving mother. She'd raised him well, had loved him with all that she had. His father had been the same, both of his parents had deserved a better ending than the one they were given.

"I couldn't imagine a little you," Adalyn admits, "you're just so big and in your face."

Killian chuckles, watching as Adalyn's cheek heat to a soft pink. "You think I'm in your face?"

"It's the whole mysterious bad boy vibe you have going on, don't shoot the messenger," she retorts, brushing a strand of hair from her nose. Killian smirks, knowing he looks the full form of arrogance.

"And do you think I'm mysterious, Addie?" He asks, arching a brow. Adalyn takes a moment to think, twisting her plump lips as she surveys him.

"I think there is a layer of mystery to you, but I also think there's much more to you than what you show me, and the others." She shrugs slightly, breaking his stare to look down at her hands. As if she'd been afraid to what she might find in his blue depths.

He smiles to himself before turning to face forward in his saddle. They'd reached the end of the descent, safely making it to solid, even ground. Adalyn sighs in relief. Killian studies the path before him, the stone path blends into dead trampled grass and dirt as they break apart and wind into the forest. Killian brings his magic forth, allowing it to guide him. It tugs him towards the one directly in the middle, the thickest part of the forest. Adalyn pulls her mare to a stop beside him, studying the forest.

"It's so alive," she whispers, leaning forward in her saddle. Killian nods.

"This is the Dathka' forest, before we enter I must warn you to not eat any of the fruit and do not go anywhere without me."

"Even to pee?" She argues, glaring at him. He levels her with a stare, showing he means no bullshit. The forest is harmless to Valarki, but a death trap to humans. It's also the only path they can take to reach the traitor and sickness.

"Even to pee. I'm serious Adalyn, this forest is no place for humans."

"Yet you're waltzing in there with me anyway," she grumbles, looking away from him. He shakes his head but taps his heels to get his stallion into motion. Killian looks towards the thick evergreen canopy, watching as the lowering sun catches the large arrow shaped leaves, lighting them from green to gold and all shades in between.

"We need to set up camp for the night," Killian calls over his shoulder. Long, thick shadows begin to unfurl on the ground around them as they grow close to thick brown trunks. Adalyn stays close to Killian's side, taking in everything around them as much as she can.

"How far in until we can set up camp?" She asks softly, carefully looking for monsters hiding in the shadows. Killian reaches out for her reins as they enter the forest, swallowed by shadows. Magic dances in the air around them, tickling his nose in greeting. He sends out a kernel of his own magic, letting the forest know he means no harm.

"Soon. There's a clearing ahead just off the path that will give us privacy. A few feet away should be a stream we can bathe in," he says absently. If Adalyn notices the magic of the forest she doesn't say a word, simply falls into silence as he leads them along. Soon enough he finds the subtle path that leads off through a thicket of brambles, they break through thick leaves with little incident to find themselves in a small clearing.

A charred circle sits in the centre, indicating the last fire hadn't been lit for some time. Killian dismounts, leading his stallion to a low branch before tying his reins loosely. His steed lowers his head and begins to pick at the grass. Adalyn follows his lead, moaning softly as her feet hit the ground.

Killian makes quick work of a fire, using the last dying rays of sunlight to his advantage as he gathers wood and gets a flame sparking. Soon enough the logs are consumed and a blazing orange and golden flame light the clearing. Warmth radiates around him, helping ease the tension in his body. Adalyn rummages through the bag she'd brought along.

"I didn't bring anything to sleep on," she says in defeat, holding a nightgown to her chest as she looks over to Killian. He turns from the fire, shaking his thoughts away.

"Don't worry. I brought two rolls with me." He walks over to his stallion, quickly unsaddling him and resting it beside Adalyn's. Killian grabs both bed rolls, laying them side by side in front of the fire.

"Why are they so close?" She looks from him to the rolls with suspicion. He huffs, digging through his bag for his own set of warm clothes to sleep in.

"Because I can't afford you wandering off into the forest, enchanted by its magic." He rises, beckoning for her to follow him. She trails behind him, huffing her annoyance but complying. They reach a small stream, Killian looks to Adalyn.

"There's only a short amount of sunlight left so we both have to bathe together." He unsheathes his blades, making quick work of peeling his long-sleeved shirt off. Adalyn fumbles for words, mouth opening and closing with no noise emerging. He cocks an eyebrow at her as he begins to unlace his pants.

"Addie, it's nothing I haven't seen before. I wouldn't insist if it wasn't unsafe. I'm not going to try anything and I'll keep my hands to myself unless you tell me otherwise." Killian steps out of his boots, pants coming off next. His skin pebbles as a cool breeze nips at his skin. Adalyn blushes, looking everywhere but at him. He chuckles before pulling his under briefs down, without wasting time he walks into the water and bites back a bark of shock at the freezing temperature.

Once he's waist level he begins to splash his face, running his hands through his hair.

"Don't look until I'm in the water." Adalyn calls out. Killian doesn't look but stays facing her way, not trusting the forest to leave her unharmed if he were to not focus on her. He listens as her clothes fall softly to the ground and as she steps out of her boots. She grumbles against the cold as she wades into the water, once she's lowered herself into the water he focuses on her.

Already her lips are a slight shade of blue and her teeth are chattering so loud it echoes around them.

"Wash quickly and then let's get out, you'll turn into a frozen Addie if we're not careful," Killian remarks, splashing water under his arm pits. Adalyn glares at him but manages to wash herself, rubbing her face roughly. Killian watches in fascination as the dying sun rays catch her hair, setting flame to reds and blends of golds. She looks up at him, her long lashes sticking together as water droplets run down her face.

"What is it?" She asks, brows dipping.

"Your hair is lovely," he offers, not wanting to share just how lovely she is in general. How looking upon her now has his heart hammering in his chest and screaming to crawl into hers and make home. She rolls her eyes at him.

"I'm done and I'm freezing." Adalyn yawns, wrapping her arms around her chest. Killian closes the distance between them, carefully wrapping an arm around her shoulder. She leans into the warmth he offers, finding her as cold as the water. He guides her onto the bank, plucking up his swords and both of their discarded clothes.

Adalyn looks up at him in confusion, clasping her clothes to her chest.

"We're going to dry by the fire before getting dressed, we'll warm up faster that way too." He holds the bushes out of her way as she walks ahead of him, his traitorous eyes wander down her curves. Her thick curls of auburn hair stop shy just at the dip in her waist, showing her luscious behind. He bites down on his bottom lip as he follows behind her, finding his cock stirring. He covers himself with his clothes, not wanting to scare her.

They reach the clearing, warmth and light greet them as the forest is well and truly thrown into the darkness of night. Adalyn stumbles to the fire, dropping down into a bed roll and holding her hands towards the blaze. Killian pulls his under briefs on before dumping the rest of his clothes with his sword beside the bedroll.

He returns with a small bag of dried meat and his water skin. Adalyn looks up at him, a blush burns her cheeks as she covers her chest with her hands. His eyes dip to the swell of her breasts.

"Killian," she whines, snapping his attention back to her face, "my eyes are up here."

He smirks, sitting down beside her. He stretches his legs out before him and relaxes as the fire burns away the exhaustion of the day. Adalyn takes a swig of water. Killian opens the pouch of dried meat and holds it out for her.

"I know where your eyes are," he remarks as she grabs a piece of jerky, "I was appreciating your other assets."

"So if I were to stare at your...your other assets you'd be okay with it?" She grunts, slapping his shoulder. He grins and grabs his own piece of jerky.

He chews slowly, "I'd be okay with you looking anywhere on my body, Addie. You only have to ask and I'd be more than happy to oblige."

"You're insufferable." She bumps her shoulder into his.

"You can get dressed now. The fires pretty warm." Killian yawns as he stretches his arms above his head. Sleep wouldn't be far off, but a thin layer of anxiety refuses to budge. Would Adalyn be opposed to the idea of sleeping by his side, with an arm securely around her waist?

While lost in his thoughts, Adalyn dresses, huddling in her cloak as she sits beside him once more. She stares into the fire, repressing a shiver. Killian dresses as well, opening his bed roll.

"Are you tired?" He looks down to where she sits, still shivering slightly. She tips her face back to look up at him.

"I could sleep. I'm a little scared though," she admits, twisting her hands in her lap. He looks at her in thought before making a decision. He undoes his bedroll all the way and folds it out so it's large enough for the both of them.

"Lay closest to the fire, I'll take the outside," he gestures. She narrows her eyes at him, defiance flaring in their depths.

"I'm not sleeping with you Killian."

He crosses his arms over his chest, "sleeping is the only thing we'll be doing. I'll have peace of mind if you're by my side."

"Do you promise we'll only sleep?" She begins to rise, taking a hesitant step onto his bedroll.

"Yes Adalyn, I'm far too tired to do more than that. I'd say once my head hits the pillow I'll be out until sunrise," he says calmly. She eyes him once more before relenting. He moves out of her way as she lays on her side, facing the fire with her cloak covering her. He unrolls her bedroll and uses it as a blanket for them both.

Sliding in beside her, he finds her tense.

"Relax Addie, it's just sleeping. We've done it before," he murmurs, already exhaustion begins to set in like a second skin. He throws the bedroll over them, sliding under Adalyn's cloak.

"I know," she whispers, "it's just intimate."

Killian moves closer to her, cocooning his body around hers. She's freezing and he'll be damned if he doesn't warm her up. She fits against him perfectly, his legs are plastered to hers while her ass is flush against him. He winds an arm under her head and over her waist, pulling her closer. He smiles as she relaxes into his body.

"I know it is. Please don't go anywhere, if you need to do anything wake me first. If the forest takes you, I'm afraid it won't give you back." He murmurs into her hair, breathing in her heavenly scent. He rests his face against her neck, closing his eyes as the thrum of her heat beat begins to lull him to sleep.

"Okay Killian, okay," she murmurs back, bringing her hands together to intertwine with his. She rests her head against his arm under her pillow. Slowly, her shivering begins to cease as he bleeds warmth into her.

Killian listens to the sound of her breathing, to the crackle and pop of the fire. He doesn't let sleep claim him until Adalyn has fallen into a deep sleep, her body completely relaxes. Killian encases the small area in a thick layer of his magic, a black circular barricade to keep them both protected.

He wants to savour this moment, wants to be awake for the entire night so he can memorise how it feels to have her so close to him. He's in deep, unrelenting shit.

Once his eyes grow too heavy to keep open, he allows himself to fall into the depths of slumber.

29. Adalyn

Adalyn

Adalyn studies Killian from where she rides behind him, his broad shoulders are strapped with his two long swords while his muscles are tense and alert. Adalyn had awoken that morning alone, finding Killian bent over a sword and sharpening it with a vengeance. She'd almost forgotten about the night before, how he'd held her. Sleep had taken her almost immediately after he'd safely tucked her into his side.

Adalyn frowns, uncertain of what is exactly happening between them.

She can't deny that she doesn't care for him, she's told him that much. Although she cares, she does not trust him. Over time she might be able to find that trust again, but for now her guard is wrapped tightly around her. Convincing herself that the chemistry between them is simply sexual tension is harder than she thought. There's no denying that they have a spark, an inferno connection to one another.

While she is still a slave, there can be no real relationship between them. She hasn't forgotten the man Killian is capable of being, nor has she forgotten the family that had been stolen from her. It's a never ending ache that can never be filled.

Ahead, a blue bird breaks from the canopy and caws. Adalyn

looks up to find it circling above them, she studies its large wingspan and shrivels slightly. Even up high above them, the bird is larger than any normal bird she'd encountered.

"Is that normal?" She asks, urging her mare forward to walk beside Killian. They'd been walking all morning along the well-worn path, the thick brown trunks and deep green canopy hadn't seemed to change with each step. It's as if they're stuck in one moment, repeating it.

Killian keeps a keen eye on the bird, hands tightening on his reins, "It's the forest keeping an eye on us."

"Why would it need to do that?" Adalyn watches as the large shadow circles lazily around them.

"Because *someone* here has made it interested in us." He glances down at her, eyes guarded from any form of emotion. Adalyn hides her disappointment, squashes down the expectations she had after being held in his arms.

"I'm a boring human, you're this dark and deadly Valarki full of magic." She arches a brow.

"I have travelled this forest many times. I am not the reason for its visit."

"Oh so it must be me then?" She rolls her eyes at him and faces forward, "I hate to break it to you Killian, but you're the only being on this continent that is putting me on a pedestal."

"Do you think that low of yourself?" He demands.

"You know exactly what I think of myself." She shakes her head, "you really can be clueless like us lesser folk."

"We—"

Adalyn raises her hand, cutting him off, "don't you dare say we are equals."

He huffs out a breath and remains silent, looking away from her. Adalyn sits back in her saddle, shaking out her shoulders. It's been two days and she's already aching head to toe from riding. Would it be this painful if she doubled with Killian?

No. She blanches at the thought of what happened when she was last in the saddle with him. That would only lead to pleasure and pain. A pleasure she could withstand but a pain that might just be the final crack in her resolve.

"Where are we going?" Adalyn prompts, needing to take her mind from the circling shadow above them.

"Osma."

"Osma...for how long?" Adalyn pushes again. Killian narrows his eyes at her, "Killian do I really look like I'm going to run away with this information? I'm a slave for crying out loud and the king made it very clear what would happen if I tried."

"Osma is still a few hours away. We'll stay at one of the taverns for a night before continuing on through the Okra forest." He relents, running a hand through his hair.

"So another forest like this one?" She waves her hand around, nothing had tried to eat them yet so it's been more than a pleasant experience. He chuckles darkly.

"Okra is very different to Dathka. You will be safe with me so don't think twice about it."

"That's much easier said than done," she grumbles in response. "This is the most I've ever seen of this world Killian and I'm experiencing it all with someone who kidnapped me."

"We're still on that?" He asks icily.

"Did you think I'd just forgotten?" Adalyn looks at him, shocked, "Killian, my entire family was murdered and I've been nearly murdered one too many times myself. I was kidnapped and taken, if anything, what I feel for you could very well be Stockholm syndrome."

"I don't expect you to forget but I did not know you then Adalyn. I was under orders from the king, I cannot just go against him. What *we* have is not you falling for your captor. I do not want to cage you." His voice is soft but his words are sharp. Adalyn has hit a nerve.

"Why does the difference matter if you knew me then or not? Innocent people have died at your hands, all they ever did was exist and *your* king despises us for it." Adalyn growls back, "do not sit there and act like you are the victim in this, I could have easily been killed with the rest of them."

"I would not have let you die," he grits out.

"Oh spare me the bullshit Killian, if Polarian had driven that sword through my chest when you'd found us in the village you would not have batted an eye. I doubt you would have thought twice about it." Adalyn trembles in her seat, batting her lashes to stop the tears from falling.

"You will always think me your villain Adalyn, so let's just leave it at that." He urges his stallion forward, leaving Adalyn behind. She takes shuddering breaths, trying to calm her heart and the hurt that burns in her chest.

What was he expecting her to do? Forgive and forget? She may care for him, but even then she will always stand for the innocents who have lost their lives at his hand. She will never justify his actions, all she can do is try to open his eyes against making those same mistakes that have landed her in this situation.

She'd do anything to be with her family once more, to live in their small home and return to the herb garden and lay in the lavender field. She'd do anything to wrap her arms around each family member she's lost, holding them tightly and telling them how much she loves them.

Adalyn gets lost in her memories of happier times and the never ending love her family had for her, so she doesn't notice that Killian has stopped ahead as the forest has ended. Or the two Valarki females that stand there talking to him.

"This is Adalyn," Killian says, gesturing behind him. Her name startles her, she looks around to find an open sky above them and a dirt road with a carriage rumbling ahead of them. In the distance she can make out the shapes of small buildings and an orange flame.

"What?" Adalyn asks, pulling her mare to stop beside Killian. She looks down to find the two Valarki females sneering up at her. Their skin is the colour of pale lavender, thick bright blue hair has been braided down both sides of their near identical faces.

"It's unusual for you to travel with a slave, Killian." The female with vibrant pink eyes looks to Killian, smirking, "does the king hate you so?"

"He must," the other female with chocolate eyes says, grimacing as she looks over Adalyn. For a moment Adalyn is stunned, half unbelieving of the things they're saying while she sits right there. She simply smirks down at them, arching a brow.

"It's nice to see even Valarki females are just as pathetic as the males," Adalyn says, her words laced with poison. "How does it feel to be so shallow?"

Pink eyes bristles, snarling up at her, "You best watch your mouth *slave.*"

Adalyn looks to Killian, feigning boredom, "Can we go now? I'm hungry and want to rest."

Although Killian's face holds no expression, his blue eyes dance with humour. She's still annoyed with him, but it's an argument she can save for another day. After riding for hours on end she desperately wants to get off this horse and have something to eat.

"Adalyn, these are our guides," he says smoothly, tilting his head to the side. His raven black hair has been pulled up into a high bun, loose strands frame his sculpted face and dark brows. The intensity of his stare is enough to make her squirm in her seat, cheeks heating.

"What a shame." Adalyn sighs dramatically, looking back to the gawking females, "Lead the way."

"You're just going to let her speak to us like that?" Brown eyes asks, scowling at Killian. Pink eyes simply stares at Killian, a flash of hurt passes across her face.

"She has a tongue of her own, trust me. I've tried *many* times to keep it in her mouth."

"The Killian we know would have killed a slave for speaking out of line," brown eyes shakes her head, turning and beginning to walk towards the distant village. Pink eyes frowns up at Killian before following her friend. Killian watches them go.

Adalyn tries to calm her heart, not wanting her fake bravado to slip.

"Tell me again why we need guides?" Adalyn grumbles, urging her mare to follow the two hateful females. She'd just about had enough of everyone thinking they were better than her.

"It's a kindness they offer whenever I pass through." Killian walks beside her, he relaxes slightly.

Adalyn snorts, "And what kindness do you *offer* them in return?"

"I am not the same man I was when I last passed through, Adalyn." His words are cold, but Adalyn swore she could detect the hint of pain. His statement has her stomach in knots as she focuses on the two females. Like all other Valarki they're stunning. Tall and lean with a warrior's body but the face of an angel. Adalyn chases away the thoughts of comparing herself to them, it would get her nowhere but a one way ticket to being miserable.

"That's not what they seem to think."

Killian chuckles, "and what do you think they think?"

"I think once we get to Osma they'll expect you to lock me in a room and then go and occupy their beds for their *generosity*." Adalyn says bitterly, hands clenching the reins.

"Are you jealous Addie, that they expect that?" His eyes burn into the side of her face but she refuses to look at him. To acknowledge him.

"Do what you want Killian, how I feel hasn't stopped you before." She clicks her tongue, her mare breaking into a slight trot. Killian curses behind her. It'd been a low blow, reminding them both of how he'd been with Alissa. Sometimes Adalyn really couldn't bite her tongue or hold back her spite.

"Adalyn slow down." Killian growls, reaching her. Ahead the two females look over their shoulders.

"What do you want?" Adalyn demands, staring up at him.

"I'm not going to go and jump in their beds for god's sake." He growls, reaching over to grab her reins. He brings both of them to stop, still leaning far too close to her. His eyes burn with emotion as he looks down at her, his breath hitting her face. She has to tilt her face back to look up at him.

"Don't let me stop you," Adalyn whispers back, wetting her bottom lip. The anger in his eyes brightens and for some godforsaken reason it has heat pooling between her thighs, her chest heaving at the sudden burst of arousal. His nostrils flare.

His pupils blow out, swallowing most of the blue Adalyn has come to like.

"The only bed I plan to be in is *ours* and if you keep letting that mouth of yours run, I will show you exactly how to use it."

Adalyn gulps, "How do you plan to do that?" she murmurs, leaning closer so her cheek brushes against his own until her lips hover before his ear, "Will you force me to my knees before you, while I take every inch of you in my mouth?"

Killian groans low in his throat, his other arm comes down to the back of her saddle and cages her in. Adalyn doesn't dare move, afraid the smallest amount of friction between her legs will have her jumping into his saddle. She refuses to let her body win this round of the sick game they're playing.

"Your pretty little mouth is perfect wrapped around me, but no Addie, I wouldn't force you to your knees." He trails his nose up her cheek and gently tugs at her earlobe, "I would bury myself between your thighs and bring you to that edge and at the last minute I'd pull away and bury myself deep inside of you, filling that tight little pussy of yours until you saw stars."

Adalyn trembles in her seat, his dirty words have her underwear drenched while her pussy clenches on open air. Begging her to take him up his offer. She can't utter a single word, no thoughts can even form in her mind. Killian runs his tongue down her throat, nipping at the sensitive spot below her ear.

"I'd take my time with you." *Nip.*

"I'd be gentle until you begged me for more." *Lick.*

"I'd give you everything and then some, I'd watch as I stretched you. You'd take all of me and I'd reward you for it greatly." *Suck.*

"Even now I can smell the sweetness of your arousal, you smell fucking divine Adalyn." Killian growls against her throat, neither of them caring about the audience ahead of them. Adalyn tips her head to the side, moaning as he sinks his teeth into her skin and sucks.

"Killian—" Adalyn gasps as his bite turns painful, he lets go and swipes his tongue over the small droplets of blood that had formed from his fangs.

"I don't just want to fuck you Adalyn." He pulls away, his arms trembling on either side of her. She stares up at him with lust filled eyes, all common sense dissolved when he'd groaned at her dirty words.

"I don't think you could give me what I wanted, not with so much resentment for me in your heart." He stares down at her lips, watching as she drags her bottom lip between her teeth, "for when I have you Adalyn, I will have all of you and no less. There will be no turning back."

"Looks like you'll have to try harder then." Adalyn raises a weak hand to her aching throat, crashing back down to earth. Adalyn internally curses herself, only Killian could make her forget the entire world around them. He smirks as he leans back, releasing her from the trance they'd both been under. Adalyn faces forward to see their two guides far ahead of them, almost at the village.

"You may want to have your hair covering your neck," Killian comments, rearranging the front of his pants. Adalyn pulls thick auburn strands over her right shoulder and hides his mark, not wanting the others to think she's just a slave he fucks.

"I'll repay that favour Killian." She glares up at him as they begin to walk forward once more. He chuckles, a small smile breaking his usually expressionless face.

"I love it when you bite back Addie, it's my favourite thing of all."

Adalyn ignores his comment, focusing on cooling the blood that now boils in her veins. There's only so much she can take before she snaps, demanding him to take all of her. She nibbles her bottom lip, staring at the two women that are now far closer than before. He'd been with both of them and the thought alone is enough to have Adalyn's stomach in knots. Would she be just another woman in his bed? Would it mean anything to him, to have her so intimately?

Would she regret giving herself to him?

They are questions she has no idea how to answer, not knowing if the answer will come after they'd finally given in to their desires for each other.

Valarki with the same light lavender skin tone bustle around the stretching village, behind the village a large stone face works as a barrier to half of the village before a thick foreboding forest covers the other half and stretches on for miles. Adalyn focuses on the village before her, not wanting to think of the forest they'll be entering tomorrow.

Wooden shacks and cottages cluster together, the pale wood faded from the constant heat from the sun. Green and white flower garlands decorate the windowsills of most cottages, a thin layer of dirt covers the glass. Small Valarki children run through the village, their magic a wild display as they play. Adalyn watches in awe as a boy flings a small fire ball over his shoulder, the girl chasing him sends a spray of water his way and douses the ball. They run off laughing hysterically, a few others follow their lead.

A majority of the Valarki stare up at her with resentment, but no one dares comment about her presence with Killian by her side. Respect shines in their eyes once they look to him, bowing their head. Killian ignores them all, focusing on leading them through a narrow dirt path and heading deeper into the village.

"Where are we going?" Adalyn asks, gripping her reins tightly. The resentful stares burn into her back and make her want to run for cover. Killian glances at her, she shifts uncomfortably in the saddle.

"To the tavern we'll be staying in for the night."

"I cannot wait for a nice warm bath." Adalyn groans, almost feeling the fresh warm water caressing her body.

"I can't wait for a warm meal." Killian continues to stare ahead, glaring at Valarki that linger too long. Adalyn relaxes slightly, purposefully riding closer to his steed. If he is her ticket for safety in this village, then she'd do anything to stay by his side.

"Will we have to cook?" She asks.

Killian shakes his head, "Dinner will be supplied by the tavern."

"Can we explore the village?" Adalyn asks hesitantly. Killian raises a dark brow as he looks down at her. She blushes, "It's still a few hours until sun down and I'd like to explore. I will most likely never come back here again."

Killian watches her silently, his face betraying no emotions. It sometimes unnerved her, how detached he could become so easily.

"Please?" she puffs out her bottom lip and widens her eyes, hoping her begging face will be enough to persuade him.

"A favour for a favour?" He asks, eyes shining with challenge.

Adalyn narrows her eyes at him, "what could you possibly want?"

"A lot of things from you, Addie," he shrugs his large shoulders, "I'll give you a tour of the village if you bathe with me."

Adalyn almost falls of her saddle with shock, "What?"

"Bathe with me and then I will show you everything this village has to offer."

"We bathed the other night in the river together," she hisses, keeping her voice low so their *two* chaperones won't overhear her. No doubt their incredible hearing has them listening to every word he says.

"Yes, we did. So what's another night bathing together?" he comments, utterly unphased by what he's asking of her. Adalyn's heart gallops in her chest, bathing in a small space...is far more intimate than bathing in a large stream. She goes over her options, cursing herself for knowing she *wants* to bathe with him and knows she'd do it even if she was getting nothing in return.

His body was sculpted by the forgotten gods, any woman would be lucky to see him in his naked glory.

"Fine, but I want a total tour of the village from the dirt beneath it to the sky above it." Adalyn warns, scowling up at him. His lips tilt up into a smirk, blue eyes shining with light. It makes Adalyn's heart twist in her chest.

"We're here," pink eyes announces, coming to a stop. Adalyn looks away from Killian, the two women stand before them and both focus on Killian. If they want to pretend she doesn't exist, that's more than fine by her. She can do the exact same back.

Adalyn looks up towards the face of the mountain in front of them, large trees with thick green foliage grow from the cracks in the stone while small taverns have been built between the trees. A rickety wooden stair case leads to the closest tavern, which is still far higher than Adalyn is comfortable with.

"Thank you," Killian rumbles. Adalyn slides from her horse, wincing as her thighs tremble violently. She grumbles to herself but pats her mare's neck, it isn't her horses fault she's hopeless on the saddle. Killian dismounts beside her. She makes quick work of grabbing her saddle bag, throwing the weight over her shoulder. Killian holds out a hand, tilting his head to the side. She shakes her head once, not wanting to embarrass herself further.

"I'll be able to take both horses," Brown eyes says warmly to him, holding out her hands. Killian hands his reins over with ease, while Pink eyes engages him in conversation Brown eyes stares daggers at Adalyn. Adalyn hands her reins to the woman, snatching her hand away before she can do anything.

Brown eyes begins to lead both horses away, back towards a large open barn that sits on the border of the village. "Bye Killie!" she calls sweetly, swaying her hips more than natural.

Adalyn crosses her arms over her chest, turning back to face Killian. Pink eyes stands closer to him, staring up at him with her large eyes.

"Will I be seeing you later?" She murmurs, "it has been too long since you've come to visit."

Killian gently grasps her wrist that goes to touch his cheek, "No, I have found someone."

Hurt flashes in her eyes as they begin to moisten, "I thought we...we were—"

"I am sorry Magdalyn, I wish you the best." He lets go of her arm, it falls limply to her side. Adalyn stands there, the entire encounter has made her uncomfortable. Magdalyn looks to Adalyn as silent tears slip down her cheeks, her top lip curls in disgust.

"You've settled with a human slave?" she demands, fury lighting those pink depths. Killian clenches his jaw.

"Who I settle with is none of your business," he says softly but firmly, still not wanting to hurt her feelings.

"Killian you've been warming my bed for months!" she exclaims, "there has been no other for me when you've been away."

"I told you that I was not interested in anything more," his voice grows firmer, "I never asked for your loyalty to me."

"You didn't have to," she cries out, turning her angry eyes to Adalyn.

Adalyn takes a step back, unsure if Magdalyn is going to take her anger out on her. She raises a hand to strike Adalyn. Killian reaches out and grabs her wrist with inhuman speed.

"You do not *touch her,*" he growls, tightening his grip on her wrist.

Magdalyn wrenches her wrist from his grip, "Fuck you Killian."

She storms off, chasing after Brown eyes. Adalyn lets out a large sigh, watching as the woman stalks away. A warm hand grasps her chin, tilting her face up to his. Killian looks down at her, eyebrow creased in the middle.

"Are you okay?" He asks, running his thumb over her cheek.

"I'm fine," she murmurs, unable to look away from him.

"I am sorry....about that. You shouldn't have had to witness that."

Adalyn rests her on hand over his, "I've survived worse than a hateful ex-lover, Killian. I'm sure it won't be the last time we have an encounter similar to that one."

"Who I was back then..." he shakes his head, letting her face go, "just know I am not like that anymore."

Adalyn walks past him, bumping her shoulder to his, "Come on, didn't you promise me a bath?"

Killian's deep chuckle chases her as they make the small walk to the first set of wooden stairs. Adalyn pales as she follows the deep ascent. Her new fear of heights is still fresh in mind.

A warm hand rests on her lower back, supporting her, "I'll be behind you each step of the way." Killian's warm breath hits the side of her throat. She straightens her shoulders and grabs the rail and makes the painful ascent. Not once does she dare look down and decides to count each step she takes to reach the opening gate for the tavern.

Killian reaches out behind her and opens the gate, pushing it inwards. Adalyn hurries up the last few steps and throws herself towards the waiting door. Killian comes up behind her, arching a brow at her dramatic display.

"This is madness, why would they think this is...this is nice?" she rasps, trying to swallow through the heaviness in her throat. Killian strokes the side of her face, smiling.

"When you've lived for as long as I have, you find that height is the last thing to scare you." He grasps her hand, leading her through the open door, "come, I'll take us to our room."

Adalyn has no choice but to follow after him, sliding her fingers firmly through his. Warmth spreads up her arm, calming her. The brightly lit hallway funnels deeper into the mountain, the wooden walls begin to turn to stone and before Adalyn knew it they're walking down stone steps.

She peers over his chest, unable to fight her curiosity. Ahead of them a large room has been carved out with another hallway continuing on. A new type of Valarki sits behind a wooden desk, their small bat like wings wrap around their bony shoulders as they fuss over papers in front of them. Their skin is as black as coal and leathery.

"Afternoon, Peri." Killian's deep voice startles Peri, who snaps their head up. His large black eyes crease at the corners.

"Killian! Oh, Killian I was wondering when you'd arrive!" He squawks, jumping down from his stool and strutting around the desk. Adalyn hides her amusement, Peri is half her height but his attitude makes him as large as Killian.

His spidery, thin body is covered in a thin layer of black material while his shape is pointed and sharp. He holds out a small hand for Killian, puffing out his small chest.

Killian grips his hand gently, encasing the entire thing.

"It is good to see you again friend," Killian rumbles, "I'd like to introduce you to Adalyn."

Peri lets go of his hand and finally takes in Adalyn. His eyes roam over her critically but not hatefully, more curious than anything. Adalyn squirms under his gaze, darting her eyes to Killian's. He squeezes her hand in reassurance.

"Hi, Peri. It's nice to meet you," she finally manages to rasp, offering her free hand. Peri eyes it warily, but places his small leathery hand in her own.

"A human hasn't stayed in my tavern before," he mumbles, "but if you're with Killian I'm going to assume you're as bad as he is."

Killian laughs deeply, the sound shocking Adalyn. Has she ever heard him laugh so *truly* before?

"I can assure you, sweet little Addie here is an angel from grace compared to me." Killian grins, winking at her. Adalyn's mouth gapes in shock, before her his metal armour has melted off and left *Killian* behind. Peri cackles, letting go of her hand.

"Well in that case I have to wonder why an angel is slumming it with a demon." Peri struts back behind his desk, jumping back up on his stool that sits his at Killian's height. Adalyn blushes as

Killian pulls her into his side, wrapping his arm around her shoulders.

"Even the angels have to dance with the devils at some point."

Peri cackles once more, grabbing a black skeleton key from a draw, "I've put you in your usual room, I expect there to be no blood left behind this time."

Killian takes the key, "It was once and that happened years ago."

"And I'll never forget it. Now, hurry along." He gestures towards the hallway, refusing to look back up again. Killian shakes his head but leads both of them towards the hallway. As they traverse the intricate system Adalyn admires the hard work that would have gone into making this place. It's large, larger than she thought it would have been.

"What sort of Valarki is Peri?" she asks as Killian finally comes to a stop down a hall with only one door. An arched, metal door encases the end of the hallway. A mural has been carved into the metal, but has been worn down over the years.

"He's a Nightmare, a type of Valarki that can never leave the confines of darkness. If he were to walk outside right now, he'd be burnt alive." Killian unlocks the doors, pulling them outwards. Adalyn breezes past him in awe at the room before them.

An exceptionally large bed sits in the middle of the room, its black silk sheets are tucked in neatly while red vines decorate the four large wooden posts of the bed frame and form a canopy over the bed. Adalyn dumps her bag on the floor and trails her hand over the silk sheet, she turns to the fire that burns brightly opposite the bed. A white fur rug sits underneath a small round oak table with two black velvet seats facing the fire.

Killian closes the doors, locking them from the inside. "What do you think?"

Adalyn continues to walk around the room, running her hands over the bookcase that is full of weathered and worn books. She walks to the open arch on the other side of the room, draw dropping at the stone bath that's been carved out of the mountain wall. Water spills from a slit in the mountain and continues to fill the bath, a medium black hole sits at the back of the bath and works as a drain.

"How..." Adalyn looks over her shoulder, finding him standing before the bed shirtless. Her eyes trail over his skin, greedily taking him in. From here she can't see the scars that cover the hard planes of his stomach, only the defined muscle and the dark hair that trails from his belly button and disappears at the waist band of his pants.

Her thighs clench as she finally looks to his face.

"Under the bath there are hot stones that are constantly heated by the Valarki that can harness fire. Most embed their flame into the stone, leaving the stone constantly hot," he explains, stalking towards her. His long legs eat up the distance in threes strides. Adalyn tips her face back, looking up to meet the intense blue eyes that hold her captive.

"This room is amazing," she manages to say, "I admire the hard work that has gone into all of this...it's truly incredible."

"They are good people," Killian rumbles, resting his large hands on either side of her waist. Her skin heats immediately at his touch and she finds herself shuffling closer to him. He leans down and brushes his nose against her own, their breath mingles as he hesitates before pulling away. Adalyn masks her disappointment.

"You promised me a bath?" He questions, spinning her around to face the stone bath. Layers of steam lick the air and spill down the stone side, curling lazily before dissolving. Adalyn freezes as Killian's hands gently run along the hem of her shirt, tugging it free from her riding pants.

He slowly begins to unbutton her shirt, his fingers an expert with each button. Adalyn's stomach coils with anticipation as he frees the garment, skimming his hands between her heavy breasts and down to the waistband of her pants.

Her breath hitches as he unthreads the lace, pulling them loose until they're barely holding onto her waist. His hot breath runs along the left side of her exposed throat, his tongue follows its path only moments later. Adalyn's nipples harden as pleasure begins to make her blood burn.

"What do you want, Adalyn?" He murmurs against her skin, pushing her pants down her legs. They fall and pool at her ankles, his hands lazily trail around her thighs as she stands naked before him. Her breathing comes in sharper as lust begins to throw a haze over her mind.

"You." She gasps as he sucks at the soft spot on her neck, nipping the skin and sending a flare of pain through her before kissing the tender spot. She leans back into him, finding him hard and straining against his own pants.

"All of me?" He rumbles, trailing kissing down her throat and over her shoulder. She wriggles against him, his hands clasp down on her thighs to restrain her.

"Killian." Adalyn whines, throwing her head back to his shoulder and giving him an open view of her peaked nipples. She'd do anything in this moment to have him touch her and claim her as his, what she feels for him is an inferno and if she isn't careful, she'll drown in their flames.

"I—I can't give myself to you just yet." His voice is pained, his fingers tighten on her thighs enough to leave bruises. She opens her eyes and looks to him, a flash of pain passes between the depths of lust that shine back at her.

"I want *you* Killian, always you." She reaches down and takes one of his hands in her own. He allows her to guide his hand between her slick folds, his fingers have a mind of their own as they begin to explore her.

"Adalyn," He growls, squeezing his eyes shut, when they open once more they *burn* with desire, "you will regret this."

"No, I won't." Adalyn bites her bottom lip as a thick finger swirls around her opening. Her pussy pulses, wanting to be filled with him. Killian groans against her skin, biting down on her shoulder. As his fangs pierce her skin he gently eases a finger into her. Her gasp of pain turns into a moan of pleasure as he slowly begins to pump his finger into her.

Adalyn pants as she throws her head back into his chest, desperately needing more.

Her legs tremble as her orgasm begins to build.

Killian lets her shoulder go, grunting as his tongue runs along his bottom lip and collects the droplets of her blood.

"More," Adalyn gasps.

Killian retracts his hand from between her legs, she cries out in protest until she's spun towards him and his lips crash down into hers. She kisses him back hungrily, desperate for more. He throws her shirt to the ground as she steps out of the pants keeping her ankles contained.

Her hands go to the waist band of his pants, he helps her tug them down without breaking their kiss. Adalyn wraps her arms around his neck as he grabs her waist and lifts him to her, her legs automatically wrap around his waist while his cock nestles between her folds.

"*Oh*," Adalyn moans, rocking her hips against him as she bites down on his bottom lip. Killian groans deep in his throat, thrusting against her as his mouth continues to claim her own.

He pulls away, pupils blown as his ragged breaths match her own. "Are you sure?"

Adalyn blinks through the pleasure, finding herself plastered to him. She thinks. Is she sure?

She finds herself feeling safer than she ever has before, a sense of *home* settles into her as she stares into his eyes. The emotion that swells in her heart threatens to spill from her lips, but she knows she is sure. She's known she's sure of Killian being her first before she cared to admit it to herself.

"I'm sure." She murmurs, threading her fingers into the hair at the base of his neck. His bun had unravelled, leaving his hair a curtain around his head. His fingers tighten on her ass, digging into the soft flesh.

"How would you like me to take you?" He leans down and

trails his tongue along her collar bone, Adalyn arches back and exposes her peaked nipple for him. Killian groans as his tongue swirls around the hardened nub, sucking it between his teeth. The small action has Adalyn rocking against him once more, her body heavy with pleasure.

"Adalyn." He growls against her breast.

"In the water," she manages to say, not wanting to walk the distance to the bed. Killian holds her close, still focusing on her breast as he steps over the stone ledge and enters the water. Moments later water pools around their waists as he sits back, leaning against the stone ledge. Adalyn straddles his waist, the warm water feels heavenly against her skin.

Her nipple pops from his mouth as he leans back, the ends of his hair stick together as he takes ragged breaths.

Adalyn trails her hands down his chest, digging her nails in and leaving thin red marks as she trails lower. Killian sucks in a breath as she wraps a hand around his thick cock, her small hand barely covers half the girth of him.

He rocks into her hand, she palms the front of his cock while rocking her pussy against the back of it and watches in awe as he rides against her. His eyes burn with emotion and desire, Adalyn moans as his hands take each breast. His fingers rub her nipples.

"I promise I'll be gentle." His voice is thick and deep, his tongue runs along his bottom lip. Adalyn bites her own lip and nods once, letting go of his cock she braces her hands on his thighs. Killian smirks at her as he takes her waist in his hands, "I need to taste you first."

Adalyn loses her words to a gasp as Killian hauls her pussy to his face, his tongue dives between her slick folds and swirls around her clit. She grasps the stone edge as he spreads her thighs wider, taking all of her weight as he feasts on her.

She looks down to find him looking up at her, the sight of his face buried between her thighs has her rocking against his tongue, he laps her up hungrily and groans into her pussy. Adalyn gasps as he inserts a finger into her, his tongue lashes at her clit as he slowly pumps into her. Adalyn can barely support her weight, each stroke of his tongue and curl of his finger has her coming undone at the seams.

Killian takes his time with her, inserting another thick finger. Pain sparks through her and he leaves both fingers inside of her, letting her adjust. Her focuses on her clit, drawing cries of pleasure from her until she's writhering against his face and silently begging for more.

He pumps the two fingers into her, sucking and nipping at her clit. Adalyn buries a hand into his hair as she rides his face harder, feeling the pleasure build and grow to something great. She desperately wants that release, begs for it.

Killian removes his fingers from her and gently lowers her back into the water, she straddles his lap. Her pussy throbs as he licks her juices from his lips and moans, Adalyn grasps his cock and lines it up with her entrance. His fingers come between them and begin to rub circles around her clit.

"Keep your eyes open, I want to watch you," he gasps, gently wrapping his free hand around her own that holds his cock. Slowly she sinks down onto him and feels something break as she takes the head of him. She bites her bottom lip as her pussy throbs with pain. She trembles against him. His wicked fingers draw her from the pain and blind her with pleasure, he sits up and the movement pulls her closer to his chest. She claims his lips as she lowers herself once more.

Inch by inch, Killian stretches Adalyn to her limits.

He groans low in his throat, his chest rumbling as he fills her to his hilt. Adalyn sits flush against him, her pussy throbs around him as she adjusts to his size. The pain only spurs on her pleasure as she breaks their kiss and presses her forehead against Killian's.

"*Adalyn*." Her name on his lips has her beginning to rise and then sliding back down onto him. The movement has pleasure building inside of her, he slides into her easily and fills her once more. She gasps as she rolls her hips against him, finding the action rubs against her clit. He wraps a strong arm around her waist as he takes a breast in his free hand, he sucks her right nipple into his mouth as his left hand gently gropes her right breast.

Slowly they find rhythm, water sloshes over the stone edge of the bath and splashes against the floor but neither of them pay any attention. Adalyn braces her hands against his broad shoulders as he relentlessly slams into her, continuing to feast on her bare breasts.

She has never felt more alive than in this moment.

Knowing that their time is fleeting has Adalyn meeting each thrust with her own aggression, winding her hands through his silk hair and tugging sharply. He growls against her chest, nipping at her nipple before pulling his face back to stare up at her.

In a sharp, swift movement Adalyn's back is pressed against the stone ledge with Killian buried between her thighs. The new angle has him hitting a sensitive spot inside of her, has her clawing at his back to escape the pleasure that is beginning to blind her.

He drags her earlobe through his teeth, his warm ragged breathing matches her own.

"You are mine, Adalyn," Killian growls, thrusting deep and hard to accentuate each word.

Adalyn moans, throwing her head back.

"Say it," Killian demands, stopping just outside of her. Adalyn's eyes fly open in desperation, her pussy throbs and clenches at the sudden emptiness.

Adalyn searches his wild blue eyes, finding the truth laid bare before her.

She is his, and he hers.

Maybe she has been all along.

"I am yours, Killian," she says, breathless, "and you are mine."

He rewards her by slowly sliding back in, stopping at the hilt. Sweat beads run down his forehead and cheeks as his lips gently take hers. This kiss is different to the others they've shared, their lips speak the words both of them refuse to say.

"I think I've always been yours," Killian confesses against her lips, beginning to move again once more.

Adalyn cries out, her mind and body overwhelmed with the pleasure and the confession that had spilt from his lips.

Killian.

Killian. Killian. Killian.

"Come for me, Addie," he groans, hands tightening on the stone edge caging her in.

Adalyn needs no more hesitation, Killian grinds his hips into and the attention to her clit has Adalyn screaming her release.

Killian slams into her erratically, riding her through her orgasm. Moments later he bruises her lips with his own, filling her up with his hot seed. They stay tangled in one another, gasping for breath. Adalyn's limbs weaken, her legs slide from behind Killian's and sink to the bottom of the bath.

"That...that was incredible," Killian mumbles, lashing out his tongue to dampen his bottom lip. Adalyn grins lazily up at him, too exhausted to move her hand to cup his face. He watches her with wonder and admiration, eyes shining with light. "That's the first time you've truly smiled at me."

Adalyn's heart kicks into gear, "I finally have a reason to smile at you Killian."

He chuckles, shaking his head. The wet ends of his hair flick at her face as a mischievous smirk overtakes his face. Adalyn steals a quick kiss from him before he leans back, sliding out of her. She moans and closes her eyes, letting herself take a moment to adjust to the pleasant ache between her thighs.

She waits for the guilt to invade her senses, for the hurt and pain to overwhelm the happiness she feels.

She waits...but it never comes.

She has given her heart and body to Killian, and has not one regret for it. He doesn't need to know the extent of how deep her feelings run, not so soon.

Killian leans against the other side of the bath, his legs encasing her own. He gently takes one of her feet in his hands, massaging the arch of her foot.

"Are you okay?" He asks, drawing her eyes open.

"I'm okay," she leans back, wiggling her toes in his grasp, "I don't regret it, I'm just not sure...what happens now."

Killian's face darkens for a split second, "I don't think I could handle another male ever having his hands on you again."

"Do you really think I want another woman touching you now?" Adalyn jabs her other foot into his toned chest, running her toes down his hard chest.

"I will never let another woman touch me now, Addie. I meant what I said earlier, I want all of you Adalyn and nothing less. A better man wouldn't have gone as far as I have, but I'm not a better man." His eyes darken, his guard going up. Adalyn sighs and wiggles herself closer to him. She clasps his cheeks, searching his eyes.

"If I wanted *anyone* else, Killian, I would have gone and found them. It's been you from the moment I laid my eyes on you and deep down I think you feel the same." She presses a gentle kiss to his nose, both cheeks and a chaste kiss cross his lips.

"I knew I kept you alive for a reason," he murmurs, stealing another kiss from her. Adalyn rolls her eyes and slips from his grasp, escaping to her side of the tub before her hands find a mind of their own and make a home of his body once more. He grins at her, winking.

"I'm tired." Adalyn admits, resting her head back against the stone.

"Come here," Killian murmurs. Adalyn opens her eyes to find a hand reaching for her. She doesn't object as he takes her in his arms, pressing her back against his chest. She settles into him, feeling his hard rod pressing into her back.

"Still eager?" She asks, rolling her head back on his chest to look up at him. He kisses her forehead but takes a bar of soap from behind him, taking her left hand he begins to rub the soap into her skin.

"I will always be eager to take you Addie. But not so soon, you'll be sore in the morning."

"I'm sore now." Adalyn smiles and closes her eyes, letting her cheek press against his chest. He chuckles but stays silent, gently gliding the soap over her chest and working on her next arm. Adalyn could get used to this treatment, the massage is doing wonders for her sore muscles.

Adalyn closes her eyes and relaxes, feeling completely safe in this moment. She trusts Killian, he'd never do anything to hurt her purposefully.

Moments later she's hauled from the water in strong arms, she nestles closer into him as he pads across the open room to the bed. With one arm holding her he expertly pulls the sheets down before sliding her under the sheets.

She moans into the comfort of the pillows and sheets, slightly sticking to the sheets from still being wet. Opening her eyes she finds Killian leaning over her, adjusting the pillows around her. He smiles weakly down at her. "Get some rest. Dinner will be brought in later. If I'm not here when you wake, I'll be at the balcony."

"Okay." Adalyn yawns, feeling blissful and closes her eyes once more. Exhaustion drags her down, distantly she's aware of Kilian pressing a kiss to her forehead, a whispered apology, but she remembers nothing as darkness claims her.

30. Killian

Killian

Killian leans against the railing of the tavern they're staying at for the night that overlooks Osma, a small Valarki village in Pantera. Osma is closest to the thick forest north east but also catches the hint of salt and sea on the breeze.

Killian shuts his eyes and inhales, if he can focus on the scent long enough he can almost see the deep blue ocean crashing against a golden shore—can almost taste the salt air on his tongue—

The sun crests the mountain, casting a golden glow over the small spread out village.

He'd escaped the room once Adalyn had fallen asleep, torn between sliding in between the sheets with her and running as far away as possible.

When they returned... and she learned of his betrayal? He doubts she'd ever forgive him again. Doubts she'd listen to him, that he'd have given himself to her regardless if the king set the task upon him or not.

The thought makes him sick, makes him want to peel his skin from bone.

"Huh. This is the most relaxed I've ever seen you," Adalyn says, breaking his train of thought. "What fantasies were you thinking about?"

He sighs roughly through his nose, reluctantly slitting his eyes to look at her. She stands to his right side, a small hand pressed against the wooden railing. Her face is masked with awe as she overlooks the village spread out beneath them, the tavern had been built on the side of a smaller mountain facing north west that encloses half the village. Their journey in the morning will take them straight into the forest, tonight will be their last night of comfort and a small sense of safety.

"The ocean." He doesn't dare voice his concern.

Adalyn glances at him, "ocean?"

"Yes. Have you never seen it?" He asks, frowning slightly. When he'd been a child his parents frequently visited its shore, it was where most of his fond memories came from.

"No. I've never left home until..."Adalyn clears her throat, looking away as her cheeks flush. Her grip on the rail tightens, Killian's keen hearing faintly hears the uneven tempo of her heart.

"I'll take you there." He doesn't know why he says it, why he would say anything in this moment for her to return back to the present with him. Adalyn looks towards him once more, narrowing her eyes slightly as she looks for any sign of weakness or deception. She would find none.

"I doubt we'll have time. We haven't even reached where we're meant to be going." She sighs, "don't worry, I'm sure I'll see it one day."

Killian looks over the village, if only to restrain himself from reaching out to offer her comfort. His chest tightens to the point of pain. She'd given herself to him, trusting him completely and yet *he* now has cold toes and wants nothing more than to protect her and keep her at distance. Would it be easier for her to hate him now or later? Could he survive either option?

"This village, these...fae. They're not like the others at the castle," she whispers, resting her chin on her palm. "Some are, like those two nasty guides, but everyone else seems...normal I suppose."

Killian's grateful for the twist in conversation. "No, these Valarki are compassionate. They still live under the kings rule but being this far out they have more room to relax."

"What's the traitor we're looking for?"

"A Valarki female, with possible conspirators. My magic will lead us to them, as will my oath to serve the king."

Adalyn turns to him, studying his side profile, "and what? We kill them, for wanting something better than this life?"

"I am oath bound Adalyn, nothing more than the king's hound," Killian says bitterly, only letting a sliver of his disdain for his life to shine through. Adalyn catches onto it though, she always does.

"You're far more than his hound Killian, far more," she murmurs. Kilian ignores the rapid pace of his heart as he looks at her, unable to deny himself the pleasure of it.

A soft, tender smile graces her lips. There's a light in her eyes, and an emotion that runs deeper than anything either of them are willing to face.

"Can't you see me for who I am?" Killian mutters. Centuries of being the king's slave have worn him down and in this moment he feels the weight will drive him from this earth and straight into the depths of hell.

Adalyn reaches out a hesitant hand, grasping his forearm gently. Her small hand barely covers the top of his arm.

He stares at her hand, shocked.

"I see who you are," she steps closer, forcing him to meet her eyes. Still bent over leaning on the rail he stands at her level.

"I am...broken," he whispers, allowing himself this small moment of peace and vulnerability with her. The week's journey with her being so near has worn him down, his cold mask of indifference has been left off more times than it has been on. Adalyn's own guards have come down also.

She is his just as much as he is hers.

"We are all broken, that's how the light gets in. Just because it is dark now, does not mean there won't be another day of light."

"Is it worth it?" Killian wonders, judging from the fire in her eyes he knows her answer before it leaves her lips.

"Yes, Killian. It will always be worth it. Is it so wrong to hope for something better, for something *more*?" she asks sadly, squeezing his arm.

He'd lost hope a long, long time ago.

But looking at Adalyn...it's almost having him believe once more.

Adalyn mistakes his silence and drops her hand, casting her eyes down even though her freckled cheeks turn a shade of red that bridge across her nose.

"I've misspoken, forget it."

Killian reaches out, wrapping his hand gently around her forearm to keep her from retreating into the tavern. He doesn't want her to hide from him anymore.

"Adalyn..." he frustrates himself, finding no words of use. If only she could peer into his heart and see his true feelings.

"It's okay," she whispers. Dejected. Embarrassed. He frowns, using his other hand to guide her face towards him. Touching her warms his skin, sends a thrill through him.

"If you could truly see the depths of my black heart, do you really believe you could still look at me with hope? Do you really believe you could ignite that light inside of me?" He towers over her now, rising to his full height. She's so small against him, a perfect match against the hard planes of his body. He doesn't tell her that he fears she is already the stars in his darkest night.

"I don't know how many times I have to tell you, Killian. I may be angry and hurt with you, but there is a part of me that cares for you as much as it infuriates me. I shouldn't...feel these things for you. I shouldn't be attracted to you." She searches his eyes, going rigid before him. "I shouldn't have such strong emotions for you, but I do. I would not have given my body to you if I didn't feel this way."

"I am truly sorry."

"Stop. I don't want your apologies. You're only saying it because it will make you feel better about yourself. I only ever asked for your honesty." Her anger deflates and leaves her raw before him.

"I have only ever given it. You will come to hate me Adalyn, it is the way our story will go." Killian takes a ragged breath, "but I am selfish enough to indulge in your kindness no matter how small an offer it is."

"I couldn't hate you." She shakes her head, "I've tried, and maybe deep down there is a part of me that does, but that isn't what we're talking about. You are not a bad person Killian, I see your cold black heart and underneath it all your blood runs just as warm as mine."

"So we both have cold black hearts?" He smirks, eyes sparkling with slight mirth. Adalyn chuckles softly, the sound is a melody to his ears. All senses focus on the staccato of low notes that fall from her mouth, a song that he wants to listen to on a loop.

She remembers herself, sobering slightly although a faint smile graces her lips.

"There you are." She presses a hand gently to his chest, raising on the tips of her toes to brush a gentle kiss across his cheek.

Before he can reply she's heading back through the propped open tavern door. Killian gathers himself, finding his thoughts and feelings settled. He looks back over the small village as the sun sets, breaking the darkening blue sky into a mixture of deep violets and pinks.

A lightness seeps into his heart as he finds himself smiling slightly.

His feelings for Adalyn solidify until his every breath seems to be for her, he vowed to never fall in love again, but for Adalyn?

For Adalyn he would destroy this world and everyone in it if meant keeping her safe. For what he feels for her, there is not a word strong enough.

. . .

Killian slides from the bed, carefully untangling his limbs from Adalyn. She sleeps soundlessly, her auburn hair decorates the silk pillow. Killian stands there for a moment, unmoving as he admires her. He studies the gentle rise and fall of her chest, how her mouth is slightly agape and her face is relaxed.

Something tightens in his chest.

He moves away from her, keeping his steps light as he pulls out his usual full body black attire. As he dresses swiftly, he finds his eyes straying back to Adalyn sleeping.

She is perfect in every form. Not once would he have imagined he'd think of any human with such fond thoughts. He never thought he'd share himself with one either, but Adalyn seems to be crafted from the same stars as him.

Killian silently straps his two long swords to his back before leaving their room, he needs to speak with Peri before they begin the next leg of their journey.

Other residents staying at the hotel give him clear berth, not daring to walk too close. He listens to their fearful whispers and silently, *guilty* indulges in them. Peri had made it very clear he isn't to use his terror on the guests, but even fear itself clings to others. It is enough to sway the cravings.

Peri mulls over a document when Killian enters the lobby, he looks towards the soft footfalls and breaks into a grin.

"Ah Killian, I should have known you'd seek me out," Peri says, disregarding the papers that sit in front of him. Killian relaxes, he'd missed his old friend.

"Yes but I'm afraid it's about a mission the king has sent me on." Killian stops in front of the desk, leaning his hip against it as he crosses his arms over his chest. Peri spits black phlegm into a stone bowl, he'd never like the king.

"Ack, what does that tyrant want you to do now?"

Killian chuckles, "you are very brave for someone who is so small."

"It's not like the king is going to waltz in here and pulverize me. I was around long before he had ever been a squirmy worm in his father's ball sack."

Killian laughs deeply, the sound echoes around the lobby. Peri cackles himself, stretches his leathery wings out and puffs his chest forward.

"I have not come to talk about the king in a ball sack, Peri. I've been sent north east because there is a sickness plaguing the Valarki and they're dying with no real cause." Killian begins, furrowing his brows, "the kings wants me to look closer and use my magic to find out what is killing them."

"I've heard a few rumours of the sickness," Peri admits, clasping his small hands together as he rests his chin on them, "I didn't realise it was that bad to send you though, why wouldn't he send one of the other mongrels?"

"It's because there is also a traitor to our kind, I'm trailing them as I'm heading towards the magic that is leading me to the sickness. The king wants them brought back to the castle alive."

Peri is silent, mulling over his thoughts. Killian looks away, studies the fire of a torch as the next words burn his throat, "It... feels wrong. A large part of me hopes I can't find them. I couldn't handle the look on Adalyn's face if she knew what was to become of them."

"How does the human woman play into all of this anyway?" Peri asks, "I know what the king holds against you Killian, you don't need to hold the judgement of others on your shoulders."

"She..." Killian's stomach turns leaden, "she is one of the ten women he has chosen for his harem."

Peri blanches, slapping Killian on the arm. He hisses as he pulls his hand away, "You're built like a stone wall."

"You brought that on yourself," Killian grumbles, turning to face Peri. Peri stares up at him, narrowing his eyes.

"Why do you have one of his women here...better yet, why do you both seem more than smitten with each other?"

Killian says nothing, knowing the hardened look on his face

will answer all of the questions that Peri wishes to ask. Peri huffs out a breath and leans back, "Do you truly care for the girl?"

"I do, but sometimes I wish I did not."

Peri looks at him sympathetically, "Do not harbour guilt for doing what makes you happy. You've been miserable for far too long, but you need to know how this will end."

"I know how it's going to end," Killian's chest constricts with pain, almost enough to take his breath away, "I know how it ends and yet I find myself unable to pull myself away from her."

"She's far stronger than you're giving her credit for." Peri chirps, he looks through the papers on his desk, "if you find the sickness, do not bring it back to me."

Killian shakes his head, shoving his hands into his pockets, "You'd be the first person I'd give it to."

"You flatter me, Killian," Peri calls after his retreating figure. Killian shakes off his sullen mood as he hurries through the stone paths that will lead him to Adalyn. Each step towards her has his muscles tensing, his heart racing and his palms sweating.

If Jurian could see how much he's effected by her, he'd laugh himself hoarse.

He opens their door to find her still draped across the bed, one hand hangs off the bed limply as the silk sheets bunch at her waist. She lays on her stomach, still sound asleep. Killian almost feels bad for having to wake her up.

He pauses momentarily before gently taking her hand, he crouches down and runs his thumb over the soft skin on the back of her hand, "Wake up sweetheart."

Adalyn slowly wakes, her eyelids flutter before those burnt golden eyes are looking at him. She smiles lazily, squeezing his hand before yawning.

"We must be leaving now," he says, unable to look away from her. She moans and sniffles before rising onto her elbows, taking her hand away from his.

"Can I bathe quickly?" She asks, raising a brow at him, "I'm sore and feel grimy."

"Of course you can, I'll gather our things and refill our bags. I'll be back shortly."

He leaves her side, gathering their water skins before slipping out of their room. He makes quick work of filling their bottles up and gathering a large cloth filled with jerky and bread. Once he returns to the room Adalyn is lacing up her boots, she'd tied back her hair and is dressed in her leather black riding pants and loose flowing white top.

She stands and tucks her shirt into her pants, Killian fills both of their bags up. Adalyn throws on her cloak and takes her bag, securing it over her shoulders.

"Where are we going after we head through the forest?" She asks as she follows him from the room, walking closer than she had the day before. Killian leads them through the winding stone hallways, most Valarki stare at Adalyn but she pays them no attention.

"I'm unsure of the village, I'll be able to tell you once we reach it," he assures her. As they walk through the lobby Peri waves a small leathery hand. Adalyn waves back before Killian is taking her hand in his. He intertwines their fingers and tugs her along.

"You're very touchy feely today," she comments, tugging her hand against his own.

"No more than usual," he remarks coolly, not wanting to admit it. He can practically feel her eyes rolling and hears the small scoff under her breath, but yet she doesn't rip her hand from his.

They reach the small balcony of the tavern, the sun shines brightly against them. Below, the village is bustling with life. Adalyn squeezes his hand and steps closer.

"I'll go first, just keep holding my hand," he assures her, beginning the deep decent to land. Adalyn stays silent, but he feels her slight tremors with each step they take. Heights don't bother him, he doesn't have much that bothers him.

Adalyn lets out a breath once her feet hit the dirt, she takes her hand from his own to adjust her hair from the wind. Killian continues to walk along the side of the village, nodding to the

Valarki who get caught staring at him. Adalyn is quick to catch up, her shoulder brushes against his own as they walk along silently.

From here, Killian can see the tall pine of the Okra forest. Above the towering sharpened canopy large black crows fly lazily, even the birds don't dare delve in their depths.

"What's the forest made up of?" Adalyn asks suddenly, breaking his train of thought.

"Pine trees and dead trees. It's no place for the living." They'd almost reached the turn from the village that will take them straight to the forest.

"Why must we go through it then? Can't we go around it?" Adalyn asks, he catches her frowning from the corner of his eye. His lips tug into a smile.

"There is no way to go around it, Okra forest covers the entire north east coast. It's the barrier between us and the ocean."

"I still think this is a bad idea," Adalyn grumbles, crossing her arms over her chest.

"Oh, it's definitely a bad idea Addie."

She pushes him slightly, he chuckles as he looks down at her frowning face. He pinches her cheek softly, earning a scowl as he leaves a small red mark behind.

"You—" her words dry out in her throat as they reach the dirt turn off. To their right the village is bustling with life, to their left there is only darkness and the occasional caw of a crow.

"Stay close to me Adalyn, this is no place for the living, hence why we must leave our horses. I will use my magic to hide our presence but even then some creatures can see through veils. I will keep you safe." He assures her, holding out his hand before they make the small walk to the forest. It almost seems to taunt them with its shadowy depths.

Adalyn hesitates, looking from Killian to the forest. After a moment she relents and slides her hand into his own. He pulls her close, needing the warmth that radiates from her to calm his fraying nerves.

Together, they begin their journey into the Okra forest.

31. Adalyn

Adalyn

Adalyn had lost track of where exactly in the forest they had been walking the moment the village behind them had disappeared. Around the forest was thick, dense pine trees. As they journeyed deeper into the forest, the trees became more unorganised; occasionally Adalyn would swear the trees would move and appear in another spot. Killian had been silent the entire time, completely on alert.

It had allowed her to relax slightly, after she'd shared herself with him the day before, she'd felt even more at home being around him. She still didn't completely trust him, but there is no other that she'd ever let herself be so unguarded with.

Adalyn keeps an eye on the random dead and gnarled tree that reaches for the blue sky, it's branches grey and leering towards the world above, as if they have a mind of their own and wish to escape this forest as well. Moss covers the damp brown earth, Adalyn spots a dark blue flower that grows drooping towards the earth.

"What sort of flower is that?" Adalyn whispers, pointing towards the small cluster that grows beneath a pine tree. Killian turns his head.

"That's a columbine. You'll find them scattered throughout the forest," he whispers back, giving her hand a gentle squeeze.

"Can we rest for five? I feel like we've been walking for hours." Adalyn admits, "I just want to sit down and stretch my legs out."

Killian stops them, turning his head slowly from side to side as he listens to noises Adalyn has no hope of hearing. So far she hadn't seen anything that could endanger them.

"Alright but only for five minutes. We don't want to be caught in the middle once nightfall comes." Killian releases her hand and stays standing, "I'll keep watch."

Adalyn sighs her relief as she walks over to a fallen moss covered log, she sits down and stretches her legs out before digging into her bag and pulling out her water flask and a piece of fruit.

She studies Killian, he stands tall and tense as his glacial blue eyes continue to skip over the forest around them, the shadow of his jaw is darkened as stubble has begun to grow. Heat ignites her veins at the burst of attraction that threatens to drown her, the shadowed jaw has her even more attracted to Killian, something she didn't know was possible.

His eyes snap to hers as his nostrils flare. Her cheeks burn but she refuses to look away.

"Where are your thoughts, Adalyn?" He murmurs, not once taking his attention away from her.

"Definitely not where they should be," she admits, tucking a stray strand of auburn hair over her rounder ear. Killian's lips tip into a secretive smile. He knows exactly where her thoughts are.

"Alright, lets continue." Adalyn readjusts her bag before walking back towards Killian. They walk side by side once more as they weave their way through the forest. Adalyn's thoughts stray away from their current task, straying to what's going to happen once they return to the castle.

There could be nothing for them once they stepped foot into the castle grounds, Adalyn is property of the king and Killian is, in his words, the king's hound.

In a sense, they are both slaves to the same ruler; bound together by the blood that's been shed and the steel that's been sharpened.

A deafening roar pierces the veil of silence that had been hanging heavily in the space between Adalyn and Killian, both caught up in their own thoughts. Adalyn startles, stumbling as the moss covered earth beneath her feet trembles.

Killian freezes, searching the shadows that surround them. The stillness that surrounds him is utterly inhuman, a tell-tale sign that he's a Valarki. Adalyn steps closer, pushing all stray thoughts aside. If she wants to survive whatever creatures stalk these woods, staying with Killian is her best option.

Curiosity over rides her fear, "what—"

Killian slowly raises a hand, a small subtle shake of his head has her sealing her lips. Adalyn's heart picks up speed as her fear grows, wanting to rear its ugly head and take any thought of common sense from her.

Her eyes strain as she peers around Killian's broad build, she's met with a moss clearing with skeletal trees lining it in a perfect circle. Her skin crawls, they have stumbled across something she doesn't want to face.

Their grey branches are slim but many, patches of furry moss and spider web like vines cover most of their branches that spiral towards the sky. High above them the dark leaves of the pine trees offer an ominous amount of shadow beneath their canopy.

Killian lowers his hand, movements slow. He sees something she cannot.

Adalyn peers over her shoulder, suddenly afraid that there's no one protecting them from behind. They'd just stepped into the clearing.

For miles there is only pine trees and the ever growing shadows as the sun leeches from the sky. Adalyn furrows her brow in confusion, she could have sworn they hadn't been walking all day.

Killian had told here these forests are no place for the living.

But yet, he'd still dragged both of them deep into its deadly hands.

Adalyn had mulled over their night in the tavern, what they'd shared and the emotions that now stir in her chest like a furious thunder storm. She'd been able to ignore them at the start, especially after the ordeal with Alissa, but now Killian had weakened her defences; she'd willingly allowed him too.

She feels like the oddity.

Killian takes a slight step back, his booted foot makes no noise. Silently he reaches for her, she takes his outstretched hand with both of her own and steps closer to him. Her skin is ghostly compared to the depths of his own deep tanned skin.

She doesn't object as he intertwines their fingers, as he pulls her tight against him.

Immediately the warmth of his body seeps into her own, working to calm her tight and rigid muscles. Adalyn doesn't know what to expect, not while he's still so quiet.

"Run."

He whispers it so softly Adalyn isn't sure she's heard him right. She blinks up at him, suddenly overwhelmed with the urge to never leave his side. His glacier blue eyes frantically search in the distance, as his skin pales as his resolves hardens.

"Run Adalyn and do not look back." He finally looks down to her, true fear lay in his eyes. Fear for her. Adalyn begins to shake her head, ready to protest.

He gently takes hold of her chin and wears his cool mask of indifference, "if you are here you'll only distract me. I can't protect you if I'm constantly searching for you."

"I don't want to leave you—I can't." Adalyn begins to panic, grasping at his hand tightly.

"I'll be right behind you, but I need you to run. Find some place safe to hide and I will find you." A stray tear slips down her flushed cheek, he wipes it away with the pad of his thumb, "I will *always* find you."

"Promise me, Killian." Her panic and sheer despair strangle

every word. If she stayed, she'd do him more harm than good. He kisses her brow, lingering for a moment.

"I promise. Now run, it has found us."

Another piercing roar vibrates the earth, sounding far too close for Adalyn's liking. She studies the planes of Killian's painfully handsome face before turning and running through the forest they'd just walked from. Low lying shrubs snag at her white shirt and coat, tearing at the free flowing strands of her vibrant hair.

Her heart is in her throat as she skids to a stop, spinning to look towards Killian. She never promised she wouldn't look behind her.

She wishes she didn't.

Killian stands before the creature without a trace of fear or hesitation, his flaming twin swords of black shadows are clasped in both hands. He had been born to do this, as if his very essence craves the danger of dancing with death. No breeze dares stir the air.

Adalyn's throat closes up as she looks at the creature that towers before him.

A creature not of the living.

It stands half the height of the trees, it's four long greyish limbs are corded with thin muscle while it's front arms are bent at the elbow. Three large white gleaming bone spikes protrude along it's hunched back, growing larger with each spike.

A shuddering breath leaves its gaping mouth, the tight milky grey skin that encases its body tightens around its large rib cage. From the distance Adalyn can almost make out the hollowness of its body, as if it harbours no organs of its own.

Adalyn feels her knees weaken, she presses a hand to closest trunk to steady herself. Killian twirls the sword in his right hand, sinking into an attack position.

The creature's narrow human like face looks down at him, eyes of darkness stretch back towards grotesque pointed ears while the skin of its jaw is covered in deadly white spikes. As it opens its jaw to scream, the skin stretches open, gaping to expose long jagged gleaming yellow teeth.

Adalyn presses her free hand to her ear as the sound rings through her mind, threatening to burst her eardrums. How Killian can tolerate it is a mystery to Adalyn.

The creature lunges a second later, moving with inhuman speed as it swipes out a large black tip clawed hand. Killian jumps and arches through the air smoothly, easily avoiding its attack.

Killian springs forward, swiping his sword expertly at the creature's back legs as he moves like liquid beneath the large spindly beast. It screeches in anger, lowering its stumpy thick neck to try it's might at grabbing Killian in its large jaws.

Killian's sword swipes through the air in a blur, cutting the creature's cheek and spraying black blood before he jumps and rolls forwards. Adalyn holds her breath as she watches them continue to try and strike each other, Killian isn't able to get an angle that can disable the creature.

It continues to roar, shaking the branches around them and clawing at the earth. Killian leaps towards one of the closest skeletal trees, jumping branch to branch until he's almost eye level with the creature.

The creature tracks him, not missing a beat as it dives towards the tree and wraps large clawed hands around the trunk just below Killian.

Adalyn is so focused on the fight before her, that she doesn't feel the hot breath on her neck until a second before it's too late. She twirls around and looks up, and up, and up until she comes face to face with a creature identical to the one Killian fights.

It watches her with hungry eyes, its half lowered head focused solely on her. Its slitted nostrils open and close as it breaths in her scent. She stumbles back a few steps, eyes widening as a scream gets caught in the tightness of her throat.

A deep groan and large snap echo behind Adalyn, she takes the chance to look behind her; finding the skeletal tree snapped in half with one of Killian's swords lodged into the creatures hand, keeping it pinned to the tree.

She runs towards him, finally her scream escapes. All eyes snap towards her, Killian's lips move as he runs towards her and focuses on the creature behind her.

She dives to the moss covered earth, rolling as Killian leaps over her and fights off the second creature with his one sword.

"Use your powers!" Adalyn yells, clawing backwards.

"They have no mind Adalyn—there is nothing for my fear to latch onto. I cannot feed off of creatures who are created from fear itself." Killian calls back, narrowly avoiding a swipe that would have knocked him across the clearing. Adalyn frantically tries to come up with a plan, looking around the clearing.

Her eyes latch onto the creature that still claws at the sword that traps one hand, it's gnashing jaws reach for her in a frenzy. Adalyn looks beyond the creature, to the jagged trunk that reaches for the sky.

An idea sparks, a dangerous idea that might just get them killed; or save them.

"Killian I have a plan!" Adalyn calls out, getting to her feet and throwing her fear aside. She needed to be quick and smart if this was going to work.

"Don't get yourself killed!" Killian calls out. Adalyn has the urge to laugh as she runs straight for the creature, at the last second she dives underneath its snapping jaws and collides with the trunk. She reaches up and heaves the sword out of the creatures hand, black blood sprays as the creature roars.

Adalyn grasps Killian's sword and is struck by deep rooted fear as his dark shadows dance over her hands, feeding her fear. *The clearing changes and morphs as thick black smoke hangs into the air; as burning wood fills her lungs with every breath.*

Distantly she's aware of someone calling her name but all she can see is the structure of her family's home burning, of blue leering eyes watching from the shadows.

Adalyn's fear transforms until she is standing in a foreign room, peering out of golden eyes and into an empty glass dome. A tan hand laden with rings reaches for the dome, tapping the glass. Black smoke bursts and rushes towards the glass, spreading and thickening. A deep chuckle reaches her ears.

Before Adalyn can comprehend where she is she's thrown back into the present world, she gasps as she falls to her knees. Killian fights against the two creatures before her, protecting her. The sword falls from her hands as she scrambles towards the trunk, she'd need the creatures to dive towards her.

"Killian I need you to take them to the other side of the clearing." She calls as she scrambles onto the tree, pulling herself towards the jagged opening with the small foot holds. Killian doesn't question her.

Adalyn heaves herself into the hollow trunk, careful as she dangles her legs into the dark depths. With a surge of bravery she free falls a short distance, landing against a soft patch of moss.

"I can do this." She whispers to herself, clenching and unclenching her hands, "there is nothing I can't do."

She stands and raises her arms above her head, grasping the sharp opening.

"Killian, take cover!" She yells. With a swift movement she swipes her palm across a sharp piece of trunk, blood spurts and bubbles from the cut as red blood begins to run down her arm and soak her white shirt.

"ADALYN!" Killian's roar shakes the world, it almost disguises the thundering of limbs that race towards her.

She curls in on herself, waiting for impact. If this does not work, she'd doomed both of them.

A large jaw clamps around the stump opening, a long grey tongue begins to unfurl as rancid breath suffocates her. In their haze for her blood, they don't realise the trap she has set.

The second creature jumps onto the first, successfully impaling its head on the sharpened spike. Black blood oozes against the wooden walls that surround her as darkness overtakes any light.

A second later the creature is ripped from the trunk, another pair of jaws begin to snap at the wood; desperate to get to her.

She raises her hand towards its mouth, swallowing her bile as a large blob of drool lands on her legs. Her closer scent has the creature going half mad, clawing and pushing its opened jaws over the trunk like the over creature had.

Inch by inch it's tongue grows closer to her, spikes gleam in the dull light that filters through a crack in the wood. If it grabs her with its tongue it will take layers from her skin.

Adalyn is almost ready to scream for help until the creature comes to a halt, above her a silver sword gleams from the top of its mouth.

Adalyn could almost cry. Killian makes quick work of retracting his sword and sawing open more of the split in the trunk. Adalyn desperately crawls out, falling into his arms. She sobs as she holds onto him tightly, breathing in his scent.

"I could kill you," he whispers, pulling her back to search her face. Adalyn grasps his cheeks, bringing her lips to his. She kisses him desperately, intertwining their tongues.

He hisses as he breaks away, paling. Adalyn steps back and quickly assesses him, leaving a bloody hand print on his cheek. A deep gash has split open his left arm from wrist to elbow.

"Oh god, wait here." Adalyn runs across the clearing, digging through her fallen bag for her skin of water. She rushes back to Killian and gently dribbles the water of his wound, he bites his lip against the pain.

"We need somewhere safe to stay." she says, hands shaking as she looks back to where the two large creatures now lay dead. A part of her is tempted to break off one of their claws, to wear it as a necklace to show the Valarki she should be something to fear.

"There should be a cabin close by," Killian grunts, holding his arm against his chest. Adalyn undoes her shirt, leaving her top half bare as she wraps it tightly around his wound. Her nipples pebble from the cold but Killian pays them no mind, focusing solely on her face.

"Let's be quick, but I just need one thing." She picks up one of his swords and rushes to the closest creature, one of their claws is the length of her forearm. She saws the knife in the joint, hacking away until one black claw rolls free. Gingerly she picks it up, holding the knife in her other hand.

"You...are everything I could have hoped you'd be," Killian murmurs as she turns back to him. She rolls her eyes but makes quick work of stuffing the claw into her bag before shouldering it. With a sword clasped in her hand she feels more protected, as if she could face anything.

Killian picks up his other sword and begins to lead the way through the forest. A sliver of light reaches them now, making it hard for Adalyn to see in front of her. The chill in the air had begun to seep into her bones, clacking her teeth together.

It isn't long before they reach an outline of a small, run down cabin. Greenery has overgrown most of the structure. Killian pries open the wooden rotted door with his sword before ducking inside. Adalyn hurries after him, pulling it closes tightly behind her.

She takes a deep breath, the scent of Killian's blood overwhelms any other scent that may be lingering in the air. A golden light sparks to her left, she hurries into the room to find Killian kneeling before a small fire. He coaxes it with a shallow breath, adding kindling. Moments later they have a roaring fire that warms the small room.

Killian leans back against an overgrown couch, leaning his head back and closing his eyes. Adalyn drops her bag and digs out another long sleeve shirt before pulling it on. She clasps her cloak tightly around her before going to Killian's side.

"We need to wrap this better." She whispers, gently taking his injured arm in both hands. He breathes heavily through his nose as she peels her blood soaked shirt back. The muscle has been cut cleanly, leaving no jagged pieces behind.

"It will take a few days to heal." Killian mumbles, "we do not have a few days."

"It's okay. You don't need to be the sole protector." She grabs her water skin, "this is going to hurt and I'm sorry."

"Those were death eaters, creatures born from fear and created by this very forest." He begins talking, distracting himself from the pain as Adalyn flushes out his wound once more.

"The forest created them? How?" She asks, looking through his saddle bag to find some clean padding and gauze. She gently packs the wound with a green poultice she found at the bottom of his bag before covering it with padding and wrapping it with gauze. She's no expert healer, but she knew the basics. She quickly flushes the cut on her hand out before lathering it with the same poultice.

"Everything around us is magic Addie, the very air we breathe is heavy with magic. I have surrounded this cabin with my own magic to keep us hidden and safe for the night, but there are creatures that have awoken now due to both of our blood. Tonight the two death eaters will be eaten by the scavengers." Killian leans forward, resting his injured arm in his lap. He takes her injured hand and gently assesses it.

"How much longer do we need to walk through this forest?" Adalyn asks, listening to the crackle and pop of the fire that warms her side.

"Only another day, time doesn't work like the rest of the world in this forest. It's something even I can't explain." He looks up from her hand, capturing her eyes with his own, "What you did...I am thankful."

"You're not angry?" She edges closer, careful of his injury as she rests against his side. He shakes his head gently, his pointed ears slip through his black curtain of hair.

"Oh, I am furious and once we are both safe and fully healed I will be bending you over the closest surface and spanking that pale ass of yours until my hand is branded into it." He growls, his promise has Adalyn biting her bottom lip. Arousal stirs between them.

"But..." she hints, beginning to smile.

"But…I am proud of you and the courage you found. You killed those two creatures and that is something you should carry with pride." He drops her hand and grasps her cheek, pressing his forehead to her own as their breaths mingle, "it was incredibly arousing watching as you hacked away a claw while shirtless and covered in blood."

"You give me the impression you like seeing me covered in blood," Adalyn whispers huskily, coming around to the idea faster than she liked to admit. He chuckles deeply.

"I like seeing you *strong*, Addie. You are no weak human, or weak woman. You outshine even the brightest stars on my darkest nights."

Adalyn gently presses her lips to his own, wishing she could mount his lap and bring them both to bliss. To forget about the fear that had plagued both of them.

"I was scared." Adalyn admits against his lips.

"Just because you are scared does not mean you are not strong, you transformed that fear into a weapon and turned yourself into a warrior. Do not think of yourself as anything less." He kisses her back, his lips slide easily against her own. She moans low in her throat before pulling away, shaking her head.

"Thank you, Killian." She leans back and looks towards the burning flames. He kisses her cheek gently before rising, he unrolls both bed rolls before laying down facing the fire. She sits by his feet, gently caressing his thigh. She needs to clean the blood from her body and change into a clean pair of pants. She'd need to help Killian change as well.

"Come on, let's change you into night clothes." She rises and pulls out both of their night outfits, more than ready to slide into her nightgown. She helps Killian stand before manoeuvring him out of his shirt, careful of his wrapped arm. She pulls a loose fitting shirt over his head before untying his pants and pulling them down to his ankles.

"I'm sorry," he says shyly, she tugs them from each foot before pulling on his loose pants. She purposely runs her hand along his impressive, thick, hardening length.

"I wish we weren't injured," she admits, stepping away from him. He studies her, shadows dance around him as she peels her own pants and shirt off. She shivers as she stands naked before him, watching as his throat bobs.

"I wish we weren't either," he says gravely, clenching a hand at his side. She reaches down and wets a cloth before quickly scrubbing at the dried blood on her skin, she uses the last of her water skin to clean herself and Killian. Pulling on her nightgown she moves around the fire and hangs the cloth out on a vine. She feels Killian track her entire move.

"Let's get some sleep." Killian yawns, laying down on his role and pulling his cloak over him. Adalyn blows him a kiss before picking up a piece of wood that holds fire.

"I'm going to explore but I'll be back soon. Only in the cabin." She doesn't waste time before slipping from the room and into the opposite one, it must have been a small bedroom of sorts. She pulls open vine covered drawers, finding decaying clothes and skeletons of small critters. Room to room she moves, grabbing a few secret items before coming back to the room Killian sleeps in. Her arm is full with a small dagger, a leather holster and a jagged blue crystal. It reminded her of Killians eyes, she'd give it to him if they made it out of this forest.

She'd never gifted a lover any presents before, she'd truthfully never *had* a lover before Killian but it feels right to give him something. Especially after what they survived today.

She hides her treasures in her bag before tucking herself around Killian, she rests her head against the back of his neck and shoulder and he gently takes her arm and wraps it around to his chest.

His warmth seeps into her, pulling the depths of sleep with it. She snuggles into him, interlacing their legs. His words replay over and over in her mind as sleep claims her, *you outshine even the brightest stars on my darkest nights.*

32. Adalyn

Adalyn

Adalyn stares up at the decaying wooden ceiling, rays of light shine through the gaps and cover the walls and floor. She's surprised the entire roof hadn't collapsed in on itself through the night, there's nothing but pure luck keeping the small building standing.

Or magic.

Adalyn peels herself away from Killian, careful to not wake him. She peers down at his face, peaceful with sleep. She gently brushes her hand down his cheek before letting him sleep some more. She dresses quickly, pulling her boots on and lacing them tightly. Her hand had almost fully healed overnight, a faint pink slice stretches from her outer palm to where the skin connects to her thumb.

Adalyn adjusts her bag over her back, she pulls out an outfit for Killian before also securing his bag onto her back as well. They'd need to leave soon, find clean water and continue on their journey.

A groan pulls Adalyn's attention from the charred wood where the fire had been, Killian blinks slowly; stretching his muscled arms above his head. Adalyn watches as he smirks, raising a dark brow at her.

"Like what you see?" He says huskily, his voice still thick with sleep. Adalyn rolls her eyes, propping her hands on her hips.

"I'd like it even better if you couldn't talk," she replies, raising her own brow at him. He shakes his head and rises from the bed, catching the clothes she tosses to him.

"Get dressed, we need to get going." Adalyn hurries to roll the bedding up, strapping it to the bags. Killian dresses silently, pulling his hair back tightly. It exposes his pointed ears, sharp jaw line and the curve of his throat. She'd never seen his face so clearly before, he'd always had hair in the way.

He's painfully beautiful. He reminds her of a serpent, beautiful and lethal with a bite that could kill.

"I can carry my own bag Addie," Killian huffs, clasping both swords onto his back.

"We need your arm to heal as fast as it can," she turns to face him, "I'm fine carrying both bags. They're not that heavy."

"A few more days and it'll be like it never happened." He takes a step forward, towering over her. She tips her face back, glaring up at him.

"I don't care if it takes a few hours or a few days. I cannot fight Killian, if straining your arm in any way delays your healing we'll both be screwed."

He purses his lips, assessing her.

He knows she's right, he's just too stubborn to admit it. She huffs and walks past him, heading for the small front door. He follows quickly behind, shutting the door behind them once they're in the open.

Adalyn takes a deep breath, relishing the fresh air. Ahead a crow cries out, circling a pine tree in the distance. Killian takes Adalyn's hand, prompting her to follow him.

"What time do you think it is?" She asks. She gives the small cabin one last glance before facing forward as they head deeper into the forest. Killian knows where they're going, so they have no chance of getting lost.

A small relief.

"Mid-morning. We went further than I assumed yesterday, we should be reaching Arden by mid-afternoon."

"Arden?" Adalyn asks. "Your people name your villages the weirdest things."

Killian chuckles, "Arden is a common name among Valarki. The village was named after the male who first built it. It's quite large and it harbours the sickness."

Adalyn is quiet for a moment, "what is the sickness?"

"I'm not sure, which is why the king has sent me to find out more information. Valarki are getting sick with no cause and dying swiftly, hopefully finding answers for the sickness will be easier than getting answers from the traitor."

"What if it's contagious?" Adalyn asks again, peering up at him. Killian sighs, licking his lips.

"You won't get sick, from what the few reports have stated it is only Valarki." He smiles weakly down at her, "nothing to worry about."

"I'm not worried about myself, I'm worried about you." Adalyn looks away from him, focusing on the defined deep brown trunks of the pine trees. Focusing on anything that isn't his intense stare that peels her layers away.

"I'll be fine Adalyn, it'll take more than a random sickness to knock me down."

Adalyn says nothing more, opting for silence for the remainder of the walk. Adalyn's thoughts pull her back to the fight with the death eaters, to the moment her hands had grasped Killian's flaming sword and she'd been thrown into her memories...at least that's what she assumed they were. Her mind snags on the last thing she saw before being pulled back to the present, a glass dome filled with black smoke.

She had never seen anything like that before in her life, she mulls over it, confused. Was it just a hallucination from Killian's magic?

"What're you thinking about?" Killian asks. Adalyn furrows her brow and takes a deep breath, tasting salt in the air.

"It isn't important. Are we close?" Her eyes strain as she looks ahead, trying to find some sort of opening in the dense thicket.

"A few more moments," Killian assures her.

Adalyn's impatience dissolves as they're suddenly stepping onto a black dirt road, a wooden rickety sign leans off to the side. They both stop once they're out of the forest.

"It's...busy for a dying village," Adalyn remarks, her eyes flicker over the deep blue skinned Valarki that continue to bustle through the wide open streets. Wooden and sandstone buildings scatter for miles. Although the villagers are dying, it's so *alive* compared to the others she'd passed through.

"There are many Valarki here," Killian murmurs, dark wisps of smoke curl around his shoulders, licking up his neck and down his chest.

"We need to take you to a healer." Adalyn begins to walk forward, Valarki peer at her curiously; no hostility in their different shades of blue and grey eyes. Killian is quick to catch up with her.

"Alright, wait up." Killian wraps his hand around her own and guides her in a different direction to the one she'd be walking. Adalyn admires the sandstone buildings, decorated with carvings of sea creatures; creatures Adalyn would never have been able to dream up.

A yellow vine wraps itself around a rope that hangs above them, flaming orange flowers blossom as they walk underneath. Adalyn giggles as a small yellow and black bee zips around her, rushing for the nectar that covers the flower.

"This village is beautiful," she says in awe as Killian leads her up a set of white stone steps, around another bend and through a blooming yellow vine arch way. He stops them while directly underneath it, Adalyn tips her head back to look at him.

Killian delicately plucks a fire orange flower from above before sliding it behind her left ear. His fingers trail down her cheek, splaying across her jaw before slightly gripping her throat.

The possessive thought has her clenching the thighs, liking the dominance he radiates as he stares down at her.

"*You* are beautiful, Adalyn." He kisses her forehead, lips soft, "thorns and all."

"Even if you bleed on my thorns?" She whispers, squeezing the hand that still captures her own. Killian brushes his nose across her own, his hot breath fills the air around her.

"Especially if I bleed, I've never been afraid of blood." He closes the distance and claims her lips, devouring her as if she is the very air he needs. She doesn't stop as he slides his tongue into her mouth, doesn't stop as the hand around her throat tightens.

He chuckles darkly as he pulls away, trailing the hand on her throat around to the back of her neck. He fists a handful of auburn strands, exposing her throat to him.

He trails his lips over her rapid pulse, "Deep down I think we both know just how dark and twisted you can be, my sweet Addie."

Adalyn is at a loss of words, can barely remember to take her next breath—Killian has a way of making her feel like the centre of his universe.

"One day we will explore it all, but until then this will be enough." Killian pulls away, smirking down at her. He tugs her along, leaving behind the flaming orange flowers. Adalyn blushes furiously as she quickly regains her bearings. Valarki smile at both of them as they walk past, no judgement in their eyes as they flicker between Adalyn and Killian.

"We're here." Killian announces, pushing open a glass door to enter a white pristine room. Adalyn is startled from the stark difference, the village outside is colourful and alive while this room is so...empty.

A small woman looks up from her white desk, her grey eyes assess them casually as they approach her desk. She wears a tight fitting deep brown shirt, a nice contrast against her blue skin.

"How can I be helping?" She asks, her accent makes her words heavy, almost melting together.

"We need to see a healer, the best one you have." Adalyn speaks before Killian can. The woman looks to Killian, squinting at him.

"Killian Abaddon?" She combs a hand through her white silk hair, it stays straight the entire time, falling back over her shoulders smoothly.

"Hello Arden," he says, nodding once in acknowledgment. Adalyn gasps, looking between the two of them.

"You're Arden?" She asks, looking back to the woman. Arden chuckles softly, smiling brightly at Adalyn; flashing her elongated canines.

"The one and only, well the one and only of my village." She rises, standing as tall as Killian. She beckons them to follow her through a white door as she pulls on a white coat. Adalyn goes first, slipping her hand out of Killian's. Sometimes it's hard for her not to feel foolish when she shows Killian affection in front of others, she is only human.

"What brings you this way? Apart from your arm." She talks over her shoulder as they walk down a long white hall. Other Valarki move silently through the halls, all wearing white coats and deep blue gloves that reach their elbows.

"I am here to look into the sickness that is spreading," Killian says, his deep voice slightly echoes down the hall. Arden shakes her head, opening a door to their right. She holds it open as they slip in. Before Adalyn a large white bed sits empty, glass cabinets line the back wall full of small glass bottles filled with more colours than Adalyn thought existed.

Killian walks past her and sits on the bed, Arden walks over to the cabinets on the wall and grabs out a long glass bottle filled with a sludgy deep green cream. Adalyn stands at the head of the bed, close to Killian but far enough away that she can still look around the room.

"It came out of nowhere, now I'm getting more than ten patients a day with signs of the sickness and dying from it." She shakes her head, rummaging through the silver tray that sits beside the bed. Arden pulls out a long silver needle and a red thread.

Killian pulls the shirt from over his head, careful of his arm. Adalyn discreetly admires his chiselled chest from the corner of her eye; not wanting to openly stare with Arden so close.

He looks to Adalyn, a smirk tugs at the corner of his lip. She flattens her brows at him and crosses her arms over her chest, he chuckles before holding his injured arm out for Arden.

As she unwraps Adalyn's bandaging she talks.

"It started with excessive nausea, hot and cold flushes which are usual symptoms for a virus or bug. Those symptoms worsen over two hours until it's vomiting, your temperature rising to such heights your organs begin to fail." Arden flushes out Killian's wound with a spray of water, it had healed slightly overnight.

"What comes next?" Killian asks, watching as she begins to scoop out the green cream. Adalyn watches as well, hanging onto her every word. The more she knew, the better.

"Two more hours after, they begin to suffer hallucinations, loss of coherent words and motor function. Temperature drops to the point their hearts begin to fail and they go into hypothermia. Usually death comes swiftly after."

"So it's claiming victims in a matter of hours?" Adalyn asks, Arden looks up to her with frustration.

"Yes. We've run blood work and tests and there is nothing that has shown us exactly what is causing this. There are no pathogens in their body, they're healthy and aren't lacking in any areas." Arden begins to sew Killian's skin together, she works efficiently and neatly, moments later the deep gash has been sealed and wrapped with another white bandage.

"Your arm will still take time to heal, it reached bone. How did you manage this?" Arden places the needle down and walks over to a small silver sink and washes her hands, Adalyn walks over to the glass cabinets and looks over all the small glass vials filled with different colours. The deep purple one is her favourite, although she has no idea what it's purpose is as she can't read their language.

"I fought two death eaters and while Adalyn was executing her plan to kill them, one nicked me in its rush to get to her." He flexes his arm out before pulling his shirt back on.

"They're nasty creatures," Arden comments, drawing Adalyn's attention. A commotion comes from the hall, just reaching Adalyn's ears.

"I need to examine the bodies of those who have died of the sickness. Is it contagious?" Killian says, rising from the bed to stand at his full height. Arden rubs a hand down her face, looking utterly exhausted despite her unearthly beauty.

"Alright. I don't know Killian. I know nothing about this sickness," Arden says, looking to him wearily. Adalyn is sympathetic and feels her pain, she suppresses the urge to reach out and comfort Arden.

The door to the room bursts open, startling them all. A wild eyed Valarki pin points Arden with his stare, "You need to come now. Three have died."

Arden runs from the room and follows the male deeper through the halls, Killian and Adalyn are hot on their heels as they rush through the halls after them.

Adrenaline surges through Adalyn as they burst through double doors and find three metal tables lined up in an empty, cold room. A white sheet covers each figure laying utterly still on the surface.

"Adalyn...you do not have to witness this." Killian murmurs, reaching out to grasp her chin gently. She pats the hand that holds her, offering him a small smile.

"I can do this." She whispers back, "they are not my people."

Killian studies her for a moment before nodding once, dropping his hand. Her heart swells, he always gave her the freedom of choice even if he didn't completely agree with her choices.

Arden pulls back the white sheet covering all three of the

Valarki's faces. Adalyn walks closer, her curiosity biting at her heels.

The first dead Valarki is a woman, her once vibrant blue hair is now dulled by death. Her blue skin is covered in small black bumps, as if something has bitten her. Red veins spider web under her skin, connecting from dot to dot.

Adalyn looks up to find Kilian studying the face of a small Valarki child, her stomach tightens as she looks at the boy who is in the same condition as the woman.

"The sickness does not care for age," Arden says dully, "it's claimed over fifty children."

"Do they suffer?" Killian's voice is soft, a tone she's only heard in private.

"They suffer greatly." Arden rests a hand against the boy's dark mop of hair, brushing back the thick strands. "I have never known a greater pain before."

A heavy silence falls over the group, every death holds grief... but the death of a child is heavier than others. Adalyn bows her head, trying to hide her rising emotions of losing her little brothers. Or losing Emilia.

"Killian...try to use your magic," Adalyn suggests, the idea hitting her out of nowhere. She doesn't know the extent of his power or the limits, but she does know he is stronger than the others. Has gifts the others do not.

Killian looks up to her, his resolve hardening.

"You beautiful, smart woman," he comments before reaching out a shadow covered hand and pressing it onto the forehead of the small boy.

His dark brows furrow and everyone holds their breath.

Seconds turn to minutes, Adalyn twists her hands together in anticipation. Killian's eyes snap to hers, their usual light blue depths darken to black and swallow the whites of his eyes.

He pulls his hand away from the boy, breaking the connection. His eyes return to their normal colour as he takes a shuddering breath. He's disturbed by something and that *terrifies* Adalyn. Killian is not one to be afraid of, well, anything.

"What is it?" Arden asks, taking a step closer. "What did you find?"

Still looking at Adalyn, Killian speaks, "It's...one of us. A Valarki of great power is doing this."

33. Killian

Killian

They leeave the village immediately after Killian discovers that a Valarki is the reason behind the sickness, is the reason behind hundreds of innocent deaths. Whoever has been doing this is hiding their tracks carefully, as if knowing he would be coming after them.

All his own magic could pick up was darkness tinted with white, a foul taste had filled his mouth and closed his air ways once he'd connected his power to theirs. They may be a strong Valarki, but he was stronger.

Adalyn had remained silent, lost in her own thoughts about the sickness and whatever else might be plaguing her unique and beautiful mind. They'd been travelling for four days now, stopping at small villages to replenish their supplies. The sickness had plagued each village to a certain extent, now that Killian had tasted the magic, it was all he could sense.

His darkness had been restless, wanting to feed from the hallucinations that are plaguing the sick. They wouldn't be able to tell the difference, no doubt their hallucinations are nothing short of terror.

So far, he'd been able to fight off his urges, but each encounter with the sickness has him slipping deeper into himself.

Over the four days he'd shown Adalyn simple defence moves, as well as simple fighting tactics. She'd asked about the different plants and how they could each be used. She kept the flaming orange lily, it still looks as though he'd just plucked it from its yellow vine.

He'd tried to teach her as much as he could, knowing she might not be able to retain all the information so quickly. It's a valuable skill to learn, knowing what plants could heal you or kill you.

"What's your favourite flower?" Killian asks, watching as Adalyn runs her hand through a bush of bright pink daisies that grow beside their road they walk on. Adalyn hums under her breath before facing him. They continue to walk, their shoulders brushing with each step.

"Blue hyacinth, sometimes your eyes remind me of them. My favourite herb is lavender though, it tops all else. When I was still living in Oakshire we had a huge lavender garden, most nights I had trouble sleeping so I'd walk across the village and lay between the rows of lavender. Their silvery green leaves always seemed to glow under the moonlight," she says softly.

"You smelt like lavender that night." Killian says, "like lavender and my undoing."

"You were my undoing," she chuckles softly, bumping her shoulder into his own, "never would I have thought this would have transpired between us."

He throws his arm around her shoulders, holding her to his side. His arm had healed a great deal over the last few days, Adalyn had made sure he'd been careful. Once healed he'd have a silver scar, a reminder of Adalyn.

"I can't say I regret that we've...grown closer. I regret the before," he replies, idly brushing his fingers over her collar bone.

"I regret the before as well," she says softly, piping up she says, "What's your favourite flower?"

"Red carnations," Killian answers, not missing a beat.

"Why?"

"Do I need a reason?" He asks, looking down at her. She peers up at him, her amber eyes shining from the reflection of the sun.

Right there and then he knows the shade of her eyes will always be his favourite colour, that nothing could ever begin to compare.

"I guess not." She thinks, "but I like lavender because they soothe me. My mother always turned them into oils and would dab it on my forehead when I was a child and couldn't sleep at night."

"Red carnations were the flowers my father always brought home to my mother...the joy on her face when he'd hand them to her, nothing could compare," Killian comments, offering a small piece of himself to her. He only spoke of his parents to Jurian and Alissa, but even Adalyn is upheaving the darkest parts of himself.

"What happened to your parents?" Adalyn asks.

"That is a story for another day." Killian presses a quick kiss to the top of her head, "we've arrived at Kola."

"Kola?" Adalyn perks up, swivelling her head back and forth as they enter the first part of the small village. Silence hangs heavily over everything, no Valarki are to be seen. No animals can be heard, while the flora has shrivelled up.

"It's another small village, there are only a few people left." Killian sends his magic out. Three Valarki are left.

"Where are they?" Adalyn asks, pulling them to a stop. Killian focuses for a moment, pinpointing the location. The sickness suffocates their location, almost making it hard for Killian to find them.

"Come." He grabs her hand and they walk deeper into the little village, careful not to make too much noise. It's as if too much noise will wake some sort of beast.

Killian stops them out the front of a large wooden home, the door hangs ajar; creaking with the light breeze that brushes past them. Adalyn lets go of his hand and hurries inside, not hesitating once.

He curses under his breath as he rushes after her, wishing her new found courage would make her stop and assess for danger before going in head first.

A soft gasp has Killian rushing down a bare hallway, the floorboards under his feet creak with each step; he rounds a corner to find three single beds. Adalyn stands in front of them, a hand covering her mouth as she looks from bed to bed.

The three Valarki are all sitting up, propped against pillows.

"Have you come to end us?" An elderly male croaks from the middle bed, his dull blue eyes sag at the corners. Adalyn shuffles towards the bed, careful not to startle the man.

"We have come to comfort you in your final hours," she says softly, her voice gentle; as if she's talking to a small child.

"What comfort can you bring a dying man?" he asks, wiping a trembling hand over his sweat covered forehead. Killian watches silently, his heart swells with emotion. She's putting her hatred aside for them.

"My company, knowing that you are not alone." Adalyn runs a hand through her hair, "is there anything I can get? Water?"

"Water, please." The man looks to Killian, his blue eyes flare with recognition. Adalyn dumps their bags and rushes from the room, Killian keeps his senses trained on her before pulling over two wooden chairs.

"I am sorry," Killian says, taking a seat at the end of the first bed. The man shakes his head, a cough rattles his chest.

"There is no reason for you to apologise, you are not the sickness in my body." He rasps, closing his eyes and leaning back. The other two Valarki wheeze in each breath, silently waiting for death to claim them.

"What happened?" Killian asks, resting his elbows on his knees as he leans forward.

"The sickness came hard and fast, wiped out half of the village on the first day. We thought we were safe, but now corpses reside in every home you see."

"It's spreading quickly, but erratically," Killian murmurs,

more to himself than the man. Adalyn is still in the kitchen, no doubt grabbing everything she can think of to help them.

"I know you, general," the man finally says. "I am Cor. We fought together a long time ago."

"Cor?" Killian studies his face, not recognising him in the slightest.

"When you were still at the battle camp training, they would send us out to smaller Valarki villages and make us fight to the death. You would remember them." Cor wheezes, opening his eyes once more.

"I remember them well," Killian says softly, the camp had shaped him into everything his mother had hoped he wouldn't be. His fate was written in the stars, before he had the choice to carve his own path.

"Your fear...is it still wild?" Cor asks, no resentment in his voice. Killian leans back in his chair, studying the old man.

"My fear is in check."

Cor chuckles, breaking into a fit of coughs.

"You haven't been feeding it," Cor finally says, patting his chest.

"I cannot feed it, not with Adalyn." Killian shakes his head, knowing not feeding his darkness will have consequences after a certain amount of time.

"There is nothing that I am afraid to face anymore. That woman, she deserves better than to be around when you explode. Before I go, take our fear. Feed your demon." Cor offers Killian a tired smile.

Killian goes rigid in his seat, his chest feels unnaturally tight as he looks at the old man. Adalyn bursts into the room before he can reply, Cor nods once before focusing on her.

She sits a large bowl full of water down on the desk at the back of the room, three cups of water are clasped against her body with one arm. She sits the cups down, wetting a cloth in the bowl.

"I'm sorry I took so long." She blushes as she comes around to the first bed, Killian watches as she gently pats the female's forehead and whispers to her.

"You never need to apologise dear girl." Cor watches her. Adalyn moves to his bed next, patting his forehead gently.

"No one deserves this death," she mutters, eyes lining with moisture.

"You do not cry for me," Cor says firmly, his voice strong, "there is dignity in death."

Adalyn sniffles but holds her tongue, Killian knows she wants to argue with him. Killian makes himself useful and grabs one of the full cups, he helps each Valarki have a few mouthfuls of water.

Soon they'd begin vomiting and their organs would begin failing, there would be nothing either he or Adalyn could do for those two hours.

"What brings you this far out?" Cor asks, once Adalyn takes the seat beside Killian, the damp cloth still clasped in her hands.

"A traitor and the sickness," Killian says. "The king has sent me."

Cor looks from him to Adalyn. "Then why bring her?"

Anxiety strikes him hard and fast, clawing from his stomach up to his this throat, strangling his vocal cords. Adalyn sighs as she rests a hand against Killian's thigh, oblivious to his internal conflict.

"He insisted I come as punishment for stopping one of the other smaller Valarki's from getting tortured," Adalyn says, nails digging slightly into Killian's thigh.

A breath whooshes from him, he composes himself before either can suspect anything else.

"You save one, only to be stuck with another." Cor chuckles, a smile breaking through the darkness of death that slowly begins to constrict.

"He isn't too bad," Adalyn comments, "after you get past his mask."

"Sometimes it isn't the person who changes." Cor looks between the two of them, "it's the mask that falls off."

"You have your own mask as well," Killian comments, resting his hand over her own. She looks up at him and offers a rare smile, all for him.

"My mask is cooler than yours," she chirps back, focusing back to Cor once more.

"You look worn from the day's travel, we have a working shower in the back if you'd like to freshen up. I will use the last of my magic to heat the water," Cor says, gesturing with a weak hand behind them.

Killian is familiar with not being able to bathe for days, sometimes weeks. Adalyn on the other hand, probably hadn't gone more than a few days without needing to bathe.

Adalyn bites her bottom lip, "are you sure?"

"Of course, I might as well use what I have left," Cor assures her. "Now go, I can smell you from here."

A deep blush covers Adalyn's cheek as she rises, she looks down to Killian in question. He chuckles, knowing the gleam in her eyes.

"Go, I will stay here until you get back," he says, watching her shoulders curve slightly inwards with disappointment. It's enough to make him smirk.

Adalyn leaves the room, leaving a heavy silence behind.

"Feed your demon now," Cor says.

"How will you use your magic while I do that?" Killian scoffs.

"The other two...they are already gone. They will not know the difference. Feed from them Killian, *you* need it more than they do," Cor demands, a sliver of the man he once was shines through. Killian sits silently, knowing he cannot say no.

He closes his eyes and cracks his neck, darkness leaks from him and gathers underneath his chair. He reaches for the first Valarki female who lays unmoving, her pulse barely stable.

Without hesitating his darkness dives under her sky, exploding with every worst possible fear she could dream of. Her fear is heightened from being ill, far sweeter than anything Killian has been able to taste before.

Not once does she move.

Not once does she acknowledge what is happening to her.

Killian drinks in her fear, feeding that *thing* deep inside of him. Sating its hunger, with how sweet her fear tastes. He will only need too feed on two of them.

Cor stays silent as Killian's magic jumps over his still body and dives into the other Valarki, Killian keeps his eyes closed the entire time as the ecstasy fills his veins. His darkness would be more than sated after this feeding, Adalyn would be safe.

Sweet, sweet Addie.

Once he's reached his capacity and his darkness is nothing more than a heavy weight in his chest, he pulls his magic back to him. It moves lazily, pouring back into him once he demands.

He opens his eyes, feeling better than he had in days.

"You look well, Killian," Cor mumbles, shuffling under the sheets to change positon. Killian listens as the spray of water shuts off.

"Thank you Cor." Killian rises and walks to his side, resting his large hand over Cor's wrinkled and frail one.

"Go clean yourself up boy," Cor says, resting his other hand over Killian's and squeezing. "The girl will keep me company. No harm will come to her."

Adalyn walks into the room, looking clean with her wet hair dangling around her. She smiles at Killian, looking down at his clasped hand in Cors.

Cor releases his hand, focusing once more on Adalyn.

"I'll be quick," Killian says, brushing his lips over Adalyn's forehead before walking deeper into the house, following her scent to the bathing chamber. She'd left a clean pair of his clothes on a brown stool with a white wool towel.

Killian wastes no time as he strips to nothing, cranking the silver lever. Seconds later warm water sprays from the silver shower head and drenches Killian, he undoes the leather strap keeping his hair secured and leans his hands against the stone walls of the shower; letting the water cascade down his back.

His muscles relax under the spray of the water, easing with each drop that kisses his skin. It had been too long since he'd truly been able to relax, months even.

Killian washes himself with the unscented soap, scrubbing deeply and testing out the scar on his arm under the spray of water. He finds a piece of Adalyn's hair on the stone wall, all thoughts of her consume him.

Her standing in this very tub, only moments before, naked and wet.

Killian groans deeply as he begins to harden, unable to deny himself the pleasure of thinking of her. Of remembering how he felt inside of her.

He grips himself tightly, squeezing the base of his shaft. He knew it was wrong, so fucking wrong while those Valarki where currently dying, but when it comes to Adalyn? Only the forgotten gods could save him.

Slowly he begins to pump himself, bracing himself against the shower wall with his other hand as he closes his eyes and lets the fantasies of Adalyn control his mind.

He imagines it's her hand that's wrapped around him, pumping him slowly.

She's the one kneeling before him, looking up at him with those doe eyes and plump lips; acting oblivious to what she does to him, how she makes him feel.

He moves his hand faster, reliving the moment he'd taken her. How tight she'd been as he'd filled her, the noises she'd made and how soft her body had been against the hardness of his own.

He hisses his release as he spills his seed into the bottom of the shower, chest heaving as pleasure releases him from its grasp. He takes a ragged breath before finishing the last of his shower.

Once dried and dressed, he heads back into the main room, finding Adalyn sitting beside Cor's bed with her faces resting against his side. She looks up at him, silent tears track down her cheeks.

Time slows down as Killian blinks, as if the universe demands he take a breath and *admire* Adalyn. Appreciate her. She sniffles, one hand clasped in Cors as he lay still.

No more conversation leaves his lips.

Killian goes to her, heart racing as he kneels in front of her.

"How do I offer you my comfort?" He asks, resting both hands on her knees.

"Stay," she whispers, closing her eyes once more.

Killian falls into silence, reading far too much into that one word alone. He would never leave her side if he had the choice, would fight any Valarki or human to be in stride with her.

As the sun sets the sick Valarki pass into the unknown, leaving a sobbing Adalyn behind. Killian holds her tightly, rubbing her back as she cries for them.

Tears line his own eyes, knowing she hurts so much for them.

"Come on, we can't stay here," Killian murmurs into her hair, still damp from the shower hours before.

"Let's just stay in a different room. It feels wrong to just...leave them." Adalyn mumbles into his chest, tightening her arms around his waist.

"Of course." Killian kisses the top of her head before swaying her back and forth gently, Adalyn finally composes herself. She steps back and wipes her cheeks, looking up at him with blood shot eyes and a red nose.

"Of course you're still gorgeous when you cry," Killian grumbles half-heartedly, earning a broken laugh from her. She takes his hand and leads them from the room, Killian scoops up their bags with his free hand before they settle down into the living room.

Adalyn curls into him as they lay down, he wraps her tightly in his arms. They stay clasped together in silence, finding there are no words that need to be spoken.

Killian closes his eyes and sends out a spark of his magic, trying to find a trace of whoever may be behind this. Underneath the oppression of the sickness, Killian finds a hint of something old; something far too similar to his own magic.

34. Adalyn

Adalyn

Two days pass of relentless walking, Killian stays close to Adalyn's side the entire time. He offers her comfort with small touches, holding her close at night while they fall asleep under the stars.

Being there for the three Valarki in their final hours had been one of the hardest things Adalyn had ever gone through, watching them suffer and not being able to ease their pain.

She had held Cor's hand the entire time, only letting go once his had grown cold and stiff. Killian had told her they'd trained together long ago and told her his name. She'd felt the weight of his death on her chest for the last two days, even now as they trudge up a small hill, she feels heavy.

If someone had told her she'd feel sympathy for *any* Valarki she would have laughed in their face, would have preferred to kill them herself if it meant finding some sort of vengeance for her family.

But...something inside of her has changed.

She has changed.

She looks over to Killian just before he crests the hill, the strong muscles in his leg move with each step while a small bead of sweat runs down the side of his tanned face.

Killian looks at her out of the corner of his eye. "You've been staring at me often, Adalyn."

"I'm just thinking," Adalyn admits, honest. Most times she'd make a joke, call his bluff or blatantly ignore him. But she needs to talk to him, confiding in him might make the heavy weight in her chest easier to carry.

"What're you thinking about?" Killian asks, waiting at the top of the hill for her. Adalyn catches up to him, taking the hand he offers her. He pulls her into him, wrapping his arms around her waist. She leans her cheek on his chest, listens to the *thump thump thump* of his heart.

"Everything that has happened from the moment we met to now. Something has changed. *I have changed.*" She closes her eyes as the sea breeze tugs at her free flowing hair. Killian runs a hand down her back, tugging gently at her auburn hair.

"You have grown, you are still *you*. There is nothing wrong with outgrowing your skin and making a home in your new one." Killian murmurs, "I have also changed Adalyn, *you* have changed me."

"What does that mean for us?" She whispers, refusing to open her eyes. Wanting to hide in the darkness, *his darkness*.

"It means we will grow together, I will always protect you. Even when you're threatening my life." He chuckles, "it means we've found something in each other that is worth fighting for. Once we return, I'm going to find a way to release you of that brand."

"Can you even do that?" Adalyn asks glumly, "I already spoke to Jurian about it. He said there was no way."

"Leave it with me." He kisses the top of her head, "I'm not going anywhere and you're not alone. The sickness is not going to get either of us and we'll deal with the traitor when we find them."

"Okay." Adalyn opens her eyes, although her vision is shielded by Killian's arm.

"Now, I wanted to show you the ocean," Killian says, squeezing her once more, "come on."

Killian twirls Adalyn in the air, earning a startled laugh from her. He places her down and spins her to face the ocean, pressing her back against his chest as they both admire the view before them.

For as far as Adalyn can see, there is only deep dark blue waters that melt and blend into light blue. A seagull caws in the distance before landing on a small sand dune. The golden sand is almost blinding as the afternoon sun rays bear down heavily in the open.

Adalyn is at a loss for words, there's *so much* water. More than she'd ever seen in her life. Killian points to their left, showing a large cliff face.

"There's a rock pool over there, come on." Killian intertwines their fingers and leads her down onto the sand, Adalyn makes a small noise of surprise at the consistency of the sand, startled by how loose and firm it is in different places.

Killian leads them along the dark sand, just as the waves break and bubble before drawing back and doing it all over again. It sprays Adalyn's legs, and the salt in the air intoxicates her.

Once they reach the rocky cliff face Adalyn notices the hidden path that's been carved through the stone. She follows Killian excitedly as he leads them through the walk way. Waves crashing and withdrawing echo through the smooth rock, Adalyn reaches out and runs her free hand along the smooth multi coloured stone.

"At night when the tide is high this entire place is under water," Killian says, smiling at her over his shoulder. It makes her heart skip a beat to see him so carefree.

"Where will we stay tonight?" Adalyn asks.

"On the dunes and then tomorrow morning we'll set back out again." He pulls her through an opening, stepping to the side so she can take in what is before them.

Adalyn gasps.

The stone pathway opens up to reveal a large body of crystal clear blue water, the jagged rocky wall that encircles the pool is just tall enough to hide leering eyes of others who might be on the other side.

Adalyn can clearly see each stone that sits under its surface, can see the small group of fish that swim lazily back and forth. A wave crashes against the stone wall, causing a small spray of water to cascade down; catching the rays of light in a flash of rainbow.

"We can swim here?" Adalyn asks, itching to get out of her clothes and dive under the calm water. Killian lets go of her hand and begins to undress, carelessly discarding his bag, swords and clothes in a pile on a smooth rock that's large enough for the both of them to bask on.

"Of course." He winks at her, dropping his briefs. Adalyn looks towards the sky, heat creeps up her neck. Killian chuckles deeply before the noise is swallowed by the sound of a splash, Adalyn looks back to find him treading water; watching her with a challenge in his eyes.

She smirks back, slowly dropping her bag and unbuttoning her top. Killian wets his bottom lip, his blue eyes track each movement of her fingers; each inhale of her breath.

His burning gaze gives her the confidence she needs to slowly undress herself, watching his reaction the entire time. He makes her feel *powerful.*

A cool breeze skims Adalyn's bare skin, causing her nipples to harden. Killian groans low in his throat, swimming closer to the edge of the stones.

"I want you to at least enjoy a swim before I take you in every single way possible." He reaches out a hand for her, "one swim and then you're mine."

Adalyn chuckles huskily, swaying her hips as she closes the distance between them. Her breasts are heavy with desire as she reaches for his hand. He pulls her into the water, holding her close to the hard planes of his body.

She moans as her breasts slide against his wet chest, he digs his fingers into the tops of her ass, the action has his hard length grinding against the front of her.

"If you keep making those noises, there will be no swim. Go explore, I've shielded your eyes so you can look underwater," Killian grits out, staring intently at her. She puffs out her bottom lip, able to push her lust aside to enjoy the water. She slides from his grasp and dives underneath, kicking out as she goes deeper.

A large silver fish swims past her, its large green eye watches her before it darts away. Her lungs begin to burn but she refuses to surface just yet, she reaches the bottom and grabs onto a bright, spiralling purple sea shell. Pushing from the bottom she darts towards the surface, breaking the surface with a gleeful laugh.

"What did you find?" Killian calls from where he floats on his back.

"A purple shell," Adalyn calls back, holding it against the different rays of light and watching as the purple deepens in colour.

"Is it empty?" He asks. Adalyn flips it over, looking for any sign of a sea critter.

"Yeah it's vacant." She swims back to the shore, pulling herself out. The sun warms her skin as she walks over to their bags, slipping the shell into the pocket that's beside the flower Killian had given her.

"Are you finished swimming?" He calls. She looks back to find him still floating, lazily moving his arms to keep him afloat. From where she stands, she has full view of his impressive muscled form.

Her body begins to burn.

"Yes," she calls back. She laughs as Killian bursts into action, swimming for her. He hauls himself out of the water, chest rising and falling heavily as he devours her with his eyes. She does the same back, unable to take a full breath as he hardens before her.

How she'd fit him inside of her the first time...magic. There's no other answer for how large he is.

"I don't think I can wait for us to go somewhere else," she

says, trailing a hand down between her breasts. Killian tracks her movements, his cock throbs.

"Come here," he orders, his voice deep and rough. Adalyn obeys, utterly his slave to command. She walks to him slowly, shaking her hands out before standing before him. He grips her chin, tilting her face side to side as he licks his lips. "I came in my hand the other night, imagining it was you working me."

Wetness begins to drip down Adalyn's thighs, mixing with the remaining droplets of sea water. His nostrils flare, inhaling her arousal.

"I imagine you often." He leans down and trails his lips over her cheek and down her throat, burning a path from her jaw to the erratic beating of her heart. He bites down on the top of her left breast, wrapping his other arm around her waist as she arches into him.

"Killian," she gasps, clawing at his broad shoulders. He sucks at the soft flesh of her breast, earning another squeal of pain mixed with pleasure.

"Do you like the pain?" he asks once he lets go of her breast, licking the mark.

"Yes." She looks up at him, finding nothing but desire in his eyes for her. She burns for him, *needs* to feel him in every part of her body and soul.

"We have many years to experiment with the fine line between pain and pleasure," Killian hauls her into the air, she wraps her legs around his waist and traps his hard cock in between them, "but for now I need to feel you wrapped around me."

He walks them towards the large stone where their bags rest, he sits her on the edge; lining her opening up with his tip. She looks down between them, bitting her bottom lip hard.

"Killian...be gentle."

"Always for you." He grasps her chin as he claims her lips, letting her control the pace of their passion. The moment their lips connect she is an inferno needing to be extinguished. She tangles her fingers through his wet silk strands, tugging his face closer as she digs her heels into the hard muscles of his arse.

Killian breaks their kiss and drops to his knees, not giving her a second of reprieve from his torture. He licks her from top to bottom, sucking on each slick fold before swirling his tongue around her clit.

Moments later she orgasms hard, throwing her head back and clawing at his shoulders. Killian leans back, his hot breath against her sensitive flesh has her squirming once more.

"Watch me," he demands, nipping at her thigh. She looks down and watches as he slowly inserts one finger inside of her, lowering his mouth to her mound once more, unbothered by the dark smatter of hair.

Adalyn moans as he begins to pump into her, slowly adding a second finger. She tightens her thighs around his head, he growls against her and uses his other hand to spread her wide once more.

"I said watch me." He ravishes her, never taking his eyes from her. She withers underneath him, thrusting her hips against his face and fingers. As he adds a third finger she arches her back, pulsing around him.

"Killian I need you inside of me right *now,*" she begs, yanking his face towards her. He kisses her savagely, the taste of her musk on his lips arouses her more than she'd ever admit.

Using a free hand she reaches between them and wraps a hand around his now fully hard cock, she begins to work her hand up and down his shaft; using her own wetness to lubricate him.

"I want to taste you," she gasps, breaking from their kiss.

He bites down on the soft skin between her throat and shoulder, blood dribbles down her chest as he pulls away; a thin droplet of blood runs down his cheek.

"I need to be inside of you Adalyn." He wraps his free hand around her hand that works his shaft and guides his tip to her slick opening. Slowly he begins to push into her.

With each inch that fills her, she cannot take her eyes from his.

The pain is a dull sting compared to the emotion that unravels in her chest, shining through every pore of her body. A body that Killian owns.

Killian licks the blood from his lip once he's rested fully inside of her. She pulses around him, panting as she grows accustomed to him.

Leaning forward she licks *her* blood from his chin before taking his bottom lip in her own and biting down. Hard enough to draw a small amount of blood.

"You are my undoing." Killian gasps into her mouth as he slowly withdraws from her, then sliding slowly back into her once more.

"Don't stop." Adalyn looks between them, watching as he slides out of her; his thick shaft glistens and throbs before sliding back into her.

"I could never stop." He rests his forehead against her as he begins to pump into her faster, the angle hits a deep spot inside of her; has her thrusting down onto his shaft.

She claims his mouth once more, loving the taste of both of them. Loving the feeling of his body moving into her own, filling her so thoroughly she'd feel him for days afterwards.

Loving him.

She opens her eyes, finding his own reflect the same feeling. The same desire that burns so deeply in her is reflected in him. She would know him blind, in death and in life.

She wouldn't want to have it any other way.

Killian reaches between them and works her clit with his fingers, driving her to that edge of pleasure. He lowers his mouth and clasps her left nipple between his teeth, sucking and twirling his tongue over the sensitive nub.

She screams her orgasm as he bites down and pinches her clit.

He roars his own release, filling her with his seed.

They breath in time to each, Killian stills sits inside of her to his hilt. Adalyn collapse against the rock, sprawling out. Killian lays his head on her chest, resting his arms down her side.

"I will never get used to this," Adalyn finally says, licking her lips. The aches and pain from their love making beginning to shine through now that the haze of pleasure is gone. Her throat aches as does her breast.

"I won't either. Every time with you feels like the first time."

"Well, it has only been twice." Adalyn runs her hands through his hair, massaging his scalp as she closes her eyes and enjoys the last of the rapidly dying light.

"Two of the best moments of my life," he says, gently running his thumb down the side of her breast. It causes her to shiver.

"Come on, let's clean up and get a fire going," Killian says, pulling out of her slowly. He makes quick work of grabbing his water skin and washing himself, he surprises her as he comes over and runs the water down her thighs and between her legs. Gently he wipes his wet shirt down her folds, cleaning away the last of their release.

"I could have done that myself." Adalyn laughs, sliding down from the rock, "but thank you."

"I'm a gentleman," Killian scoffs, tossing her a wink. She rolls her eyes and gets dressed, wrapping her cloak tightly around her shoulders. Her thighs tremble with each step she takes, she couldn't wait to curl into his arms and fall asleep. It's been a perfect day.

"Come on." Killian wraps an arm over her shoulder and guides them through the walk way, the sun has half set by the time they reach the sand. Adalyn watches as golden rays burst through the sky, a final declaration before sinking behind the ocean.

"You won't get pregnant either," Killian says as he leads them to the closest hill that's covered in grass, "I use my magic to ensure my sperm stays sterile."

"I can't say I even thought about it. Lucky you're thinking ahead." Adalyn blushes, feeling foolish she hadn't spared a thought at the consequences that would have hit her if she did fall pregnant.

Could a Valarki and human fall pregnant?

"This spot should be fine, take a seat and relax. I'll gather wood for the fire." He kisses her forehead before heading towards the dark trees they'd walked through that morning. Adalyn sits down on a soft patch of grass, dropping her bag and unrolling their bed rolls.

Once she's set up their bedding she sits up, watching as Killian walks up the hill towards her. He smiles, light enters his eyes as he seems to glow with pure, undiluted happiness. She begins to smile as well, feeling her heart melt in her chest.

Wherever Killian is, she shall be.

"This should be enough to keep us warm through the night." He drops the wood in a pile, his shirt gapes open and exposes the muscles of his stomach. "Eyes up here, Addie."

Adalyn laughs, "I was just admiring my view."

"You're—"

Killian's eyes widen in shock, his smile falters.

Adalyn looks down to his chest, to where a silver arrow head now protrudes. He opens his mouth to say something but his knees give out. A blue substance coats the arrow head along with his blood.

Someone is screaming.

Adalyn is screaming.

"*Killian!*" She hurtles towards him, crying as her hands hover over the arrow head. He gasps a painful breath, his eyes full of fear.

Run, he mouths.

His eyes flutter closed and he slumps forward, she takes all of his weight and gently lays him on his side. She can barely see through the tears that coat her cheeks.

She looks up to find a large, grey skinned Valarki standing down the hill; their split open mouth is far too wide as they grin and begin to stalk up the hill, the bow is now strapped to their broad naked chest.

Fear ignites her veins, her instincts scream at her to run.

But she can't.

She can't.

As the Valarki grows closer, Adalyn covers Killian's body with her own, trying her best to shield him from any more harm. She breaks the end of the arrow off, sobbing as blood gushes from the back of the wound.

Already his back is littered with silver scars.

Her heart breaks.

She won't accept something could kill him so easily. She can only hope and pray that he will come for her, because this Valarki is going to take her.

A large rough hand wraps around her throat and squeezes, hauling her from Killian's barely breathing body. She claws at his hand as he cuts her air supply off and assesses her, his bright green eyes are slitted with black pupils.

His nose is nothing more than two slits on his angular face, his mouth reaches from ear to ear with jagged sharp white teeth clacking together. A long, pink tongue slips between his teeth and licks her tears away.

He nods to himself, deciding her fate.

Adalyn fights to stay conscious but her lungs burn, she uses the last of her energy to look towards Killian, wanting him to be the last thing she sees before it all goes black.

His chest stops rising and falling.

Adalyn falls into darkness.

35. Adalyn

Adalyn

Adalyn keeps her eyes shut as she comes back to consciousness, she keeps her breaths steady as the muffled noises around her begin to become more crisp.

A wad of thick cloth is wrapped around her face, stuffed into her mouth to keep her from making any noise. Each breath through her nose reeks of the old metallic tang of blood. How many others had this gag been on?

She wiggles her hands, finding them bound tightly with rope along with her ankles. She's immobile. A soft moan interrupts her thoughts, Adalyn opens her eyes to find a large roaring fire in the middle of the camp.

A metal frame is propped over the fire, a large piece of meat sits to one side. The Valarki who had grabbed her now flips the meat over with a silver rod, he wears a thin strap of material around his waist but is bare from the chest up.

Adalyn has no idea what sort of Valarki he is, because he is nothing like the others she's met on their journey. From the little amount of information she can gather, he can't speak their language and is alone.

Adalyn cranes her neck, desperately looking for Killian.

He isn't there.

Adalyn doesn't know if she's relieved or terrified. He's in range though, because if he wasn't, the brand on her wrist would have her screaming in pain. It's a small comfort.

A soft sob causes Adalyn to focus back on the camp, two human girls lay bound near her. The girl closest to her has tears streaming down her blood splattered face, her brown eyes full of fear.

The girl that's closest to the fire doesn't move, the only indication she's alive is the steady rise and fall of her small chest. Adalyn squirms in her restraints, trying her best to squeeze a hand through the restraints.

The Valarki swings its large bald head towards the limp girl while chomping down the piece of meat it just cooked over the fire.

Its mouth opens even wider than Adalyn had first thought, the meat is gone after three large chomps. The small camp is bare of anything besides the Valarki's weapon, a large bag and the three women.

Killian where are you?

Adalyn goes utterly still as the Valarki crouches down and grabs the limp girl with a fistful of hair. She doesn't wake, Adalyn spots a large gash on the side of her face as blood steadily streams down and stains her shirt. She hangs from his hand.

In a swift movement the Valarki grabs a large hunting knife from his boot and begins to saw at her throat, the tearing of flesh and bone has Adalyn screaming against her gag.

The girl beside her begins to thrash as well, eyes locked onto the girl. Blood runs down the front of her chest while only half her throat is still attached to her body.

With another brutal cut her body falls to the ground, the Valarki walks over to the fire and throws her head into the embers.

Adalyn watches in shocked horror as he begins to cut her limbs off at the joints, discarding her clothes into the fire until she is nothing more than chunks of near unrecognisable meat.

The Valarki whistles a soft tune as he props the chunks of meat onto the metal grate, entirely unphased. Adalyn forces the bile down her throat, knowing she'll choke if she lets her stomach get the best of her. She'd seen death before.

This is no different.

Adalyn squirms backwards, towards the darkness that borders the camp. The other girl is still thrashing, completely lost in her fear.

The Valarki looks towards her, narrowing its bright green eyes. Adalyn freezes, just as the Valarki stands. The other girl screams around her gag and steals his attention. Adalyn watches him closely as he walks over to the other girl.

He crouches down and rips her pants from her, exposing the tan skin of her behind. Adalyn watches in horror as the cloth around his waist is pulled upwards and exposes a large ribbed membrane; not fully a penis as it wriggles like it has a mind of its own.

He slams into her, wrapping a thick hand around the back of her throat as he continues to take her from behind. Adalyn cries silently, knowing that soon this will be her fate.

After a few more thrusts the girl stops screaming and resisting, she goes limp. As the Valarki roars his release he crushes her throat with his hand, the snap echoes around the fire and rings in Adalyn's ears.

A rough hand grabs Adalyn by the throat, hauling her into the air until she's dangling and struggling for air. The Valarki looks up at her, grinning madly. Adalyn kicks her legs out, hitting the Valarki right between his thighs. He grunts and hunches over, his hand jolts around her throat and loosens the gag that covers her mouth. She spits it out and uses her last breath to scream.

Her scream breaks through the silence of the night.

The Valarki closes his hand around her throat, black spots begin to dot her vision as she gapes. Her lungs burn for that next breath of fresh air.

Just as she's on the verge of falling into the darkness, the

Valarki is ripped from her. She falls face first into the hard ground, grazing her cheek. She gasps for breath, coughing and spluttering around the tightness in her throat.

Through watery eyes she looks up to see Killian standing with his back to her, the arrow is gone from his chest but the wound still oozes blood and a blue substance.

He sways slightly on his feet, his skin pale and dripping with sweat. Adalyn manages to get her wrists unbound as magic pulses and the rope flays, a last lifeline for her. The Valarki charges at Killian. He meets the grey Valarki full force and bellows in pain and fury.

He had come for her, but now she had to save him.

Adalyn rushes to get her ankles out of the bindings, her hands tremble and shake as she does her best to loosen the rope. She looks up in time to see Killian stop the Valarki from driving a silver rod into his chest, his face twists in pain as he snarls; exposing his elongated canines.

Adalyn often forgot all Valarki had the sharpened canines, another tell-tale sign they aren't human. Adalyn scrambles towards the dead girl, the large silver dagger sits beside her body; still coated in blood from the other girl that cooks over the fire.

Careful not to touch the dead woman she reaches over her chest and grabs the dagger, quick to saw through the bindings on her ankles.

She could cry in relief as the blade slips easily through the rope, freeing her.

Adalyn jumps to her feet, dagger in hand. She angles it like Killian has shown her over the last few days, she may not be able to face the Valarki head on but she had another idea.

Killian rips the rod out of the Valarki's hand and punches him in the face, the Valarki is larger than Killian and while Killian is still injured his punch barely moves the creature.

Adalyn sprints across the small distance, Killian meets her eyes as she leaps into the air on quiet feet. She wraps both hands around the hilt of the dagger as she brings the blade down, right into the back of the Valarki's neck.

She screams as blood sprays towards her, but not from fear.

From *rage*.

She withdraws the blade as the Valarki stumbles backwards and tries to grab at her wildly, she keeps her legs wrapped around his waist as best she can.

He bellows in fury as she drives the blade back into his throat, twisting the blade as it tears through flesh and bone. She can't stop herself from smiling as his blood splatters her face, as he falls to his knees.

She continues to stab into his neck, each thrust of the dagger is more forceful than the last.

Once he's lying face down, still gurgling, she digs her fingers into his eyes sockets and pulls his face backwards, Killian watches with wide eyes as she begins to saw into his throat.

The Valarki lets out a pathetic croak before she cuts through his oesophagus, ripping through the last tendons with ease. Her chest rises and falls heavily as she stands, clasping the Valarki's head in her hand.

"Adalyn..." Killian murmurs, stumbling towards her.

His voice breaks her from her murderous thoughts, she throws the head into the fire before rushing towards him. She wraps her arms around his waist as he leans into her, his blood coats the front of her as he falls to his knees.

"Killian, stay with me," Adalyn whispers, carefully laying him down on his back. He coughs and takes a deep, rattling breath. Dull blue eyes meet her own, before closing once more.

"*Killian!*" She cries out, tapping his cheek gently. He does not stir.

His chest barely rises with each breath.

She looks around the camp desperately, her eyes land on the Valarki's large leather bag. She doesn't hesitate as she rushes over to it, opening the straps to dig through the clothes and little bottles that litter the bottom. In the end she hauls the bag back over to Killian, digging out the water skin and a shirt she begins to gently wipe around the wound on his chest.

The blue substance burns the skin of her fingers, causing her to flinch away and wipe her hand desperately against her pant leg.

"Poison?" Adalyn murmurs, digging back through the Valarki's bag. If he had poison, he'd have to also have the antidote for it. Adalyn refuses to accept anything else as she scrambles through the multi coloured glass bottles.

"Killian you've been poisoned, what would the antidote look like?" She asks, even though he can't hear her. She needs to talk, needs to keep him here in any way she can.

Her hand brushes against a small leather pouch, she pulls it out and undoes its bindings. A small, glass vial falls into her open palm containing a milky substance.

"Could this be the antidote?" Adalyn asks, holding the glass to the light of the fire. It hadn't been scattered with the rest, so it must be.

She doesn't have the time to waste to figure it out.

"Killian, I don't know if you need to drink this or if I need to put it in your wound, so I'll do both." Adalyn uncorks the bottle and leans over his chest, gently tipping a small amount of the liquid onto his chest. His back bows upwards as his eyes fly open. "You're going to be okay."

He thrashes against the ground, Adalyn cries as she watches; unsure what she's meant to do.

"You can't die on me," she cries out as the thrashing stops. She brings the rest of the bottle to his lips and leans his head upwards. Trickling the liquid into his mouth slowly, she begins to count backwards from ten.

His throat bobs as he swallows the liquid, he doesn't thrash again. Which Adalyn hopes is a good sign. Once the bottle is empty she places it back in the bag and rests Killian's head back on the ground. She begins to wipe around the wound, watching as the white liquid begins to dissolve the blue liquid and sizzling the blood that had been mixed with the blue poison.

"You're going to be okay, I've got you." She whispers, gently stroking his cheek. She rests her forehead against his own, letting her tears fall onto his cheek.

This has been too close.

She is in far too deep, if Killian dies...she doesn't know if she'd make it. He is the blood in her veins and the air she needs to breath, he has shown her he is capable of change and when he's with her, there is no one else in his world.

Wherever he goes, she will follow.

They can figure out the complications at the castle with the king, Killian would fight for her. He always has, now she had to do the same back.

"Come on, wake up." She sobs, opening her own eyes to find his still closed. His breathing had evened out and the colour has slowly begin to return to his cheeks, it's a small relief.

Adalyn looks around the camp, bile rises in her throat.

She crawls away from Killian and throws up, heaving until there is nothing left in her stomach. Blood still coats her face, neck and arms.

She breathes through her nose, squeezing her eyes closed. She needs to pull her shit together, she can't spiral out of control now; not when Killian needs her so badly.

Adalyn crawls back to his side, holding one of his limp hands between her own. The fire roars in front of them, keeping them both warm as the night grows colder and darker.

Adalyn's head falls forward as sleep begins to overtake her, Killian still breathes soundlessly beside her. She shakes herself, yawning.

If only she could just shut her eyes for five minutes...

A snap steals all traces of sleep as her head snaps upwards, across the fire two glowing eyes watch her from the darkness.

Adalyn drops Killian's hand and grabs the dagger once more before rising on unsteady legs. She'd had the element of surprise with the other Valarki she'd killed, but she had to try.

For Killian, she'd always try.

"What do you want?" She shouts, hands trembling as she points the blade towards the glowing eyes. The rise higher from where they'd been crouched.

Adalyn takes a startled step back as a woman Valarki steps out of the shadows, dressed in ripped mismatched pieces of deep green clothes that blend into her surroundings. Deep blonde dread locks hang down to her waist, exposing both of her pointed ears covered in silver piercings. Deep red tattoos cover her face and throat, running over her shoulders and down her bare arms in swirls and Valarki language.

"I am not here to hurt you," she says, stepping towards the light on silent bare feet.

Adalyn doesn't dare take her eyes from the woman.

"I won't let you hurt him," Adalyn says, resting the back of her heels against Killian's side.

"I can help you," the woman calls, holding up both hands free of weapon, "he needs medical attention."

"How can I trust you?" Adalyn demands, torn between wanting to keep Killian here to look after him herself or letting this stranger help them.

"You can't, but I will help you. I've been tracking the grey Igor you killed. It looks like you beat me to it." She smiles proudly at Adalyn, causing her to blush.

"He...he's been poisoned. I gave him the antidote but he's not getting better." Adalyn relents, slowly dropping her hands to her side. She keeps a wary eye on the woman as she walks over, crouching down beside Killian.

She clicks her tongue as she hovers her hand over his chest wound.

"Come, we must get him back to my home. The antidote has helped stop the spread, but poison still runs through his veins." The woman gently picks up Killian, the muscles on her arms flex as she cradles him to her chest. Adalyn grabs onto the Igor's bag, strapping it to her back before walking beside the woman. She constantly checks on Killian as they begin to walk, not wanting to take her eyes off of him for too long.

Keeping a hand clasped on the dagger she follows the woman into the darkness, hoping she's made the right choice for Killian's sake.

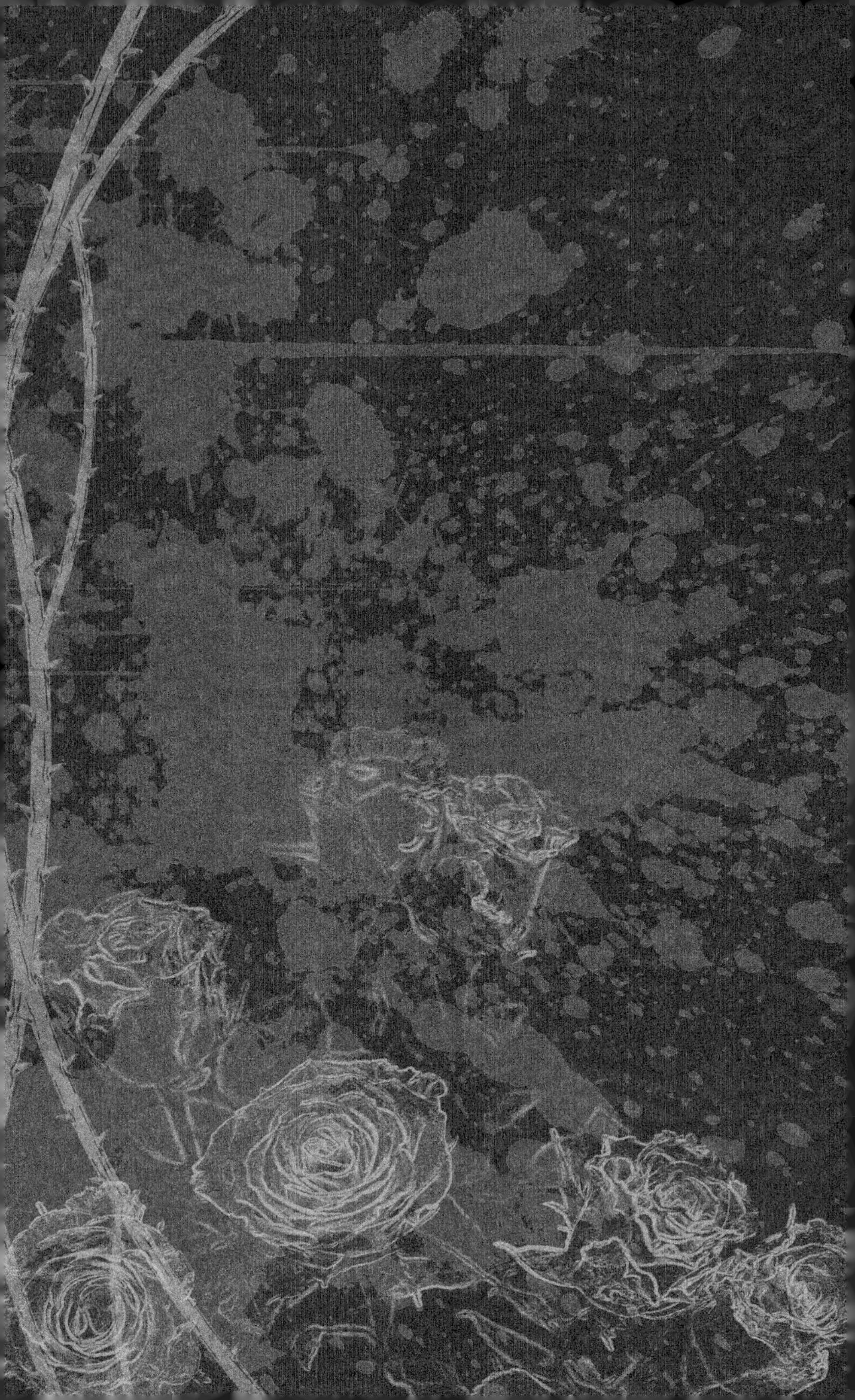

36. Killian
Killian

I stand with my back against a barrack wall, the wood bites into the bare skin that still bleeds from my recent lashing. I hold my tongue against the pain. I will not be weak, I will not show weakness. Jurian stands to my side, in far better condition than I.

"How in the unforgotten god's name did we end up here?" Jurian murmurs, keeping his red eyes narrowed on the rumbling grey sky above us.

"Because you decided to follow me you prick, you could be inside where it's warm." I curse back at him, shaking my head.

He'd followed me secretively as I crept through a gap in the barrack wall that surrounds our camp to meet one of the human slaves they'd been beating. I'd given her a small ration of food and a balm for her wounds. Jurian had scared her off, and we'd both been found arguing outside our camp.

Immediate punishment followed. I was lashed fifty times, taking Jurian's whippings to save the smooth skin of his back being tainted.

I am already stained, there's no reason for me to shy away from the pain. From the lesson they're trying to ingrain in my mind.

"I couldn't let you suffer alone, brother." Jurian begins to chuckle as the first large droplets of freezing rain start their assault.

"You're a fool," I groan, resting my head back against the wood. Somewhere in the buildings in front of us, where golden flames flicker from hearths, there is one person watching us. They'll retrieve us once they believe we've suffered enough.

"Why did you feed the human anyway?" Jurian tilts his head towards me, his blond hair is long and tangled with mud, matching my own raven strands which now stick to the gashes in my back.

"She took a beating similar to one countless of us take, I'm surprised she lived," I say softly, shaking my head. "The punishment is worth the pain."

"You aren't this cold, hard bastard everyone thinks you are." Jurian grins, his face youthful as all white teeth shine.

"Oh, I'm definitely that." I find myself grinning back, despite the pain, despite the punishment.

"He's opening his eyes!" A soft, female voice calls out in desperation. Killian's surroundings are a blur as he struggles to keep his eyes open. His entire body feels as though it is melting from the inside out. He recalls nothing but the fire, the pain.

"Gah you stupid bastard, let the antidote do its job," another female hisses, their words seem to just reach his ears. He feels the darkness beginning to claim him once more, tempting him into its slumber.

His right hand is warm, someone is holding his hand.

A wet drop hits his cheek as soft lips trail over his own, "I am here. I am with you."

Who is she?

Killian succumbs to darkness once more.

"Get up!" Jurian screams, hoisting himself under my right side. I groan as blood spills from my mouth, everything hurts.

"I..." I can't form words as more blood spills from my lips.

Blood and chaos descend around us as Valarki butcher their way through the humans who have thought to fight back with weapons. Foolish, we'd been foolish to think they were weak.

"Leave me," I finally manage to rasp. Blood spills from a deep gash between two ribs, coating my battle suit. A small human had caught me off guard, sticking his dagger into my side.

"I'm not leaving you behind, you fucking asshole." Jurian hauls me towards our own camp, towards safety. We have no healers with us, but it won't stop him from trying his best to keep me alive.

"We have a mission to complete." I press a weak hand to my slick side, blood spills between my fingers. Jurian gets us to my carriage, flinging the doors open with his magic as he drags me inside. I lay on my back with blood dribbling from my lips. It doesn't take a healer to know my fate.

"I don't give two rats asses about the mission, my loyalty lies with you, Killian. It has always been with you. Now be a stubborn bastard and live." Jurian hurries to undress my top half, compacting the wound at my side with balm and gauze. I shut my eyes as the warmth of his words wrap around my heart. My friend. My brother.

"How long will he be like this?" The same, soft feminine voice asks. A hand is still wrapped around Killian's own, slowly caressing the back of his hand. His eyes refuse to open, but he is just there in the present moment.

"Depends how long the antidote takes to eat away the poison. I'm surprised he survived as long as he did," the other, grouchier female voice replies. Something *zings* and scrapes.

"Do you really need to do that now?" The voice to his side growls, tensing her small hand against his own.

He knows her...*who is she? Why can I not remember?*

"There's never not a good time to sharpen your sword," the grouchy female retorts, continuing to sharpen her blade. Killian would chuckle if his body allowed, she's right. Anytime is a good time.

"Well, it seems inappropriate," the soft voice says, she sounds closer to Killian now. As if she hovers near his face, her breath is warm against his cheek.

He feels freezing, as if his body is solidifying from the inside.

"Why are you travelling with him?" The grouchy female asks.

Silence.

"Because...I was sent by the king. I would rather wait until he awakes to have that conversation." Warmth is pressed against his cheek and his body hones in on the sense. If only she could coat his whole body.

"Ah, that is a conversation for once he awakes. You know I can't let him take you back, Adalyn."

Adalyn.

"I will not leave him."

"Even if it means your demise?"

Adalyn presses a tender kiss to his cheek, "even if it means my demise. Where he goes, I follow."

I soak in the hot springs under the castle, soothing the wounds I'd acquired from the newest conquest. It's nice to be home, even if it's only for a short reprieve. The recent conquest had been hard, bringing those women back. What could the king need them for?

I sink lower into the bubbling water until my face is the only thing above the surface. Soft footfalls enter the hidden chamber, I look towards the carved door as my wife enters. Her golden hair frames her soft curves that are shrouded in a pale blue silk dress. She smiles, lighting up the entire room.

"I thought I'd find you here." She takes a seat against the stone ledge, reaching out a tanned hand to clasp my cheek. Her golden eyes shine with love as I lean into her hand, covering it with my own.

"I will not be home for long I'm afraid," I say, unable to take my eyes way from her. She tucks the strands of her flowing hair

behind pointed ears before leaning forward and pressing her lips against my own.

"I know honey, I just wanted to spend whatever time I could with you." She leans back, stroking his cheek.

"I don't deserve your love," I murmur, opening up my vulnerabilities to her once more. She always soothes my pain.

"You deserve my love and more, and I could never imagine loving another as I do you." She releases my face, "now come on, let me wash your back."

I move forward until my back faces her, the newest lashing had just crusted over. She releases a pained moan before gently grabbing a wet cloth. I close my eyes and brace my hands on the floor beneath me as she begins to wipe my back down.

"You are so much more than your scars, Killian," she whispers. "I could not love you more for them if I tried."

Killian gasps awake, the lingering pain in his back is a phantom touch as he remembers his wife. His dull heart aches as he ultimately remembers *he* was her undoing. He blinks through the haze, refusing to let the darkness drag him through his memories again. A green, forest rood is above him; small cracks let the sunshine through and dance around the wooden fort room.

His chest aches with a burning but bearable pain, he presses a hand to find his middle wrapped with gauze. He sits up, grunting with effort.

"Where the hell am I?" He murmurs, swinging his legs to the wooden floor. Peering through a crack he finds himself high above the ground. He looks around the room, his bag and swords lean beside the open arched doorway. The bed is soft beneath him, filled with feathers.

"Addie?" He calls out, ears straining.

Pounding feet fly towards his room, not hesitating over the height. She's terrified of heights, yet she's up here. With him. Running towards him.

Her body bursts through the arched doorway and she pauses, gasping for breath. Her auburn hair has been braided down the middle of her head, a few loose strands frame her soft face. Her amber eyes fill with tears as she closes the distance between them, collapsing to her knees before him and wrapping her arms around his waist. Her warmth shocks him into action as he rests a hand on the back of her head and rubs circles on her back. He doesn't dare lean over too much, not wanting to irritate his chest wound.

"I—I thought you weren't going to wake up." She says softly, clinging to him. He stares down at her, perplexed. He knew things had shifted between them, had known for some time but *seeing* and *feeling* the change is jarring.

"I'm stronger than I look," Killian says roughly, his throat dry and aching.

"You *idiot* you could have died!" Adalyn pulls back, her sadness masked with her anger, "You could have died!"

He leans back slightly, "Addie—"

"No, you don't get to joke about this! You were close to dying Killian, it was up to your soul if you chose to come back or not."

Killian cups her face with his hands, brushing away her stray tears with his thumbs. "I came back, I'm not going to die."

Her amber eyes widen as more tears spill from their depths, "you cannot leave me now, Killian."

"I am not leaving you." He presses his forehead against hers, "where you go, I follow."

Adalyn takes shuddering breaths, regaining her calmness. He feels the change in her as she wrangles with her emotions, regaining her calm. She pulls back and presses her lips to his own. He doesn't hesitate as he slips his tongue into her mouth and fire ignites in his veins.

He groans as she pulls away, both of them breathing heavy. She smiles shyly up at him.

"We can't get ahead of ourselves. You need to heal." She presses a gentle hand to his chest, earning a jab of dull pain. He groans as he lays back on the bed, resting a hand against his forehead.

"What happened? I can barely remember anything."

Adalyn lies down beside him, curling into him. He welcomes her warmth, wrapping his free arm around her. It feels so natural to have her so close.

"You were shot through the chest with a poisoned arrow by an Igor. I was knocked out and taken and woke up at this small camp. I was bound and gagged and I couldn't get free. There were two other human girls but he killed and cooked the first one and raped and killed the second." Adalyn goes still, breathing heavily, "He almost killed me and then you appeared and fought against him as best you could."

Blurry imagines begin to resurface in Killian's mind as Adalyn lays the pieces out before him. He remembers waking in the cold, the arrow still pierced in his chest. He'd pulled it out and staggered to follow her scent.

"I got a hold of his dagger and I just went crazy. I had so much built up anger inside of me and it just exploded. I killed him, but I don't feel guilty for it.

"I found an antidote in his bag and I'd given it to you but it wasn't working well and then she appeared and promised to heal you and I followed."

"We're up fairly high," Killian murmurs, running his hand down her braid. "You came all the way up here for me?"

"Yes, I did." She huffs, "don't expect me to do it again. I still don't know how I'm meant to climb down."

"You climbed up here on your own?"

"Of course, she was carrying you so I didn't have much of a choice." Adalyn looks up at him, reaching out a pale hand to trace the line of his jaw, "we're okay now. We're safe now."

"As long as you're safe, that is my only concern," Killian murmurs, kissing her fingers. She giggles, flicking his nose before leaning on her elbow to look at him. He traces her face, memorising every inch.

"We have to stay here for a few days so you can heal." Adalyn intertwines her fingers with his own. "I'm going to learn how to make poisons while you heal. I kept the Igor's bag and it was full of them."

"Great, so I need to watch out for a dagger and now poisoned food?" Killian jokes, grinning up at her.

"Careful, I might go through with my dagger."

"You know I'd like that," Killian leans forward as best he can, brushing his nose along her cheek until his lips press against her ear, "just as much as I know you'd like that too."

"Am I interrupting something?" That gruff female voice breaks their heated moment, Adalyn blushes furiously as she pulls away but still keeps her hand intertwined with Killian's.

She sits up on the bed, helping Killian sit up as well.

His eyes narrow as he takes in the woman's leather covered feet to the mismatched knitted deep brown material that covers her strong legs.

Her dark skin is covered with red intricate tattoos, swirling and disappearing under her singlet from her face down to her throat and arms. A pink raised scar adorns the skin at the base of her throat, only managing to make her look more dangerous.

She grins, exposing her two elongated canines. Her blonde dreadlocks have been tied back to expose her silver piercings that dangle from pointed ears.

A green and blue eye glows with recognition as Killian finally looks at her face. His magic snaps into place almost painfully.

"Hello, Killian."

For fuck sake.

"Hello, Farikha."

Traitor.

37. Adalyn

Adalyn

Adalyn looks between Farikha and Killian, his eyes harden as he grips her hand tighter; not daring to take his eyes from where she leans against the archway. Farikha grins wickedly, cocking her head to one side as she taps a sharpened nail against her arm.

"Am I missing something?" Adalyn asks, unable to place why there's tension in the room now. Farikha breaks their heavy stare first, looking towards their clasped hands. She'd dealt with enough of her questions while Killian had been in and out of consciousness.

"I once fought side by side with your general here," Farikha says, "back when Valarki began hunting down humans and burning down their villages."

"*Farikha.*" Killian hisses, baring his teeth up at her. Adalyn hides her hurt by pursing her lips, wills her bleeding heart to cease beating for this moment. She does not want to be weak anymore.

"What? Are you annoyed about the general part or the slaughtering part?" Farikha asks, looking back towards him. The tension in the air thickens and Adalyn knows if it isn't diffused soon there may be trouble.

"It's okay Killian," Adalyn murmurs, tugging his hand to grab his attention. He looks at her, brows creased. She looks back to Farikha.

"You once fought with Killian and succumbed to the king's orders. Obviously something happened since you are here and not back there," Adalyn says calmly, finding herself curious about the woman in front of her.

"I went rogue." Farikha shrugs, "fairly simple. I refused to slaughter innocent lives and I fled the castle."

"Are you branded?" Adalyn asks, tracing her eyes over her bare arms looking for any sign she may have belonged to the king once. Farikha laughs without humour.

"Valarki are not branded, only the cattle to the king's eyes are." Her eyes soften as she looks to Adalyn's arm, to where her brand hides under the loose fitting white shirt. Adalyn doesn't hide her shame.

"How did he let you leave?" Adalyn asks again, wanting to know more.

"He came after me to start with. I was a very powerful asset to his conquest team. My magic is a mimic of Killian's, but in light." Farikha raises her palm to the roof, white light sparks in her palm and glows, "Whatever Killian can do, I can do the opposite. We were once a united team with our gift."

"Why did you rebel?"

"Because the guilt got the best of me. I grew a consciousness. I refused to slaughter innocent people, no matter what race they are. Doesn't seem fair to me." Farikha looks to Killian, "but Killian stayed. And now he's here, with a human by his side. Why?"

"The king sent me on a private mission." Killian relents, running a hand through the dark strands of his hair, "I was to gather information on the sickness infecting the Valarki and find the traitor."

Farikha smiles, "you've found the traitor I assume?"

"Farikha...I do not want to take you back to the king." Killian pinches the bridge of his nose, "he would rip you apart."

"As if I would let you take me back Killian." Farikha stands tall, gesturing for them to follow her, "I'd flay you alive before you could lay a hand on me, boy."

Adalyn rises, watching as Farikha disappears. Killian stands, letting go of her hand to go to his bag. Adalyn twists her hands together, biting her bottom lip.

"Killian, what are we going to do?" She watches as the muscles on his back quiver as a loose black shirt is pulled down. He ties his hair back into a loose bun, leaving two strands to frame either side of his face.

"I'll figure it out." He closes the distance between them, claiming her mouth. She melts into him, gripping his biceps as her tongue dances with his. He pulls back, kissing her forehead before taking her hand and leading them from the room.

Adalyn ignores the rise and fall of her stomach as they walk along the intricate hallway system Farikha had built high in the trees. The wooden boards underneath their feet are sturdy and reinforced with thick rope that runs underneath the boards and ties to the trees. Each hallway is framed with thick mesh and vines have grown around them, making them almost unmoveable.

They reach a forked intersection and Killian leads them towards the left, ascending higher into the canopy. Adalyn squeezes his hand, with each step her anxious thoughts threaten to consume her with fear. She's explored a few pathways while Killian had been out, but refused to leave his side too much.

They reach a large open room, half carved into the trunk of a huge tree. Green and red vines cover the mesh walls and deep grey trunk, orange lilies bloom and pulse under the light.

Farikha sits on a large round pillow, a few other pillows are spread out in a circle while a small fire rages in a large metal bowl.

"Aren't you afraid it'll catch flame to everything?" Adalyn asks, stepping forward. Farikha laughs, leaning back in her seat.

"Magic my dear, take a seat."

Adalyn releases Killian's hand and takes a seat on a large square blue pillow, tucking her hands into her thighs as she faces the woman. Killian sits beside her, stretching his long legs forwards as he leans back on his hands.

"What is this place?" Killian asks, peering at the other half of the room that is entirely trunk. The room is adorned with trinkets and carvings, as well as herbs strung up near the mesh wall. A dark doorway sits at the back of the trunk, leading to some place deep within the tree.

"This is my home. I have spent many, many years building this safe haven and warding it from prying eyes." Farikha grabs her dagger and a stone, beginning to sharpen it once more.

"I see that, and what is it you do now?"

Farikha looks up at him, still working her blade, "I am rescuing the humans and sending them to a safe place that only I and one other Valarki know of."

"You rescue humans?" Adalyn pipes up, sitting forward. "Have you seen my sister? I think she escaped the raid on my village."

Adalyn slams her lips shut once she realises the information she's just given Killian. She had kept that secret close to her heart, not wanting to risk her sister's safety if she is alive.

She feels the burn of Killian's eyes but refuses to look towards him.

"What was your village's name? Sometimes I remember faces and places, but this fortnight alone I've recovered and rescued two hundred." Farikha offers her a gentle smile.

"Oakshire. Her name is Emilia and she's only young, she has blonde short curly hair and emerald green eyes." Adalyn feels the tears dripping down her cheeks and splattering her hands.

This is opening wounds she wanted to conceal.

"I am sorry, Adalyn. I cannot be sure. How many of your family were taken from you?" Farikha is the first person to make her feel as though her family were people, people who mattered and had purpose.

"My mother and father and my twin brothers. They were only

toddlers." Adalyn wipes her cheeks, looking down at her quivering hands, "they even killed my cat."

"Valarki are not kind, not all of them anyway. I am truly sorry for your loss but just know that your family walk by your side every waking second and you are never truly alone."

Adalyn looks back to her, unafraid to show her tears or the pain that is spread across her face for all to see, "Thank you, Farikha."

"So you're in the king's harem?" Farikha curls her lip. "God, I hate him."

"Yes but he hasn't...used my body yet. The most we've done is dance and he used his magic on me for that." Adalyn wipes her tears, blinking through the heart ache. She needs to spark the anger for the king, for her vengeance.

"I cannot wait for the day that he is six feet under and pushing daises." Farikha sighs, "or rotting in the depths of hell while his body is torn apart by rabid animals."

"I cannot wait either," Adalyn whispers, finding the courage to finally look towards Killian. He shows no expression as he studies her, his lips pressed into a tight line. He knows how deep her pain runs, he's never been hidden from it.

"I've been rescuing humans for years now Adalyn and I in good conscious cannot let you leave with the general." Farikha grabs both of their attention. "I can remove your brand and you can be free, child."

"How?" Adalyn asks, a small seed of hope sparking in her chest.

"I...would have to cut off your arm from the elbow down."

"*No. You will do no such thing to her.*" Killian snarls, his anger wafting off of him in waves. Adalyn sours, wanting the brand gone but not wanting to lose half of her arm in the process.

"You do not speak for her, Killian," Farikha snarls back, pointing the sharpened end of her blade towards him.

"No...I don't want to lose my arm. Plus, I can't leave the others behind." Adalyn breaks through the fire. "They need me."

"Going back is a death sentence." Farikha declares, "Killian if you had any good sense in you or a beating heart and cared for this woman even a bit, you would not let her return."

"It is her decision to make, but I will not let you cut off her arm for the sake of it. Does that method even work?" He demands.

"We would find out, I've never taken one of the brides from the king before," Farikha admits, tapping her chin with the dagger.

"I'm not going to be an experiment for the sake of it," Adalyn grumbles, crossing her arms over her chest. "I will return with Killian. That is *my* choice."

"You will never be free of him." Farikha gestures to Killian, "he's a stain on your soul."

"I am already stained," Adalyn whispers, hardening her resolve. She had been stained and tainted from the moment she'd crawled into her burning home, "I deserve my vengeance and I will get it."

"I would never take that from you, but it is a suicide mission. Is vengeance more important than your life?" Farikha asks calmly, assessing Adalyn as though she is her opponent on the battle field.

"I will get my vengeance from the steel of my blade and through the blood of my enemies. If my life is taken because of it, then so be it. My family will be avenged."

"What of your sister?" Farikha sits her dagger and stone aside, clasping her hands together. "Will you simply let her wonder what happened to you?"

Adalyn feels torn, "I...I'm not sure."

"She will get her vengeance. I will ensure her safety," Killian says quietly, staring at Farikha with the promise in his words.

"The next obvious problem, what is the relationship between the two of you? You reek of one another." Farikha growls, narrowing her eyes in disapproval at Killian.

"We are still figuring it out, not that it's any of your business."

He grinds his teeth together. Adalyn rolls her eyes at his protectiveness.

"We've been together, yes. It's only recent and I'm still a bit murky on the details but I'm...happy with where we are," Adalyn says, a blush rising to her cheeks. "He will protect me as I will him, and he is right. This is none of your business."

"You're both idiots, but I cannot cure that." She waves her hand, dismissing the heavy weight of their conversation, "I want you to meet my friend."

On cue, a tall female Valarki emerges from the darkness of the doorway in the tree trunk. Her deep golden hair swims around her, two small braids hang down the sides of her angular face as she steps into the light. Dark brows frame her large almond shaped eyes, their hazel depths warm and inviting.

She grins, the two canines indenting her plump bottom lip. A crescent moon necklace hangs around her throat, its opal depths complimenting her slightly tan skin.

"I am Sanveeka, friend and ally to Farikha." Her voice is soft and welcoming, relaxing Adalyn. She walks over with ease, the deep green skirt swirls around long lean legs as she bring four cups and a large tea kettle towards them. Her shirt is short, exposing the indent of muscles near her ribs.

"Here, let me help." Adalyn rises, taking two ups from her and sitting back down. Sanveeka grins and takes a seat between Farikha and Adalyn, sitting the two cups and kettle down.

"It seems you've had quit the journey," she comments, filling Adalyn and Killian's cups up with a sweet vanilla scented tea. Adalyn passes Killian his cup before taking a deep sip of her own.

"They're here to take me to the king," Farikha drawls, waving a hand in the air as she leans back into her seat. Sanveeka laughs, covering her mouth.

"I would pay good coin to see that happen." She grins, sipping from her own cup. Farikha rolls her eyes but takes her own cup.

For a moment they all sit in comfortable silence, sipping their tea. Adalyn studies Sanveeka as discretely as possible, not wanting to be rude and stare straight out. She taps her toes along to a beat no one else can hear, but the very air around her seems to vibrate with life. As if she glows.

"I'm assuming you heard everything?" Killian asks, breaking the silence.

"Of course, I was just waiting for my introduction." Sanveeka smiles at Killian, "it is nice to finally meet you. Farikha has spoken of the dark one on a couple occasions."

"I thought that nickname died years ago," Killian grumbles.

"Maybe for those outside of this haven." She gestures with a free hand around them, the bracelets on her wrist clink with the small movement. Small crystals adorn green rope, while some bracelets are a deep gold carved with words Adalyn can't read clearly.

"I would hope once I leave, the nickname will die with my absence." Killian leans back on his free arm, sipping from his tea. Adalyn giggles at the image he makes, looking utterly innocent with the small tea cup between his large hands even though he radiates the promise of death. Killian catches her eyes, a million things unsaid pass between them.

Later, Adalyn mouths, looking back to the two women once more.

"Mmm I might have to think up a new nickname for you," Sanveeka says mischievously, "you do not paint the image of the all mighty dark one right in this moment."

Adalyn smiles into her tea cup, having thought that only moments ago. Farikha chuckles across from them as does Killian, his chuckle runs over her skin and ignites a small fire in her veins. How has he come to have this effect on her?

"Addie tells me she's going to learn poisons over the next few days while I recover, who's teaching her?" He asks, looking between the two, strong Valarki women. Farikha grins and looks towards Sanveeka.

"I am," Sanveeka says, "I know my way around a poison or two."

"Please—"

Sanveeka raises a hand and cuts Killian off, "she is safer here than you are, you have nothing to worry about."

Warmth blossoms in Adalyn's cheeks as she sits her empty cup down. She tucks her hands under her thighs as she looks above them, the sun still sits high and warms the air around them.

"Adalyn, how about we go and get started on these poisons?" Sanveeka offers, sitting her own cup down. Adalyn looks to Killian in question.

"I'll be fine, you're safe," he says, reaching out. She squeezes his hand and shakes her head.

"It's not my safety I was worrying for." She lets go of his hand and begins to follow Sanveeka's retreating figure, heading straight for the darkened doorway in the trunk. Excitement sparks as she begins to smile, she always loved learning new things. Knowing how to make poison and counteract them is going to be a hidden weapon once she returns to the dreaded castle.

Adalyn doesn't spare Killian or Farikha another glance as she descends down the carved wooden steps. A golden light below lights her way as she slowly takes the steps. Both hands support her as the air grows slightly thicker.

Sanveeka's cheerful face pops into the stairwell, "this way!"

Her voice echoes around Adalyn as she makes the last few steps. She enters another carved room with only the back wall being mesh covered. Fresh air fills the room as Adalyn looks around, gobsmacked.

Sanveeka stands before a large wooden table, the Igor's bag is resting against its surface with the small bottles all placed neatly side by side. Wooden shelves run from floor to ceiling and cover half of the room, the mesh wall being spared.

"I like to collect things," Sanveeka says, turning towards Adalyn, "I have all sorts of goodies on my shelves. You really never know when you may need them. I have ten jars solely for different teeth I've come across."

"This is amazing," Adalyn says as she begins to walk around

the room. There's another wooden table set up near the mesh with multiple stains covering its surface with multiple glass vials resting in little metal clasps.

"That's where I create the antidotes," Sanveeka says, "and there's a large book in its drawer where I document everything. I'm not very artistic but I try my best to draw what I use in poisons and their cures."

"I can't read the language you write in," Adalyn says, turning towards Sanveeka after studying a large, yellow disfigured skull on one of the shelves.

"Ah, I forget you're different. That's alright, are you able to learn quickly?" Sanveeka asks, leaning against the main wooden table. Adalyn stands opposite her and looks down at the array of poisons.

"I don't have much of a choice. I can't carry knowledge in physical form with me when I return." Adalyn looks to Sanveeka, "I will learn as much as I can over the next few days. I may not be skilled with a sword but I will sharpen my mind into a blade and wield it as my choice of weapon."

Sanveeka grins, "a warrior at heart. I like it."

"Alright, were do we begin?" Adalyn looks down at the twelve different bottles, three are blue, four are purple, two are black, one is pink, one is red and one is green.

"Blue bottles. That is a magic poison." Sanveeka picks up one of the blue bottles, swishing the contents back and forth, "this is what coated the arrow head and crippled Killian. Once in the blood stream it works as a paralyser to the body while it mutes the user's magic, no matter how strong you are."

"Killian still found me," Adalyn whispers, only now realising the full effects of the poison that could have killed him, "he still came for me and fought."

"He might be the dark one, but he does have a heart." Sanveeka chuckles, "it must have been pure emotion for him to do what he did. Most Valarki die in hours once injected with this concoction."

"What's in it?" Adalyn asks, picking up one of the other blue bottles. It seems harmless as it swishes around in the glass.

"Curare is extracted from the root of a strychnos plant and then mixed with water, once they've combined you add powdered blue nightshade and a dash of silver shavings." Sanveeka looks to Adalyn, "a strychnos plant lives in the Okra forest, so it's a bit of a walk to make this poison. One I think would be too much of a trouble, but you'll be taking these poisons with you; even if Killian has to say they're his own."

"What are their names?" Adalyn asks, knowing the blue poison would be perfect for her revenge once Jurian gave her the names of the Valarki who slaughtered her family.

"Okay, the blue poison is Paradona, a mild paralysis and magic muter which leads to death. The purple poison is an hallucinogenic which can last up to four hours, it's called Kompa." She places the blue bottle down and picks up the purple one, "sometimes in small doses it can give you a nice high. A friend of mine sometimes chews on the leaves of the sycamore tree to experience the hallucinations safely."

"I'm not really into that." Adalyn shakes her head, "it would most likely get me killed not having my wits about me."

Sanveeka picks up the black bottle, "this is an immediate death. Stops the heart and organs before you know what's got you. There's no antidote for this one because it works instantly. It's called Cynda."

"Is it painless?" Adalyn asks, not wanting to pick the bottle up. Sanveeka shrugs, placing it back down to pick up the green bottle.

"I think so, I've only ever found the bodies afterwards and never during." Sanveeka looks at the green one with loving eyes, "this is Jura, one of my favourites. It works on the nervous system, so you can inject it and they feel nothing, Combined with Paradona it's a deadly combination."

"Have you used it before?" Adalyn asks, half scared to know her answer. Sanveeka chuckles.

"Yes, on a few enemies of mine that had it coming." She picks up the pink and red bottle, the last two poisons. "Which one do you think is deadlier?"

"Ah, the red?" Adalyn asks, nibbling her bottom lip.

"Wrong, the pink. This is Sundoo. It sticks to your red blood cells and boils them, takes an hour until death." She places the pink one down, "and the red is Killer. Very original, I know."

"Killer? But you said it was the least deadliest." Adalyn purses her lips.

"That does not mean it isn't deadly dear one. Killer is a poison you slip into wines. It works as a type of drug and pulls the person into unconsciousness, it's effects last about two hours until the person comes to. It doesn't kill them."

"What should I know to make?" Adalyn asks, running a hand down her braid, "I have limited supplies in the castle but I do have access to the library in the catacombs."

"I've told you how to make Paradona, now I will tell you how to make Killer and Jura. If my assumptions are correct you can find most ingredients around the castle." Sanveeka grins, leaning forward, "I will also show you how to make each antidote, they are very simple. Are you ready, Adalyn?"

"I have never been more ready in my life." Adalyn sits the vial down, looking over the array of poisons as a calmness settles over her, "whoever killed my family is going to pay with blood and pain."

38. Killian

Killian

Farikha leans back, watching Killian with far more wariness than she had while Adalyn had been beside him. He meets her stare with the force of his own, sitting his empty tea cup down beside Adalyn's.

"We've come to a joint problem," Farikha finally says. "You cannot take me back as the traitor."

"No, I cannot." Killian mulls over what his options are. The magic that ties him to completing this mission are slithering under his skin, demanding to be fulfilled. He would need to return to the castle with Adalyn by his side soon, they only had just shy of two weeks of their journey left.

"What shall we do then? I'm assuming it's a death sentence if you return empty handed."

"Or he will punish someone I care for." Killian grunts, rubbing a hand down the rough stubble that's begun to grow on his cheeks and down his throat.

"Adalyn?" Farikha asks, eyes twinkling, "she is a pretty little thing."

Killian narrows his eyes on her, "I am not using her."

"No, but something has happened that has you acting this

desperate. The Killian I had left behind wouldn't have bedded a human unless there was something vital at stake. So tell me, what would have happened if you didn't?" Farikha leans forward, dancing light between both of her open palms. Killian tenses but remains silent.

Disappointment creases Farikha's stunning features, "what have you done, Killian?"

"It's more complicated than that," he says gruffly, "it is not black and white anymore. There is so much grey."

"I will not tell her Killian, I will not be the one that breaks her heart." Farikha points towards the darkened archway Adalyn had disappeared down, "you do not realise the extent of her feelings."

"I know the extent of them! I know her feelings like I know my own. I feel as deeply for her as she does me. Do you remember Polarian?"

"Of course I do. What does he have to do with this?" She demands, glaring at him.

"He has been keeping an eye on her, had the pleasure of humiliating her on the journey back to the castle. They had an incident at the castle and he ended up injured by her, which I had no problem with, but the king did. You know Polarian's perversions." Killian watches as Farikha processes the information, "the king forced my hand, Farikha. I had no choice."

"What were your options?"

"If I didn't bleed Adalyn before we returned, he would let Polarian have her for twelve hours. Free rein, he could fulfil every dark desire he wants. She wouldn't have lived. I couldn't hand her over to him." Killian looks away from her, "I know I have fucked this up, but I am trying to protect her. I was not meant to develop any feelings for her, and I know once the king forces his hand and *checks* to see if I've finished this mission she will hate me and never forgive me."

"Killian..."

"I don't want your pity. I have enough of my own. I hope

once the truth is revealed that she hates me." Killian breathes deeply through his nose, letting his emotions war inside him. He would be better off if Adalyn hates him, she deserves the world and he cannot give it to her. He will only bring her pain.

"Don't you think telling her the truth yourself will be easier for her to digest?" Farikha says softly, "if you're protecting her from Polarian surely she can understand."

"You don't realise that she is not one to be protected and coddled. She is strong and she burns with fury. If Polarian had her for the night I doubt he would have come out of it in better shape." Killian laughs dryly, shaking his head.

"If that's the case, why did you sleep with her?"

"Are you asking because you want the answer or are you spiting me?" He looks towards her, thankful Adalyn can't hear any of this conversation. He had decided telling her himself isn't a good idea, because he is selfish and if it means her loving him longer than he will take it.

"I want the answer," Farikha says evenly, clasping her hands under her chin as she watches him.

"Because I have fallen for her, there's been fire between us from the moment I first had to deal with her. Every encounter escalated into something more and when we were in Osma we finally crossed that line." Killian speaks quietly, fondly remembering their first time.

"I am truly sorry for the pain that is going to come your way Killian." Farikha rises, offering him her hand, "my judgement was misplaced, with the both of you."

Killian takes her hand, nodding once.

"What are we going to do?" Farikha asks, standing at his level.

"I will need some sort of proof, right now the magic is alive in my veins. It needs to latch onto your essence for me to accomplish this," Killian mutters, sifting through his many years of life to find a loophole.

Farikha taps his hand, clicking her tongue as she thinks.

"What if we kill another Igor?" Farikha says, beginning to grin, "you can take the head back and I can get Sanveeka to make a potion with my essence to cling to the head. Do you think that might work?"

Killian begins to smile, "I think it might. Do you think it will work?"

Farikha shrugs, letting go of his hand, "I have no idea, but I'm willing to try it. Come, those two will be busy for the rest of the day. We'll hunt down another Igor, you watch and I do all the killing. You still need to heal."

"Fine but if you get into trouble I'm helping," Killian grumbles, but follows behind her. Farikha cackles.

"We both know I won't need the help," she sings sweetly over her shoulder.

"Should we tell them we're leaving?" He questions, pushing through the throbbing pain in his chest to keep up with her. Farikha hurries along, bringing them to an enclosed room. She opens a vine covered door and ducks inside, retrieving a large spear adorned with carvings. Killian peers inside, admiring the array of swords, daggers, spears, bows and arrows.

"I could live in this room," he says, itching to strap himself with weapons. Farikha straps the spear to her back, shoving two small daggers into her boots.

"It was one of the first rooms I built, the only room that reminds me of my past. Reminds me of my purpose." She finishes her final look with another dagger strapped to her waist.

"I'll need my boots and I'll bring a sword, just in case," Killian says, raising a brow. Farikha rolls her eyes and locks the room once more.

"Fine, but I'll ignore the insult to my expertise for now," she says, hurrying through the intricate system once more. Killian follows easily, finding himself enjoying the safe haven she has built.

It's freeing, although he wouldn't admit it to anyone. Jurian would have loved it here, would have enjoyed the two women.

Once they reach the small room, Killian hurries to pull his boots on and his cloak. With a sword in hand and looking more capable than he feels, he follows Farikha to the entrance that's also their exit.

"The only thing is we'll need to climb down, Farikha says as they reach a large oval intersection. In front of them a wooden door sits on circular rope and wooden opening. Farikha pulls the hatch open with ease, peering down.

"Lucky I'm not afraid of heights," Killian mutters, walking over. He looks down and blanches. The drop...*holly hell the fucking drop.*

"Yeah, lucky that," Farikha says, rubbing the back of her neck.

"How did Adalyn climb up here?" He demands, pointing down, "she is utterly terrified of heights."

"Because you were dying and she would literally do anything for you. I had to carry you up here Killian, I could do nothing for her human fears." Farikha says, "she climbed behind, although she cried the entire way."

"You do not tease her." Killian growls, narrowing his eyes on her, "she could have fallen to her death. Why did you not have her climb first?"

"So if she slipped we'd all fall and die?" Farikha barks a laugh, "don't be a fool Killian. I don't have the feelings that you do for the girl. She climbed up and lived and she'll be climbing right back down on her own."

"I will carry her," Killian says, beginning to lower himself through the open doorway and sliding his feet into the rungs of the wooden ladder. He begins to climb down, one rung at a time.

"You're still healing Killian, I doubt you'll be carrying her." Farikha calls down, "she climbed up here, she is capable of climbing down."

Killian bites his tongue, refusing to reply. The warmth he feels for Adalyn is almost suffocating, she'd put aside one of her greatest fears for him.

Would he do the same for her?

Yes, I'd do the same in a heartbeat if it meant being by her side.

Killian keeps his mind busy for the lengthy climb down, his chest throbs and aches with each step but his perseverance keeps him clear minded and able bodied. He wouldn't become a useless bystander just because she demanded him to be. He's the shadow of death, a poisoned arrow to the chest is the last thing that'll take him down.

Reaching the bottom, Killian moves out of the way for Farikha. He looks skywards to find no trace of the safe haven, only the ladder that blends well into the thick grey trunk. Around them the forest is littered with thick grey trunk trees, their canopy high above the forest floor. Killian feels tiny against their trunks.

"This forest is magnificent. How do you not get lost?" Killian asks once Farikha reaches the floor beside him. She adjusts her weapons before walking away from the tree, beckoning him to follow.

"My magic surrounds this safe haven I've built, I could find my way to it blind. It also keeps unwanted visitors out, just how I need it and prefer it," Farikha says, her multi coloured eyes survey the forest ahead of them. Killian keeps his sword ready in both hands, ears straining. He only picks up their own soft foot falls as they travel along.

"Where is another Igor?" Killian asks softly.

"Most likely at the camp where I found you. There was a human girl cooking over the fire and another dead one waiting to be cooked when I came across Adalyn protecting you." Farikha looks at him sideways, "I still don't understand why her feelings are so strong for you. Apart from being dashing, you're quiet sour."

"I think she prefers my sour side," Killian jabs back.

"She'd be the only living and not living person to," Farikha snarks right back. "Your back is still covered in scars. Do you have any inch of skin that isn't scarred?"

Killian growls, "Why must you bring up my past?"

"Because it angers you," she says simply, as though his trauma is a simple topic to talk about.

"Obviously," he grits out, flexing his fingers on the handle of his sword.

"What does Adalyn think of it?" she asks.

"I haven't asked." Killian shakes his head, "she carries scars of her own so I can only imagine she would think the same of my own."

"That girl is smitten with you, I'm sure she thinks they're lovely," Farikha says more seriously.

Killian remains silent, not wanting to comment more on the subject. He reflects back to his memories of when he stumbled upon Adalyn in the grasp of the Igor. He hadn't noticed the other girls there, had only focused on her.

They walk at a swift pace for hours, finally breaking through the forest. The sea breeze greets them in a warm embrace, ahead Killian sees a large fire roaring at a camp. They come to a stop as a large Igor lumbers around the camp, swinging the body of a human around. Killian snarls his disgust.

"Alright, let's go in full force. I can't be bothered waiting it out," Farikha says, taking off full speed moments later. Killian curses as he runs after her, still too far behind to help her if it goes wrong.

Farikha releases a battle cry as she leaps across the clearing, slamming her dagger into the chest of the female Igor. The Igor screams, using the deceased human girl as a weapon against Farikha. Killian skids to a stop in the clearing, his stomach heaving as he sees almost unrecognisable cooked pieces of human over the fire.

Adalyn had to suffer this, so he will suffer it as well.

"You big knuckle head bitch!" Farikha yells, pushing from her back and flipping in the air. She skids along the ground, looking up to the Igor. The Igor hurls the girl towards Farikha, who dodges the lifeless body with ease. Killian winces as the body folds in on itself, bones snapping from the early onset of rigor mortis.

He looks back in time to see Farikha charge towards the Igor with her spear, grinning madly as the Igor runs straight for her.

Farikha impales the Igor, who continues to struggle against her hold. Farikha is stronger than she looks and every inch equal the warrior Killian is. She laughs wildly as she rips her dagger from the Igor's chest, and jumping to the end of the spear she still holds.

"Killian, can you use your magic at all?" She calls, glancing over to him. The Igor is a mindless beast impaled at the spear, still chomping and spilling blood from its wide lips.

"A little, not much," he calls back, summoning the small kernel of magic that will come to his call. He uses the small portion to shoot across the clearing, inflicting the creature with fear. It freezes immediately, consumed.

"Just know I could have done it without your help!" She calls back, beginning to saw the Igor's head from its body. Killian watches blankly, blood sprays towards Farikha as she hacks through the skin and tendons and eventually bone of the Igor's throat.

"Ah ha!" She shouts in victory, holding the Igor's head up by its long ear. Killian chuckles and shakes his head, crossing his arms over his chest.

"Disgusting," he calls as she re-sheathes the dagger to her waist and then rips her spear from the Igor's lifeless body.

"All in a day's work." She swaggers towards Killian, proud of her kill, "I hunt these creatures leisurely, let's hope it's our saving grace."

Killian and Farikha make the walk back in silence, moving quickly through the forest as the sun begins to set. She carries the Igor's head for the journey, eager to return to Sanveeka to experiment. Once they reach the base of the tree Killian climbs the ladder first, moving swifter than he had the first time climbing down.

The hatch is a small struggle, he screams in pain as he heaves it open and climbs out. Warm arms wrap around his waist, the scent of Adalyn invades his senses and dulls his pain.

"You're back," she whispers, resting her head beside the wound on his chest. He hugs her back, resting his chin on the top of her head.

"I had to get an Igor head. They're going to see if they can put Farikha's essence into the head so I can take it back to the king without giving her up." He murmurs into her hair.

"I'm glad you're safe." Adalyn pulls away, blushing as she remembers their company. Killian's lips twitch into a smile as she steps away from him, scowling as she focuses on the lifeless head in Farikha's hand.

"Rest for two more nights Killian and then I give you my blessing to leave. I'm sure an extra night won't hurt either of you, you're safe here." Farikha says softly, smiling. "Now come along, I'll take you back to your room."

Adalyn stays silent as she follows after Farikha, Killian taking up the end. His eyes betray him as he looks over Adalyn's curves and finds himself craving the simplicity of holding her, curling his large body around her own and breathing in sync with her.

It's the small things he's finding himself craving, which he's finding more dangerous. Farikha drops them off to their room, bidding them goodnight before disappearing back into the night.

Adalyn pins a thin sheet over the door way, giving them a small piece of privacy. Killian undoes his cloak and leans his sword against the wall, wanting nothing more than to eat and lay down. Spend some time with Adalyn.

Two bowls of soup sit on a small wooden table that hadn't been there earlier, two pieces of bread sit on a separate plate. Killian grabs a bowl and a slice before sitting on the bed, leaning back against wall as he eats.

"What a day," Adalyn huffs, stripping down to her underwear before pulling on a dark green thin strapped nightgown. She joins him moments later, bowl and bread in hand.

"How did the poison learning go?" He asks around mouthfuls.

"I think I know what I need to," she says around a mouthful of soup. "I really like it here."

"Thank you for climbing all this way for me," Killian murmurs, bumping his shoulder into her own. She smiles up at him.

"Please don't expect me to do it again, once in this lifetime is enough."

Killian chuckles, shaking his head. "It's okay, I won't indirectly ask it of you again. I promise."

Adalyn sighs and leans into him, "what will happen to us once we return?"

"We will still be us, although it will need to be hidden from the king. I am sorry to ask that of you, I would never hide you away if I didn't have to," he says softly.

"I know what we have puts us both in danger." Adalyn reaches over and places their empty bowls onto the table before gently pushing Killian to lay down. The small glow in the room dulls, which Killian puts down to Farikha's magic. Killian lays back, pulling the thick blanket back and climbing under the covers.

He inches over, allowing room for Adalyn to lay by his side. She climbs under the blanket, tangling her legs with his own as she drapes her arm over his lower waist. He rests his arm around her shoulders, relaxing as their warmth seeps into one another.

"I will miss this." She mumbles, resting her head against his chest.

"I'll sneak into your room every night if I have to," Killian murmurs, kissing the top of her head. She leans back and steals a quick kiss before nestling into him.

"I'll lock the door, give you a bit of a challenge," she murmurs. He smiles into the darkness of the room as he closes his eyes.

"You're too kind to me," he says back in a hushed tone.

"Will we be okay, Killian?" she asks drowsily.

"I can only hope so Addie, I'll try my best for us."

Adalyn begins to hum a nursery rhyme under her breath, it has sleep grasping him and pulling him under faster than it ever had before. Her voice is the last thing he hears, safe and warm and *home.*

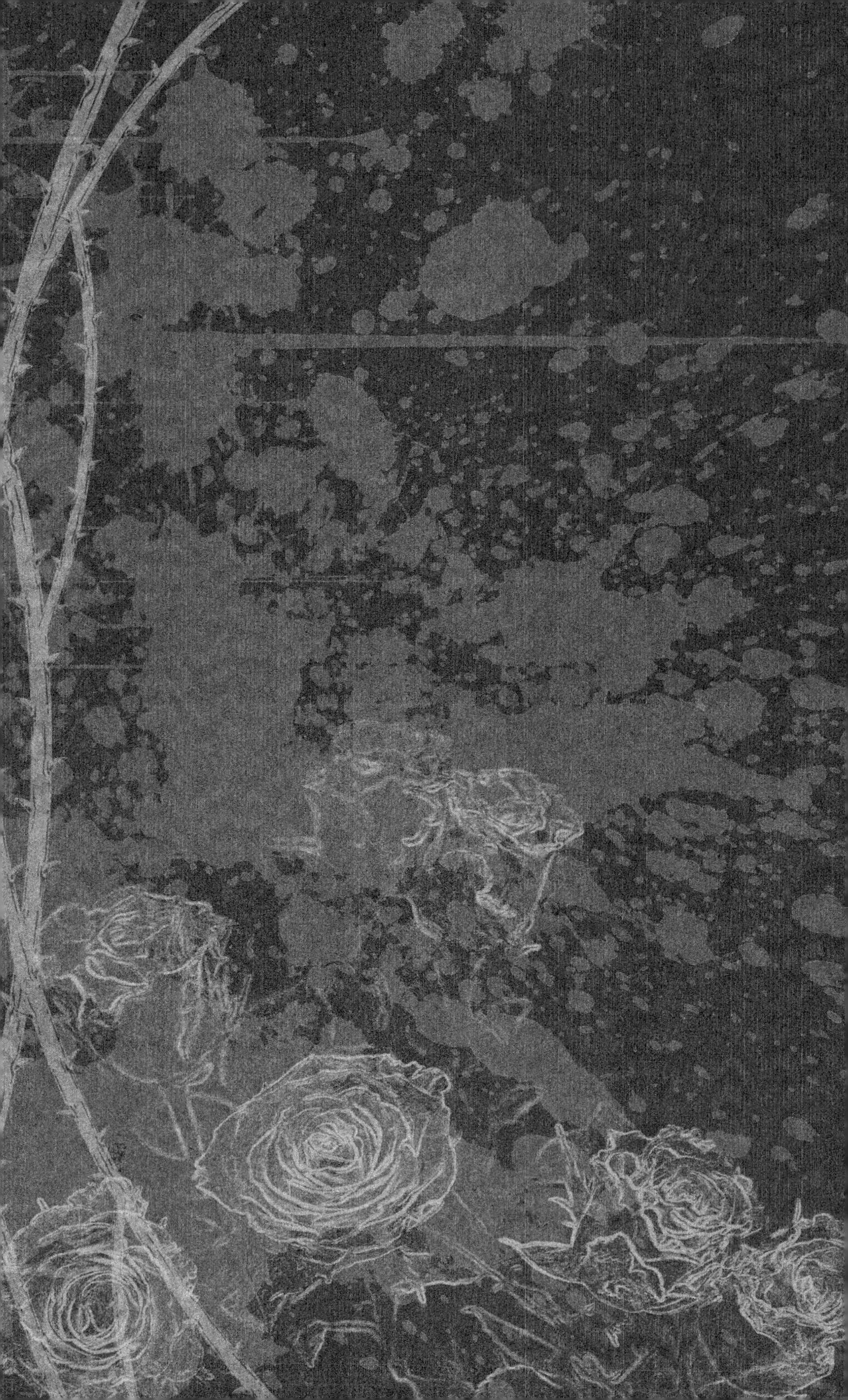

39. Adalyn

Adalyn

Two days later, Adalyn finds herself standing on the outskirts of Okra forest, hand in hand with Killian as the early morning sun basks them in its light. They'd left the safe haven after waking, with an enchanted Igor head in tow. Adalyn avoids looking at the grey bag that's now clasped to Killian's waist, not wanting to remember the horror she'd witnessed that night.

Killian had used his magic to get them to this point, allowing them to ride the horses back to the castle and find some sort of balance for once they returned. Adalyn had decided she couldn't show any other emotion than hatred, it's what she thrived on before they'd left. If the king or Polarian could see her happy, they'd do anything to rip it away.

Adalyn waits for the nausea to subside, "I don't like using your magic like that."

"When you've done it for as long as I have, you get accustomed to it fairly quickly." Killian tightens his hand on her own, watching as Osma comes to life before them. Valarki begin to fill the streets and the bustling reaches their ears even from the distance.

"Are you ready for this?" Adalyn asks, voicing her own small doubt.

"Well one of us has to be, and by the sound of it, it's not you." He smirks down at her, a dimple appearing his left cheek. It makes her swoon on the inside, but she chooses the feign annoyance on the outside.

"I'm just thinking." Adalyn jabs her elbow gently into his ribs, finding any reason to touch him. She can't seem to keep her hands off of him, wanting to bury herself under his skin.

These feelings are dangerous, but looking into his crystal blue eyes she knows she'd risk anything to feel what she is when he looks at her.

"You're overthinking, Addie." Killian begins to lead them towards the village, holding her hand tighter. She revels in the comfort of it, leaning into him. Adalyn takes a deep breath, trying her best to ignore the anxiety that's growing with each step that leads them closer to the castle.

"I can't help it." She grumbles in response, "how are you not thinking?"

"I thought we discussed this." He loops their intertwined hand around her shoulder, suctioning her to his muscled side.

"Well not really...only that you'd sneak into my room every night. We didn't really discuss much else."

"What is there to discuss? My hands are tied until we can figure out a way to get that brand off your wrist. Once we return, I'm going to try my best to get you out of the king's clutches." He murmurs into her ear, his breath and igniting all her nerve endings.

"What if...what if the king wants me to service him?" She asks in a soft voice, only now realising what is expected of her.

"I don't want to be sent into a darkness just yet, darling." Killian growls, "no one touches your body but me."

"I know that you fool." She scowls up at him, "what am I meant to do? Oh, sorry your majesty you can't touch me, even though you own my body."

"If he touches you Adalyn, I will not be able to keep my composure." He brings them to a stop, staring down at her, "I will raise that castle from the ground and skin the king alive."

Heat curls low in her belly, burning through the anxiety that had begun to overwhelm her. "I didn't realise you'd kill for me."

"I'd do much more than murder for you, my sweet Addie." He steals a kiss before she can reply, tugging her along faster. She chuckles and shakes her head but follows without complaint.

They approach the wooden stable structure, pausing as a large brown stallion is lead out of the open barn doors by one of the stable boys. Adalyn hides her distaste when Pink eyes and Brown eyes approach her and Killian. She hadn't bothered asking for their names, had no care knowing them.

"Killian, what a pleasant surprise," Brown eyes comments, grinning at him with suggestion in her eyes. Adalyn feigns boredom, equipping her armour of cold indifference. She'd allowed herself to simply *be* while she'd been with Killian, not wanting to keep him too far from reach.

"I wish I could say the same," Pink eyes murmurs, curling her lip as she looks at Adalyn.

"Don't be rude," Brown eyes says, narrowing her eyes at her friend, "it's always a pleasure to see the general."

"Morning, ladies. We're just coming to collect our horses and finish the journey home," Killian says, blunt but pleasant. Adalyn peers up at him, catching his eye; he winks at her before looking back to the women.

"You're not staying the night?" Brown eyes asks, frowning slightly.

"No. We're best needed at home," Killian says, tightening his arm around Adalyn's shoulders.

"What for?" Pink eyes asks, unable to help herself.

"The information is for the king only I'm afraid, I'm just following orders." Killian looks down to Adalyn, "I'm going to grab our horses. Stay here."

Adalyn shrugs, untangling her hand from his own. Shee hides

her fear behind her mask, not wanting the two predators in front of her to pick up on the scent.

"Pleasure seeing you both." Killian nods politely before stepping past them and striding into the stables, leaving Adalyn to face them on her own.

"What does he see in you?" Pink eyes asks, looking down her nose at Adalyn. They wouldn't have been so intimidating if they weren't so tall. Adalyn shrugs, arching a brow.

"Your guess is as good as mine," she says, looking between both women. "You're best off asking him why he likes me."

Brown eyes snorts, "I wouldn't say he likes you. You're simply a human play thing until he grows bored, and he will grow bored."

"He might have grown bored with the both of you, but I can't say the same will happen for me." Adalyn smiles, although her heart threatens to burst from beating so hard, "I'm not Valarki, I am human. I'm *very* different to the both of you, a fact I pride myself on."

"Humans break," Pink eyes says, "you always break. You're as weak as a foal finding its feet. If the world doesn't break you, he will."

"Enjoy his attention while it lasts," Brown eyes chirps before walking away. Pink eyes follows. Adalyn watches the women leave, the conversation hadn't been as bad as she was preparing herself for.

"Everything okay?" Killian asks, approaching her with the two horses at his side. Adalyn smiles as she looks upon her mare, finding her plump and happy.

"Everything's fine. Let's get out of here." Adalyn takes the reins, brushing her hand down her mares nose. She breathes in her heavy scent, enjoying the smell of leather and horse.

"We will arrive at the castle at sunset. I will enchant the horses to move with speed and use my magic to avoid the narrow path ascending the cliff." Killian mounts his steed, tying the grey bag to the horn of his saddle. Adalyn mounts. Although still clumsy, she mounts smoother than she had the first time. She adjusts herself on the saddle before taking the reins in her hands.

"Alright. Let's go then," she says, looking to Killian once more before clicking her tongue. His stallion breaks into a gallop and her mare is quick to follow. Valarki cheer and clap as they bolt past, avoiding trampling any bystanders. By some miracle they make it through the village without any casualties.

Adalyn lets go of all thoughts and doubts as they approach Dathka' forest. Once they return to the castle the first thing she'll be doing is running a hot bath and soaking for an hour.

Maybe with Killian to keep her company...

He rides ahead of her, sure and confident with each stride his stallion takes. His raven hair whips in the wind, he'd opted to leave it down. The lengths had grown slightly, now grazing below his collar bones.

Adalyn could find him attractive with short hair or long hair. She wonders if he'd still find her attractive with short hair; not that she'd be cutting it anytime soon.

They ride through the forest, encountering no problems. Adalyn grimaces as a portal ripples ahead before the large cliff.

"Straight in!" Killian shouts over his shoulder, riding straight for the opening that exposes the skeletal and grey land that surrounds the castle.

Adalyn squeezes her eyes shut just before her mare rides through the magic, the once fresh and clean air stales and fills with poison.

Adalyn coughs into her elbow as she adjusts to the change of scenery. Her once calm composure begins to crack as she lays eyes on the grey, looming castle that's far closer than comfortable.

The sun has begun to dip behind the castle, casting shadows across the land. Adalyn rides harder, her thoughts escaping her and thinking of all the monsters that might come out once there's no light.

Killian slows his stallion to a trot, Adalyn reaches his side and hides her trembling hands by gripping the saddle's horn. She doesn't want to show Killian how afraid she is to be back at this awful place.

"Home sweet home," he says bitterly, narrowing his eyes as they reach the castle wall. Adalyn peers to their side as the ride along, heading towards the large gates guarded by stone gargoyles and Valarki trained to kill.

She wishes more than anything she could jump back in time, to when it was her and Killian and nothing else. No worries, no looking over their shoulders. Just simply enjoying one another.

She may never get that again.

"Are you ready?" Killian asks, looking down to her. His eyes hold warmth and worry, she looks away and focuses on the path ahead. Soon, they'd be in the castle. Soon, she'd continue living her nightmare.

"No." She answers honestly, "but I have to be."

"We will need to go to the king once we put our horses away," Killian murmurs, straightening his shoulders as Valarki on the wall begin to shout his arrival.

"And then take it day by day?" Adalyn murmurs, narrowing her eyes on the Valarki that guard the high wall. They hold no kindness in their own, only darkness and death.

"Day by day," Killian says softly before he slips underneath his cold mask. Adalyn watches as the air around him changes, as the cold practically oozes from him. She does her best to stay composed, not wanting anyone to think he broke her on this trip.

"General Killian, welcome!" A Valarki shouts before working the lever to open the gates. Killian nods once, wearing no expression as they ride underneath the arch way. Adalyn wipes her forehead, eyes flittering around at the commotion as Valarki bustle around the castle grounds.

It feels as though she never left.

Killian leads them down the side of the castle, heading for the stables. Two stable boys run forward, their transparent wings flutter nervously as Adalyn and Killian come to a stop. Adalyn dismounts, groaning at the protest in her thighs.

"Thank you," she says, handing her reins over the boy that approaches. He nods once, his white silk strands flowing with a gentle breeze. Adalyn watches as the horses are lead away, she doesn't know when she'll see her mare again.

"Coming?" Killian asks, arching a brow. He has both hands tucked into his black buckskin breeches, painting the picture of disinterest.

"If I must." She avoids looking at him as they walk side by side into the castle, she doesn't dare walk too close to him. She isn't sure what the consequences would be if anyone found out about their relationship, but deep in her bones she knows it wouldn't be good.

Killian hums to himself, a nursery rhyme she is all too familiar with. Her heart twists violently as memories of her mother come to mind, loving warm eyes and gentle smiles.

"How do you know that?" she asks once they walk down a deserted hallway.

"You were humming it to me," he answers simply. "I like the tune."

"My mother would sing it to me when I was a child, every night before bed." Adalyn crosses her arms over her chest, feeling the burn of his eyes on the side of her face.

"I would have liked to meet her," he whispers, nothing but kindness in his voice. Tears burn her eyes but she refuses to let them free.

"Too bad you killed her."

They fall into silence, although she knows he fights the urge to say something. Before he can, they enter the throne room, walking through gilded golden doors. Adalyn slowly trails her eyes over the marble floor, until they land on the king as he lounges in his bone throne.

"You've returned," he says, not displeased, although not pleased either. Adalyn can't pin point his tone, so she opts to stay silent as she watches him stand.

Killian approaches the king and hands him the grey bag

before stepping backwards, his shoulders are tense as he focuses on the king.

Adalyn holds her breath, if the king figures out this is not the traitor...

"What is this? I told you I wanted them alive," the king says angrily, pulling the Igor's now rotting head from the bag. Adalyn gags as the smell reaches her.

"I didn't have the choice to bring them back alive," Killian says simply. "I had nothing to restrain them with and they were incredibly violent, feasting on human flesh. It was safer to bring back their head."

"I am not pleased, but my magic has accepted it." The king's expression sours as he places the head in the bag once more, throwing it to one of the armed guards that line the walls. "What of the sickness?"

"It...is a Valarki's doing. I picked up hints of their power but nothing that could point me in their direction. It kills within a day. It hasn't reached Osma yet, only the coastal villages."

"Is there any way we can prevent it from reaching us?" The king growls, falling back into his throne. Killian clasps his hands behind his back.

"I'm afraid not."

"At least we know where the source of the sickness has come from," the king finally says, turning those golden eyes to Killian. "Thank you, general."

"It's been my pleasure." Killian bows his head, although his entire demeanour screams at him not too. Adalyn wouldn't have noticed if she didn't know Killian.

"Little bird, did you behave?" The king asks, focusing on her.

"Yes, your majesty. Thank you for allowing me to go," she says, refusing to smile but doing her best to look kind. She doesn't want to be interrogated, she wants to climb into a bath and sleep.

He studies her, head to toe. She isn't sure what he sees but it satisfies him.

"Adalyn you may leave, I wish to speak with Killian in private.

You have pleased me," The king says, smiling down at her. Adalyn nods once, not sparing a second glance at Killian before leaving the throne room. She isn't sure why the king wishes to speak to him in private, she can only hope he isn't in any trouble. Adalyn is sure he'll tell her once he finds her.

Once she's certain no one can see her, she bolts for her room, finding her way with ease. An odd sense of comfort comes over her as she closes her door, leaning against the wooden foundation.

What am I going to do?

She walks to her cupboard, gently putting her bag towards the back. Removing a dress, she drapes the deep red material over the bag that carries all of her poisons. Her time will come, she just has to strike when she's able.

Adalyn walks into the bathing room, surprised to find steaming water already to the brim.

This must be the king's doing, she ponders but doesn't complain. Removing her boots and clothes has her feeling more comfortable, especially once she lowers herself into the water.

Adalyn leans her head back against the side, shutting her eyes.

Someone opens her door, soft footsteps hurry towards the bathing room. Adalyn sits up just as Allison walks into the room. Her deep, rich brown skin is on display; her dress thin and barely covering her most sensitive parts.

Adalyn smiles at her friend, Allison falls to her knees and hugs Adalyn to her. Adalyn inhales her berry scent, resting her head against her.

"I have missed you so much, I wasn't sure if you were going to return in pieces. Tell me everything." Allison murmurs into her hair. Adalyn finds herself smiling as she leans back, cheeks heating.

Allison grins, "You and Killian?"

"It's not like that," Adalyn groans, sinking back into the water. Allison chuckles, rising and sitting on the edge of the tub as she lowers her feet into the water.

"By the redness in your face I'm going to assume it is exactly like that. There's no judgement here." Allison swirls a hand through the water, "you haven't missed much. Alissa was in a bad mood for the first week after Killian left with you, but Jurian's been worried."

"Why has he been worried?" Adalyn asks at the mention of her friend.

"I'm not sure, we've only spoken a hand full of times. I'm not even sure he knows who I am." It's Allison's turn to blush as her deep black curls spill over her shoulders.

"I can introduce you if you like," Adalyn suggests, winking at her friend. Allison laughs.

"I'm still tied to the king."

Adalyn loses her smile, casting her eyes down to the soapy water, "I am too."

"Start from the start, from the moment you met Killian at the stables," Allison says, nudging her leg into Adalyn's.

"I was furious..." Adalyn begins, replaying the memories.

Allison stays by her side as she tells her everything in hushed whispers, from the fight they'd had in the forest to the love making. She hadn't been able to bite her tongue, enjoying the fact she could finally speak to her friend about what's happening between them.

Allison listens while Adalyn talks and as the night grows darker, Adalyn finds herself feeling more than content. Less restless. All she needs now is for Killian to sneak in and complete her night.

40. Killian

Killian

Silence falls over the throne room as Adalyn leaves, the echo of her soft footfalls reaches Killian's ears, his lips twitch upwards as he hears her run down the hall; heading for safety. Golden eyes narrow, reminding Killian the purpose of him being here and not trailing *her*.

The king taps his long fingers on a gleaming skull, his hair sits flat against his chest tonight; no sign of it having a life of its own.

Killian sighs through his nose. "What did you wish to speak about?"

"I simply wished to know more about the trip." The king begins to smile, stretching his cheeks too wide, "I wish to know if you completed all missions I set upon you."

Out of the corner of his eye, Polarian grows restless stepping from foot to foot. At least Killian can take great pleasure in knowing he'll never get his hands on Adalyn.

Killian opens his mouth to tell the king he has completed every mission, but his tongue is lead in his mouth. Words refuse to slip between his lips.

This is betrayal. You are betraying her.

Killian opts to stay silent, staring up at the king with nothing but cold detachment on his face. The king doesn't need to know his heart is beating faster than it has before, doesn't need to know how badly he wishes to be with her instead of standing here.

"Well?" The king prompts. He leans forward, the tapping of his fingers stops. His golden eyes swirl and glow faintly as he calls his magic forth.

Killian knows the king can use his magic to see if he completed all tasks. He wishes to humiliate him in front of the guards and Polarian and his rookies. Killian grits his teeth.

The shadow of death, sworn off human females, has fallen.

The king begins to laugh, pure shock overtakes his handsome features, "My god, you actually did it."

"What?" Polarian's long legs eat up the distance as he comes to stand near Killian, his orange eyes flare as he narrows them at Killian. Killian pays him no mind, ignoring him.

"Killian has slept with the human woman." The king chuckles, "I have to say I am impressed, Death Bringer. I didn't think you had a soft bone in your body for the humans anymore."

"You gave me a mission to complete." His own words have his stomach twisting with disgust but he refuses to endanger Adalyn even more. If the king and others think he only did it for the king, she will be safe from their wrath.

"That I did." The king looks to Polarian. "The deal is off. Killian came through, you don't touch her."

"You promised I would have her." Polarian grinds his teeth, trying his best to hide his anger, "I am due what I'm owed your majesty."

"I only said you could have her if Killian failed," the king snaps. His hair flares to life and begins to float from his body. Polarian takes a small step back. Killian feigns boredom, he's learnt what masks to wear in their presence.

"What's your obsession with this human anyway?" Killian asks, tilting his face towards Polarian, "you've been hot on her trail like a hound from the moment you found her."

"I am not obsessed," Polarian spits, snarling at Killian, "I simply laid claim to her when I found her."

"You knew she was to be the king's." Killian turns away from him, "when will you...check her?"

"I think I'm going to leave that as a surprise..." The king nods to himself, "yes, a surprise. I'm no fool Killian, I know you wish to have a few more moments with her."

Killian keeps his mouth shut, staring up at the king.

"Considering you haven't disappointed me, I will grant you this small victory. Enjoy your few moments." The king waves a hand towards the exit, ignoring the rage that spills from Polarian. "Now be gone. I wish to dine in peace."

Killian spins on his heel and stalks from the throne room, his mood darkens with each step. He can't protect Adalyn from the king, he can't tell her what is to come.

But he will steal their moments with her, eating up whatever time they have left together. It will be the last time she looks at him with...*love* in her eyes. The last time she will trust him, but he can only hope that one day she will forgive him and see he did it to protect her and because he cares.

Killian runs a hand through his hair, deciding to bathe before going to Adalyn's room. He needs to shave the stubble from his cheeks and wash his hair, soak in hot water and ease his tense muscles. With the king wanting to surprise Adalyn when he checks her, Killian is going to be in a constant state of hidden anxiety.

Not to mention there's still the sickness spreading with no cure in sight. There's still the brand on Adalyn's arm and the ritual the king needs the ten women for.

Could Adalyn be viable to...use anymore? A woman in the ritual must hold hate in her heart and from the way Adalyn has been looking at him for the past week, there is no hate anymore.

Well...maybe a little.

He did kill her family, after all.

Killian climbs the steps one by one, dragging his feet slightly as the weight of his responsibilities come crashing back down.

A small part of him wishes he hadn't come to care for Adalyn, it would make his life a hell of a lot simpler. She's better off without him. All he is contrasts against all she is. He is darkness and she is light, she deserves someone who can give her equal light back.

Killian shakes his spiralling thoughts from his mind, opening the door to his room to find the fire roaring in the stone fireplace, keeping the room warm.

"Jurian's doing?" He murmurs, smiling slightly. Jurian. He would definitely need to catch his brother up on the entire trip and ask for advice. Jurian was always the better one at dealing with...*feelings and emotions.*

Killian strips to nothing, climbing into the scalding hot bath water that waits for him. He relishes the pain as his tanned skin begins to turn a shade of red, a small punishment for letting his heart get the best of him.

He ducks under the water, scrunching his eyes as the water burns his face. He grabs a bar of scented soap and scrubs his scalp, wanting to be clean and needing the pain to bring his mind back to focus.

He knows once he lays eyes on Adalyn he has no defences... but he still must try.

Killian washes quickly, rinsing his hair out before wrapping a towel low on his waist. Grabbing a bar of soap and the small sharpened blade that hides behind his mirror, he makes quick work of getting rid of all his stubble.

He splashes water over his face before staring at his reflection. His bright blue eyes, a shade darker than ice, skim over his now clean face. Physically, he looks the same.

His heart is to blame for his change.

"Bastard thing," he curses to himself, pushing from the sink and stalking back into his room. He looks up to find Alissa spread naked over his sheets. Once the vision would have stirred his cock...but as his eyes trail over her large breasts and the curled hair between her thighs, he has no reaction.

She grins, her black hair fanning his pillows.

"What are you doing here?" He asks, turning from her and going to his chest of drawers.

"You've been gone for nearly a month, I've missed you Killian," her sweet voice says. "You've completed your missions, so now we can have some fun."

"Alissa, you're one of my best friends but I'm not sleeping with you anymore," Killian says gruffly back, pulling a long sleeve black shirt on. Exhaustion is setting in, and he just wants to curl into Adalyn and forget all his problems.

"Why not?" She asks, the sheets ruffle and heavy footfalls head towards him. He keeps both hands securely on the towel at his waist as he turns to find her standing in front of him.

"Because I do not want to sleep with you anymore," he says. "I don't need a reason."

Hurt flashes in her eyes. "Killian...it's been years. How could you not want me anymore?"

"Alissa you will always be a close friend, you've been there for me through my darkest moments. But, my loyalties have changed," he says softly, not wanting to bring her pain. He hadn't realised that their casual sex had meant so much to her.

"Killian, I don't want to give this up. Please, please. I'll stop sleeping around, I'll do whatever you want." She reaches out and presses her hands to his chest. His heart squeezes, he never wanted to hurt her.

"Alissa...please don't make this harder than it has to be." He begins to step back, but she reaches down and palms his still soft cock.

"You're...not even hard seeing me." He removes her hand firmly.

"I am sorry, I truly am." He lets her go and stalk across the room, quickly pulling on a woollen pair of sleeping trousers. He discards the towel on the bed. "I am leaving now. I am sorry I've hurt you."

"Where are you going?" She demands, pulling her deep blue dress over her head before fixing her hair.

"You know where I'm going," he says quietly, already beginning to walk to the door.

Why does this happen to me, I can never just have a simple damn life.

"You're going to Adalyn's room?" She yells, "what, you've finally fucked her and now she's all you want to put your dick in?"

"You do not speak ill of her," Killian growls, now finding her standing in front of him with her hand on the doorhandle.

"Oh, now you're protecting her too." Alissa spits, "disgusting, Killian. How you could lower yourself to sleeping with mortal filth is beyond me, but let's see what she thinks of the truth."

Alissa sprints from the room, her anger and hurt almost choking him. Killian growls as he rushes after her, if she tells Adalyn of the mission...*no, I will not let her take that from me.*

Killian makes it to Adalyn's level to find Alissa already in the room, yelling at her. Killian barges through the door. Darkness dances at his finger tips and it *rages* when he sees Adalyn trembling in front of the fire. Her white nightgown hugs her body, exposing the scar on her breast, shoulder and near her throat.

"What does he see in you?" Alissa yells, "you are *human.* You are weak and you are nothing compared to me. I have been by his side for years and you come and suddenly he has a change of heart?"

"You need to stop, Alissa." Killian stalks forward, Adalyn catches his eye. She's scared, he can feel her energy wrapping around him.

"I don't think I will Killian," Alissa turns to him, "this is ridiculous."

"You're hurting and I understand that, but taking out your anger and pain on Adalyn is not the right way to go about this. It is not her fault, it is mine." Killian begins to reach for her. Although she's acting irrational, she is still one of his closest friends.

"No, Killian. It is her fault." Tears begin to stream down her cheeks a she lifts the hand that faces Adalyn.

"I have done nothing!" Adalyn speaks up, although her voice shakes she finds her courage, "I care for Killian, but I didn't ask for him to have a change of heart. I wasn't the one sleeping with him to pass the time."

Alissa glares at her, snarling.

"I heard of your reputation, you don't warm one bed for too long. Don't punish Killian because he wishes to only warm mine." Adalyn still trembles, but she holds fire in her amber eyes.

"You do not speak down to me, you mortal filth." Alissa clenches her fist and Adalyn begins to choke. Her hands reach her throat, clawing at invisible bonds.

"Let her go!" Killian yells, reaching to grab Alissa. He can't control his darkness, for the first time in a very long time his darkness overrides his control.

Black tendrils explode from him, wrapping around Adalyn. A single tendril breaks from the churning mass and spears into Alissa's mind.

She begins to scream and her fear fills Killian. It's sweet but there's a sour aftertaste, he isn't sure what nightmares are being shown to her but they can't be good.

Killian struggles to harness his darkness but it refuses to let Adalyn and Alissa go. He goes to Alissa and lifts her from the ground, she stumbles against him whimpering, but her screams die in her throat.

"Killian..." she groans, keeping a hand fastened to his arm as he leads her from the room. Once they step into the hall, the darkness falls from her and travels back to Adalyn.

"You do not touch her, speak to her, look at her or even think of her again." He lets go of her, taking a step back into the room. The guards in the hall don't pay any mind to the commotion.

"But..."Alissa reaches up, wiping her tears away.

"You have crossed a line, Alissa," he says firmly, "you hurt her.

You were supposed to be a close friend and this is how you repay me once I find loyalty to someone else?"

"Killian please," her voice is pleading but Killian can't find it in himself to forgive her so soon.

"Go. I don't want to see you again. If I forgive you, I will seek you out for *friendship* and only that." He closes the door on her, taking a deep breath. He turns to find his darkness slowly opening. Adalyn peers out of the churning depths and smiles faintly.

"Crazy ex, huh?" She says weakly.

It brings a smile to his face.

"You put up with far too much of my baggage." Killian slowly prowls towards her, finally alone. She must realise it too as a blush begins to burn her cheeks.

He's glad to see he isn't the only one affected when they're together.

"We all have baggage Killian," she murmurs, taking a step forward. She brushes a hand through the darkness, smiling as it gently caresses her hand, "I think it likes me."

"I think it more than likes you." He rests both hands against the chaise, the seat is the only thing that separates them, "I am sorry for her. I didn't realise she was going to take her anger out on you."

"You couldn't have known. She was hurting." Adalyn shrugs, looking up at him, "I know you are friends Killian, and I'm never going to sit there and tell you not to be because you've slept together."

"She hurt you. No friend of mine would do that."

"Well lucky you only seem to have Jurian left now, and he would do the opposite of hurt me." She winks, reminding him of the kiss they shared. Killian shoves the chair away and closes the distance between them.

He wraps a strong arm around her waist, stepping into the darkness that now hugs them both. He tangles his free hand in her hair and tips her face towards him.

A lazy smile graces her damp lips as she moulds herself to him. "Someone's a bit possessive."

"The only person giving you pleasure is me." Killian growls, dipping his face down to run his lips across her jaw. She shivers against his touch, digging her nails into his chest.

"You're addictive." He murmurs into her ear, gently nipping at the heartbeat in her throat, "and there is no other drug I wish to be addicted too."

"Killian..." she groans as he sucks at her neck, biting down firmly. He kisses the tender mark before claiming her lips, she opens her mouth and their tongues tangle with desperation.

"When I'm with you I have no defence." He breaks their kiss, leaning his forehead against her own, "there is only you and I."

"You think you have no defence," she says, half breathless. "I should...hate you. But I don't. I *can't* hate you Killian and it terrifies me."

"You will, one day," he murmurs, kissing her nose.

"I don't think so." She nips at his jaw, "you clean up nicely."

"Mmm is that a compliment?" He drags her towards the bed, wanting to wrap himself around her. His darkness fills him up once more, content now that she's safe.

"I don't think you need my compliments to know how good looking you are." She shakes her head, "your ego would explode."

"Your compliments are the only ones that matter to me." He falls back into the bed, pulling her down on top of him. She smiles softly down at him. Resting on her elbows, she begins to trace his face.

He's captivated as he watches her, his heart beats wildly in his chest.

"I think...you have a face carved by the gods themselves. That...was my first thought when I saw you, kneeling before Polarian. The gods carved you from their stone and gave you the voice of silk, deep but intoxicating." She blushes and refuses to meet his eyes, focusing on his jaw.

"Addie," he murmurs, trying to draw her attention.

"You are handsome, Killian. Far more beautiful than any man I've ever laid eyes on. There is not one part of you that I see as a flaw." She finally looks up at him, "your back, your scars? Even they are beautiful. I wish I could take that pain from you. You have suffered more than enough for this lifetime."

"I am not a good man, Adalyn," he says, voice thick with emotion. "I deserved every lash against my back. If you knew of the man I once was, you would not look at me as you do."

"I never asked or wanted you to be a saint, Killian." She cups his cheek, brushing a light kiss against his lips, "I won't run from your darkness."

"I have done bad things. Unspeakable things. I can't take them back and they are a part of who I am. Most of the time, they seem like the only thing I am." The truth of his words is freeing, it has been some time since he has opened up his festering wounds.

"Oh Killian," Adalyn's eyes fill with tears, "you think you deserve the pain. You don't. I will spend every waking moment showing you that. You are not only your darkness."

He brushes her hair from her face, tucking it behind her round, human ear, "You are not your darkness either."

Adalyn's bottom lip trembles, "Only you would say that."

"Isn't that what you've been saying?" He murmurs, "that there is more to me than this...this entity of emotion?"

"Yes, but your darkness has served its purpose already. Mine has not." She studies him, "I will avenge my family, Killian. It will not be pretty and I will take my time making them suffer how they have made me suffer. Does that not scare you? That I...want to do these vile things?"

"I could never be scared of your darkness Adalyn, I've never run from pain before. I'm not about to start." He studies her, tracing a finger down her jaw, "you have nothing to fear with me."

"I know." She kisses his finger as he runs it over her lips, "It can be heavy, suffocating. The sooner I have my revenge, the sooner I'll be able to breathe more freely."

"What will you do?" He asks. "I'm not going to stop you, as long as I know you're safe and have no air to get hurt."

Adalyn laughs dryly. "Trust me, I will be safe. More than safe."

"Is it disturbing that this is making me hard?" He smiles up at her, she grins down at him and purposefully rubs her breasts against his chest.

"I'd be offended if it didn't." He groans low, shutting his eyes. Adalyn peppers kisses along his jaw, trailing down his throat to where his pulse beats rapidly.

"I'm sure we have time..." Adalyn murmurs into his ear, pulling the lobe between her teeth. Killian bucks into her, his hard length rubs into her thigh. Her own breathy moan fills his ears.

"You're not tired?" He asks, opening his eyes, "you don't want to wait? After earlier..."

"I'll be satisfied once I'm fully seated on you." She bites her bottom lip, he watches as she sits up and straddles his waist. Slowly her hands skim down her waist, fisting the hem of her nightgown she removes it in one movement.

Her bare breasts beg for him, their hardened peaks have his mouth watering. He could never get enough of her, of this. Of her wanting him.

He rests his hands on her thighs, digging his fingers into the soft flesh.

"I like how you look at me," she whispers, trailing her hands over her breasts and down her waist.

"How do I look at you?" he asks, unable to take his eyes from her hand that begins to rub his hard length.

"Remove your clothes, Killian." She helps as he rips the shirt over his head, giggling as he lifts his ass up to pull his trousers off.

"Eager?" She purrs, nestling his hard length between her slick folds. He pants as she slowly rocks her hips against him, the sight has him almost spilling his seed.

"Always for you." He lifts her waist, she wraps a hand around his thick length and lines him up with her opening. Their moans fill the room as she sinks down onto him, taking every inch of him. She throws her head back, breathing deeply as she adjusts.

He sits up, wrapping his arms around her waist as he takes a peaked nipple in his mouth. He swirls his tongue around the nub, licking and sucking and pulling every sound of pleasure from her.

Adalyn begins to ride him, rubbing against him with each down ward thrust to hit her clit. Killian meets her with each thrust, supporting himself with one hand as he reaches around and grabs her round ass.

Adalyn fists his hair, riding him in a frenzy.

"God, I'm already close," she moans into his ear.

"Adalyn...." He claims her lips, needing to taste her. She indulges him, slipping her tongue into his mouth as he begins to pound into her harder and faster. He swallows every moan of pleasure, every gasp and plea.

Reaching down, he trails a finger down her ass and wets it with their slickness. He gently rubs the tight ring, she breaks away from the kiss and looks down at him.

"Do it," she whispers, her voice heavy with lust. Killian pulls out of her, as he slowly fills her once more he pushes his finger through that tight barrier.

Adalyn cries out, throwing her head back, "More."

Killian bites down on her breast, unable to stop the heat from building as he fingers her ass and pounds into her. Adalyn begins to pulse and clench around him.

"I'm...I'm coming." She cries out, wrapping her arms around his head as she constricts around his cock. Killian thrusts twice more before spilling his seed inside of her. He slowly pulls his finger from her ass as they sit there, breathing uneven. Sweat coats their bodies.

"That was," she looks down at him, "amazing."

"You didn't mind the finger?" He asks, stealing a kiss before standing with her still wrapped around him. He walks them into her bathroom, using his magic to heat the water.

"I…think I'd like to try it one day. You know, with your *other* hard length." She rocks against him, still inside of her he begins to harden again. She scrapes her nails down his back.

"I am trying to bathe us so I can hold you while we sleep," he chuckles, thrusting into her. "If you keep this up, we won't be sleeping tonight."

"Then let's not sleep." She looks down at him, warmth filling her amber eyes. "Make me yours, Killian."

He lowers himself into the water, reminding him of the first time he'd taken her body. The first time she'd given in to him. He fists a hand in her hair, fire floods his veins as she grinds against him.

"That, I can do."

41. Adalyn

Adalyn

Adalyn admires the red roses as the late morning sun shines down on them, causing the red of their petals to deepen. She'd escaped to the kings garden shortly after attending a breakfast with the king and the other nine girls. Most seemed content, accepting. The other half still shielded the hatred with quick smiles and charming words.

She'd been quiet at the breakfast, opting to listen. It's not as though she had anything to contribute to conversation. Nothing that could cheer the women up or help them. Adalyn's yet to find Jurian and see if he's found who murdered her family. Although Killian supports her, she can't risk him getting involved. If she can shield him from the wrath of the king, she will.

He has suffered enough.

It's almost been a week since they'd last spent a full night together, exploring *every* part of each other's bodies. She could spend the rest of her life indulging in him, filling herself up to the brim.

Adalyn knows there will be a catch, the other shoe will drop soon; she notices the tension between his eyes, the tightness in his limbs when he finds free time to find her.

There's something troubling him, but she doesn't push. Its

best she knows little about what the king asks of him, she just wishes he'd trust her enough to help with the weight he carries.

Adalyn turns to find Killian standing before her, his black dress shirt leeches the light around him. The sleeves roll up to his elbow, exposing his deep caramel skin.

"I thought I'd find you here," he says, looking around the garden. She shoves her hands into the pockets of her dress, glad she'd found a dress that even had pockets.

"It's peaceful here," she says, walking over to him. "Is everything okay?"

"Everything's fine. The king has dismissed me for the day, claiming a headache." His lips twitch into a smile as he looks down at her, "I want to show you something."

Adalyn hums, "What could the general possibly need to show me?"

"The general wishes to show the beautiful woman a secret of his." Killian reaches out and cups her jaw, his warm breath hits her face and tangles with her own. She leans into him, smiling.

"A secret? What will it cost me?" Adalyn murmurs, loving the game they play.

"You will have to trust me." Killian takes a step back, eyes dancing with mischief. "Do you trust me, Addie?"

Adalyn rolls her eyes, "Show me this secret and then I'll answer your question."

"Come then." She walks beside him, a large hand rests against her lower back as they leave the garden and begin to walk the many halls of the castle. Guards pin point his hand, but not once does he remove it from her back. Not once does he let their stares unnerve him.

Adalyn narrows her eyes as they enter the deserted hallway that leads to the catacombs, to the hidden library she's fond of. "Killian, why are we here?"

"The secret is in the catacombs."

"Those hounds are down there," she hisses, crossing her arms over her chest. "They nearly ate me last time I was down here."

"And why were you down here?" He asks, holding open the door that leads down to the catacombs. She sighs as she begins to walk down the steps.

"I was in the library, looking through the books."

Killian is quick to step in front of her once they reach the first hallway. As before, both black skinned hounds stand before the library door. Their ears perk towards Adalyn and Killian, but they make no move to attack.

"You control them?" She asks, knocking her shoulder against his. Killian chuckles as he takes her hand, leading her past the hounds and deeper into the castle.

"Of course I do." His deep chuckle echoes down the dark path in front of them. "They won't hurt you again. I've made sure of it."

"Were you following me?" She demands, looking up at him. Although she can barely see him with the fading torch light, she still catches his grin.

"I was making sure you didn't become their dinner," he says, "I didn't stalk you or lurk. I simply made the hounds docile so you could enter the library. I entered their minds and made it known you were not to be harmed."

"I didn't even see you," she grumbles, secretly loving that he went out of his way to keep her safe, even though she resented his presence at the time.

How long had they been destined to fall together?

"How much further? I can't see," Adalyn whispers, keeping her other hand wrapped around Killian's bicep.

"Not much further, just around this corner and through the hidden passageway." Adalyn follows him blindly, in the distance she can hear the faint flow of water. The air begins to fill with moisture and her curiosity grows.

"Just through here." Killian guides her through a hall, a soft blue light glows from the room ahead, filling the smooth stone hallway with light. Adalyn's eyes widen as they exit the passageway to find the high ceiling covered with bright blue glow worms.

A large rock pool takes up the entire room, water spills from a large gash in the wall and fills the pool up. The water never spills over the stone edges, draining through a large hole at the back of the pool.

Steam curls over the edges, dissolving as it hits the cold stone floor. Killian lets go of Adalyn's hand and walks to the water, dipping his hand in.

"This is my secret hiding place. I've been coming to this hot pool for many years." He looks over his shoulder at her, "I have only ever shown my wife this pool."

Adalyn's stomach churns with angst, this is the first time he's ever spoken of his wife. "What happened to her?"

Killian's sad smile breaks her heart. "She chose to love me. I chose to make bold choices and the king saw fit to punish me accordingly."

Adalyn gasps, "he killed her?"

"Yes. She...was heavily pregnant with our child. Neither survived." Killian looks back to the water, "I learnt my lesson that day."

"I'm so sorry Killian. No one deserves that on their conscience." Adalyn closes the distance and wraps her arms around his waist, resting her cheek on his back. She breathes his scent in, "you do not deserve to carry that pain."

"It is my fault." He wraps his hands around her own, breathing deeply.

"She wouldn't want you punishing yourself, Killian." Adalyn murmurs, "I know if I was in her position, I would never want you to blame yourself."

"You are too good for me, Addie."

Adalyn says nothing, only holding him tighter; as if she could piece back together all his broken pieces if only she could hold on long enough.

She knew he carried scars and held secrets, punishing himself for the path he's been forced to walk upon. When someone breaks, a piece of their soul is stained. Living with that stain is hard and there will always be dark days that feel as though there will never be light again.

In this moment, Adalyn can only hope her being here with him will help lessen the dark days he faces. The fact he even shared this piece of himself with her...she shuts her eyes.

After a few moments he turns in her arms, looking down at her with sadness and pain in his eyes. Her own eyes burn, feeling his pain.

"I don't want to think of the pain every time I visit this place anymore." He kisses her forehead gently. "I don't want to be haunted when I come here."

"Let's take a dip then," Adalyn says, forcing herself to smile although her heart is hurting for him, "I bet I can beat you in."

He chuckles and lets her go. Adalyn pulls the dress over her head before discarding her underwear, Killian growls as he looks down at her naked body; taking in every imperfection and blemish.

The way he looks at her...makes her feel powerful.

"I'm surprised to see you still clothed, Killian." Adalyn saunters past him, trailing a hand across his chest before climbing over the stone ledge. Warm water greets her, she sighs in relief as she lowers herself into the pool. She turns and watches as Killian undresses slowly, taking his time to unbutton his shirt; revealing his chiselled chest.

Adalyn licks her lips, reaching between her thighs as her blood thickens. He removes his shirt, not once taking his eyes from her as his muscle flex and strain with the movement. His body is a blessing from the gods.

Adalyn begins to circle her clit as he unties his pants, pulling them down with his under briefs to reveal his hardening length. Standing naked before her, he wraps a hand around his length and slowly begins to pump himself.

Adalyn's fingers rub faster, feeling the pleasure begin to build low in her stomach until she's aching to be filled. Killian continues his slow tease, drawing ragged breaths from her as she fixates on his hand.

"What do you want, Adalyn?" His deep voice skitters over her skin.

"You." She looks up at him, pausing her hand.

His blue eyes are intense as they capture her. "How do you want me, Addie?"

Adalyn rises from the water, finding her courage as she slowly walks to the edge of the stone, "I want you to join me in the water. I want you to fill me to the hilt and have me screaming your name."

The pupils in his eyes expand, he prowls to her and effortlessly stands in the water. Adalyn takes his face in her hands as he picks her up, holding her ass as he brings their bodies together. She wraps her legs around his waist, excitement building as he makes her wait.

He holds her tightly with one arm, grabbing his length with his free hand; he runs the head of his cock between her slick folds and teases her opening.

"Killian." She groans, trying to force her ass downwards. He chuckles darkly, nipping at her jaw.

"Mmmm?" he murmurs against her skin, biting down on her shoulder gently, "What is it darling?"

"Why do you tease me?" Adalyn presses her breasts against his chest, her body burns with anticipation and she aches to be filled.

"Because you love it...." Killian lines his cock up with her wet opening, "you love being filled by my thick cock."

He slides into her slowly, she clenches around his length as he buries himself inside of her. She grinds her hips against him, her clit rubs with each thrust against him. *Gods I'm not going to last long.*

"Yes, Killian." Adalyn is breathless, barely able to form sentences. His dirty words have her bouncing against his cock, using her legs to anchor her to his body. His wicked lips begin to suck and nip at her breasts as he thrusts his hips faster against her.

Killian moves a hand down to her ass, Adalyn's movements turn feverish as her body begs for his finger. He circles the ring before beginning to slide his finger into her, grunting as she clenches him tightly.

"Fuck I can't wait to take you here," he growls against her skin, leaving red bite marks across her breast.

"I can't either." Adalyn begins to pulse, "I'm close."

Killian takes her lips, sliding his tongue into her mouth. They kiss desperately, hot and passionate. He pulls away at the last second, taking her nipple between his teeth, "Come for me."

He bites down on her nipple, shoving her over that edge.

Adalyn screams his name as her body explodes with light, euphoria fills her veins as he continues to thrust into her; riding her through her orgasm.

Moments later he roars his own release, filling her with his seed. She collapses against him, resting her head on his shoulder as his limbs turn to jelly.

He lowers them into the water, wrapping his arm around her waist as he leans against the stone wall. He runs a hand up and down her back, catching his breath.

They enjoy the silence for a long while, not needing to say anything. Eventually Adalyn moves from Killian, floating on her back in the warm water. She watches the glow worms on the ceiling, fascinated by their glowing blue bodies.

"Who do you think is spreading the sickness?" She asks, breaking the silence. Killian floats on his back beside her, linking their fingers together.

"I'm not sure, it...felt familiar. As if my magic recognised what remnants were left behind." He murmurs, "I did not tell the king this, though. Otherwise I fear he would suspect I was behind it."

"Are you?" Adalyn asks.

"No, Addie. It's just weird that my magic recognises their

magic, whoever it is. I have no living relatives, there is not one person that walks this earth that has my power."

"Is there a piece of you missing?" Adalyn turns her face, needing to observe his reaction. He frowns slightly.

"I...I'm not sure." He looks at her, his blue eyes clouded with concern. "If there is a part of me *missing*, it will be the king's doing."

"Do you feel whole?" Adalyn asks. Something nags at the back of her mind. A memory, but she can't pull it forward.

"Well I don't feel empty. I suppose..." he frowns, "I don't feel that suffocating darkness. The rage that feeds my magic."

"When was the last time you felt it?"

"I don't know."

They fall back into silence, Adalyn is sure she's uncovered something vital but there are still too many pieces missing for her to make a connection.

A thud echoes through the room, Killian goes utterly still. Adalyn follow suit, not daring to breath. Her heart thunders in her chest as the echo of footsteps walks past their hidden hall and grow distant.

"What is someone else doing down here?" Killian murmurs, more to himself than her. Adalyn sits up in the water, looking towards the dark passage way.

"Could they have a hidden pool too?" She whispers back, desperately hoping that's what it is. But looking at Killian's face, she knows it's going to be something more.

"No, this is the only one. There are other tunnels..." He shakes his head, "care for an adventure?"

"I have a feeling I'm not going to have a choice." Adalyn huffs, letting him drag her from the water. They dress quickly and quietly. Killian holds her hand as he leads her from the room. Darkness encases them.

Adalyn walks along blind as he leads, she doesn't dare speak as the air thickens the deeper they head into the forgotten tunnels.

She tries her best to hide her fear, knowing Killian will protect her if it comes to that.

"There's a large iron door ahead, give me a second." Killian releases her hand, her ears strain as she listens to his grunt; suddenly golden light spills into the hall. Adalyn blinks rapidly as her vision adjusts.

Killian grabs her hand once more, leading them into the room.

High stone walls are covered in deep gouge marks, to their left there are stone cages. Most metal bars have been bent and broken. Dark red stains the floor underneath them, drag marks from the cells through to another door have Adalyn shivering.

"We shouldn't be here," she whispers, as the urge to flee begins to suffocate her. They shouldn't be here, they shouldn't have discovered this place. It wasn't meant to be discovered.

What have they just walked into?

"It's okay....I need to know why someone was here." Killian leads them towards the end of the hall, chains reinforce the door.

"Killian...I don't think we should open that door. It looks like whatever is on the other side needs to stay there." She pleads, tugging at his hand, "I have a bad feeling."

"I need to, something is calling to me on the other side." Killian drops her hand and begins to remove the heavy chains. Adalyn wraps her arms around her chest, looking over her shoulder. The room they're in is narrow, only holding the damaged cells. What could this room have been?

"Addie, look." Killian's whisper has her peering around his large frame, the circular room is large; covered with white stone floors and golden, cracked walls.

"What's in there?" She whispers, taking a few steps into the room, it's incredibly large and most of the room is covered by thick shadows. Killian walks to a pile of bones close to the door, crouching down to inspect them.

Adalyn walks to a crack in the wall, finding a large sharpened nail suck in the crack. The gleaming silver nail is as large as her thigh.

She reaches out, running her hand against the surprisingly smooth surface.

"What the hell..." she whispers, what creature did this nail come from?

A hot breath hits her, her hair falls over her chest from the force. Fear roots her in place and she fears her heart might just fail. Her hand trembles against the nail.

"I found fresh blood." Killian calls, still engrossed, "it looks as though something is being fed."

Killian you stupid faerie bastard turn around!

Hot breath hits her again and something large inhales, pulling at her hair and dress. Her stomach bottoms out as she slowly turns, not wanting to startle whatever the hell she's about to face.

Adalyn's throat dries up as she comes face to face with a large silverly purple scaled snout. She meets the golden eyes of the dragon that watches her. Its body is hidden by the shadows, but she can tell it's extremely large as she spots the swift movement of a scaled tail.

A jagged scar runs down the creatures snout, mangled scales cover most of its snout as Adalyn studies it closer. It's been tortured, multiple scars cover is face. Her eyes travel down its thick neck, but the rest of its body is cloaked in darkness.

A dragon.

She is staring down a dragon, who only has eyes for her.

Adalyn doesn't dare move as it brings its large snout closer, inhaling her scent.

How has Killian not noticed yet? She screams into her mind, wanting to look for him but afraid to take her attention from the burnt honey eyes that focus on her.

The dragon hasn't eaten her. Yet.

"Addie—" Killian's voice comes to a halt. Adalyn has the irrational sense to laugh at the situation they're in, because of course they'd find a dragon hiding in the catacombs.

She was never lucky, not in her past life or this one.

The dragon opens its mouth and bellows, shaking the foundation around them. It steps out of the darkness, iron chains restrict its stunning purple and silver veined wings.

It bellows...as if it is pain.

Adalyn screams as heat begins to fill the room, the dragon directs its pain towards Killian; its chest begins to glow red and orange underneath the iridescent scales.

"Killian!" Adalyn runs towards him, the scorching breath of the dragon singes the edges of her hair.

Adalyn wraps herself around Killian's body as she hears the dragon exhales its fire.

She waits for death to come.

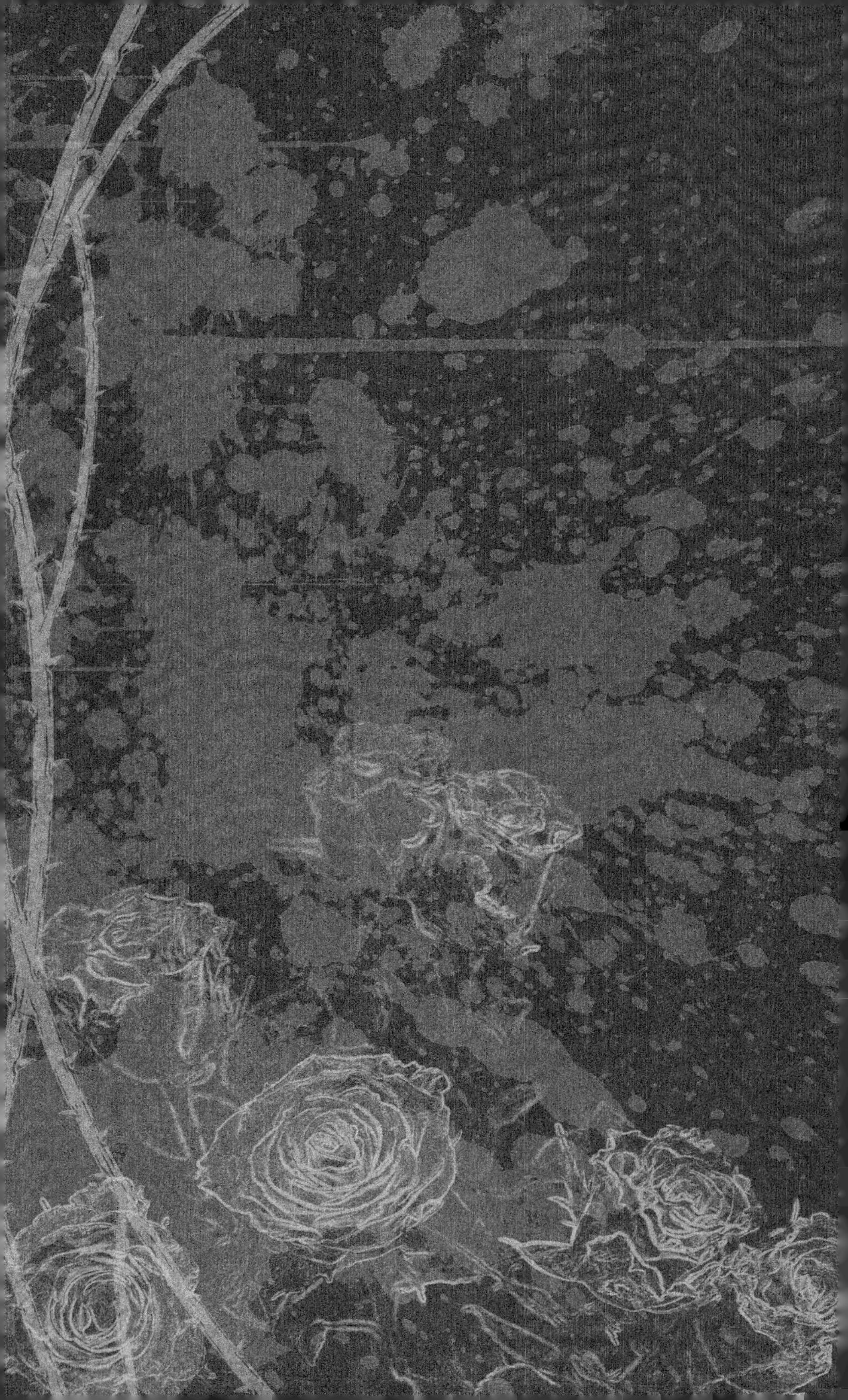

42. Killian

Killian

Adalyn's screams fill his ears moments before she propels her small body into his, grappling and straddling his waist as she protects his front. Killian releases his darkness mere seconds before the dragon was going to turn them into its next meal.

The heat in the room retreats slowly, Killian keeps one arm around Adalyn's waist as he levels one hand towards the dragon. Black essence swallows his hand as his power funnels into the dragon, calming the creature.

He has no idea how he missed the dragon when they'd entered this room, had he let curiosity get the best of him? Or was there something more?

Killian is fascinated with the mighty beast before him, slowly it lowers its large stunning face to the ground before slumping over and falling into a deep sleep. He releases a small amount of his magic, not wanting to take the chance it will wake once more.

What is a dragon doing down here? He hadn't seen one since he was a child, and even then they'd been a dying race. Beautiful, misunderstood creatures. His mother had told him stories of when their kind were plentiful, coming in a kaleidoscope of colours with defining shapes.

Shackles keep the dragon's wings restrained, as well as cuffs around each large scaled ankle. Scars dent the creature's silvery purple scales, covering most of its body.

Steam puffs from its nose, curling in the air.

Adalyn trembles in his hold, her warm breath draws him from his thoughts and back into the present.

"What...what is going on?" She whispers.

Killian helps sit her down, "I don't know. I haven't seen a dragon since I was a child. I didn't even know she was down here."

"How do you know it's a girl?" Adalyn asks, taking a small shuffled step towards the sleeping dragon. Wonder rounds her eyes as she takes in its mighty size.

"The snout." Killian points towards the scarred snout, "female dragons have stumpier snouts whereas males have long and thin snouts."

"She's beautiful." Adalyn looks over her shoulder to him, "how did they even get her down here?"

Killian looks around the large room, no sun shines down here. He isn't sure where exactly this room is under the castle, unless it's just under the earth.

"I'm assuming they built this around her, maybe had her here as a baby."

"Is there any way to get her out?" Adalyn asks sadly, wrapping her arms around her waist. Killian sighs.

"Not unless we want the entire castle and Valarki in the surrounding area to know there's a dragon. She might be the very last of her kind."

"Do you think the king has a purpose for her?" Adalyn takes slow steps towards the dragon's large face, after hesitating a moment she gently runs her hand down a scaled cheek.

"He would, but he hasn't told me of his plans or that he even has her down here." Killian stuffs his hands into his pocket, mulling over this new information.

"Could the king be making a move against you?"

Her question unsettles him.

She'd asked only hours before if he felt like a piece of *him* was missing.

She's questioning his position with the king now.

"Do you know something I do not?" He asks quietly.

Adalyn frowns, but refuses to look at him .

"I don't think so..." she says slowly, still stroking the dragons cheek, "I feel like there's something nagging at the back of my mind but I can't figure it out."

"About me?" Killian furrows his own brows, "What could you possibly know?"

"I don't know, Killian. That's what I'm saying. I...I keep having this dream that feels like a memory of a glass dome, and when I touch it my hand isn't my own, but..."

"But what?" Killian feels his heart begin to race as he focuses solely on her. He isn't sure why he feels panicked, or like he wants to shed his skin.

"Every time I touch the dome, *your* power appears and rushes to the surface."

They fall into silence.

Killian tries and fails to figure out what her dream may mean, he scours his mind and comes up empty. He'd never once seen a glass dome, or anything similar to his power. He doesn't rule her dream out for now, wanting to keep an open mind in case Adalyn is onto something.

"I'll try my best to remember more details and I'll let you know what I come up with." Adalyn steps away, dragging her eyes from the dragon. "We should go, though. I don't want anyone to know we're here."

"Come."

Killian takes her hand in his own, relaxing at her touch as he leads them back through the darkened hallways, away from the dragon and away from the questions he can't answer.

Adalyn doesn't speak as she walks beside him, occasionally squeezing his hand in reassurance.

Killian needs to find the king, keep his ears and eyes open for any information. His eyes flitter to Adalyn in the darkness...she has access to his private chambers, to information not even he has access to.

For years, he'd been willing to follow his king blind; not questioning any of his real motives and playing the role of a good general.

How many times had he been lied to?

Deceived?

Not once had he questioned his loyalty like he is now, it simply became as natural as breathing; do what you're asked and avoid punishment.

Ahead, the hounds perk up at their footsteps. Adalyn shrinks into Killian's side, not daring to look at the terrifying beasts.

He chuckles internally, but keeps her tucked neatly into his side. Anything to touch her, have her touching him.

His body rolls with tension as they ascend the stairs leading to the main castle, his anxiety had dissolved as he'd taken her in the hot pool.

He'd lost all worries and doubts, thinking of only her.

Once they enter the hallway she drops his hand, putting a respectful amount of distance between them. Killian knows they must be careful, but all he can feel is her absence.

Does she feel the same?

Adalyn keeps her features neutral as they enter a busier hall, human slaves keep the halls as they stumble back and forth; Valarki guards snarl in their direction, jabbing them with their spears.

He narrows his eyes on them, sending out a small tendril of his magic. He'd keep them in line, if only for Adalyn's sake. She stiffens as one guard stares at her a beat too long.

"Got something to say?" The guard taunts, overlooking Killian. It darkens his mood.

"Mmm," Adalyn taps a finger to her cheek, pretending to think, "I've just come to the conclusion you must not be well hung enough if you feel the need to stab your spear at every human that walks past."

Killian narrows his eyes on the guard, his top lip peeling back into a snarl.

The guard growls, ready to say more until he notices the darkness that now spills into the hall. He falters, snapping his mouth shut.

"They're simply doing what they're forced to do." Adalyn begins walking past him, "you don't need to make it harder for them because you're miserable with your own life."

The second guard across the hall smirks, looking at Adalyn in a new light. Killian feels his possessiveness grow, not wanting any other male, human or Valarki, to take an interest in her like he has.

Adalyn doesn't notice though, sparing Killian a glance once with an arched brow. He catches up to her, walking by her side. He tucks his hands into his pocket, supressing the urges to take her hand.

They reach a rounded hall, Killian cuts her off and to others it looks as though he's whispering directions to her as he points with his hand.

"Seeing you feisty makes me hot all over," he whispers, nipping at her earlobe. Her dark chuckle skitters over his skin, sending all his blood to his hardening cock.

"Killian, you're not being a good sport," she whispers back, tilting her face towards him. "I can see your erection from here."

"You undo me, Addie." He presses a quick kiss on her forehead before straightening, readjusting the front of his pants. He arches a brow down at Adalyn as she stares up at him, cheeks flushed and eyes wide.

"Mmm?" He hums, tucking his hands back into his pockets once more. Adalyn bites her bottom lip but shakes her head.

"I'm going to sit in with the king, will you be okay?"

She blows out a breath, stirring the hair on her cheek, "I'll be fine. Bored, but fine."

"I'm sure Allison or Jurian would be willing to keep you

company," he comments. He's still yet to catch up with his brother and gather insight.

Adalyn grins, "maybe I can make another trade with Jurian."

Killian narrow his eyes at her, chest rumbling.

She laughs, patting a hand to his chest before sauntering away from him; her hips swaying with each step, "I'm joking, Killian. You're lucky you're the better kisser," she sings sweetly over her shoulder before turning and leaving him standing there flushed head to toe with a raging hard on.

He chuckles as he walk in the direction of the throne room, only Adalyn could tear him two ways and still have him hot and bothered.

Polarian enters the hallway, immediately his orange eyes blaze. Killian keeps himself composed, half praying he doesn't notice the bulge in his pants.

"What will you do once she finds outs?" Polarian asks, coming to a stop. "I respect you as my general, Killian, because you're a splendid fighter and you're good at dealing death."

"What do you need, Polarian?" Killian asks, wanting to save the small talk and the reminder that he has more blood on his hands than Polarian.

"Do you know why I've taken an interest in her, Killian?"

Killian narrows his eyes, but stays silent. Polarian grins, winding a hand through his long, straightened brown hair that rests around his waist.

"Because you have placed her on a pedestal. The first human female that has ever caught your eye." Polarian tilts his head to the side, brushing his eyes over Killian, "you know I deal in torture, revel in it. You've always known how dark it is inside my head."

"What does she have to do with your perversions?" Killian growls, clenching his hands at his side. Polarian simply shrugs.

"Deep down, I think she secretly likes the fight and the pain."

"You will *never* touch her, do you understand?" Killian takes a threatening step forward, his darkness clouds his vision and the rage begins to boil deep in his veins. "If you touch her, you will have me to answer too. I can assure you I will not be as merciful as our king."

Polarian has the good sense to pale slightly, he simply shrugs one before stalking off. Killian struggles to contain his anger, the thought of Polarian touching Adalyn makes him want to listen to his screams and bathe in his blood.

Killian had become too complacent as his feelings had grown for her, he'd released the handle he once had over the fellow Valarki that look up to him.

No more will I be walked over. For Adalyn's sake, I need to be feared. She will be protected if everyone knows she belongs to me.

Once he reaches the throne room, Killian has calmed himself down and donned his favourite mask of cool calm. The king looks up from his throne, no women from his harem are to be found; only the guards that line the throne room walls.

"Ah, Killian. Just who I was looking for." The king's deep voice rolls towards him, "we have much too discuss."

"What have I missed?" Killian asks, taking the king's right side. He straightens, clasping his hands behind his back. The king relaxes back into the throne.

"There is trouble stirring in the human lands once again," the king sighs, drumming his hand on the white skull in the arm rest. "I was being generous, leaving them with the small amount of land they have. I'm afraid I will have to make the final blow."

"What are you saying?" Killian questions.

"Do you think the human males can be trained to make good soldiers?" The king asks instead, "do you think their frail bodies have it in them?"

"I'm unsure, your majesty." Killian keeps his face neutral and voice bored. "It would entirely depend on the human and their dedication to training."

"Do you believe they'd fight against their own kind?"

Killian's stomach tightens. "It would take...persuasion. They have loyalty to their own kind."

"Hmmm."

“Why do you ask?”

The king leans forward, rubbing his temples, “because hard times are upon us, Killian. Word has come from Oktavia, the continent across the sea. Their human lord wishes to form an alliance. In exchange for the human lives that remain in the human lands, he will offer us trade.”

Oktavia...a human country. Killian can’t remember the last time they’d been in contact with anyone from a different country, let alone a purely human country.

Dread coils in his stomach, closing his throat.

“Do you believe it? They really think I’m just going to simply hand over the few humans who remain for trade. We are a sole sufficient country, we’ve never needed to rely on another country.” The king slams his fist onto the skull, sending a crack down the middle.

“What is your plan then?” Killian asks. “If you don’t wish to trade, what do you wish for?”

“An invasion, Killian. Once I have all of Pantera in my grasp... the world will be my oyster and I its victor.”

Killian stays silent, clicking together the pieces. The king has kept the dragon under the castle as an aerial attack weapon that can fly across the ocean, forced with his magic to do his bidding.

One dragon wouldn’t be enough to begin an invasion... Killian studies the king's side profile, thinking of the full training camps that border the north west mountain where he had trained.

“For today, we will be listening to requests from our people. Tomorrow I will begin to plot and plan.” The king chuckles, resting his ankle against his knee, “maybe I will even allow you to rule Oktavia, Killian. You have been good to me, loyal and honest.”

“It would be an honour, your majesty.” Killian bows his head slightly, although the king doesn’t see it. The proposition has thrown Killian from his first train of thought. If he ruled an entire country...would he be able to have Adalyn by his side? Would he be able to enforce the humans to slavery and murder them until he had his handle?

Could he resist the power that comes with the weight of a crown?

Furthermore, how far could Adalyn's forgiveness stretch for him?

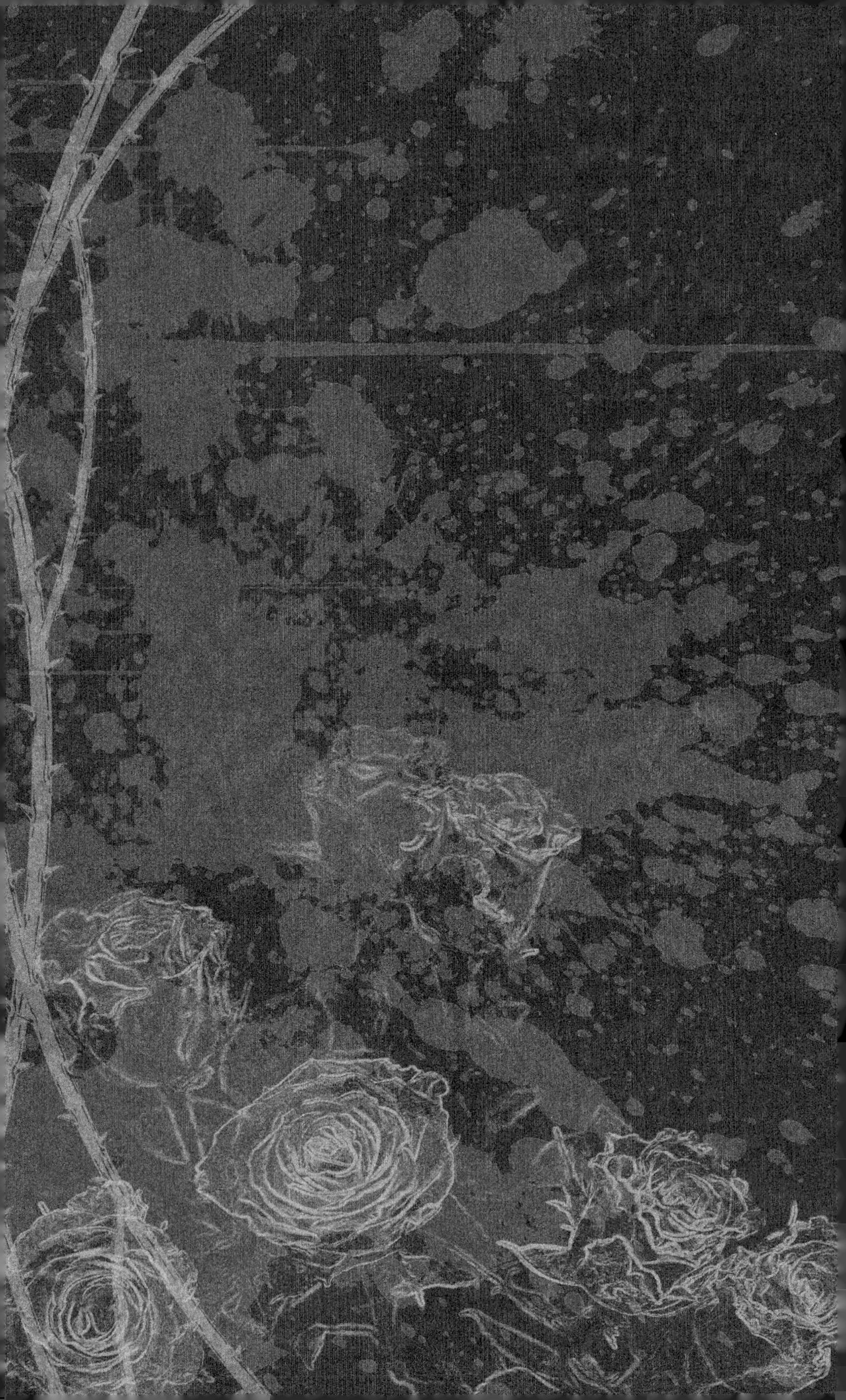

43. Killian

Killian

Killian internally groans as another Valarki male steps forward, holding a small child to his chest. He hadn't realised the king was going to take so many requests in one day. Now, well into the late evening Killian is restless to return to his chambers and dine in peace.

All afternoon he'd mulled over the conversation he'd had with the king before the first Valarki had been presented. No blood had been shed yet, and if it had, he doubts he would have even paid attention.

"What is your case?" The king asks, leaning forward. "This will be the last one for the day so I am hoping it is good."

The man straightens, raising his chin although a sliver of fear shines in his eyes. It captures Killian's curiosity.

"My...my child."

"What of your child?" The king asks, growing impatient. The man pauses, looking down at the child still hidden in the dark peach blanket. His brown hair is curled in ringlets, held back by a leather clasps. It hangs just past his shoulders. His lean body is tanned from the many hours in the sun, doing god knows what. Killian had never taken it upon himself to learn about what his own kind did outside these castle walls.

"I wish for you to pardon my child."

Killian frowns.

"You want me to pardon your child?" The king barks a laugh, "I do not need to pardon Valarki children, they are a blessing."

"As all children are a blessing." The man takes a steady breath, "I wanted to go about this the right and correct way, I did not want to hide and cower."

"You're testing my patience," the king growls.

"My child's mother...is human."

Silence falls over the room, the king wraps his mind around the man's statement faster than Killian can. Killian is still grasping at the fact as the king rises, calm fury rolls off of his large frame.

"Why have you bred with a human?" The king asks, clasping his hands in front of him. "They are our slaves, you can have your way with their bodies as much as you wish but you *never* keep their child."

"I know the rules your majesty. It was a mistake." The man pulls down the peach sheet to reveal a rather human looking child, her tan skin shines under the light and illuminates her rounded ears.

"She looks human," Killian states.

"She...has magic." The man cradles her to his chest, although she peers out and a childish giggle leaves her small mouth.

Killian's heart convulses in his chest.

This is what his child with Adalyn would look like.

It has him losing his breath, knowing what the king is going to ask of him.

"Pass her to me," the king demands, holding out both hands. The man hesitates. "I said *pass her to me.*"

Killian can't look away as the man places his child into the king's arms. She paws at the kings hands as they hold under her arms. Already six months old, if Killian could guess.

"She is already quiet aged, why have you not presented her sooner?"

The man brushes a hand over his face. "The child's mother

died in child birth. I could not bring myself to take her from this world."

The king tilts his face, golden eyes narrowing.

Killian breathes deeply through his nose, unable to stop the rolling of his stomach. He doesn't want to witness what comes next.

He never has the choice.

The king arches a brow, two guards come forward and take hold of the man's arms. He looks at the king with wide, panicked eyes.

"Please–please do not do this. Pardon her, *pardon her.*" He struggles against the guards, trying his best to get to his child. Killian feels pain radiating off the man, who still struggles to fight. A third guard comes forward, pressing the tip of his bade to his throat.

The king sighs. "You have left me with no choice. I will not have half breeds living and breathing in my country."

The baby girl begins to cry as the king squeezes his hands together.

Killian looks away as the cries turn to screams, ringing and echoing around the throne room. The father cries and yells his fury at the king, begging for forgiveness and pardon. It falls on the king's deaf ears.

A sickening crack and squelch has the baby girls cries abruptly cutting off. A soft thud hits the marble floor as the father cries out his grief.

"*No, no, no, no,*" his voice breaks as he screams.

Killian struggles to stay present, his own screams of a distant but raw memory keep resurfacing. It had once been him, forced on his knees as the king took his blade and slit his wifes throat.

It had been his own screams of grief for the child that he never got to meet.

For a future he had been robbed of.

Blood surrounds the baby's broken body, Killian can't take his eyes from her small, still form. Only moments ago she'd been alive, giggling. Full of life.

Now, there is only darkness.

There has only *ever* been darkness in this castle, in these wall, in the hole where Killian's heart is meant to beat.

"This is your punishment," the king says calmly, utterly unphased as the man sobs. "For future, I suggest you keep yourself infertile or carve out the slave's uterus. Make it well known the king does not allow half breeds to live."

The king turns and stalks back to his throne. "Killian, take the body to the burn pile. Guards, clean up the floor."

The man is dragged from the room, sobbing into his peach blanket. The guards throw him from the room, snarling as he walks away defeated.

Killian moves on heavy legs as he descends the stairs, walking over to the small body. He bends down, acid crawls up his throat as he gently takes the baby girl into his arms, holding her to his chest.

She does not stir, her light green eyes open and unseeing.

Killian feels the king watching him, gauging his reaction. Killian forces himself into boredom, "What is it, your majesty?"

"I am sending another conquest and you will lead it with Alissa."

Killian freezes, looking over his shoulder to the throne, "Why Alissa? I always take Jurian."

"Is that your only concern, Killian?" The king grins, wiping his thumb along his bottom lip. "Jurian will go as well, then."

"Why are you sending another conquest? We have only not long returned." Killian grits his teeth, knowing he'd be torn from Adalyn once more with no idea how long he'll be gone for.

"Because I am not the only player in this game, Killian. Do not think I am the only one in this world who holds great power. I simply hold the pieces to keep myself in the most important spot."

"When do I leave?"

The king grins. "In due time, general. In due time. Now leave, I wish to be left with my thoughts."

Killian leaves, glancing down at the child in his arms. Blood drools from her gaping pink lips and runs down her chin, splattering the daisy jumpsuit she'd been dressed in.

Resolve and rebellion overtakes Killian as he walks through the castle with speed and agility, tracking down the man who had brought his child here, in hopes of being redeemed.

Killian finds the man about to exit the castle, his broken sobs echoing with each beat of Killian's heart. He pauses once, doubting his next move.

The man looks over his shoulder, his red rimmed eyes spill tears as he look down into Killian's arms.

"Does the king wish to have me relive my pain?" He asks, clutching the blanket to his chest with white knuckles. Killian struggles with each breath, this has hit far too close to home.

"He does not know that I am here," Killian says, his words deep with his own grief. "Take her and give her the right burial. Mourn her life."

"The king...the king told you to take her to the fires."

"I know what he has asked of me," Killian growls, holding his arms out. "Take her now and mourn her or leave and regret the decision. It is your choice to make."

The man walks forward, uneasily. "Why are you doing this, General? I've heard of you."

"There is only so many truths to the whispers that reach your ears." Killian gently places the girl in the peach blanket, skin prickling as the man covers the baby and cradles her to his chest. "Do not speak of this to anyone. You should have fled with her."

"I was trying to do right by the king," the man says, shaking his head sadly.

"There is only death and darkness in this castle, you will not find your redemption here. Now go, before you land both of us in graves six feet under," Killian growls, gesturing to the door beyond. The man nods once, rushing from the castle without another word.

Killian's hands tremble, he looks down to find small droplets of blood on his left hand.

He isn't sure when he returned to his room, or how he undressed himself and scrubbed his skin red raw. He isn't sure if he spoke to anyone between the time from seeing the blood on his hand to the time he blinked back into the present to find himself aching and raw in his steaming bath.

He holds his head in his hands, breathing deeply. He'd lost hours, trapped in his own grief and supressing the pain that had consumed him.

Killian drags himself from the tub, throwing the first items of clean clothing on and leaving his room. His mind is empty, no thoughts occupy the vacant space as he walks to Adalyn's room on autopilot.

He opens Adalyn's door, finding her curled on the chaise in front of the crackling fire. Warmth consumes him as her scent drifts towards him, he inhales her lavender scent and finds the fog clearing from his mind. He shuts and locks the door behind him.

Adalyn looks away from the flames and frowns, "are you okay?"

Killian shakes his head, swallowing the lump in his throat as he walks to the chair. She moves her legs and allows him to sit. He takes her hand and pulls her into his lap; burying his face into her chest.

His heart *aches*.

"Killian...you're worrying me," she whispers, wrapping her gentle hands around the back of his neck. She keeps herself straddled to his waist, holding him close.

"I...I just need you to hold me," he whispers back, closing his eyes and inhaling all that she is. Adalyn reminds him that he is *here* and *alive*.

Grief is a deadly shadow that is constantly lingering, it holds no discrimination for human or Valarki; once you experience a loss that rips your heart from your chest, it digs its talons in.

Grief reminds him that once, he had a heart capable of that. That *he* was capable of being loved in return.

Adalyn holds him tightly, whispering sweet words into his ears and combing a hand through his hair. She is warm, she is *here*.

With him. Holding him. *Loving him*.

He has made the mistake of restarting his heart when he casts his gaze upon her, has made the mistake of letting her fire breath warmth into his veins.

"Killian...do you want to talk about it?" She whispers, kissing his forehead gently. Killian sighs against her, wrapping his arms around her waist.

He's made a mistake, but the grief of losing Adalyn...it will be worth every second, every minute of his suffering.

"I...I can't." He leans back, peeling open his dry eyes as he looks into her amber ones, even now her own grief clings to her shadow; darkening her burnt golden and brown depths.

Yet, she still offers him comfort; even though he is the source of *her* grief and pain.

"That's okay," she cups his face in her hands, leaning forward to press a gentle kiss to his lips. "Stay the night with me."

"I can leave if you wish," he murmurs against her lips, nuzzling his nose into her cheek.

"I don't want you to leave, Killian. Stay. Stay with me, you're safe here." She slips from his lap, taking his hand with her own. He allows her to lead him to her bed, the sheets are cool as he slides into them.

She huddles against his side, wrapping an arm around his waist as she leans her head against his chest. He stares at the ceiling as he runs a hand through her hair.

"The king wishes for war," he mumbles. "I have no power to stop him, I can only do what he commands."

"A war with who?" Adalyn asks, drawing patterns against his clothed chest.

"Another country, they're wanting to make a trade but he wouldn't delve into details. I believe he keeps all his paperwork in his private chambers."

"Do you have access to them?" Adalyn asks, her hand now runs up his chest and trails against his throat and jaw. His hand tangles in her hair.

"No, only the women of his harem are allowed into his private chambers. I wouldn't be able to tell you the colour of his walls." Killian leans into her hand and closes his eyes. The thudding of a headache begins in his temples, reminding him of the multiple curve balls that are going to be thrown his way.

He wants to be prepared, to have the upper hand, when it all catches fire and comes crashing down.

"I...I could go into his room," Adalyn says, propping herself up on her elbow. "I'm not sure what I'm looking for, but I could try and find some information for you."

"Addie, I can't ask you to do that—"

She presses a finger to his lips. "You're not asking me to do anything. The king wants to invade a country that simply wants to trade. I can't allow innocent people to be murdered because he's a tyrant."

"You don't understand what that means, to go into his chambers," Killian says, gripping her chin. "He will expect you to give him something and I can't live with that."

"Killian, you don't have a choice." Adalyn whispers, "I'm not too excited about the idea either, but my father always said sometimes we have to make choices we don't wish to, for the greater good. Let me do this for the greater good."

"Your father sounded like a wise man," Killian whispers, looking into her eyes. "I am truly sorry I have taken him from you."

Tears gather in Adalyn's eyes, spilling over her cheeks. "Killian...I can't say I forgive you, but I can learn to live with the heart ache. My family wouldn't want me to be miserable, they'd want to me to thrive and be happy. You had your orders and you've lived this way for years, longer than I've been alive for."

"I don't think I will ever change," he whispers, surprised to find warmth dripping from his eyes.

"Sometimes it's not the person who changes, Killian, it's the mask that falls off." She brushes his tears from his cheeks, licking her lips.

Her statement unravels him, from the start Adalyn has challenged him and forced him to see the world through her eyes; she's forced him to look beyond his cold indifference and walk beside her.

She's only ever tried to make him *see*, to feel what she feels. Human or Valarki, they both share the same emotions. Killian has worn a mask for many, many years. He has bent himself into the shape others expect of him and has rarely showed his kindness to others who he does not care for.

"Let me do this for you, for *me* and for those who don't have a say." She grasps his hand that rests on her chin, "let me do this, even if it is the last thing I do."

Looking into her eyes, he knows he cannot deny her.

"Adalyn...thank you, for pulling my mask off in the time I needed it most."

Adalyn kisses him, her lips warm as she seems to breathe life back into him, reaching out her hand unafraid of his darkness. "There is nothing wrong with being vulnerable, Killian. Sometimes, it is our greatest strength in our darkest moments. To face our shadow and still be able to stand on our own two feet. To share that shadow with the people who mean the most to us."

Killian claims her lip once more, his heart pounding louder than ever before.

Thud. Adalyn. Thud. Adalyn.

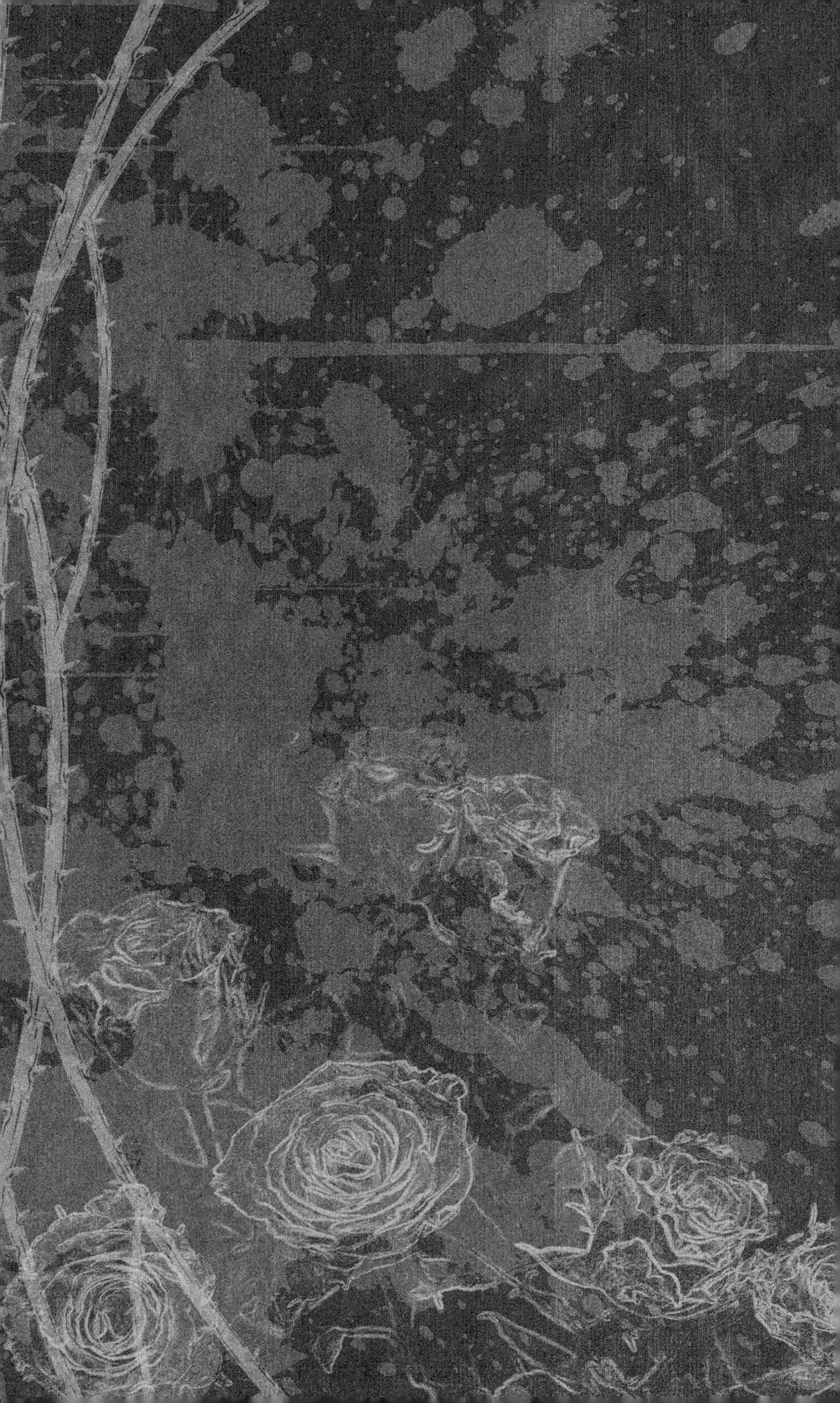

44. Adalyn

Adalyn

Adalyn runs her fingers lightly over the cold, golden doors that are closed before her. Her mind empties with each slight caress, craving the confidence from the night before when she told Killian she would help.

She wouldn't admit it, but a small part of her regrets her choice.

After Alissa bursting into her room and trying to choke the life out of her, Killian's confession and the soft side he'd shared with her, Adalyn had felt brave; bold even.

She had vowed to make them regret their choice of keeping her alive, but from the moment she set foot in this castle nothing has gone to plan. She'd been sent away with Killian, had grown far too fond of him to the point that craving him was her addiction.

She hadn't made Polarian pay for his sins against her, and the small part of her that craved to see his blood spilt was beginning to grow restless.

Adalyn slips her other hand into the hidden pocket of her deep red dress, finding the small glass vial still corked. Knowing the red liquid, *Killer*, was still safely in her hands gave her the confidence to knock.

The king hadn't summoned her, hadn't gone out of his way

to find her once she'd returned with Killian. Adalyn wasn't sure if seeking him out was even allowed, or if she'd get punished for interrupting him.

Killian needed certain papers, and Adalyn couldn't read their written language. The small potion would give her two hours, she'd grab the papers and hand them over to Killian in her room, then she'd return to keep an eye on the King. They'd discussed the plan in the early hours of the morning before Killian had shown her just how much he appreciated her doing this.

Adalyn knocks again, firmly hitting her knuckles. The king may not even be in his chambers, but it's a gamble she had to take.

"Come in." His deep voice slips through the door, muffled. Adalyn takes a deep breath and plasters on a hesitant smile before she gently pushes the doors inwards.

A small gasp escapes as her eyes flitter over the room, unable to focus on one section for too long. A large, rounded red velvet covered bed sits at the back of the room with thick, black bed posts anchored to the ceiling. To her right a large fire roars in the golden fireplace, crackling and popping.

The king sits on the chaise, wearing a thin cloth to hide his most intimate parts. He takes a sip of his red wine, golden eyes roving over Adalyn as she stands there. Golden hair flows around him, seeming interested to see her as well.

Adalyn feels her cheeks burn as she closes the doors behind her, concealing her to her fate. There's no turning back now, she'd have to face whatever came her way. The room smelt of the king, smoked sandalwood mixed with the smoke curling from the burning logs.

It was intoxicating, even though her heart and body belonged to Killian.

"What brings you here, petal?" He asks, resting his elbow on his thigh. The glass seems small clasped in his large hands, he swirls the liquid contents.

"I wished to see you, if you would have me." Adalyn says softly, the blush in her cheeks real. She could admit to herself the king was handsomely wicked, Killian had known what might transpire if she entered this room and he had let her control her own choices.

Looking into the king's burning golden eyes, she knows she will be begging for forgiveness.

Her eyes skim to the left of the room, not surprised to find a golden study desk lined with papers and other little trinkets scattered on the top.

A wooden room divider sits beside the study, Adalyn catches a glimpse of a glass dome sitting on top of a white marble stand.

"Indulge me," the king draws her attention away from the dome, gesturing for her to take the empty space beside him. He relaxes his legs in front of him, allowing her to sit.

She tries her best to relax into the seat, stealing glances towards his wine glass. Her plan might work too perfectly, so far everything had fallen into place.

"How was the journey?" The king asks, staring into the fire that warms the front of them. Adalyn rests her hands in her lap, staring into the fire as well.

"It was pleasant, I enjoyed seeing more of Pantera," she admits honestly. "The forests were beautiful and the people were all so different."

"I take much pride in my country, in my people and in the appearance," the king says. "I have ruled for many, many years."

"Do you ever get lonely?" Adalyn asks, unable to help herself. Curiosity always got the best of her at the worst of times, but showing an interest could only work in her favour. She needed to get to that study table.

"That is why I have you and the others," the king chuckles. The sound dances over Adalyn's skin as she feels the warmth of his magic begin to curl around her.

"You're using your magic on me again," Adalyn says, looking at him. He tilts his face as he studies her.

"You're the only woman who notices." He takes a slow sip of his wine, his tongue darting out to catch the red droplet on his bottom lip. "I'm not going to influence you to do anything you do not want, but you do need to relax."

"I'm sorry—" Adalyn runs her thumb over her bottom lip, "I will admit I'm slightly nervous, I can't say we've shared a private moment."

A faint smile graces the king's lips as the glow of the fire dances off his darkening golden eyes. "You sound as though you wish that will change?"

Adalyn finds herself biting her bottom lip, his magic has definitely relaxed her – so much so all she can do is stare at him and appreciate how alluring he is.

He reminds her of the mighty lions who once roamed the land, golden and fierce but beautiful in the silence. Beautiful in the slaughter and covered in blood.

"You've surprised me, Adalyn. I was expecting more fight from you." He leans forward, grasping her chin in his large calloused hand. His warm breath hits her face as he studies her intently, tilting her face to the left and right. "You truly are beautiful for a human woman."

Adalyn is surprised by his comment.

"It is a shame you aren't Valarki, you would have made a formidable woman and warrior. I see the fire that burns behind your amber eyes." He releases her chin but remains close to her. Adalyn is aware of every breath he takes, she inhales his scent and her thoughts begin to muddle.

The crackling and popping of the fire echoes in the silence of the room as they continue to stare at one another, Adalyn is too caught up in the moment to remember her true purpose of being here, too high on the king's magic to care.

"Would you like a drink, Adalyn? You look...parched," the kings says, his golden eyes dip down to her lips before looking into her eyes once more. His glass was still half full, resting on his knee.

"Please." Adalyn leans forward, resting one of her hands on his corded thigh. His golden eyes flare with pleasure as she runs her lips along his jaw, nibbling her way towards his throat. A low rumbles comes from his chest, getting caught in his throat as her hand begins to trail up his thigh.

He leans forward and rests his glass of wine on the table before them. In slow movements he grips her hips and guides her onto his lap.

Adalyn's body burns as he pulls her flush against his almost naked form, she feels exactly how eager he is for her to be in his chambers. His large hands trail under her dress and up along her bare thighs, Adalyn arches into his touch as she bites down on his shoulder.

He chuckles, gripping her ass tightly.

"You do have fire in you," he whispers into her ear, nuzzling her throat with his nose, "and you smell divine. I can only imagine how sweet you taste."

Adalyn blinks through the haze of magic and lust that had begun to fill the room and suffocate her, she suddenly remembers the point of being in the king's chambers and realises it isn't to get into his bed.

She forces her body to relax as the king's hands run back down her thighs, extremely close to the vial that rests in her pocket. Thinking clearer, she pulls her face away from his shoulder.

He tips his face back to look up at her, Adalyn can't help but noticing the differences between the king and Killian. Killian's face is more narrow while the kings is more chiselled, Killian's nose is more straight while the kings is slightly crooked.

"Do you like what you see?" He asks, running his fingers over the top of her thigh. Adalyn can't deny the attraction she feels towards the king, she can't deny that her body aches for his as she sits flush in his lap.

Her body burns for him in this moment, but her heart yearns for Killian. It is the only thing that stops her from free falling over the edge she currently stands on.

"More than I should," she whispers, clasping his face with

both hands. Adalyn wets her lips, watching as he follows the slow movements of her tongue. "I am parched though."

"I was going to get you a glass of wine." He smirks, squeezing her thighs, "there is no rush."

Adalyn brings her lips to his own, closing her eyes as her body hums. The kiss is gentle, hesitant. It quickly begins to turn into something more, the king is a very, *very* good kisser.

Adalyn curls her hands at the back of his neck as their tongues tangle, as her body begins to rub against his own. His hands roam from her thighs and trail towards her chest, one arm wraps around her waist and holds her steady while his free hand pulls down the strap of her dress and exposes her right breast.

Adalyn whimpers into his mouth as he rubs the hardened nub between his fingers, tugging it gently.

This shouldn't feel as good as it does.

The callouses of his palm scratch at the soft skin of her breast as he begins to massage it, his fingers still rolling over her nipple. She grinds her hips into his hard cock as it rests between them.

The king bucks into her, reaching up and fisting a handful of her hair to keep her restrained. He dominates her, forcing her to submit to his will.

Adalyn continues to grind into him, feeling heat and pleasure burn in her veins. It's intoxicating in the moment and all she craves is release.

The king bites on her bottom lip, groaning into her mouth as she rocks into him faster. He trails kisses down her throat, biting down on the soft flesh between her neck and shoulder. She gasps as a trickle of blood runs down her chest.

He pulls back, red staining his lips. Golden eyes burn and darken with lust as he licks away her blood, savouring every drop.

The sight is erotic and has wetness pooling between her thighs.

"Do you wish to enjoy that drink, Adalyn? Because if we do not stop now, I will not be stopping at all." He says roughly, squeezing her breast for emphasis. She sits back, heaving in breaths.

"I will take that drink, your majesty." Adalyn manages to squeeze the words from her throat. He grins before leaning forward and grasping her nipple between his teeth.

Adalyn moans, her head falls back as his tongue assaults her nipple before sucking and licking at her breast. He is wicked through and through.

He releases her breast with a *pop* before sliding her from his lap. Adalyn pulls the strap of her dress over her shoulder as he rises, finding his thick, hard and long erection almost jutting from the scrap of material that keeps it concealed. He chuckles down at her before turning and walking towards his bed side table, Adalyn hadn't noticed the bottle of wine resting in a pitcher of ice earlier.

With trembling hands, Adalyn pulls out the vial and empties the red liquid into the kings glass. She shoves the empty vial back into her pocket before resting back in the chair once more. Her heart beats erratically as she tries to shove down the desire and lust for the king. Without his body so close, she can think with a clear head.

Her eyes trail over the king's back as the muscles flex, she finds no scars.

Killian.

His name alone is enough for her to rear back from the heat she'd felt only moments ago, could she have gone as far as having sex with the king to get these papers?

She forces herself to smile as the king walks back towards her with a fresh glass, she takes it with ease and takes a large sip.

Adalyn would need the liquid courage to see out the rest of the night. The king takes his glass from the table before sitting back down, taking a large gulp.

"What's your real name?" Adalyn asks, resting the glass to her lips. The king looks at her and arches a brow.

He rests his glass on his knee, tapping his fingers. "Why do you wish to know?"

"Well you'd have to have a name. Everyone refers to you as your majesty, or the king." Adalyn shrugs, looking to the fire, "I was curious."

"Maybe one day I will indulge you with that information, until then I do enjoy hearing *your majesty* come from your lips."

Adalyn continues to make small talk, mentioning the garden and the stables. The king is polite enough to listen and not send her on her way. Adalyn isn't sure how much time has passed when the king yawns, sitting his now empty glass down.

"Are you okay, your majesty?" She asks, resting her hand on his thigh. He sighs, shaking his head.

"I'm afraid I will have to cut our night short, I'm rather tired." He rises from the chair, swaying slightly. Adalyn jumps up, wrapping an arm around his defined waist.

"Allow me to help you into bed," she whispers, guiding him towards the large bed. She pulls the sheets back with her free hand before helping him. His magic falls from her as his hair spread on the pillows before him.

His handsome face relaxes and Adalyn knows the potion has worked. She tucks him in and rushes to his study table, she tugs at her hair as she realises she can't even decipher which documents might be important.

Screw this, Killian can come in here.

Adalyn slips from the room, leaving the doors slightly ajar as she runs into her own room; the guards don't look away from their post. Killian looks up from where he sits on the corner of her bed, his hair knotty as if he'd spent the last few hours running his hand through it.

"Come on, I need you in there." She hisses, gesturing for him. Killian doesn't hesitate to take her outstretched hand. His nose crunches as they slip back into the king's room, sealing the doors behind them.

"You smell like *him*." He growls, pulling her into his chest. Adalyn's heart skips a beat at the darkness and possessiveness that dances in his eyes.

"Someone sounds jealous," she teases, standing on her tip toes as she captures his lips with her own. Killian gives in to her, devouring her mouth as though he can replace the king's taste.

Adalyn groans into him, digging her nails into his shirt as his hands lower to her ass. Killian pulls back, breathing heavy. No blue in his eyes can be seen.

"You are mine, Addie. In every sense, you belong to me." He captures her lips in a bruising kiss before letting her go and stalking over to the study table. Adalyn burns with pent up pleasure, if she didn't get release soon she'd combust in fury.

Killian looks through the papers, his hands working fast as he skims through each page. Adalyn walks behind the wooden panel divider, finding the glass dome sitting there.

Empty.

Adalyn sucks in a sharp breath as she *remembers* where she's seen this before. When Killian's shadows had a hold of her in the Okra forest, she'd seen this exact dome. She reaches forward, resting her palm on the cold glass.

A spark ignites in the centre before the jar begins to fill with withering shadows as dark as the night sky. Adalyn can't take her eyes away from the dome as the darkness fills the emptiness, dancing against the shadow of her hand.

What the hell is this?

"I've found the letter!" Killian's harsh whisper startles her, she stumbles away from the dome and watches as the darkness disappears once more. Adalyn opens her mouth to tell Killian about what she's found, but the look of fury on his face stops her.

Adalyn rushes to his side and looks down at the piece of paper clasped in his tightened hands. She can't understand the scribbled writing, but the designs on the edge of the dark cream paper look vaguely like water dragons.

"What is it?" she asks, peering up at him.

"This is the trade letter the human leader of Oktavia sent to the king. He wishes to beginning trading resources with our country." A muscle in Killian's jaw tightens, Adalyn still isn't sure why he's so angry.

"What's the matter then?" She asks, twisting her lips.

"He wishes to send the king human slaves in a show of good faith. Ten women, men and five children. His last request is that the king's harem is to be replaced with women of his own country. He goes into great detail about their *experience and finery*."

"Isn't that a good thing?" Adalyn asks, "If the king releases me from the brand we can finally be together Killian!"

He refuses to look at her. "The king wishes to send me to Oktavia with our first battle fleet. He wants me to raise hell and tear their country apart so he can expand Pantera."

"But..." Adalyn frowns, "I can come with you if I'm free of the king. Convince him to accept the treaty and then he can go back against it and we can figure out a plan."

"Adalyn..." Killian looks down at her, his eyes barely masking his pain and sorrow. "I could not let you come with me to another country. I will be forced to slaughter them all."

"Killian..." Adalyn takes a step back, rubbing at her chest to ease the ache in her heart. "I thought we could work together. I thought..."

"You thought I'd stop killing innocent humans?" he asks softly, his eyes so sad that it brings tears to her eyes as it breaks her heart.

"Yes," she whispers, feeling stupid.

He wraps his arms around her, holding her tight. "Addie, if I ever had the choice I would not slaughter another human again unless it was to protect you. The king's magic will force me to and won't let me go until I have fulfilled the debt."

Adalyn says nothing as she buries her face into his chest, breathing in his scent. She can't form any words, so opts to stay silent.

"I am so, so sorry. I would not be able to live with myself if you started looking at me with absolute disgust like you did at the start."

"What happens if you leave, what about us? Me?" Adalyn asks, gripping the back of his shirt tightly. If Killian leaves, there is no one to protect her. She will be left with her own devices and the king's need for her.

"I am not selfish enough to ask that you hold out hope for me, Adalyn." He murmurs into her hair, "I will stay strong for you if I am sent away, but I'm afraid I may return as a man I don't wish for you to know."

They fall into silence, grasping each other as though their lives depend on it. Adalyn thinks that maybe, they do. If she could only hold on tight enough, this unravelling nightmare will be just a bad dream.

"Did you find anything else?" Adalyn whispers, pulling away. Killian keeps one arm around her as he rearranges the papers once more. He runs his hand through his hair before leading them both from the room.

Once the doors are sealed shut he relaxes slightly. "I've found his plans, no mention of the dragon though. I'll need to do some research in the library to confirm a few other things I'm unsure of."

"Stay with me the night?" Adalyn asks as she opens her door. He smiles softly down at her, kissing her nose.

"I was going to, anyway." His eyes darkens as he stalks her into the room, shutting and locking the door behind him, never taking his eyes from her.

She backs away slowly, fire curls low in her stomach as he grows closer. Her body kicks into fight or flight mode, adrenaline pumps through her veins like molten lava as he grasps a handful of hair and pulls her head back.

He licks her throat, growling at the bite mark the king had left her with.

"I am going to lick, suck, bite and *fuck* every trace of him out of your system until I am all you know," Killian says hotly into her ear before biting down over the king's bite. Adalyn moans as she leans into him, fisting her hands into his shirt. He rips his mouth away, not bothering to wipe the blood from his chin.

"Do you understand, Addie?" He forces her face back, staring down at her with nothing but possession in his eyes. Adalyn burns under his gaze.

"Yes, Killian," she says breathlessly, squeezing her thighs together. Killian studies her once more before spinning her around and forcing her face onto the bed sheets. She cries out as her dress is gathered at her waist, exposing her ass and drenched undies.

He trails a finger along her slit, circling her clit through her underwear. "Is this all for me?"

"Yes." She groans into the sheets, burying her face as she sticks her ass out for him. He chuckles darkly as his finger disappears, Adalyn is about to protest when his palm slaps her ass.

She hisses at the sting, whimpering as he rubs the tender skin.

"You only ever get wet for me." His hot breath hits her tender cheek, he gently bites down on the skin and sucks. Adalyn shakes her ass into him, silently begging for more.

"Use your words, Adalyn." Killian licks her from her clit to top of her ass, swirling his tongue in her wetness.

"I want you to taste me Killian." She tilts her face to the side, taking a shuddering breath as he slowly slips her underwear down her legs.

"What else?" he asks, spreading both cheeks as he dips his tongue into her. She cries out, her back arching as his tongue continues to taste her.

"What," *suck,* "else." *Lick.*

"Punish me, Killian. Own me." Adalyn begs, aching to be filled.

Two fingers slide into her, curling and pumping as he focuses on her clit. Adalyn bucks her hips into him, an orgasm takes her by surprise as Killian gently bites down on her clit and tugs; resting his thumb over the tight ring of her ass.

She screams out, tensing around him as she falls forward into the bed. Killian allows her a moment to catch her breath before beginning the slow, torturous assault once more. Already Adalyn can feel her orgasm building, needing him to bring her to that high.

"I need you, Killian." Adalyn begs, gripping the sheets above her head, "I need this dress off of me and I need your body against me."

Killian smiles against her before he pulls away, leaving her empty and aching. He rips the dress in half down her back, throwing the two scraps to the side.

"Like this?" he asks, grasping her hips as lines himself up with her wet heat. Adalyn's breathing falters as he slams into her, he rests at the hilt as she adjusts to his size. A warm hand wraps around her throat and pulls her upwards, Killian grasps one of her legs and guides it onto the bed.

Adalyn leans her face and claims his lips, his hand begins to tighten around her throat as his other hand begins to rub her clit.

She rolls her hips as he continues to slam into her, hard and fast. He fills her to the hilt each time, forcing her to take him. Adalyn reaches up a hand and fists his hair as their tongues tangle together, their breaths combine as their hearts begin to beat side by side.

Killian tightens his hand, cutting off her air flow. Fear taints her pleasure as he works his fingers faster, thrusting his heaps in a frenzy. Adalyn's lungs burn but she refuses to give in so soon.

As darkness begins to creep into her vision Killian releases her throat, his roar of pleasure shakes the bed frame; her own scream escapes her as the orgasm takes her in its grip and squeezes.

Wetness gushes down her legs, leaving her feeling light headed and dead limbed. Killian holds her close, resting his sweat covered forehead on her shoulder as he catches his breath.

"*Mine.*" He whispers against her skin, gently kissing the spot.

"*Yours.*" Adalyn whispers back, letting him carry all of her weight. She whimpers as he slides from her, leaving her feeling empty and hollow. He holds her to his chest as he walks into the bathroom, steaming water waits.

Adalyn closes her eyes as he lowers them both into the water, positioning her between his legs before he gently begins to wash her.

"We'll figure it out Killian, I promise," she murmurs, resting her hands against his knees as she rests her head on his chest.

He kisses her temple, his beating heart is erratic as the staccato notes echo into Adalyn. Every time she's shared her body with him, it has led her to feel nothing but pleasure; she thinks tonight is only the tip of the ice berg to what Killian has leashed, waiting to release himself onto her.

"I know we will, Addie." He whispers, "I just hope it isn't too late when we do."

45. Adalyn

Adalyn

Adalyn leans against the large marble kitchen counter as Allison busies herself with filling a woven basket with fruit, bread and a few pieces of aged cheese. Adalyn smiles as her friend curses under her breath, adding an extra piece.

"What's the special occasion for?" Adalyn asks, tapping her nails against the marble top. She'd woken to an empty bed, vaguely remembering Killian kissing her goodbye in the early hours of the morning. Adalyn had needed to busy herself, knowing if she was alone, her thoughts would drift back to the king and what had happened between them.

She wished she could tell Allison all about what has been happening. She wished she could confide in her friend about the worries and all the trouble that is going to come their way.

"I'm going for a picnic." Allison finally straightens from the pantry, a human slave moves numbly around her into the dim light. Allison casts her eyes down and steps back into the main area of the kitchen.

"Who with?" Adalyn teases, "where was my invite?"

Allison's cheeks tinge red, a nice compliment to her dark skin. "Well...the king wanted to picnic in the garden at the back of the castle."

"His private garden?" Adalyn asks, losing her smile.

Allison shakes her head, "no, he won't share that garden with me. The other garden is out of the castle, I can only imagine it's just as nice."

A foreign emotion stirs in Adalyn's chest, knowing the king allows her and no others to enter his private garden. Was it a ploy to get her into his bed? After last night, she isn't sure how much longer she'd be able to postpone their joining.

Adalyn is a part of his harem, even if she doesn't want to be.

"What do you have planned for the rest of the day?" Allison asks, gathering the basket in her hands. She'd left her curls out today, framing her soft face and bringing out her caramel eyes.

"I'll probably wander for a bit." Adalyn pushes from the counter and walks side by side with Allison from the kitchen. Her stomach twists as human slaves walk past them, completely oblivious to the world around them. Adalyn wonders what would happen if they were released from the magic, would they remember their time under the influence? Would they remember who they are?

"Be safe, maybe you can find Jurian or Killian to spend time with?" Allison suggests, bumping her shoulder into Adalyn's.

"Yeah I'm sure I could track one of them down if I wanted to," Adalyn tucks her hands into her frilly white laced gown. She'd wanted to dress nicely today. The dress hugs her chest and waist before exploding in lace layers and frills that trail behind her as she walks.

Allison wears a nice golden gown, similar in style to Adalyns.

"We need to see each other more now that you're back, the others girls can't even remember your name." Allison mutters, shaking her head. Adalyn shrugs.

"I'm not too phased if they don't know my name, Allison. I haven't exactly been too forthcoming myself." Adalyn isn't sure if she can even remember the other girl's names.

"Yes, but we're all in this together. We should be confiding in each other."

Adalyn stays silent, unable to comfort her friend on this topic. She isn't even sure what the point would be, leaning on one another. When she'd lived in her village before her world was torn apart, Adalyn had barely socialised with any others her age. Of course, she'd kissed a boy or two but not once had she ever formed a genuine friendship outside of her sister.

"We'll have a cup of coffee soon and talk, I'll invite a few of the others girls. I think you'd like them." Allison says with determination.

"Alright, I'll do it for you," Adalyn grumbles, fighting a smile. Allison chuckles, licking her lips.

"I knew you'd come around."

As they enter another large hallway Polarian rounds the corner, fixing the cuffs of his tight black armoured shirt. Allison stumbles a step, blushing deeply before looking anywhere but at him.

Adalyn scowls, running her eyes over him before he notices their approach. His large, lean frame is covered in the black material, similar to the one Killian wears when leaving the castle.

He'd pulled his long chestnut brown hair back in a high pony tail, a few wispy pieces frame his sharp featured face, complementing the slant of his orange eyes. Adalyn *hates* him more than anything, and hates that even though he is one of the most vile creatures she's met, he still is rather handsome.

He finishes with his cuff, orange eyes cut right to them. Both girls come to a stop as he approaches, stalking them as though he's a predator. Adalyn refuses to cower beneath his stare, opting to cross her arms over her chest to avoid the urge to lash out at him.

Allison fiddles with a lost piece of the woven basket, eyes roaming over him.

"Well, what a pleasant surprise," he drawls, stopping in front of them. Adalyn tilts her face up to his, annoyed that he towers over them.

"I wish I could say the same," she snaps back. Polarian

narrows his eyes before looking to Allison, heat enters his gaze as his eyes roam over her body.

"It's always a pleasant surprise to see *you* at least," he says, directing it towards Allison.

"As it is you, Polarian," Allison says quietly, sucking on her bottom lip. Adalyn looks between them, feeling the tension thicken. She narrows her eyes before the pieces begin to click together.

"Have you...are you both..." she scrambles for words, in shock that Allison might have been in Polarian's bed. Allison stays silent, refusing to look at Adalyn.

Polarian grins, looking back to Adalyn, "Run along Ali, the king awaits you."

Allison spares Adalyn an apologetic glance before stepping around Polarian and continuing down the hallway. Adalyn watches her go, losing her edge of anger. If Allison is sleeping with Polarian...*no, no one will stop me from getting my revenge*, Adalyn thinks.

"I've been busy while you've been gone," Polarian says, drawing her from her thoughts.

"I can see that." Adalyn takes a step forward, glaring up at him. "If you hurt her, I will cut every appendage from your body starting with the most important one to you."

Polarian moves swiftly, pinning Adalyn to the wall. He presses his body into hers, shoving his thigh between her own. She pushes at his chest, baring her teeth up at him.

His orange eyes dance with amusement and something deeper...danger.

"Very soon, Adalyn, I'm sure you'll be begging me for that appendage," he purrs, keeping her caged in. Each breath she takes has her breasts rubbing against his chest, she almost refuses to breath. His sweet scent of cinnamon and butterscotch fill her nose, reminding her of the first falling leaves in autumn.

"I would never beg for you, Polarian."

"I love how humans lie; you do it without even knowing

you're doing it." He leans down, running his nose down her jaw. Adalyn freezes, stuttering a breath as she digs her nails into his chest. "You reek of *him.*"

"I don't know what you're talking about," Adalyn bites out.

"You don't know yet, do you?" He chuckles, leaning back. He studies her face, grinning. Adalyn tries her best to hide her curiosity and suspicion.

"I don't know what you're getting at Polarian, but I don't care what you have to say. You've done nothing but be awful to me from the moment you found and *stabbed* me," Adalyn says, frowning at him. "Why do you think I'd indulge you now?"

"I've only ever shown you my true nature, Adalyn, it's a lot more than I can say for the others." He leans back, allowing her room to breathe. "You'll come for me, if only for spiting another."

"I'd rather fall on my own blade."

Polarian grasps her chin, running his thumb over her bottom lip. "I'll still have you even though you're ruined, even if it means killing you afterwards."

"Let me go, Polarian." Adalyn wraps her hand around his wrist, done with this conversation. She'd already paid him too much attention, and he is not one that would let her go under his radar.

"You heard her you big headed asshole," Jurian growls from her right. Adalyn struggles against the hand that grasps her chin, wanting to look towards him. She could only imagine how their position looks to others. Polarian smirks, leaning down to run his lips along her jaw.

Adalyn squeezes her eyes shut, but he lets her go and steps away. She hurries to fix her dress, fisting her hands at her side as she glares at him.

"It wasn't what it looked like, Jurian," she says, quickly glancing towards him. He scowls at Polarian, narrowing those blood red eyes.

"Why don't you go harass someone else, Polarian?" Jurian says, walking closer to them. Adalyn steps into his side, feeling a hell of a lot safer now that Jurian is there. Polarian backs away with his hands in the air, although he doesn't lose the devilish smile.

"I'll be seeing you around, Addie," he coos before spinning on his heel and stalking off. Adalyn presses a hand into her chest, watching him leave.

"God he's like a cockroach, nothing will kill him," Jurian grumbles, wrapping an arm over her shoulder. Adalyn leans into his embrace, closing her eyes. "What did he want?"

"Nothing really, just to intimidate me like always," Adalyn replies, wrapping her arm around his waist. Jurian chuckles and turns them around, leading them deeper into the castle. Red carpet runs down each hallway as torches light their way.

"I've missed you, Red," Jurian says, squeezing her shoulder. "You haven't come and found me since you've been back."

"I've been busy," Adalyn admits. "When I do have the spare time I can't find you anyway."

"I think Killian is hogging you all to himself." He pouts, looking down at her with wide eyes. Adalyn chuckles, shaking her head.

"I don't think you'd know what to do with me if you had me, Jurian," she chirps back, smiling sweetly up at him. Her mind drifts to the passionate kiss they'd shared, how her blood had sung for his. His eyes flash, remembering the moment they'd shared as well.

"I'm sure I'd figure it out." He winks before facing forward once more. Adalyn leans her head on his chest, feeling content and safe and *happy*. Jurian had become one of her first friends, not expecting anything from her and he'd been there for her when she had needed him most. Had needed *someone*.

"Where are we going?" She asks, noticing he's wearing loose casual clothes. His white shirt gapes open, exposing his toned tanned chest.

"To the library. Killian has been down there since this morning."

"Did he tell you what happened?" She feels her cheeks burn, hoping Killian didn't tell Jurian about her fondling with the king. Jurian chuckles, twisting a strand of her auburn hair between his fingers.

"He informed me of the human king sending the trade letter and the dragon and has informed me we're knee deep in shit we can't climb out of." He chirps, seeming unphased.

"Aren't you afraid?" she queries, peering up at him He grins down at her, a dimple appearing in his chin on the left side.

"I've lived far too many years of my life being afraid, Adalyn. Never give your fear truth or it will own you before you can own it."

Adalyn huffs, digging her fingers into his side, "you're annoying."

"Annoying but *wise.*" He tugs at her hair, earning a whine of protest. They bicker back and forth until they reach the door that leads them to the catacombs. Jurian holds the door open for her, gesturing.

Adalyn takes the steps two at a time, waiting at the bottom for Jurian to join her. The two black hounds look towards them, sniffing the air once before resting their large heads on their paws.

"Do they have names?" Adalyn asks as Jurian walks by her side towards the large doors they guard. The hounds pay them no mind, although they keep an eye trained on them.

"I don't think so." Jurian shrugs, "you can name them if you want."

Adalyn hums, pointing to the hound on their left. "That can be cupcake," she points to the hound on their right "and that can be princess."

Jurian laughs as the doors open for them, revealing Killian hunched over a book; piles and piles scatter the table, some open.

"I don't think they suit their names, they are hounds from darkness," Jurian comments, drifting to a spare seat at the table. Adalyn huffs and walks directly for Killian, pausing at his side to look at the passage he reads; in Valarki, of course.

"Have you found anything?" Adalyn asks Killian, drawing his eyes from the text. He offers her a strained smile, running a hand through his hair before leaning back in his seat.

"Nothing that I don't already know I'm afraid." His deep voice runs over her skin, enticing her. Adalyn smiles at him before looking down at the books.

"I told you this morning that you wouldn't find much," Jurian comments, resting his feet on the table as he stretches his arms above his head. Adalyn traces the grooves of his stomach with her eyes. He winks at her.

"I'm not just going to sit back and do nothing," Killian grumbles. "You know I like to be prepared and have a plan set in place."

"I don't think you can plan for this, brother," Jurian drawls, waving a hand in the air. "By the sounds of it, the ball's in the king's court and until he starts making decisions you can't plan anything."

Adalyn turns to Killian, "I think Jurian is right. I know how much you want to be prepared, but we need to wait for the king to make the first move. We already have an idea of what we're facing, so already we're better off than we were before."

Killian reaches for her, she allows him to pull her onto his lap, she straddles him and runs her hands through his hair as she leans her back into the table.

"Why do you have to always be right?" Killian hums, grasping her waist.

"If I recall, I said it first," Jurian says.

Adalyn smirks down at Killian. "Did you hear that?"

Light begins to enter his eyes as he gazes up at her. "Hmm. I don't think I heard anything."

"You two are so annoying," Jurian grumbles, huffing under his breath. Killian chuckles breathlessly, resting his head against Adalyn's chest. His scent entraps her, his warmth burns her.

She squeezes her thighs against his waist, feeling the ache for him emerge. Killian stiffens slightly, digging his fingers into her waist.

Jurian goes quiet as Killian pulls his face back far enough to look up at her, his blue eyes burn as he studies her face. Adalyn can't find it in herself to be embarrassed that Jurian can no doubt smell her arousal, if she's honest with herself it turns her on even more knowing he's there watching.

Killian growls, as if sensing her thoughts. "You're playing a dangerous game, Addie."

"I...I want to play, if you do," she whispers, trailing her lips over his cheek to his pointed ear. "Only if you're comfortable sharing."

Adalyn feels Killian beginning to grow hard against her, pressing into her thigh. He leans into her ear, nipping at the lobe.

"I will share you, but just know I will make your body my own once we're alone again." He trails kisses down her throat, "my name will be a prayer to the gods before I'm done with you."

"So...are we doing this?" Adalyn asks, dragging her hand down his chest. Excitement sparks in her chest as the idea of having both of them, not knowing exactly how it's going to work but wanting to experience it with them. The two men she trusts with her life.

Killian leans around her, Adalyn begins to trail kisses down his throat as he addresses Jurian. "You can leave, or you can stay."

Adalyn pulls away from Killian and looks over her shoulder, finding Jurian standing as if he'd been about to leave. He looks at her, obvious lust in his eyes.

"Are you sure, both of you?" Jurian asks, swallowing hard. "If you choose to hand my ass to me afterwards, I would say it's worth it."

Killian leans back in his chair, fisting Adalyn's dress between them. "I would never deny Adalyn anything."

His answer warms her heart, she faces Killian and kisses him quickly, darting her tongue into his mouth before pulling away and sliding from his lap. Nerves begin to set in as she walks towards Jurian, his eyes track her every movement.

“Do you want me, Jurian?” she asks softly, standing before him. He gazes down at her, his golden hair flat against his chest.

“Yes.” His answer is a whisper, but is enough for her. Adalyn wraps her arms around his neck and brushes her lips against his, her heart beats wildly in her chest as his hands grasp her waist.

Jurian kisses her with the same hunger, sucking and nipping at her lips as his hands begin to trail over her ass. He groans into her mouth as his large hands squeeze, pulling her into his erection.

Adalyn gasps as another pair of hands trail down her back, moving her hair to the side and begin undoing the laces at the back of her dress.

Jurian moves his hands to her front, gently grasping her breasts as Killian undoes her dress and helps her out of it. Her nipples pebble immediately as she stands naked before them. Killian trails kisses over her shoulder, pressing his now bare chest into her back.

“Naughty girl,” he growls, biting down on her shoulder. Adalyn groans as she arches back into him, jutting her breasts out for Jurian. He dips his face to her right breast, sucking the nub into his mouth.

Killian trails a hand between the front of her thighs, sliding his fingers along her slick folds. Already, she’s wet for the both of them. The heat in front of her and behind is intoxicating, knowing they both want her as badly as she wants them.

This might be a once in a life time experience, and she is going to enjoy every single second of it.

Jurian's hand replaces his mouth as he claims her lips and devours her. Adalyn kisses him back, ripping his shirt from his body. Her hands trail down the hard planes of his stomach, palming his erection. He growls into her mouth, biting on her lower lip.

Killian grinds into her ass, the material of his pants the only thing stopping him from sliding into her. Adalyn breathes feverishly, needing more. Wanting more.

“Will you take us both at the same time, Addie?” Killian asks, his voice deep and lust filled. Adalyn pushes Jurian's pants down, he makes quick work to be rid of them.

"Yes." She whimpers, wrapping a hand around Jurian's cock and slowly works her hand up and down his length. His red eyes burn as he watches her hand, his chest heaving.

"Good." Killian dips two fingers into her, curling them to hit that soft spot inside of her that melts the blood in her veins. Adalyn grabs his arm with her free hand, rocking her hips into his fingers.

"I need you to relax, okay sweetheart?" Killian murmurs against her throat, sliding his wet fingers towards the tight ring of her ass. She tenses for a moment before relaxing, focusing her hand as she works Jurian faster. He goes back to sucking and licking her breasts, helping her relax.

"This is going to sting a little." Killian slowly inserts a finger into her ass, resting it there as she adjusts to the burn. Adalyn nods once as he pulls it out and begins to pump it slowly. Killian kicks his pants off, running the head of his cock down the slit of her ass.

"Killian..." she moans, throwing her head back into his chest. He looks down at her, biting his bottom lip as he watches Jurian devour her breasts.

"You are so beautiful," Killian says, claiming her lips with his own. Adalyn kisses him back with feverish passion, loving the way he dominates her mouth and body. Killian is her ultimate undoing, working her into oblivion.

He inserts a second finger into her ass, pumping slowly before inserting a third. Adalyn squeezes her eyes against the deep sting, but relaxes against him.

Killian removes his fingers, leaving Adalyn trembling for more. He grasps her thighs and hoists her into the air, she grabs Jurian's shoulders to anchor herself between them. Killian presses into her back as Jurian grabs her thighs to help support her as well. Killian reaches behind them and guides himself into her wet heat, slowly rocking his hips into her.

Jurian grinds his cock between them, groaning as he watches her breasts bounce with each thrust; his grip is bruising on her thighs.

"You're going to take my cock in your ass now," Killian groans, sucking on her throat as he reaches between them once more and positions himself against her tight ring. Adalyn closes her eyes as she pushes himself into her, stopping after his head has just entered. Adalyn pants with pain and pleasure, digging her nails into Jurian's shoulder hard enough to draw blood.

"That's it, be a good girl." Killian inches into her slowly, until he rests fully at the hilt. "*Fuck.*" He leans his forehead against her shoulder, reaching around to grab both of her breasts in his hands, pinching her nipples.

"Jurian..." Adalyn rocks her hips against him, earning a grunt from Killian. Jurian releases one hand from her thigh to positon himself at her opening.

He rubs the head of his cock in her wetness before forcing himself inside of her. Adalyn gasps with pleasure as he fills her to the hilt. With both of them seated inside of her, she feels close to exploding.

Killian begins to thrust into her, sliding a hand down to circle her clit. Jurian finds tempo against Killian, one enters her and leaves as the other enters.

Adalyn *burns* with pleasure and euphoria as they worship her body, thrusting their hips faster and leaving kisses and bites wherever they can reach. Adalyn twists her head towards Killian, claiming his lips.

His tongue slides into her mouth as he pinches her clit. Adalyn shatters against them as her orgasms rips through her, Killian swallows her screams as her body tightens and she gushes. Heat and pleasure explode behind her eyes, feeling euphoria.

"Oh fuck, I'm not going to last." Jurian works faster into her, taking her left breast into his mouth once more. Adalyn moans with each thrust, whimpering as Jurian's hips stutter and still inside of her.

He pulls out of her, their joint wetness slides down his throbbing cock as he steps back. Killian spins and pins Adalyn against the top of the table, he pulls out of her and flips her over before slamming back into her ass.

Adalyn arches off the table as Killian wraps a hand around her throat, squeezing. God, she loves this. Loves how he owns her body.

Killian leans over her body and kisses her, intertwining their tongues as he pulls another orgasm from her. As she tenses and wraps her legs around his waist, Killian slams into her once more and roars his own release.

The sound rattles the books on the shelves, the torches flicker. He lays against her chest, throbbing inside of her. Adalyn goes limp against the table, closing her eyes as she tries to catch her breath.

That was amazing.

Killian kisses her forehead, "you did amazing, darling."

Adalyn grins up at him, still lost in the haze of the orgasms she'd had. "I'm glad you learnt to share."

Killian chuckles before sliding out of her, her grabs her dress from the floor and manages to redress her as she continues to lay there. Adalyn peers over to where Jurian now leans in a chair, redressed with his shirt open. Nail marks spot his two bare shoulders.

"Did I hurt you?" she asks, resting on her elbows to look at him. Jurian grins with hooded eyes.

"You couldn't if you tried, Red."

Killian redresses, smiling gently down at her as he guides her from the table and holds her to his chest. He runs a hand down her head, kissing the top of her head.

Adalyn wraps her arms around his waist, "I'm sore and tired."

"You need rest now," Killian murmurs, pulling back to look into her eyes. Something troubles him, but Adalyn is far too worn out to ask what it is. She simply nods once and kisses him softly.

"I can walk her back to her room if you want to remain down here," Jurian says.

"I will walk her back," Killian says, a hint of possessiveness in his voice. Adalyn chuckles, as well as Jurian.

"I was simply offering, with no hidden motives," Jurian remarks. Adalyn shakes her head but allows Killian to lead her towards the door. Jurian falls into step behind them and hums a tune to himself.

"Are you sure you're okay?" Killian asks, lifting her face to look up at him. Adalyn smiles, her heart stuttering in her chest.

"I've never been better," she admits, hoping the raw emotions she feels are shining through her eyes in adoration. He kisses her nose and faces forward once more, allowing her to rest her head on his chest.

Adalyn knows her heart now belongs to him and for once she isn't afraid to face the consequences that come with loving someone you shouldn't.

Loving someone she didn't think she ever could.

46. Killian

Killian

Killian inhales Adalyn's sweet scent as she curls in his arms, her small body flush against his own. He strokes a hand through her hair, closing his eyes as he relaxes. They'd returned to his room earlier that evening after a day of adventuring through the catacombs, avoiding the path that would lead them to the dragon.

Killian had found a bottle of wine sitting in an ice bucket on his bed side table, open and ready to be poured. He'd assumed Jurian had left it for them, a thank you for what transpired between the three of them only a few nights before.

Adalyn had seemed happier and more content in the last few days, as if something had finally solidified inside of her mind. He wishes he could peer into her mind and hear her thoughts, still finding her a mystery.

She sighs as she twists her face towards his, kissing along his jaw. "Do you think it'll always be like this?"

"I could only hope so." Killian opens his eyes, feeling the full effect of the wine take control. He'd lost track of how many glasses they'd shared, but if he looked over he would find the bottle empty.

"I think someone was in my room the other day," Adalyn murmurs.

"Why do you think that?" The weight of his magic begins to recede, leaving a vast hollowness in its wake. Killian struggles to call his magic forward, finding not even a spark will rise.

"My dresses were scattered over the room." Adalyn frowns up at him, "are you okay?"

"My—my magic." Killian sits up, the world spins around him wildly as he presses his palms into his eyes. *What on earth is happening? Where has my magic gone?*

"What do you mean?" Adalyn sits beside him, rubbing a hand down his back. Killian can't even begin to form words as his magic disappears, the weight in his mind is gone. The absence of his magic leaves him feeling like a shell of his former self.

"It's gone." Killian looks towards his front door, faintly hearing multiple boots marching towards his room. He looks at Adalyn desperately, grasping her cheek in his palm. "They're coming."

"Who is coming?" She asks, wide eyed with fear. Killian kisses her once more, ingraining the feel of her lips into his mind; savouring each hot breath that touches his cheeks.

His heart beats wildly in his chest as he pulls away, he searches her eyes. "I hope you can find it in your heart to forgive me."

Adalyn screams as the doors burst open, slamming into the wall and rattling the hinges. Two golden armoured guards hold the doors open as six guards dressed in blood red enter. Killian jumps to stand, needing to protect Adalyn until the last moment.

He stumbles, arms reaching out blindly.

Two guards grab Adalyn by the biceps, ripping her from his bed. Her white nightgown rides up her thighs as she struggles against their grip, trying to keep her eyes trained on Killian.

Before he can react a metal collar is shackled around his throat, in the next breath his wrists are chained. Four red guards hold his chains, keeping him restrained.

"Adalyn..." his voice is hoarse as she's taken from his room, forced to follow behind. She continues to struggle and spew insults at the guards, they pay her no attention.

Killian stumbles along, trying and failing to gather his bearings. He knows what is to come next, knows that if he could think clearly they'd be on the path towards the king's throne room.

Towards his demise that he crafted himself.

The two guards open the golden gilded doors of the throne room, closing them once everyone has entered the room. A large, stone slab has been positioned in the centre of the room in front of the throne of bones.

Killian falls to his knees as his chains are tightened by the guards, his head snaps backwards as he's forced to watch as the two guards guide Adalyn to the stone slab.

Faceless guards line the walls of the throne room, while Polarian stands off to the left with a sadistic smile painting his features. Sweat runs down Killian's temples, he'd been wearing loose night pants when the guards had broken in.

The king narrows his eyes on Adalyn, his golden and silver streaked hair floats in the air around him as he rises from his throne. Today he's dressed in finery, every inch of his body is covered with a deep green tunic and pants to match, golden thread has been woven along the trimmings.

He looks every piece the king he is.

Killian trembles as a wave of the king's magic presses into every empty inch of the room, without his own magic to combat it he is crushed under its force. Adalyn continues to struggle, continues to fight.

"It is truly a pleasure to have you all here today," the king begins, clasping his hands behind his back. "I will address two matters at hand. The first is the next conquest."

Killian trains his eyes on the king, breathing heavy through clenched teeth.

"Killian, tomorrow you will be leading the next conquest to wipe out the remaining human villages south of the continent. I want the children, adults and elderly slaughtered. I want their villages burnt to ashes with nothing but cinders remaining."

"You can't do that!" Adalyn shouts, going still in the grasp of the guards.

"I can and I will." The king spears her with his churning golden eyes. "For too long I've sat back and allowed this country to rot. I will not sit back any longer."

"They're innocent," Adalyn says, voice full of pain. "They have done nothing to you but simply existed."

"Just because you were chosen for my harem, does not mean you have any special privileges. You are still *human* and you will remain so."

Adalyn stays silent, her rage seeps from her fisted hands and the defiance set in her shoulders.

Killian can do nothing but watch as his undoing begins to unfold before him.

"I sent Killian on a mission weeks ago, with you as his own personal slave," the king begins, taking a step down the dais. "I gave him *two* tasks bound by magic to complete. Do you know what they were?"

"To look into the sickness and find the traitor." Adalyn's voice is strong and sure, she risks a glance towards Killian and he finds nothing but loyalty looking back at him.

This is worse than the pain he'd felt when his wife was slaughtered, worse than when he'd been tied to the whipping pole and tortured for his defiance.

"Correct, for one of them. I asked Killian to seek out the sickness, but it was not a magically binding task." The king descends towards Adalyn, his eyes turning cold and cunning as he stops before the opposite side of the stone slab. "Do you know what the other task was?"

"No," she grits out, slightly trembling. The king grins, malice in his eyes.

"I tasked him with taking your first blood, or risk punishment."

Silence suffocates the room. Killian struggles against his chains, his betrayal is a sharp, hot blade through his chest as Adalyn remains silent. He had done this to protect her from Polarian's wrath, had *wanted* to give his body to her because he cares.

He would have given her the world in the palm of his hand, if only she asked.

"You're here today for me to see for myself if he went through with his task." The king nods once and the guards drag Adalyn to the stone slab. She begins screaming once more, withering and kicking out her leg as she's thrown on top of the slab; before she can scramble away the king's magic crashes down on top of her; pinning her.

"Adalyn..." Killian's voice is a hoarse whisper, blood runs down his wrist and splatters the white marble beneath him; he continues to fight for freedom. She needs him *now*.

He has doomed her.

"Stop! Please!" Adalyn cries out, making one last desperate attempt to break free from the confines of the king's magic. Her arms are yanked above her head as her legs are spread, the white night gown bunches at her waist revealing her white underwear. Adalyn buckles under the pressure, gasping for breath as tears streak her cheeks.

She turns her face towards Killian.

It ruins him.

"Please—" a broken plea, for him, to help.

To save her.

The king laughs, "Killian, I'm assuming your mission was successful?"

Guilt claws its way out, dragging him under. He doesn't take his eyes from Adalyn, hoping she can see beneath who he portrays himself on the outside. His body desperately fights against the poison coursing through his veins, but he's afraid it'll be too late.

"Your silence is answer enough." The king walks forward,

flicking a hand towards Adalyn's night gown. The material rises higher and gathers above her pale stomach.

"Please don't do this." Her voice breaks as fresh tears spill, still she struggles against the weight of the magic layering her.

"You will face far worse than this in your lifetime." The king runs a hand up her bare leg, looping his fingers through her underwear and ripping them from her body; leaving her bare. Adalyn squeezes her eyes shut as her body trembles.

Polarian crosses his arms over his chest, glaring at Killian with triumph. Killian may have completed his task, but he had ultimately lost in the end.

"Aren't you curious, little one?" The king purrs. He pulls the scrap of underwear to his nose and inhales, sighing as he lets the piece flutter to the floor, "I can smell him on you."

Killian feels the acidic bile rise up his throat, horrified.

Adalyn turns her face towards Killian once more, finally opening her eyes. Amber eyes burn as they meet his as that *hate* sparks.

"I'm surprised Killian, I never thought you'd complete this task. I know how much you detest the humans." The king leans between her thighs, trailing a hand over the curve of her knee and dipping between her legs.

Adalyn steels herself, refusing to beg and cower before him.

Her face pinches in pain as the king licks his lips, Killian's roar of rage is trapped inside his mind as the king pulls his glistening fingers out of her.

"Still as tight as anything, but she has been bled."

Oh god what have I done. What have I done. What have I done.

The king looks towards Killian as he takes his seat on the throne once more, sucking on his fingers, "Do not forget who I am, Killian. The power I hold. I am no fool. I learnt of your interest for the slave through multiple resources. I will always be one step ahead of you and I will make you burn if you ever try to cross me. I know who you truly value now." His gaze goes to

Adalyn, she lays still on the slab with her eyes open but unseeing. Her eyes are void of emotion, no tears streak her cheeks. A hollowness roots itself inside of her, making home in the bones of her torment.

Wherever her mind has gone, it is far away from this place.

Hot tears fall from Killian's eyes.

What have I done to her?

"If you disobey my orders, she will be the one that suffers. I learnt that killing someone you love is far too easy. For you to truly suffer, Killian, I will pull every scream from her until she is hoarse."

"I...understand," Killian manages to whisper. Defeat sinks into his bones. Tomorrow he leaves and there is no doubt in his mind that he won't see Adalyn until he returns, many weeks or months from this moment.

"Polarian, take the girl to your chambers." The king waves his hand towards Polarian, who grins and stalks towards her. Adalyn closes her eyes as Polarian picks her up from the slab and cradles her against his chest. She tilts her head into the crook of his arm, refusing to look at Killian.

He begs her silently to look at him, to see how sorry he is.

She doesn't.

Killian watches as Polarian leaves with her in his arms. No one hears the crack of his heart; the noise echoes in his ears with each step she gets further away from him.

The guards pull Killian to his feet, forcing him to walk out of the throne room.

"You leave with Jurian and Alissa in the morning, Killian. Do not *fail* me. You know the consequence." The king's voice haunts him with each step, the poison still in full effect.

Adalyn would never forgive him for what he has done.

He would never forgive himself.

47. Adalyn
Adalyn

Adalyn blinks into existence, ignoring the ache between her thighs and absence of her underwear. She blocks the flurry of images that want to assault her mind and drag her into darkness. She takes all her pain and locks it behind a door in her mind, leaving only the bitter taste of hate behind.

Killian had betrayed her.

"I was wondering when you'd return to the living," Polarian drawls, dragging Adalyn's attention to where he lounges on the chaise that sits in front of a raging fire. His chestnut brown hair gleams in the fire light as it lays flat against his chest, his orange eyes glow as he looks at her.

"Why am I in your room?" she asks, voice hoarse from screaming. Polarian rolls his eyes, leaning his chin on the palm of his hand.

"King's orders. You're not allowed to see Killian again."

Adalyn looks away from him, finding herself not caring she's in his bed, tucked in nicely. She inhales, replacing the scent of Killian with Polarian.

"Do you want to see him?" Polarian asks.

"No."

He chuckles, "I did try to warn you the other day."

"It wouldn't have mattered if I believed you or not," Adalyn grumbles, fisting the sheets in her hands. "I'd still end up here, wouldn't I?"

"Yes."

"I don't want to talk." Adalyn rolls on her side, facing her back towards him. She closes her eyes and prays sleep will take her, if only to relieve the ache in her heart momentarily.

"I like it when you snap back at me, even threaten my life. Especially when you threaten my life." Polarian says, "why won't you bite? Demand to be returned to your room?"

"I don't fucking care, Polarian. Shut up," Adalyn grits, squeezing her eyes shut. He's no help, but knowing she's far away from Killian is a soothing ointment to her torn apart soul.

"You humans are pathetic," Polarian spits. "I can't stand you on a good day, and yet you still cry and wallow in your own self-pity."

"I can't recall asking for your opinion," Adalyn snaps back, feeling a small spark of fire in her chest. *Damn him! I want to forget, I want to ignore the pain and simply not exist!*

"You're really going to wallow in your own self worthlessness because of him?" Polarian laughs to himself, "I will never understand how naïve humans are. You knew what he was from the start but you still chose to turn a blind eye."

"He-he isn't all he appears to be," Adalyn whispers, feeling tears well in her eyes. She had once thought that he had layers to him, so much depth that she would need a lifetime to figure him out.

Now? Now she simply wishes to forget he exists, he had asked for her forgiveness but had done nothing to earn it.

"He has always been exactly what he shows the world. I've known Killian since I was a teenager, mortal, and not once has he changed." Polarian grunts.

"What makes you think you're so much better?" Adalyn demands, rolling back to face him once more. Polarian leans his elbows on his knees as he looks at her, his orange eyes more intense than she'd seen them before.

"I never said I was better, but I don't lie and deceive others to make them believe I'm something I'm not. I'm all sorts of fucked up and not once will you find me apologising for it. I am unapologetically myself and it's all I ever will be. I harbour darkness inside of myself and I *love* making others cower before me."

"Why are you so intrigued by me? From the start you have done nothing but humiliate me." Adalyn presses her lips together, feeling the ire of her hate for him surface. He'd put her through hell.

He simply smiles devilishly, "I wish to make you bleed, Adalyn. I wish to peel back your skin and make you scream."

"Fat chance of that happening." She snorts, hiding her unease. She doesn't doubt for a moment that Polarian would prove his words with actions.

"Maybe, but I have other ways to make you scream." He winks, "but I will also require a fair amount of blood shed and a threat to my life to enjoy it."

"I'm not going to fuck you, Polarian." Adalyn glares at him, "I'd rather run back to Killian."

"Will you?" He questions, tilting his head to the side. His hair creates a curtain and shadow his features, revealing only the gleam in his eyes.

A predator.

Adalyn steels her spine, refusing to be his prey any longer.

"No."

Her word echoes and solidifies in the air between them and she can't figure out why he cares, can't find it in herself to care that he's asking so many questions.

Tomorrow, Killian would be gone. For weeks or months, but his presence wouldn't suffocate her. She wouldn't break under his will or be forced to hear his plea for forgiveness. Adalyn could finally focus on her one goal she had set when coming to this place; make them all pay.

Polarian breaks into an easy smile, licking his lips. "I have a feeling we're only just scratching the surface for all of your own darkness that lingers behind those awful amber eyes."

"As if your eyes are any nicer," Adalyn snaps back, resting her head on his pillow. "I hope you don't expect me to share your bed tonight."

Polarian leans back into the chaise, opting to look into the fire. The dancing flames are mirrors to his own eyes, aglow and burning with hunger. Always demanding more.

Polarian may be hungry forever, never eating his fill of pain.

"I'm under strict orders from the king, you are safe in my room for the night but once the sun rises I can't say the rules apply."

"If you touch me, I'll gut you," Adalyn threatens, closing her eyes. "I told you I didn't want to talk."

"Yet you're still indulging me," he snaps back, his annoyance flaring. "This is a punishment for me, having you in my bed and unable to touch you."

"Looks like it's the night for punishment," Adalyn says, relaxing into his sheets. If the king has ordered him to not touch her, she's safe for now.

She would still go through with her threat of spilling his entrails if he thought for a second he could touch her. Having him so close is already grating on her nerves.

"I didn't do anything to deserve punishment," Polarian says, "and I've been kept from going on the next conquest. Do you know how much I crave to slice the throats of mortals and bathe in their blood?"

"No but it doesn't paint a pretty picture." Adalyn pops one eye open, studying him. Polarian drums his hand on his knee, refusing to look her way.

She still hates him and knows her curiosity is coming from a place of current vulnerability. Tomorrow, she'd go back to planning his murder, tonight she'd allow a sort of truce to form.

"I don't paint pretty pictures and happy endings, Adalyn, I paint the harsh truths you are all too afraid to face."

"I've never shied away from the truth, Polarian," she says quietly. "I was there when you invaded my village and slaughtered people I knew before my very eyes. People I had grown up with."

"Save me the sob story, you're not the only one who has suffered." He finally looks at her, a shadow of a ghost haunts him; darkening the flames in his eyes to cinders.

"At least I've learnt from my suffering." Adalyn glares at him, "I have suffered and instead of letting it rot me from the inside I am learning to wield it as a weapon."

"Are we any different?" he muses. "I may be rotten, but where will your hate run once you've avenged your wrong doings? There will be nowhere but inside for it to sleep and decay."

"I will never be like you." Adalyn lays on her back, looking up at his high ceiling. This is the most conversation she'd ever had with him before, with only minimal threats to inflict bodily harm.

"You don't understand." He grumbles, his stare burning the side of her face, "the decaying has already begun."

The room is plunged into silence, only the crackle and pop of the fire and the howling wind that rattles the window is to be heard.

Adalyn closes her eyes, forcing herself to end the conversation. She'd get nowhere with him, but she could appreciate the truth he has given her. The others had lied and deceived her and she'd played her hand like a fool in love. Had Jurian known as well? She'd taken both of them at the same time, and they'd both betrayed her.

No more would she allow herself to be weak, to be vulnerable. If they wish to make a monster of her, she vows to be the meanest of them all.

A darkness unfurls in her soul, the events of the night have been her tipping point. She would never slaughter innocents like Polarian, but she would cut her blade through any throat that has painted their hands with the blood of those who didn't deserve it.

For once she is unafraid of facing her darkness and she welcomes it with open arms, she has nothing left to lose and everything to gain. Adalyn will make any sacrifice if it means getting her justice.

A war is brewing between Pantera and Oktavia, between the Valarki and innocents. How long will it be until the scale tips in someone's favour?

Will her soul be rotten by the time she's forced to make a choice?

Adalyn falls into her darkness, allowing it to mould her into the creature she needs to become in order to protect herself. Polarian may be right after all.

Maybe her hate will decay and rot inside of her, but she's certain of one thing; if she goes down, she's taking every single one of them with her.

48. Adalyn

Adalyn

Adalyn stands on the hidden balcony, peering down at the large conquest that spills from the castle walls and into the dead and barren land. Patrons of the castle gather around and cheer, excited for the blood shed that is to come. An announcement had been sent out through the night, alerting all of Pantera that the southern human lands will fall in the coming months.

She'd left Polarian's room before the sun had risen, finding him scowling at her from the chaise; he hadn't moved through the night and had kept his word of not touching her.

She hadn't dared say goodbye, had simply left his room with her head high and eyes dry. Adalyn would allow the hurt and betrayal to rise to the surface once Killian had left, she's come to the conclusion it will be easier to heal from the havoc he's caused when he isn't around to twist his words and work his way into her heart once more.

A cool breeze bites at her cheeks as she leans over the balcony, spotting Killian on his black stallion. Jurian sits astride a chestnut mare, looking towards Alissa who walks towards them on a white stallion.

A twang of jealously courses through Adalyn, knowing that

Alissa is going to take the advantage with Killian now that they are done.

Adalyn's eyes burn as she grips the railing, her heart begging for her to do *something*.

There is nothing I can do. He betrayed me, he used me and manipulated me to believe he is someone better. She pleads with her heart, wanting her thoughts to take control. She refuses to lead with heart, from now she would turn it to ice and stone and throw away any resemblance of warmth.

Killian turns in his saddle, surveying the balconies that hang over the high towers. Adalyn steels her gaze as their eyes connect, and her heart thunders. She may love him, but she will never be with him again.

"I hate you." She whispers to the wind, imagining it carries her words to his ears. "I allowed myself to fall in love with you, but there are no actions you could show me that will ever let me forgive you. Now you go to battle, to slaughter more innocent humans. You have not changed, Killian, you have always been exactly *who* you showed me from the start."

Adalyn turns and slips back into the castle, slamming the door behind her. She stalks through the castle, clenching and unclenching her fists. She hadn't returned to her room, afraid his scent would linger. That their joined scent would still hang heavy in the air and perfume her sheets.

Maybe she could burn the room down, beg the king for a new room far away from his. All she has are the memories and they demand to haunt her. Inside of her mind a countdown begins, ticking away with each second she wastes.

Time is running out but she's unsure as to what exactly will happen when the clock chimes midnight.

Ahead voices fill the hall, Adalyn scurries into an empty room and gently clicks the door shut as she falls into darkness. The voices grow louder as they reach her hall and stop, Adalyn holds her breath.

"Is it done?" The king's muffled voice rumbles through the door.

"Yes, your majesty," a slithering voice answers, skittering over her skin and leaving goosebumps in its wake. Adalyn frowns as she tries to figure out *who* owns the voice.

"Good. I've sent the general away so his suspicions will leave with him. After last night's events he's returned to himself. When he returns, he will be the bringer of death once more." The king replies, deep in thought. Adalyn's mind whirls with the information as the anxiety that something is coming begins to weigh on her shoulders. What is the king up to? Killian may have betrayed her, but she knows deep down he has a soft spot for the humans.

"I have kept Polarian behind, much to his disgust." The king chuckles, "but I think once he learns of what I have in store he will be glad he stayed, especially with the red head."

"When do we begin?" The other voice asks, hissing at the end of their words.

"Soon, my friend. Once the first fleet of Oktavia arrives in the coming weeks we will begin phase one. If Killian knew the depths of my plan, he would have fought more." The king sighs, "it is truly a shame he is yet to realise that not only do I now hold his heart in my hands, I also hold his soul in an invisible prison."

"He's always been blind."

Another slithering voice comes from behind the door. "Too trusting."

"Too eager to please," a third voice chimes. It gives Adalyn the chills, but she refuses to move from the door. Fear of being heard keeps her rooted in place, forehead resting against the wooden door.

"He fell in love with a human, who holds only hate in her rotten heart. I don't have to move against Killian to ruin him, he does it himself." The king confides, "if he knew his child lived, imprisoned and alone, he would tear this world apart."

Killian's son is alive?! Adalyn hides her gap of surprise with her hand, biting her tongue.

"You kept his child?" The voice hisses.

The king chuckles. "Oh yes, a simple illusion and trick of hand. I enjoyed killing his wife, but his child holds potential. A secret I will keep to myself for now, but just know he will rise soon."

"Where does the son reside?"

"In the darkness or light?"

"When I introduce his son to this world, there will be nothing but ruination left in his path. He craves blood and demands death, but he still needs time." The king muses, "a delight, really. He will be everything his father wasn't."

The slithering voices hiss, but say no more. Adalyn's heart beats in her throat, unable to comprehend the fact that Killian's son is *alive* and the king has kept him hidden all these years.

When does he come into play in this never ending game? How does Adalyn intertwine with their sick and twisted demands?

"But first, we begin our invasion towards Oktavia. Rally the members of your community and wait for my call."

"What about the girl?" One voice hisses, turning Adalyn's blood to ice. She can only assume they speak of her.

"Polarian is going to keep her occupied, much to his delight and hate," the king replies, sounding bored. "She will be no problem and if she is, I'll simply perform the ritual earlier."

What ritual?

Adalyn takes a sliding step away from the door, not wanting to hear the rest of the conversation.

"Does she carry hate in her heart now? Can you feast on her blood and life source?" A voice asks, they all sound the same to her ears.

"She breathes hate now, she will be the one that feeds my hunger. Her hate will taste sickly sweet, similar to the taste between her thighs."

The hissing voices laugh, shame burns her cheeks as she's

assaulted with the memory of the king forcing his fingers into her; she'd been a fool. A complete, utter fool.

"In time, the pieces will fall together. Come, we have much to discuss." The king strides away from the door, his footfalls muffled but sounding further away than before. Adalyn breathes heavy as she presses a hand to her chest to ease the ache. Not only does she need to deal with her broken, tattered heart that has left her soul in pieces; but she must stop the king from sending back his forces to Oktavia.

Adalyn slips from the room after a few more moments of silence and finds the hallway empty. She scurries from the room on light feet and winds her way through the castle.

All the pieces are on the board, now she must move her piece into position.

Adalyn slips into her mask of cold indifference, similar to the one Killian has always worn and learnt to live and breathe. She will no longer survive in this castle as a mere mortal seeking revenge, no, she must mould herself into a Valarki; become as cunning and deceptive, conniving and blood thirsty.

Vengeance will be hers in the form of blood and she's willing to sacrifice whatever it costs. For her sister and her family, she will make their blood rain.

Killian may have had a hand in crafting her into the monster she's destined to become, but Polarian will be the one that sees her grow into her skin; fangs and claws.

Adalyn smiles as she walks through the castle, finally feeling every bit the predator she has always hoped to be when setting foot in this castle. First things first, she must play the part of the innocent human girl who will crawl to the king's every call, obey every command without hesitation.

Killian's betrayal had been her final breaking point, dooming her to become everything he hoped she wouldn't.

"If you could see me now, Killian...would you still see *me?* Or would you see a reflection of yourself staring back at you?" She whispers into the empty hall before entering the king's private garden. Adalyn closes her eyes as the sun warms her face.

"The eyes are said to be a mirror of our souls..." Adalyn clenches her fists, opening her eyes as her chest burns with the chaos of her emotions. "My soul has long ago given up residency, leaving darkness and hell behind."

I will become the darkness and I will become the flame.

I will become the blade and I will inflict pain.

Those who have wronged me will feel the steel of my blade, and as their blood spills I will scream out my rage.

Adalyn solidifies her vows as she stares at the garden, seeing the world in all the shades of grey. No longer will she see colour or light, she will feed her darkness until there is nothing left of her to give.

The door jerks open behind her, Adalyn spins to find Polarian glaring down at her, a snarl twisting his plump lips as his eyes shine with the promise of violence. "You're fair game now, *darling*." He mocks the nickname Killian had called her in private. "Your protector has left the castle."

Adalyn begins to smile, a hint of malice shining in her eyes. "A game I hope you're prepared to play, *darling*, because this time I will not leash my rage."

Polarian's scowl turns into a grin, for she's finally become his match.

Vengeance will be hers, and Polarian is going to be the first to taste her wrath.

Acknowledgments

I want to start by thanking my readers. Knowing you've made it this far makes me beyond elated. I'm so grateful to each and every one of you, your support doesn't go unnoticed and reading your words of encouragement get me through the writing blocks and hard times. Knowing you care that much fills me with warmth.

A special thanks to Shalika, my soul sister. Honestly, if it wasn't for you this book never would have been finished. I'd still be one chapter 12 struggling with what the hell was going on. For someone who doesn't read, you were more on my ass about writing it than I was because you desperately wanted to know what happened. So, this one's for you. I love you to death, and I can't begin to express how proud I feel knowing you approve. If you didn't show up at my house and stand over my shoulder with that last chapter, it never would have happened. YOU did this.

I also want to thank Trinh Kim, from the get go you've been a huge support, reading the unedited version and expressing your love for the characters and the story. You make me realise that even though I may not reach many people, the people I do reach are worth more than a million.

Thanks to the author community, you guys are amazing. Seriously. Your support is never ending and the encouragement is surreal.

Writer's Retreat: my own little slice of heaven. Abra, Elena, Brittany, Emmie, Jessica, K E Barden, Karlein, Kay, M.J, Maddison, Olivia, Phoebe, Stephanie and Melina. You guys go above and beyond, from general questions to the more difficult topics to every day chit chat. Without you all, I'd still be second guessing everything and having no idea what comes next. Each of you are amazing, and it wouldn't feel right if I didn't express that. Love you guys.

A special thanks to Acacia from Ever After Cover Design. You captured the cover PERFECTLY. And thanks to Mallory for making the inner workings look beautiful.

Thanks to my family, and Nonna, you'll probably be clutching pearls after getting to this part, considering how different it is to my last five books you've read, but I truly hope you enjoyed it. I love sending you my books and I love hearing the good things you have to say about them.

Also, a big thanks to B. You know who you are, your support has been endless and the late night chats have kept me sane while working on this. Thank you so so much.

Big, big thanks to my editor, Tara Routley. You've once again worked your magic and made this book worthy of being read. Thank you so, so much for doing this for me once again. I know it was a big project, and I loved giggling with you in Coles about *that* particular scene.

Last but not least, thank you to Lawson, although you came along after I'd written this, your love and support keeps me from crumbling. I love you. Thanks for giving me my happy ending.

About the Author

Shana J. Caldwell is an Australian self-published author from the Western Downs, who is either knee deep in reading or crouched over her laptop with her trusty cat, Luna, as her writing companion. When she's not writing she's got her nose stuck between the pages of a book or can be found with a coffee in hand. She loves morally grey characters and villains who have the chance of redemption.

Find her on Instagram @shanajcaldwellbooks
Find her on Facebook @Shana J. Caldwell

Other Books By This Author

THE IMMORTAL SERIES

Immortal Awakening

Immortal Sufering

Immortal Reckoning

ENCHANTED SERIES

Enchantment of Darkness

Enchantment of Thorns

FAE OF PANTERA

Blood & Steel

Printed in Dunstable, United Kingdom

63529216R00292